CAT PAY THE DEVIL

Center Point Large Print

Also by Shirley Rousseau Murphy
and available from Center Point Large Print

Cat Playing Cupid

**This Large Print Book carries the
Seal of Approval of N.A.V.H.**

CAT
PAY
THE
DEVIL

A JOE GREY MYSTERY

Shirley Rousseau Murphy

CENTER POINT PUBLISHING
THORNDIKE, MAINE

This Center Point Large Print edition is published in the year 2009 by arrangement with William Morrow, an imprint of HarperCollins Publishers.

The text of this Large Print edition is unabridged. In other aspects, this book may vary from the original edition. Printed in the United States of America. Set in 16-point Times New Roman type.

ISBN: 978-1-60285-567-0

Library of Congress Cataloging-in-Publication Data

Murphy, Shirley Rousseau.
   Cat pay the devil : a Joe Grey mystery / Shirley Rousseau Murphy.
      p. cm.
   ISBN 978-1-60285-567-0 (library binding : alk. paper)
   1. Grey, Joe (Fictitious character)--Fiction. 2. Cats--Fiction. 3. California--Fiction.
      4. Large type books. I. Title.

PS3563.U7619C3525 2009
813'.54--dc22

2009016714

To the young men
in the Orange County Corrections Department's
Literature-N-Living Program, Orlando, Florida

With best wishes for each of you, always

"They say of some temporal suffering, 'No future bliss can make up for it,' not knowing that Heaven, once attained, will work backwards and turn every agony into a glory. And of some sinful pleasure they say, 'Let me but have this and I'll take the consequences': little dreaming how damnation will spread back and back into their past and contaminate the pleasure of the sin. Both processes begin even before death. . . ."

C.S. LEWIS, *The Great Divorce*

1

At the edge of the sea, the small village, even among the shadows of its lush oaks and pines, seemed smothered by the unseasonal summer heat that had baked into every stairway and crevice and shop wall. The rising coastal temperatures, mixed with high humidity from the sullen Pacific, produced a sweltering steam bath that had lasted through all of July, and was not typical for the central California coast. The scent of hot pinesap was mixed sharply with the salty stink of iodine at low tide. And from the narrow streets, the scent of suntan oil rose unpleasantly to the three cats where they sprawled on a cottage rooftop, in the ineffectual shade of a stone chimney, indolently washing their paws— avoiding the crush of tourists' feet and the scorching sidewalks, which felt like a giant griddle; if a cat stood for a moment on the concrete, he'd come away with blistered paws—Joe Grey's white paws *felt* blistered. The gray tomcat sprawled, limp, across the shingles, his white belly turned up to the nonexistent breeze as he tried to imagine cool sea winds.

Near Joe, the long-haired tortoiseshell lifted her head occasionally to lick one mottled black-and-brown paw. Kit had the longest coat of the three, so she was sure she suffered the most. Only dark tabby Dulcie was up and moving, irritably pacing. Joe watched her, convinced she was fretting for no reason.

But you couldn't tell Dulcie anything; she'd worked herself into a state over her housemate and nothing he could say seemed to help.

Below them on the narrow streets, the din of strangers' voices reached them, and the shrill laughter of a group of children. Tourists wandered by the dozens, dressed in shorts and sandals, lapping up ice cream and slipping into small shops looking for a breath of cooler air; the restaurant patios were crowded with visitors enjoying iced drinks, their leashed dogs panting beneath the tables. Strangers stared in through the windows of shaded cottages that were tucked among bright gardens, into shadowed sitting rooms and bedrooms that looked cool and inviting. Lazily Joe rose to peer over at a pair of loud-voiced, sweating joggers heading for the beach to run on the damp sand, as if they might catch up to an ocean breeze.

With a soft hush of paws, Dulcie came to stand beside him at the edge of the roof, silent and frowning, looking not at the busy streets below but up at the round hills that rose above the village—hills burnt dry now, humping against the sky as brown as grazing beasts.

They could see nothing moving there, no human hiking the dusty trails, no rider on horseback; the

10

deer and small wild creatures would be asleep in the shade, if they could find any shade. Even among the ruins hidden among the highest slopes, the feral cats would be holed up in cool caverns beneath the fallen walls. For a long time Dulcie stood looking in that direction, her peach-tinted ears sharply forward, her head tilted in a puzzled frown.

"What?" Joe said, watching her.

"I don't know." She turned to look at him, her green eyes wide and perplexed. "I feel like . . . As if they're thinking of us." She blinked and lashed her tail. "As if Willow is thinking of us, as if *she* knows how I feel." She narrowed her green eyes at him, but then she rubbed against his shoulder, brushing her whiskers against his. "I guess that makes no sense; maybe it's the heat."

Joe didn't answer. He knew she was upset—and females were prone to fancies. Who knew what two females together, even at such a distance, could conjure between them? Maybe both Dulcie and the pale calico had that fey quality humans found so mysterious in the feline. Maybe their wild, feral friend, with her unusual talents of perception and speech that matched their own, maybe she did indeed sense that Dulcie was worried and fretting. Who knew what Willow was capable of?

But Dulcie was worrying over nothing, as far as Joe could see. Dulcie's human housemate had gone off before, for the weekend, driving up the coast to the city, and Dulcie had never fretted as she did now.

Now, Dulcie thought she had reason, and Joe looked at her intently. "Prisoners have escaped from jail before, Dulcie. That, and the fact that Wilma is later than she promised, does not add up to disaster. You're building a mountain out of pebbles."

Dulcie turned, hissing at him. "Cage Jones better keep away from her. Wilma's done with supervising him and too many bad-ass convicts like him, done with the kind of stress they dumped on her for twenty years. She doesn't need any more ugly tangles and ugly people messing up her life."

But despite what either Dulcie or Joe thought, tangles were building, complications that would indeed snare Dulcie's housemate. The scenario had started two months earlier on the East Coast, when an old man entered the continental U.S. When Greeley Urzey stepped off that plane, he set in motion events that would weave themselves into Wilma Getz's destiny as surely as a cat's paw will snarl a skein of yarn.

The old man's flight from Central America entered the States officially at Miami, where passengers would connect with other flights after lining up to go through customs inspection. Deplaning, Greeley smiled, sure of himself and cocky. He'd slip through customs clean as a

12

whistle, as he always did, not an ounce of contraband on him, this time, for the feds to find. Even if he'd had anything tucked away, he'd have waltzed right on through slick as a greased porker, always had, always would, he'd never yet got caught. And, he thought, smiling, there were better ways to bring what he wanted into the States.

He'd gotten most of it through over a period of years, tucked in among household furnishings in them big metal overseas containers. Them feds couldn't search everything.

Well, that part was behind him now. Half of it already cashed out and stashed away, and in a few days he'd have the rest, all *he'd* ever need. He didn't live high like some of them fancy international types: high on the hog, and dangerous.

He fidgeted and shuffled through the long, tedious customs line with its pushy feds and too many nosy damn questions, but after that hassle he still had a good share of the four-hour layover to do as he pleased; enough time for the one important phone call, make sure his contact was in place. Then a couple of drinks and a decent meal instead of them cold airline snacks you had to pay for. Sure as hell not like the old days on Pan Am, free champagne if he flew first class, a nice filet and fancy potatoes all included in the price of your flight, good Colombian coffee and a rich dessert. Now it was pay, pay, pay, and lucky to get a dry sandwich. Even customs, in the old days, didn't make all this fuss. Boarding was the same way—all this new high-powered routine they said would stop terrorists. So high tech that for a while there they were stopping babies in arms from boarding, refusing to let toddlers in diapers on the plane if they didn't have all the right ID. Sure as hell the world had seen better days.

He'd boarded in Panama City at seven A.M. and now, approaching the Bay Area and nearly suppertime, his whiskers itched and his rough gray hair tickled under his collar. The flight from Central America seemed longer every time he took it, though he didn't return to the States often. He'd gone to work for the Panama Canal Company when he was twenty, and then later for the Panamanian government, a forty-year hitch all together. Now, at last, with a little fast footwork, he was getting together the kind of retirement money that would let him laugh at the rest of the world.

Well, he sure as hell wasn't retiring stateside. A visit to California every few years was plenty. Better living in the tropics, better weather, better people. Hell of a lot more opportunities. Too bad a man had to come up to the States to sell his take—if he wanted to sell it safe, not get a knife in his ribs.

They'd taken off from Miami in early afternoon, the sun over the left wing blazing in his eyes as they banked to head west. Full of a good meal in an airport café, he'd leaned back in his seat, in a

14

better mood, going over his moves. Planned to pick up a rental at San Francisco Airport, better known as SFO. Get the montly rate, and he could use a car that long. Check into some airport motel, hit the road early tomorrow morning—first, the short drive down the coast to Molena Point. Couple of hours, get in and out of the village nice and easy, not run into his sister. He sure didn't want to see Mavity now, she asked too many questions. She always had been too damned judgmental. Then head south for L.A., on 101. Long trip down and back, but that couldn't be helped if he wanted cash in his jeans—wanted cash in the bank, in big numbers. He didn't look forward to those megalane city freeways in southern California, he was too used to the slow, crowded streets of Panama and the narrow jungle roads.

When he'd gotten back to San Francisco and took care of business, he'd make one more quick trip to Molena Point without Mavity's knowing. Later on, though, he planned to spend some time in the village, and camp out at his sister's.

He'd waited a long time to make this sale and he wished the price was higher now. But the time was right, and his contact to the fence was available now—or would be when he got to L.A. Strange, Cage Jones in and out of prison all those years and leaving his half of the stash hidden like he did.

Well, Greeley thought, he had salted his own share away, too, while he was out of the country.

But in a safer place. Sometimes, you had to trust a bank.

But Cage never did. Well, everyone to his own. Question was, where had Cage hidden it?

Greeley smiled. He'd find out; might take some time, but he had time.

Right now, the hard part was done. They'd both got their share into the country. Now, once he picked up Cage from prison, selling his own share would be a piece of cake.

Somewhere along the way he'd buy a car, maybe one of them old-fashioned-looking PT Cruisers; that old thirties era look suited his sense of humor. He wasn't never no high roller to be buying some fancy convertible, he wasn't out to impress no one, and he liked doing things his own way.

Looking ahead, he could see the lights of the Bay Area now blazing out of the dark. Hell of a lot more lights spread out than you saw over Panama City. Propping his feet on his wrinkled leather duffle, Greeley settled into the feel of the big 757 cutting speed and dropping altitude. Soon felt the little bump as she let down her landing gear. Pilot's tinny voice over the loudspeaker said the city was sixty-five degrees and foggy, and that made him shiver. He wished this coast had warmer summers; here it was May and he doubted it would get much warmer except maybe a few scattered days in July. Pulling his coat around him, he settled deeper into his seat as the plane hauled back and touched down; deafened by the roar of the plane on the runway, then waiting to deplane, he went over his schedule again to make sure he hadn't missed anything.

The minute the door opened, everyone stood up and crowded into the aisle. Greeley stood, too, but didn't move out, picked up his leather duffle and set it on the seat beside him, watched them crowd out like a flock of brainless chickens.

The next days went smooth as glass; he'd missed nothing in his planning. When it was over and he had the cash, he headed down the coast in the rental car, for Molena Point; but again he didn't call his sister. He closed out his now empty safe-deposit box, and in three other village banks he opened modest checking accounts and new SD boxes, each in a new and different name for which he had obtained new IDs in the city. He filled the boxes with sealed envelopes containing bound packages of hundreds. Then he took himself back to the city for a little vacation. Nice but modest hotel room where he watched stateside TV, read the papers, enjoyed room service. Didn't do no shopping, fancy clothes meant nothing. He'd buy a car later, in Molena Point, after he'd made his presence known to Mavity.

She wouldn't be happy to see him. She lived with three other women now. Strange thing to do, putting her bit of money from the condemnation sale of her marsh-side house into a fourth share of a house big enough for the four old women. The chicken feed she called her savings. Said she wanted to keep her independence, not go into a home. Well, he could understand that—but likely she'd gotten scammed somehow in that house deal and just didn't know it yet.

It was nearly a month later, in mid-July, that Greeley was ready to return to Molena Point and move in with his sister. He booked the short flight from SFO on a one-way ticket. He didn't call Mavity; she'd figure out some reason he couldn't stay there with her. He'd take a cab from the airport, give her a nice surprise.

At least the weather had turned hot; even on the coast it was up in the high nineties, hot as hell itself, just the way he liked it. On the short flight, and again as he swung into the cab outside the little peninsula airport, he thought about them two village cats. Them talking cats—he'd had his share of those snitches. Hoped they kept their distance, this time.

He sure didn't want them hanging around him, nosing into his business. Them cats saw too much. They got into too many places, always snooping, damn near as nosy as his sister. And talk about judgmental. Them Molena Point cats . . . Not judgmental like the black tom who used to run with him, who'd used to break into stores with him. Azrael'd been opinionated, all right, and he sure as hell said his piece. But that black tom, he wasn't never hot for law and order.

That Joe Grey and his tabby friend, those two thought they were God's gift to law enforcement.

Somewhere he'd heard, maybe from his ex-wife, there was a third cat hanging around with them. Another snoop, you could bet. Well, he didn't want no truck with cats, no more than he did with cops. Just wanted to be left to his own affairs, thank you.

2

Now, as Joe Grey and Dulcie stood on the scorching rooftops looking up toward the old ruins, Dulcie frowning and wondering, up there among the fallen stone walls, they could see no creature. If they'd been nearer, an occasional small shadow might have been glimpsed flitting through the tall dry grass and brown weeds. But among the ancient oaks, no deer grazed; the deer had left in search of water. Only the wild little cats slipping stealthily among the rubble, only they knew where to find water, deep in hidden cellars and chambers beneath the fallen walls of the crumbling old estate: ten sentient cats prowling through the ruined mansion, wandering through its moldering interiors that now stood open, like ancient stage sets, the faded wallpaper curling down in long, dirty strips.

Atop a ragged wall, Willow paused in her nervous pacing, her bleached-calico coat blending into the colors of the fallen stone; thinking of Dulcie, she stared down across the dry hills, to the far village. "Something's wrong," she told her two companions. "Dulcie's troubled, she is afraid and troubled."

"Even if she was," said the long-eared tom skeptically, "what could we do? We could do nothing."

But the white tom said not a word; he hated the village, he had still not recovered from their entrapment there and their panicked escape.

The other seven of their small wild band had already vanished at Willow's mention of trouble, fleeing among the basement caverns; and soon Cotton and Coyote slipped away, too, leaving Willow alone, shivering and wondering.

And down in the village, Dulcie turned away from pacing the hot shingles, restlessly counting the hours until Wilma would be home. Her housemate had been gone only three days, but to Dulcie it could as well have been three months. She'd never felt like this before at Wilma's absences. She thought of going home again, thought maybe Wilma would be there now. Or she could stay home and wait for her in the relative coolness of their stone cottage—but she'd been home just an hour before; the bright rooms were too empty, their cozy cottage echoed with loneliness; she had left again quickly, her skin rippling at the desolation of the empty house and the fear that gnawed at her.

Her increasing panic was wearing her into a near frenzy; she was so wired that Joe, who had lain down again, collapsing in the one small patch of shade on the hot roof, raised his sleek, silver-gray head to stare irritably at Dulcie, the white strip down his nose narrowed in a frown, his slitted yellow eyes flashing his annoyance.

"Will you calm down? What do you expect? The woman's shopping. Give her a little slack."

"But she might not know that Cage Jones escaped from jail this morning!" Dulcie stared at Joe, her tail lashing. "She might be wandering innocently around the shops, without a clue. Don't you care?"

"She's a trained federal officer, Dulcie. Even if she is retired. You don't give her much credit. She's armed, and she isn't going to let some sleazy escaped con slip up on her."

"But Jones *hates* her. He has to hate her now, after she testified to send him back to prison. Don't you think he's in a rage! *That's* why he broke out, Joe! To get at Wilma!"

"You can't know that!"

But Dulcie looked away, toward the clock in the courthouse tower; it seemed ages ago that it had struck five thirty. "She promised to be home by early afternoon, and now it's nearly suppertime!"

"The clock struck five thirty ten minutes ago. In

21

my book, that's late afternoon. A woman shopping should punch a time clock? When *we're* hunting rabbits, do you come home right at suppertime? How many nights has Wilma paced the cottage worrying about *you?*"

The kit had awakened and was listening, licking her long, mottled fur. She gave Dulcie a round-eyed gaze. "You know what shopping's like. *We* dream of shopping, of being human shoppers . . . The silks, the cashmeres . . . And she's not only buying clothes for herself, she'll buy presents for us, and for Charlie. Wilma always buys presents." Charlie was Wilma's only niece, the only family Wilma had, besides Dulcie—but Wilma was *Dulcie's only* family! And now, when Joe and Kit refused to understand, Dulcie turned her back on them, lay down, and closed her eyes.

Ever since Dulcie had discovered she could speak and could understand human language, she and Wilma had shared all confidences. Almost all, Dulcie thought. Some things, like teasing coyotes or leaping long distances from tree to tree, would unnecessarily worry a human. They shared most of their meals and certainly they shared the special treats from Jolly's Deli that Wilma liked to bring home. They shared the blue afghan on the velvet couch, and they shared the big double bed in Wilma's bright bedroom, where they curled up to read, both from the same page, while a cozy fire blazed in the small red woodstove in the corner of the bedroom. Or Wilma would read to her; that was how Dulcie had learned to read, by following the pages as Wilma said the words. She'd had no idea, when she was a kitten, that those strange papers Wilma stared at for hours could offer up such wonderful worlds for a cat to explore. Dulcie's discovery of her latent talents, of her ability to master the human language, had opened gigantic worlds for her—just as that discovery had revealed amazing new worlds to Joe Grey; together the two cats had stepped into realms of history and myth and human endeavor far beyond their own feline world.

The kit, on the other hand, had always known she could speak, from as far back as she could remember, from the time when she was an orphaned kitten tagging, unwanted, behind a band of feral cats; though those wildly roaming cats had seldom spoken to her, keeping their conversations among themselves. Except when they said cruelly, "We don't need that straggly weanling. No one wants a tortoiseshell around. Chase it away, there's hardly enough garbage for the rest of us."

Dulcie tried to think about the tortoiseshell's precarious kittenhood, to think about anything besides Wilma, but she couldn't. *Wilma will be home in an hour,* she told herself. *Wilma can take care of herself, she* is *trained and she* is *armed and she* is *clever.*

But maybe she should just go home once more.

Each time she'd raced home, she'd tried to reach Wilma, leaping to Wilma's desk, punching the speaker button and then the one-digit number for Wilma's cell phone. Five times, the voice mail came on. Five times, she'd left the same message. "Cage Jones has escaped from jail! Have you turned on the news or seen the paper? He escaped this morning, about the time you left the city. Please, please watch out for him! Please, come home! Now! Please, please be careful!" Wasn't Wilma checking her phone?

And why wasn't she?

If she'd gotten Dulcie's frantic messages, she would have replied.

If she could reply. And terror gripped Dulcie. No one had any idea what Jones would do. The ex-con would be wild with fury not only at Wilma but at her partner, too. Both Mandell Bennett and Wilma had testified before a federal judge to send Jones back, and Dulcie knew enough about that kind of offender, from Wilma herself, to know that Jones would be hot for revenge. She had left three messages on Bennett's tape, too; though his office was in the city and he surely would have heard that Jones had walked out of jail using a false ID. Probably laughing to himself, the bastard.

This would be the second time Wilma and Bennett had helped send Jones up; the first time was ten years ago, just before Wilma had retired as a U.S. Probation Officer. This time, he had come out of federal prison in early June on conditional release. He'd stayed clean for all of a month, then been arrested the first week of July for transporting a stolen car across the state line. The judge, after looking over Jones's files, had, in an unusual move, requested the testimony not only of Mandell, who was his present probation officer, but of Wilma, who had supervised Jones before her retirement.

Dulcie had seen Jones's picture, and she knew from Wilma that the beefy, big-boned convict found the idea of rehabilitation a huge joke. Jones pretended to reform, lied and made a big show, then went his own way, following his own lawless agenda, forcing Mandell Bennett to send him back before the judge.

Bennett had been a green young officer when Wilma first met him; his first assignment was as her partner. Now he covered Molena Point out of the San Francisco office, and when he made a trip to the village, they often had lunch together. Wilma had driven up to the city four days ago, meeting Mandell there, in court, to testify at Jones's revocation hearing. The hearing had lasted two days; Friday afternoon, after the sentencing, Jones had threatened both Wilma and Bennett, and had been forcibly hauled out of the courtroom and locked in the San Francisco city jail to await transport back to the federal prison at Terminal Island.

Wilma had stayed in the city Saturday, seeing

friends. Her plan was to leave for home early this Sunday morning, in time for several hours of shopping at the discount mall in Gilroy—and this morning Jones had walked, mistakenly released when he presented the officer on duty with borrowed identification. Had walked out free, and dangerous.

Pacing the hot shingles, lashing her tail, Dulcie created such turmoil that Joe hissed and growled at her. "Will you stop! She's all right! She'll be home before dark. Between the heat and your fussing, you'll work yourself into a frothing cat fit."

"But she keeps her gun locked in the glove compartment, she won't take it in the stores while she's shopping, and a lot of good that will do her!" Dulcie lashed her tail harder. "Jones is as volatile as a pit bull jabbed with hot pokers. Armed robbery. Seven assaults on guards while he was in prison. Solitary confinement half the time, for fights with other inmates. And in this heat . . ." The tabby sighed. "You know how a heat wave affects the unstable ones. Three weeks of scorching weather, every nut in the world is on the prod! The papers are full of it—petty thefts turning violent, family arguments escalating into rage and battery. Add all this heat to Jones's anger, you don't know what will happen!"

Joe looked at her, and stretched in the sun's baking heat, and he licked a white paw. But then he rose and nuzzled her ear and said he was sorry—

and he had to admit that in hot weather there was always a jump in the crime rate. Ask any cop, Joe saw the reports and arrest sheets on Chief Harper's desk. Or ask the highway patrol—CHP could tell you about the increase in road rage. And all up and down the coast, the unseasonable heat had escalated silly pranks into acts of hate, prodded simmering resentments into mayhem, exploded friendly arguments and familial conflicts into violence. And now, just two nights ago, a brutal murder in the village.

Both of Chief Max Harper's detectives and the chief himself were working long hours overtime, as were their street patrols, who yearned for additional men and women on the force. The three cats, intent on their own input into police matters, with their own unique ways of discovering evidence, wished they could lead double lives. Or, given that cats have nine lives anyway, they could use several of those lives now, all at once. This late-afternoon's nap on the roof was the first time Joe had been still in days, the first time he had not been lying on the dispatcher's desk listening to radio communications or snooping into apartments or homes where the police did not yet have sufficient evidence to enter. He was idle now, waiting for additional information on the break-in murder to come into the station, just as the detectives were waiting. The village woman, whom everyone knew and liked, had been shot and

27

killed in her bed at three in the morning. She had been alone, her husband on a business trip.

Perhaps she had awakened, surprised the burglar in her bedroom and maybe screamed or in some way alarmed him, and he'd fired at her in panic; the coroner's report said she had not been molested. The event created unusual fear in the village; suddenly everyone was security conscious. Doors and windows were being kept locked at night despite the killing heat, and all five village locksmiths were working overtime to replace credit card locks and weak window closures that should have been tended to long ago.

After the police left the crime scene, the three cats had slipped into the house through a roof vent and down through the attic trapdoor; they had gone over the scene carefully, searching particularly for scents that the officers couldn't detect. But they had found nothing suspicious, no smell that did not belong to a cop or to the householders, no tiny overlooked item that the police hadn't listed and cataloged. Ordinarily Dulcie was as eager as Joe and the tortoiseshell kit to track a killer, but now she couldn't even keep her mind on the appalling murder. Every fiber of her little cat body resounded with missing Wilma, she *knew* that Wilma was in danger or was soon to be; now, nervously, she rose. "I'm going home again."

Joe looked at her with strained patience. But then

he gave her a whisker kiss and licked her ear. "Shall I come with you?"

"No. I just want to go home and see." She was panting with the heat but shivering, too, all at odds with herself. "I'll be right back. If—if she isn't there." And she turned away. But at once, Joe was beside her again.

"Don't, Dulcie. Don't be angry. I know you're worried. I just . . ." The tomcat's fierce yellow eyes looked naked for a moment. "I just don't know what to do about it." He looked deeply at her. "I could call Clyde, we could go to Gilroy to look for her. But we could miss her on the highway. We could call the station, tell the chief she's not home yet, but it's—"

"I *know* it's too soon," Dulcie said. "And I know that every cop is looking for Jones—CHP, the county sheriffs." California Highway Patrol always provided excellent backup. "I *know* there's a warrant out for him. Maybe—maybe she's pulling into the drive right this minute. Or . . ." She stared hopefully at Joe. "Or standing in the garden, calling me!" For a moment, she leaned into him. Then she took off across the rooftops, running flat out—and praying hard.

3

She's shopped all day! **Dulcie thought,** racing
home across the roofs. *All she ever buys are jeans
and sweatshirts; Wilma doesn't linger over satins
and velvets the way I would—so it couldn't take
her this long!* Dulcie loved soft, beautiful garments; when she was younger, she'd often stolen
silken scarves or nighties, a cashmere sweater or a
satin teddy from their good-natured neighbors, had
dragged each item home to snuggle on—only to
see Wilma return them with an embarrassed
apology.

But such luxuries wouldn't delay Wilma.
Dulcie's tall, silver-haired housemate would have
left the city early; she liked to hit the road before
work traffic grew heavy, would probably have left
before breakfast, planning to stop for a bite on the
way or to eat at a favorite restaurant in Gilroy.
Now, though the long summer evening was still
bright, it was nearly six—*twelve hours,* Dulcie
thought. *Oh, she'll be home by now! Home when I
get there! Oh, Wilma, please be sitting on the
couch with your shoes off, your packages strewn
all over.* And she leaped from a tree to the next
roof, dropped from the shingles onto a storefront
sign, then down to a bench, and finally to the sidewalk, landing lightly between a bed of petunias

and a metal news rack. Crouched to sprint across the street and up the block for home, she stopped, staring.

Even in the heat radiating from the sidewalk, suddenly she felt cold all over. She stood facing the news rack and the afternoon edition of the *Molena Point Gazette* in its metal holder, feeling as sick and weak as if she'd eaten poison.

ESCAPED CONVICT SHOOTS FEDERAL OFFICER

Dulcie couldn't breathe, couldn't move. Didn't know what to do but stand shivering and staring.

But then common sense took over—if the victim was Wilma, she'd already know, the police would have been to the house, Joe's housemate would know and would have found her and Joe even on the rooftops. It wasn't Wilma, couldn't be Wilma. But then when she scanned down the first column, again her heart pounded with hurt and rage.

The lead article might ordinarily have been of interest only to San Francisco readers, for the shooting had occurred in the city where the victim worked—but it was in the *Gazette* because he was well known in Molena Point as well. Mandell Bennett was in intensive care in San Francisco General Hospital. He had been found early this afternoon by a coworker, in the underground parking garage of his San Francisco office, lying beside his car. The paper did not identify the

31

shooter, and no suspect had been apprehended. Dulcie stood staring up at the newspaper, unable to move—until a giggle behind her made her spin around.

Two people were watching her, two fat, fleshy tourists in shorts staring down at her, cackling with amusement. "What's that cat *doing?* Reading the *paper?* What kind of animals do they keep here? Dogs in the restaurants, cats reading newspapers . . ."

Leaping at the paper rack, Dulcie snatched at an imaginary moth, batted it around the back of the stand, and took off running and dodging as if chasing it—reading the paper in public was a blunder the little cat would never, ordinarily, have committed. Behind her, the tourists laughed louder; but then when she glanced back, they had lost interest, had turned to admire a dreadful painting in a gallery window—and Dulcie raced for home.

Wilma Getz had indeed left the city early, heading out around six A.M.; after two days in court, she was looking forward to a rare binge of shopping. Having gassed up her car the night before, she drove south on Highway 101, enjoying a cinnamon roll from the hotel's continental breakfast bar, sipping coffee, and listening to a favorite Ella Fitzgerald tape that included "Lorelei" and "Too Darn Hot." She seldom had the time or patience for a shopping spree, and didn't pay much attention to clothes; she was happy in jeans and well-chosen sweatshirts. But her jeans were growing threadbare, her sweatshirts baggy and faded, and every few years the mood hit her for something new, even for a bit of elegance. As she drove, she left her phone off, and had not glanced at a paper or turned on the news. Once she'd fulfilled her courtroom responsibilities, the extended weekend was a welcome vacation. Her governmental duties behind her, she didn't want to spoil her drive home with some local reporter's warped version of the revocation hearing, or with the sour sensationalism of national or world news that could leave one filled only with questions. With her mind on a breakfast of a Mexican omelet in the small town of Gilroy, and then a grand and restorative few hours trying on and buying new clothes, she kept the music at a sensible level, the air conditioner turned to high, and enjoyed the smooth curves of the passing hills burnt dry by the hot sun, their winter emerald changed to summer brown. She planned to pick up a few early Christmas presents for her redheaded niece, too, to put away until the holidays, and of course she would find gifts for the three cats; Dulcie and Kit so dearly loved a new blanket, something soft and fresh. Joe Grey, just like a human male, was the hard one to shop for.

She'd had dinner last night with Mandell, a few hours to visit. He still covered Molena Point and the central coast, and she often saw him then, but dinner in the city had been special. Mandell was fun, and he made her laugh, though he was a no-nonsense officer. Bennett was from Georgia; he was half Cherokee and had retained in those sturdy genes not only a quick wit and a powerful instinct and skill for survival, but an easygoing humor that, no matter the circumstances, never seemed to fail him. Because of this and his inner strength, and the fact that he'd always been there for her, he was more like family than merely a friend. And though she'd tried, when he'd lost his wife six years ago to cancer, she had never felt that she'd been able to do anything significant to help ease his distress. No one could help much, that was a pain one must bear alone, a pain Mandell would carry to the end of his life.

During the hearing, Mandell had weathered Cage Jones's sullen anger with the cool equanimity he always mustered, while she had inwardly fumed. Their quiet dinner afterward had lifted her spirits, had helped her to get centered again. Maybe she'd grown soft, in retirement. The likes of Cage Jones disgusted her far more now than when she'd dealt with him and his caliber of criminal. Dulcie had asked her once why she had chosen probation and parole as a profession, and she hadn't really had a good answer.

"Wanting to change the bad guys—until I learned that most of them wouldn't change, had no desire to change. And then wanting to keep them off the street, keep them from hurting others."

She'd looked at Dulcie's wide green eyes. "Maybe a bit of a predatory streak in me? A bit confrontational? A streak of the cat in my nature?"

"Maybe," Dulcie had said, laughing. "Maybe that's why we get along so well. And," Dulcie continued, "that should help you understand why Joe and Kit and I love what we do."

"I guess it does," Wilma had said, diffidently stroking Dulcie's sleek tabby back, tracing a finger down her dark, silky stripes. "I guess I understand very well."

The drive to Gilroy took her an hour and twenty minutes, from hotel parking lot to the sprawling discount mall. Her first stop was to gas up her car, and then to her favorite restaurant where she enjoyed a large and decadent breakfast. Locking her car, she'd made sure her glove compartment was safely locked, too. The .38 Smith & Wesson had been important when she worked corrections, but now, with those years long past, the revolver was simply insurance in case her car broke down or something else unexpected occurred, such as a carjacking or attempted robbery. Life bloomed with the unexpected, and she felt more comfortable prepared. Though the gun wasn't likely to be needed for a simple day of shopping; and her only known enemy of the moment was safely cooling his heels, watched over by San Francisco's finest.

She thought of checking the messages on her cell phone before she hit the stores; but she had called her close friend Clyde last night, and then called Lucinda and Pedric Greenlaw. Dulcie had been there with the elderly couple, tucked up on the couch with Kit as Pedric recited an old Celtic fairy tale for the two cats. Pedric was an authority on Celtic myth and, as the cats' heritage lay within that distant and mysterious realm, they loved hearing his stories.

She supposed she could check for a message from Dulcie, but she'd talked with her just last night, and she'd be home in a few hours, even if she hit every store in the complex; she was trying to break herself of worrying about Dulcie. Ever since Dulcie and Joe discovered they could speak and understand the human language—were, as Dulcie put it, thinking like real human persons—Wilma had worried over the little tabby to the point of driving Dulcie crazy. Just as Clyde worried over Joe. When the two cats launched themselves into a life of spying and snooping, she and Clyde had worried big-time. The inherent dangers of such an occupation for two little cats had nearly undone them both.

From the first, Dulcie hadn't liked Wilma fussing, and had set her straight with such insistence that she'd backed off. That hadn't been easy. But the thought made Wilma smile, because soon the tables were turned. When the tortoiseshell kit arrived on the scene, a starving orphan kitten then, and had taken up with the Greenlaws and with Joe and Dulcie, she had proved to be far more of a handful than either of the older cats had ever been—and soon it was their turn to worry. Kit was fascinated with criminal investigation, and she was fearless.

Molena Point might be small, but there was a lot of money in the village—multimillion-dollar homes; wealthy estates on the outskirts; a handful of movie stars, retired and otherwise. And there were moneyed tourists drawn not only by the charm of the village but by fine golf courses, antique-car competitions, and a world-class horse show. When Kit joined Joe and Dulcie's clandestine investigations of burglaries, thefts, and the crimes of passion that occurred beneath the sleepy facade of a small town, her approach was wild indeed; she launched into the investigations with all four paws, ears back, and tail lashing—too often putting herself in harm's way, so that Dulcie and Joc did indeed fret over her.

"Payback time," Wilma had told them, though she, too, worried about the kit. But at least now the older cats understood what such worrying was about.

Finishing her coffee and paying her bill, she left the restaurant. The mall parking lot was only half full, the shop doors just opening, but already the heavy July heat was enervating. She hoped it was nicer at home, that the sea's fog had moved in to cool the village, to cool her cottage that, even with thick stone walls, could in this weather grow too hot for her taste or Dulcie's. Moving her car over in front of her favorite discount stores, sitting for a moment looking at her short shopping list, she had a fierce, empty feeling of missing home; felt an unaccustomed nostalgia for her cozy living room with its soft blue velvet chair and love seat, the huge, bright landscape above the stone fireplace between the walls of books, her cherry desk before the window where Dulcie liked to sit. She felt empty suddenly, as if she'd been gone for months.

But she'd be home in a few hours. She was just tired, and feeling bruised after the court hearing, after having to dredge up all Jones's ugly history and listen to his squirming protestations. She was just wanting to be snug at home, where she could restore her sense of the goodness of the world. Annoyed with herself, she swung out and locked the car, and, mustering a bit of shopper's eagerness and excitement, she headed for the first row of stores.

4

Racing home, Dulcie couldn't get Mandell Bennett out of her mind, a vision of the strong, dark-haired, soft-spoken man falling beneath a blaze of gunfire—and she imagined Wilma falling . . . falling . . . But that had not happened! She had to stop this, she mustn't think this . . . Courting bad luck, Lucinda would say.

Wilma's car was not in the drive, and there was no scent of exhaust as if she had pulled into the garage. Dulcie pushed resolutely through her cat door into the service porch then into the kitchen.

Crossing the blue linoleum, there was no scent of Wilma. She padded into the dining room, stood beneath a dark, carved chair, her paws on the Persian rug, looking through to the living room. There was no one there. The vivid oil painting over the fireplace, with its red rooftops and dark oaks, seemed faded; the blue velvet love seat, Wilma's cherrywood desk, the potted plants, the bright books in the bookcases—all seemed abandoned without Wilma, diminished and forlorn.

She knew she was being melodramatic, overreacting. Turning away, she hurried down the hall to Wilma's bright bedroom, stood looking in at the cheerful flowered chintz and white wicker, the red iron woodstove—then she fled back to the living room, leaped to the desk, and again pressed the message button.

Nothing, no message. Punching the speaker button, then the one for Wilma's cell phone, she recorded a few listless words. The effort seemed useless, she'd already jammed Wilma's cell phone with messages. Shouldering quickly out through her cat door again, then through Wilma's wildly blooming garden, she leaped once more to the rooftops and raced through waves of rising heat across the hot shingles and tiles, straight to Joe Grey and Kit. Above her, the sky was deepening into evening, the gleam of the low, slanting sun glancing golden across the roofs ahead of her. She found Joe and Kit atop a little penthouse where the faintest breeze fingered their fur. The kit was curled on the high roof, dozing, but Joe Grey paced, now as restless as Dulcie herself. As if, having had a restorative nap, he could no longer stay still.

She knew it wasn't Wilma that Joe was fretting about—he was yearning to get back to Molena Point PD, to the dispatcher's desk and its rich sources of information. Joe's whole being was focused on last night's break-in murder; something about this shooting had deeply puzzled the tomcat, had taken hold of him from the very beginning. He'd been grumpy and preoccupied all day, waiting for the lab reports, waiting to cadge a look at whatever information might come in over the wire.

. . .

Joe was indeed growing grumpy. The murder had occurred at around three A.M. There had been no sirens, and he hadn't learned about it until that morning over the radio while Clyde made breakfast—an omelet for the two of them, the usual canned feast and kibble for the three family cats. Halfway through the news, Joe had pawed the morning paper open across the breakfast table, and there it was.

While Linda Tucker's husband, a real estate agent, was in Santa Cruz at a training conference, Linda had been shot once in the forehead, with a small-caliber bullet, while she slept.

Clawing the page over to read the rest of the article, Joe had quickly devoured his breakfast omelet and taken off, up to the roof and across the rooftops to Molena Point PD, where he slipped in on the heels of two officers coming on duty. Leaping to the dispatcher's desk, he had rolled over and purred, making nice, picking up what news he could—and when that source dried up, when no more information seemed forthcoming, he had headed for the murder scene.

He had found Dulcie and Kit already there, having heard the news when Kit's humans, Lucinda and Pedric Greenlaw, turned on the TV before breakfast to see if the weather might cool off.

No such encouraging weather report was at

hand, but when reports of the murder came on the screen, and before Lucinda could stop them, Dulcie and Kit had fled out the dining room window and across the oak branch to Kit's private tree house, where they scrambled backward to the ground, claws raking the oak bark, and headed for the murder scene. There, Joe and his tabby lady, and Kit, had waited, hidden and watching, until Detective Garza and three other officers had secured the scene and left, at around ten A.M.— and quickly they had slipped into the house, past a uniformed guard and under the yellow tape, to search for scents that the police had no way to detect, and for any tiny, hidden items that the officers might somehow have missed.

The Tucker house had been torn apart, drawers pulled out and dumped, furniture turned over. And yet, for the first time in all the crime scenes the cats had prowled, they'd found nothing of value that the law hadn't already photographed and bagged as evidence; they had detected not even the scent of the intruder, a clue that human officers would, of course, miss. The house reeked so of the husband's cigar smoke that they could smell nothing beyond it. Even the scents of the three other cops and Detective Garza, laid back and forth across the house, were muddied by the stink of cigars. The only other notable smells were a spoiled onion in the kitchen cupboard and the unpleasant odors associated with the death of the deceased.

Later in the day, Joe had returned to the PD twice to prowl the dispatcher's desk and then the chief's office. He knew it would take a few days to get the ballistics report. As far as the cats knew, the police had not found the gun; the bullet was from a .22 fired at point-blank range. It had made an ugly, torn wound at the back of the head. Not that the deceased cared; if Linda Tucker was looking down from heaven, she probably cared only that she was dead and wanted to see her killer apprehended and punished.

Joe Grey wondered sometimes about the dead. *Did* they look down, watching the investigations? And if they did, why couldn't they, one way or another, give a sign? Why couldn't a murdered woman point a ghostly finger? How convenient that would be—if a cop knew how to read those unearthly signals.

The ransacked Tucker house was a mess in the crime photographs, which Dallas Garza studied later at his desk, going over and over them. Yet, for all the mess, according to the bereaved husband only jewelry had been taken, and some cash from Linda's purse. Tucker had arrived home about five A.M., an hour after the Santa Cruz police located him asleep in his hotel room in that small coastal town. There had been some mix-up at the desk about his reservation, and he had been moved from one hotel to another because of overbooking, so it had taken officers a while to find him. When he did arrive home, and when at last he pulled himself together sufficiently to go through the mess in the house, he was certain that nothing else was missing. Linda's body had been taken to the county morgue, where it would remain until disposition of the case.

It seemed a cut-and-dried case of break-and-enter; perhaps when Linda woke up she had made some move that caused the thief to think she was reaching for a gun, perhaps she had slipped her hand under the pillow or toward a drawer, and in panic he had shot her.

And yet, the murder bothered Joe Grey. As, he thought, it seemed to bother Detective Garza and Captain Harper. Now, sixteen hours after the killing, the tomcat paced the shingled roof, his mind totally on the dead woman.

"Something isn't right," he muttered, turning a narrow yellow gaze on Dulcie. "Garza missed something at the scene, and we missed it, too."

Dulcie knew Joe hated to muff a case, but it was all she could do to pay attention, her own mind on Mandell's brutal shooting and worry over Wilma. Joe looked at her intently.

"Why would a real estate agent go to a training conference?"

"I don't know, Joe! To learn something new. Or maybe to train others. How would I know? I just saw the afternoon paper, and—"

"Garza's report said Tucker was certain nothing

else had been taken. Very certain. Garza watched Tucker go through the house, through all the junk dumped out of the dressers and her jewelry box and the desk. He—"

"Joe, I—"

Joe's short gray fur gleamed like silver in the falling light of evening. "Garza said Tucker was very certain nothing else was taken, and that's what bothers me—just like it bothers Garza. No hesitation, just a steady reassurance that nothing else was missing."

He looked intently at Dulcie, his yellow eyes blazing. "Is that normal human behavior? How many people can tell right away that nothing is missing, no little bauble, a forgotten necklace—his wife shot to death and the house a mess, he should have been all at loose ends, confused and uncertain, unsure of anything." He was so wound up that Dulcie gave up trying to tell him that Mandell had been shot.

"After the death of a loved one," Joe said, "most folks are totally befuddled, all rage and grief, and their senses go bonkers. Their perceptions are all unhinged, they can't remember anything clearly. But not Clarence Tucker," the tomcat said, hissing. "He seems to have a total grip on reality."

"He's a real estate agent," Dulcie said softly. "And a very deliberate kind of man. Precise. I've watched him, in restaurants. Hardly ever looks at a menu. Knows what they have and exactly what he wants."

Molena Point's patio restaurants welcomed well-behaved village cats just as they welcomed leashed dogs; and it was amazing how much information a cat could pick up along with the bits of lobster and steak that might be proffered by cat-friendly diners. "Such a man *might* act logical and have his wits about him, Joe, but still be hurting bad inside."

Joe just looked at her. He wasn't buying that. "Garza's report . . . Garza thought there was something off about Tucker." The tomcat reared up, staring away over the rooftops in the direction of Molena Point PD. "Maybe something more has come in, a fax or an e-mail. Maybe Dallas has something more. Come on, Kit, get a move on." He looked hard at Dulcie. "You coming?"

Dulcie turned her back on him. "You go," she said shortly.

"Wilma's fine!" he said, frowning so hard the white strip down his forehead was a narrow line. "She'll be home soon, tired, will probably stop at Jolly's Deli to pick up supper for the two of you. Come on, we'll only be a few minutes."

Dulcie sighed. She wanted badly to tell him about Mandell; she longed for Joe's help, but he was too preoccupied. And the fact was, how could a cat stop Cage Jones? If Jones was set on . . . "Oh!" she said suddenly. "Oh! The sheriff's

46

office!" And she fled for home, chagrined that she hadn't thought, sooner, of the Santa Clara County sheriff.

Watching her race away, Joe shook his head. Cage Jones, if he had a lick of sense, would be miles from the Bay Area by now, probably on a plane, under an assumed name. Why would he hang around where every cop in the state was looking for him? And dismissing the escaped prisoner, his mind fixed on the Tucker murder, Joe headed for Molena Point PD and its electronic world of fast information. He assumed Kit was behind him—but Kit followed neither Joe Grey nor Dulcie.

No one seemed to care where she went. Looking from one fleeing cat to the other, both deep in their own concerns, she felt hurt and abandoned—and disappointed in Joe. She knew Joe's mind was on the murder-burglary, but Dulcie was so upset, and Joe Grey didn't see the dark tabby's distress—or did he just not care? Frightened and unsettled, her heart filled with Dulcie's fear for Wilma and with Joe Grey's disregard, Kit leaped after Dulcie, racing to catch up, her mottled paws flying over the shingles, her yellow eyes huge and anxious.

5

The old man had been home in the village two weeks, staying with his sister—home in the sense that it was where he grew up, not where he chose to live. Mavity didn't welcome him real warm, but that didn't bother him none. It was where he needed to be at the moment, and a sight cheaper than these rip-off California motels. And he had to say, the food was tasty. Those four women sure could cook. They refused to do his laundry, though, and that ticked him off big-time.

In Panama he'd had a black woman to do his laundry and make his meals. Everyone down there had a maid. Several if you were rich. All these years he'd had a woman come in to shop and clean, wash and iron and cook supper. There was plenty of cheap labor, black people descended from the Barbadian families that'd been brought in to build the canal during the early years of the last century.

The last century. Christ that made him feel old. Ever since he'd hit Central America as a young man—and that was some years back, he had to say—ever since he was twenty and stepped off that ship in Cristobal the first time, there'd been blacks in the streets, blacks cutting the lush green lawns, cleaning the houses, driving the cabs while talking to you over the back of the seat in Barbadian accents that he'd had trouble understanding back then. Barbadian descendants picking bananas in the interior, too, working alongside lighter-skinned Panamanians.

That Creole woman who lived here with Mavity, though, she was something else. Nothing servant-like about her. Good-looking woman, even if she didn't seem to have much use for him. None of the four women did. Well, hell, it was free rent, and he wouldn't be there long.

Just long enough to figure out where Cage'd hid his half of the stash. And figure out why Cage'd been so closemouthed with him all the way back from L.A. to San Francisco. Then silent and sour when Cage took him to the fence in the city, not easy like they used to be. Too long ago, maybe, when they ran together. Or maybe prison'd changed him.

Well, Cage'd got him to a fence, like he'd promised, and he'd got a fair price. Could have waited, but who knew how long till the market went higher, right along with inflation?

The day was nice and hot, and he'd walked down into the village to look at cars, that high-class Beckwith dealership. He thought he better be careful about paying cash in there, though. That friend of Wilma Getz, the one who owned that gray tomcat with the smart mouth, he had the

49

mechanic's shop there. Didn't need to be flinging cash around in front of no friend of Wilma Getz, it'd get back to her. Get straight to Mavity, too, the two of them thick as thieves. And all of them thick with the cops. Well, the hell with it. He'd set up a loan, then next month, pay it off. The dealer wouldn't check on that, and he hated paying interest.

He was just crossing Fourth, looking for a place to have a cup of coffee, when he stopped, staring up at the roofs across the street, and then he stepped back quick, into the shadows of a door-way.

A cat had gone racing over the roofs. A dark-striped tabby, he could swear it was that gray tom's female. That Getz woman's cat, another of them special ones, and her damn near as smart-ass as the tom. He didn't need them cats knowing he was in the village. The longer he kept them out of his hair, the better off he'd be. Take care of business and get out of here. Them cats could muddle up everything.

Well, the tabby was gone now, flying over the roofs in a hell of a hurry—scorching away like a streak, in the direction of the Getz house.

He hadn't seen anything chasing her, but she was sure as hell stressed about something. And that made Greeley smile. Whatever her problem, the worse the better. Maybe it'd keep her and that Getz woman both busy.

Kit, racing across the rooftops, her paws hitting only the high spots, careened against Dulcie—but the racing tabby spun on her, in sudden temper. "Go back, Kit! Go home! Why didn't you go with Joe? I don't want company!" Dulcie felt too shaky and upset for company, felt like she'd fly apart any minute.

Kit wilted, creeping away, and stood forlornly watching Dulcie drop down through the branches of an acacia tree to her own street, then disappear. Joe had been short with her, and now Dulcie, too. *What did I do? Why does no one want me?*

Kit, of all cats, knew she should understand about sometimes needing to be alone when you were frightened or upset, when you needed to collect your wits. But right now she had wanted, had badly needed, to be close to her friends; she stood on the roof looking away after Dulcie, puzzled and alone. And as evening tucked itself down around the village, Kit sat hurt and lonely for a long time, staring away toward Dulcie's house, and then toward Molena Point PD where Joe would be nosing into everything on the dispatcher's desk.

But then she looked, even longer, up at the silent hills where the shadows were fast gathering. Something unseen was pressing at her from up there, pressing and insistent, pressing and pushing, the same something that had held Dulcie, earlier in the afternoon, the same sense of someone listening and watching. It was Willow. The feral calico surely sensed trouble, sensed Dulcie's distress; Kit felt almost as if Willow reached out her paw, offering whatever help she could give.

The shops of the discount mall finessed Wilma along from one inviting window to the next as skillfully as strippers beckon to their audience—and, once she'd entered, finessed away her cash just as readily. Well, she didn't shop often.

The day was too hot for Wilma's taste, but the mall gardens were rich with flowers, the streets clean, and the shops offered discontinued items in all her favorite brands. She told herself she might not shop again for another ten years and that she really did need clothes. She purchased, as Dulcie had suspected, mostly faded, well-fitting jeans in the soft stretch denim she liked, and sweatshirts and T-shirts in her favorite colors—powder blue, yellow, lots of soft tomato red, a shade that was not available every season. She bought sandals, boots, one long flowered skirt and a couple of bouclé sweaters for more dressy occasions. She purchased one indulgence, a silver-and-topaz necklace, with a matching clip for her long gray hair.

And the gifts she found . . . A soft cashmere throw for Dulcie in pale blue, though Dulcie had throws all over the house. For the tortoiseshell kit, a bright plaid cotton blanket for Kit's new tree house.

She bought for Joe Grey a new glazed bowl with a gray cat painted on its side and a stainless-steel liner to hold food or water. She didn't trust ceramic glazes, didn't know what chemicals they might release to be innocently ingested. The painted cat looked very much like Joe, with its white nose and chest and paws, except that this cat's tail was long, not docked like Joe's.

Joe had lost his tail as a half-grown stray, in San Francisco, where Clyde had then been living. A drunk had stepped on his tail and broken it. Clyde had discovered him in a gutter, sick from the infection, and had taken him to a vet, who removed all but the last jaunty stub. Clyde nursed Joe back to health, and the two remained together, soon moving back to Molena Point, where Clyde had grown up. Where, when he was eight years old, Wilma thought, smiling, she was his neighbor and, he said, his first love. She had been in graduate school then.

Using her credit card with abandon, Wilma took packages to her car three times and locked them in the trunk. The ordeal in court had left her feeling unaccustomedly flat, and this spree was definitely making her feel better. Cage was such a manipulator, his big face all soft and smiling, hardly revealing his brutal nature.

Jones had irons in a dozen fires, many of them strange and off-key. He enjoyed scams and angles that few other offenders would bother with, from rigging up fake ATM machines, which he labeled DEPOSITS ONLY, hauling them to a new location in the small hours of the night and switching them for real ones, then collecting the take every day, to several interesting confidence games over the years. In Judge Bailey's view, society would benefit greatly if Cage Jones spent the rest of his natural life behind bars. *Preferably,* she thought, *without the amenities of telephone and e-mail with which to pursue his scams.*

The court's unusual request that Wilma, retired for ten years, should return to testify along with her partner clearly showed its view of Jones. Cage's was the last case Wilma and Bennett had worked together before she retired. At that time, they had searched his Molena Point house with a team of DEA agents, turning up enough heroin and stolen cash to net Jones a twelve-year sentence, ten of which he had served before he came up for parole. The parole board, which was now disbanded, had, in Wilma's view, made a serious error in judgment when they'd turned Jones loose in society.

But that wouldn't be the first time a parole board had wrung its hands with pity over an undeserving prisoner, ignored the safety of ordinary citizens, and set a felon free to seek out the most vulnerable victims. Such was bureaucracy, Wilma thought, shrugging to herself in the mirror as she tried on a gold silk sheath. The lovely dress was very slimming, not that she needed it; she kept herself in fair shape. And she had no occasion to wear such an elegant dress. But it would look smashing on Charlie. Wilma and her redheaded niece wore the same size, and she knew the cut was right. This, she thought with excitement, was the perfect Christmas present—even if Charlie, like Wilma herself, lived most of the time in jeans, sweatshirts, and boots. A police chief's wife didn't have much occasion to dress in fancy clothes, nor did Charlie have the desire to do so. But when Charlie's new book came out, she might need just such an elegant gown for a gallery opening and book signing. This was Charlie's first book, which she had both written and illustrated—written with clandestine feline help.

That secret was well kept by the tortoiseshell heroine of the story. Kit and Charlie shared the confidence only with Joe and Dulcie, and their few human friends who knew they were not ordinary cats: Clyde and the Greenlaws and Wilma herself were all privy to the cats' secret.

After buying the dress for Charlie, Wilma found a lightweight summer blazer for herself to wear over jeans, then decided she was done with shopping. She'd hit the stores she liked best, and the afternoon was waning; the sun was low in the west as she headed for her car.

She clicked the trunk open and fit in the blazer package between the other purchases and her overnight bag; she could not have bought much more, she already felt like she'd made a grand haul. Shutting the trunk, she clicked open the car door, was leaning forward to put the long dress box in the backseat and wondering if she should just check out the two shoe shops she'd missed, when she was grabbed from behind. Big hands jerked her around, bending her arm back painfully and forcing her keys from her fist. Enraged that she'd been caught off guard, she kicked backward, hard, ramming the heel of her shoe down his shin and jamming her elbow into his stomach. He hit her so hard across the neck that she reeled, and saw blackness. In a frantic move she slipped her credit card from her pocket, bent it double, swung around in his grip, and slashed his face with the sharply folded corner. He swore and shoved her in the backseat on top of the dress box. She knew it was Cage before she saw him, but only then did she get a look at him. Cage Jones was grinning coldly at her as he leaned in. He had a rope in his fist.

"Bend over. Put your hands behind you! Now!"

She fought him, tried to kick him in the crotch. His weight was too much on top of her, he was too strong. He jerked the rope so tight around her wrists he probably took the skin off. How the hell did he get out? How did he get out of jail?

6

Dulcie didn't see Greeley Urzey as she
raced across the roofs above him; she was too preoccupied. *It's nearly dusk. She* will *be home! No
need to call the sheriff in Gilroy, she'll be in the
bedroom unpacking her overnight case and that
thin little hanger bag. She probably stopped in the
kitchen to put on a pot of coffee or make a drink,
and she's wondering where I am. Right this minute
she's home and everything is as it should be!*

There! Her own shake roof, where she sunned,
where she caught birds. And lights on in the
kitchen! Yes! She couldn't see the bedroom windows, but she could see the reflection of their
lights across the hill that rose close behind the
house. And even as she looked, lights came on in
the living room, reflecting across the oak trees
beneath her; leaping down the oak to her own
driveway, she smelled car exhaust. Oh, the wonderful perfume of that ugly exhaust stink—tonight
it smelled as sweet as catnip. Madly she bolted in
through her cat door, all purrs and mewls and
wanting to shout Wilma's name.

But something stopped her. She stood in the
middle of the kitchen, very still. Something wasn't
right—the wrong smells, and when she reared up
to stare at the tops of the counters and the tabletop,

fear filled her. She leaped to a chair, looking. Wilma never left the kitchen like this. A mess of smeared jam and butter mixed with toast crumbs. The bread out of the bread box, its wrapper ripped raggedly and three slices of bread left to dry among the crumbs; the half-full juice bottle on the sink, its lid missing; the tub of butter atop the toaster, lid off, the butter smeared with crumbs and jam.

But when she peered through to the dining room, the dining room table was piled with bags from Liz Claiborne, Chico's, all Wilma's favorite shops. Had Wilma dropped her packages and, very hungry, stopped for a hasty piece of toast before she unpacked, and left that mess behind her? Dulcie cocked her ears toward the bedroom, listening.

The house was deathly still. She started to shiver. Had someone been in here when Wilma got home? Someone who'd hidden and waited . . . ?

Dropping silently to the floor, she slipped toward the living room—and stopped: the scent of strangers, two men. And the living room had been trashed, the couch cushions thrown to the floor, Wilma's beautiful Jeannot landscape rudely jerked from its hook and jammed against a bookcase. The Persian rug was flipped back at three corners—as if the burglars thought there might be a hidden safe sunk in the floor? And the rug scuffed up into folds where Wilma's lovely cherry desk had been shoved away from the window, all the drawers pulled out and tossed in a heap, their contents a jumble—bankbook, erasers, pencils on top of a tangle of files marked CDS, STOCKS, and BONDS. One man's smell was all over the files, his testosterone-heavy scent overlaid with the stink of greasy potato chips.

Now she knew how their friend Kate Osborne had felt when her San Francisco apartment was broken into and ransacked; the same shock of invasion, of being defiled, a hot tide of helplessness and rage.

But the burglar in Kate's apartment had been after jewels, searching for a rich inheritance that Kate had not, then, known the true value of. Wilma had nothing like that. A silver hair clip, one or two small precious stones, and the one valuable hair clip Kate had given her—but not enough to warrant this kind of search. And, what about the packages? If Wilma's purchases were here, so was Wilma. Or, she had been.

Dulcie's paws were sweating, her mouth dry. Trying to steady herself, she sniffed all across the floor searching for Wilma's fresh scent, but she found only the sour smell of the two men. When she paused again to listen, she heard from the bedroom a drawer being pulled out softly, then a man's hushed voice, low and angry . . . "It's not here . . ."

Silently she padded into the hall that connected

Wilma's bedroom and the guest room, pausing in the shadows at more thumps, and a second man's voice—and she glimpsed a broad figure that made her draw back. That was Cage Jones. It had to be— he was just as Wilma had described him. And was Wilma in there, held captive? Swallowing back terror, Dulcie tensed to leap at him . . .

She knew she should spin around and go for help. She was no match for Jones, he was huge. If he killed her, there would be no one to help Wilma. But she had to see. She was slipping through the shadows toward the beefy man when she heard her plastic cat door swing and flap. Terrified they'd hear, she spun around . . .

The tortoiseshell kit stood behind her, her yellow eyes widening at Dulcie's soft hiss for silence. When the voices came again, Kit dropped to the carpet, backing away in alarm.

Dulcie, creeping to the door, could not smell Wilma. She peered in, saw the two men. Wilma wasn't there. She slipped away with Kit, to the living room, where Kit licked Dulcie's ear just as, so many times in the past, Dulcie had comforted the tortoiseshell.

"Who are they?" Kit asked. "The burglars who killed that woman in the middle of the night? Oh . . ."

"It's Cage Jones," Dulcie whispered. "He shot Wilma's partner this morning."

"Mandell? Oh, he didn't shoot Mandell Bennett! How . . . ?"

"He's alive. Intensive care." Bennett had been to Wilma's house only a few times, but he was gentle in the way he spoke and stroked a cat, was the kind of human a cat liked and remembered.

"We need help," Dulcie said, glancing at the phone that had, surprisingly, not been knocked off the hook; its receiver was still in place—but if they called 911, Jones would see the extension's red light blinking in the bedroom. For several years, Wilma had had a second line for her computer, with two-line extensions where a red light blinked when one line was in use. That light would be a dead giveaway.

But what if Wilma *was* in there, and hurt, maybe tied up in the closet? Abandoning the phone, the cats headed back for the bedroom, Dulcie thinking, *So what if they see us? We're cats! What're they're going to do? Shoot a couple of house cats mindlessly looking for our supper?*

7

The beefy man sat on the bed going through the overnight case Wilma had taken to the city; her thin hanger bag was thrown on the floor, the clothes spilling out. Dulcie stared in at his long, heavily angled face, long upper lip and heavy features. Jones must be well over six feet, big boned, big hands, thick shoulders. The other man was smaller, tall but of light frame. Thin face, maybe thirty. Thin shoulders, thin long hands, long brown hair under a brown baseball cap. Both men seemed, to Dulcie, parodies of what humans should look like. She could not bear to think how they might have hurt Wilma, what they might have done with her.

Wilma's flowered chintz coverlet was wadded up on the floor, the white wicker night tables over-turned, the door to the red iron stove flung open and ashes scattered over the flowered rug: Did they think Wilma hid her valuables in the woodstove? But, what valuables? What did Jones think she had? Finished with the overnight case, he dropped it on the floor, stood, and began going through Wilma's closet, throwing clothes out into the room, running his hands over the wall behind. The white wicker dresser had been jerked away from the wall, cosmetic jars scattered on the floor, as were the contents of her traveling makeup case. What would she hide in there? The case she kept in her overnight bag, neatly supplied, ready for an impromptu junket, a habit learned when she was a probation officer and so often had to travel. Dulcie, seeing that Wilma wasn't in the bedroom, backed away toward the guest room, Kit pressing close.

The guest room had been trashed, too, closet doors flung open, drawers pulled out and dumped, guest sheets and towels spilled on the rug, the bed shoved aside, the covers pulled off. If they thought

Wilma kept valuables in the house, a large stash of money, or jewelry, why would they look in her luggage? And if they had Wilma, why had they brought in her luggage and packages? This made no sense. If Jones wanted it to appear that Wilma had come home, why bother to trash the house?

Did they want it to look like she'd been here, then was forcibly taken away? Did they want the cops to think that the housebreaker who'd killed that woman last night had done this? Take advantage of the moment, make it seem that Wilma had come home, had a snack, started to unpack, and then the break-in or forced entry had happened?

"Her car . . . ," Kit said. "Is her car here?"

"I smelled exhaust. It . . . She . . . I didn't look inside!" Racing for the laundry and the door to the garage, Dulcie leaped up the door, scrabbling her paws to open the dead bolt . . . But it was open. Those men had been in the garage, had left the door unlocked. She could smell them. Swinging on the knob, she kicked at the wall until the latch gave and the door carcened in, carrying her with it.

She saw Wilma's car as she dropped to the concrete, could feel heat still radiating from it, smell the stink of oil and exhaust. She did not want to look inside, *could* not look inside that car. Kit stared at her, waiting, then reared up, trying the doors, but they were locked.

Ever since Dulcie and Joe Grey discovered they could speak and were thinking like humans, ever

63

since they'd helped trap their first killer, not much in the human repertoire of assorted evil shocked the cats; their clandestine roles as police informants had hardened Dulcie to most human viciousness. But now fear held Dulcie as cruelly as she, herself, had ever gripped a mouse between sharp teeth. And it was Kit who leaped to the hood first, and pressed her nose to the windshield. Ice cold, Dulcie followed.

The hood was warm beneath their paws. Pressing her nose to the bug-splattered glass, Dulcie shivered with relief at the empty front seat and floor. She stared into the back as far as she could see, then leaped to the workbench and stretched out across space, her back paws on the bench, her front paws on the side window, to see the dark floor of the backseat.

Empty. She began to breathe again—but then she caught the faintest scent of blood and stiffened, studying the pale leather upholstery.

There was no dark stain, and the scent was so faint she wondered if she was mistaken, if it might be a blood smell that the tires had picked up. Dropping down to the concrete, she examined the warm tread, but she could detect no blood scent there. She watched Kit sniff at the trunk, her mind awash with every grisly kidnapping she'd ever heard about—and Kit *did* smell something, she was sniffing intently.

But then she dropped down again, lashing her

bushy tail, and turned her round yellow eyes on Dulcie. "Only gas fumes," she said quietly.

Dulcie went limp. "Is her cell phone in the car?" Both cats flew to the hood again, peering in at the seat and dark floor; then over the curved metal roof and onto the trunk to look in through the back window, pressing their faces against the glass, leaving smears that would puzzle the police but couldn't be helped. They could not see Wilma's little phone, not dropped on the floor, not fallen in the crack of a seat—and Cage Jones wouldn't stay in the house forever.

"Going to chance the phone," Dulcie said boldly, and she streaked for the living room again and onto the desk, and hit the speaker button. Her paw was lifted to press the button for the police dispatcher when she thought, How *could* she call the station? Why would the phantom snitch, whom Harper thought was a human person, be in or near this house? How would the snitch know that the house had been trashed, that there were two men in the bedroom, and that Wilma had disappeared? Only someone who had a key would know that.

Captain Harper himself had a key. As did Joe's housemate, Clyde. And Wilma's niece, Charlie Harper.

Swiftly Dulcie punched in the key for Charlie's cell phone. Charlie would have to lie for her, would have to pretend she'd come in here, herself.

Three rings, and then she got the voice mail. She

tried the house, but again no answer, only that canned voice telling you to leave your name and number. Fidgeting from nerves, she punched the digit for Clyde's cell phone. *Answer,* Dulcie prayed. *Oh, please, Clyde. They won't be in the bedroom forever. If they see the light, they'll be after us. And if they don't . . . Once they're gone, the cops might never find them, and they're all that can lead us to Wilma.*

But Clyde didn't answer, not on his cell, or on his home phone. She left frantic messages on both. If he was at the automotive shop, which was closed on Sunday, he'd be in the very back, in his own exclusive garage, working on one or another of the classic and antique cars he collected, happily puttering away, no phone to disturb him, not knowing anything was amiss. And Dulcie did the only thing left to do. She'd have to conjure up a whopping lie. She tried to think of a good one as, heart pounding, she pressed the key for 911.

One ring, and the dispatcher picked up. Dulcie was glad it was Mabel Farthy. She was describing the trashed house, explaining that Wilma was missing and that two men were in the bedroom when Chief Harper came on the phone . . . Mabel had summoned him, or had turned on the speaker. At the same moment, as Dulcie started to describe the two men, Kit stared toward the bedroom, hissing, and slipped behind the couch. Dulcie leaped after her as harsh footsteps pounded out, running. The two men raced past, through the dining room and kitchen and out the back door. As the door banged, Dulcie leaped to the window, looking, leaving Mabel shouting into the phone. She heard a car start on the side street, heard it peel away, but couldn't see it. At the same moment, two trucks rumbled past, loud and intrusive, hiding all other sounds.

"They're gone," she shouted at Mabel. "A car raced away a block over, I never saw it, I can't hear it now, can't tell which way it went." That sounded so lame, like she was making the whole thing up. "I couldn't see!" she told Mabel in frustration.

But even as she pressed the disconnect button, she saw the first squad car pull quietly to the curb. Bless Harper's men for being so fast! They must have been nearby, even closer than the station, men already in their squad cars, their engines running. Two more units sped past the house, racing to spot the fleeing car.

"You didn't describe the men," Kit hissed. "Tell her—"

Moments later, a second squad car halted at the curb, and Max Harper swung out as four uniforms took off running, to surround the house. A key clicked in the front door; the door banged open so fast, the cats only had time to back against the shutters. Chief Harper and two uniforms moved fast, toward the bedroom. The instant they were past, the cats streaked through to the laundry and bolted out Dulcie's cat door; they just missed being trampled as the two other cops moved quickly up the steps, their hands on their weapons. Dulcie and Kit dropped from the porch into a flower bed, Kit's eyes wide. This was not the usual procedure for a break-and-enter—but the law didn't fool around when it came to an escaped convict. And Max Harper didn't play gentle when a close friend, and his wife's own aunt, might be in danger.

8

When Dulcie frantically phoned the station, Joe Grey was asleep in the chief's empty office, sprawled across Max Harper's desk; he snored softly, less than thirty feet from the dispatcher's cubicle, so deep under that he didn't hear a thing until Mabel shouted. He heard Harper double-time up the hall from the coffee room, then, as if she had turned on her speaker, heard the voice on Mabel's phone. Joe woke up, alarmed, leaped from the desk, and peered around the door, up the hall.

Mabel Farthy never lost her cool, the amply built older blonde was totally in control in any emergency as she juggled radio, phones, fax, computers, and officers milling around her counter. But not so now. Her voice shook and she was swearing. She stood gripping the chief's arm, upset indeed, as, from the shadows of the hall, Joe listened to Dulcie's frightened voice on the phone and tried to play catch-up, his every muscle tense with alarm.

An hour earlier he had been lounging on the desk in Detective Dallas Garza's office as Dallas and the chief discussed a second break-in killing, another woman murdered in her bed. Joe had come into the station, on the heels of Detective Garza, to see what new information might be forthcoming on the first death, and now they'd been discussing a second one. What was coming down here? Some deranged burglar who wasn't satisfied simply to steal and get out, but who got his thrills in other ways? The coroner had already told them that the first victim hadn't been sexually molested—just sadistically blown away. And as the officers began to put this second killing together, they waited for autopsy and fingerprint reports on the first one, for which they had two sets of prints besides those of the dead woman and her husband. But there had been workmen in the house, a carpenter and a plumber repairing a bath-room, and the officers expected the prints would turn out to be theirs. Now, with a second, similar case, questions had multiplied like jackrabbits. Joe had lain curled up in Dallas's in-box, sharply alert beneath shuttered eyes, watching Dallas lean back in his desk chair, put his feet up on the blotter, and flip open a file.

The square-faced Latino detective's usual sunny

smile had vanished. "Marital trouble in both cases. Five domestics at the Tucker address since the first of the year, four at the Keatings'. Linda Tucker was a shy little thing, real quiet and reclusive. But Elaine Keating . . ."

"Right," Harper had said. "She was bad news."

"Three of those call-outs, Linda pressed charges for battery, and was told how to get help and find shelter. Didn't do much good. She took him right back."

The detective had sipped his coffee, reaching to stroke Joe Grey, giving Joe a look of amazement—whether amazement that the cat hung around the department, or surprise at his own friendly feelings toward a feline, Joe wasn't sure. For a dog man, Dallas Garza was coming right along, and that made the tomcat smile. Dallas had, when Joe first met him, considered cats about as appealing as gutter rats.

"We could have a kinky burglar," Harper had said, "or a copycat murderer. Common knowledge Tucker was sleeping around. Maybe his wife threatened to walk."

In that case, Joe thought, she didn't handle the problem very well. Even a cat could have told her that a battered woman should keep her plans to herself, get her own affairs in order, put her money where the man couldn't reach it, and then quietly get out. Follow her escape plan and lay low, not telegraph her intentions. No different from a sensible cat quietly stealing away from a pack of coyotes, no disturbance, no movement through the grass to give himself away, just gone. And this sure would be true if a woman had children to get out safely—or pets. It hurt Joe deep down when a fleeing wife, in her haste and terror, left a dog or a cat behind. The poor creature was nearly always abused; most abusers would do that to get back at a woman.

"Elaine Keating had some money of her own," Max said. "A small inheritance she kept in a separate account. Trouble was, she put his name on the account."

Dallas shook his head. "If this is a copycat murder, I hope to hell it doesn't start a rash of wife killings." The detective studied the gray tomcat sprawled across his papers. "What does he find so fascinating? We don't have mice in here."

Harper shrugged. "This is one of the coolest buildings in the village, with these thick adobe walls."

"And in the winter?"

"One of the warmest." Max stared at Joe. "His visits couldn't be because Mabel feeds him, hides away little snacks for the cats?"

"Then why isn't he on Mabel's desk instead of mine?"

"Likes your company," Harper said. "If we get an article or two in the paper, to head these guys off . . . Help them remember we keep a list of wife abusers from past reports . . ." Harper rose to refill his coffee cup from the pot on the credenza.

"And maybe enlighten the abused wives," Dallas said. He scratched Joe Grey's ear. "Put those women on alert—without inviting a lawsuit. I'll call Jim Barker, he's a good reporter."

"Who would sue us? We won't be printing their names." But Harper grinned. These days, some people would try to sue the cops over a traffic ticket.

The chief rose and moved away down the hall on some errand, and in a minute Joe heard him going downstairs, where the emergency center and shooting ranges were located. Dallas had picked up the phone and was making a date with Barker for a private lunch; but when the detective turned on his computer and started filling in tedious travel sheets, Joe leaped down and trotted along to Harper's empty office, which was darker and quieter; he never had liked the click of computer keys.

Now, an hour later, having been awakened by Mabel's shout from the dispatcher's cubicle, he listened, alarmed, to the canned female voice from Mabel's speakerphone—Dulcie's voice, talking to both Mabel and then to Harper when she knew the speaker was on.

". . . isn't in the house, I'm sure. But the house has been ransacked . . ."

"How do you know this?"

"I . . . The door was unlocked. I thought I'd

glimpsed her car go in the garage, so I knocked. When she didn't answer, I tried the garage door. It was locked, but I smelled a whiff of exhaust, like she had just gotten home. I thought it strange that she didn't answer, and knocked again. When she still didn't come, I got worried. That's when I tried the back door.

"It was unlocked, and I stepped into the kitchen. I was about to call out when I saw the house was all messed up, furniture overturned; then I heard men's voices from the back. But I didn't hear Wilma. I ran out, called you on my cell. I saw two men run out . . . One was—"

The line went suddenly dead. Dulcie had hung up or bolted away. Harper snatched the phone, shouting, "Give me your name. You're Wilma's neighbor? Where . . . ? Your address . . . ?"

He turned away at last, came pounding down the hall past Joe, shouting at Garza; the detective swung out of his office, and as the two headed for the back door and a patrol unit, Joe slipped up the hall to the front, where Mabel was dispatching squad cars—she paused long enough to punch in a phone number. Her voice, sharp with dismay, was obliterated as three police units sped away from the station. When they'd gone, she was saying, ". . . in Wilma's house. Two men. They ran, but . . . All right, but be careful. You tell anyone I called you, Clyde, you're dead meat!" She listened, then, "You'd better cover for me, or the chief'll have my hide." Silence. Then, "Said she was a neighbor. Hung up before she identified herself. I . . . Max would fire me, I swear he would."

Joe was strung tight as four more officers hurried up the hall and out the front door; he streaked out behind them, leaped scrambling up the overhanging oak to the roof and headed for Wilma's house. Racing across hot shingles and tiles, he forgot the two murders and the disquieting prospect that they might not be the last. Dulcie needed him, and Wilma needed them both—and he guessed Clyde, too, could use a little support. Wilma was like Clyde's older sister, the only family Clyde had.

Sailing across space and into an oak that bridged the narrow street, Joe scrambled up it to a higher roof. Max Harper was nearly as close to Wilma as was Clyde; they'd both known Wilma since they were boys, the two kids spending hours in Wilma's kitchen eating peanut butter and bacon sandwiches, awed by the beautiful blond graduate student, talking with Wilma about life in a way neither boy could talk with his parents.

Roof after roof; the blocks had never seemed so long. At last, backing down a jasmine vine to the sidewalk, Joe fled across Wilma's street, between parked squad cars and through Wilma's tangled garden. He was headed beneath the bushes for Dulcie's cat door when Dulcie and Kit materialized out of a forest of lavender, Dulcie looking as miserable as he'd ever seen her. Her sleek tabby fur was bedraggled, her peach-tinted ears twitching with distress.

"She's gone," she panted, pressing against Joe and mewling as pitifully as a lost kitten. "Somewhere . . . ," she said. "Those men . . . Cage Jones . . ." And she collapsed against him, trembling.

9

The old man was sitting at a sidewalk table in front of a hole-in-the-wall café enjoying a beer when half a dozen police cars moved swiftly up the street. No sirens. Two cops in each car. He watched with interest as they turned onto the street where that Wilma Getz lived. Several blocks up, they slowed. Looked like them cops was headed for that Getz woman's place, sure enough. Fancy stone house. Cottage, they called it.

Pretty fancy place for a retired parole officer. Hard-assed old bitch. She'd throwed him out of that house when he was trying to visit his own sister, Mavity, sick in there, near to dying. Threw him right out, or tried to. Two years ago, that was. Just because he'd had a couple of drinks. Dried-up old prune . . .

Well, Mavity was just as judgmental. Raised a

hell of a fuss this afternoon when she saw him drinking an innocent beer.

A person had to walk into the village, pay through the nose—tourist prices—if he wanted to have a drink in peace. Open a beer in that house or let 'em see a bottle of whiskey, all hell broke loose, Mavity fussing and the other three scowling like he'd made a bad smell. One little drink . . . What the hell did *they* do for recreation?

Gulping his beer, watching for more cop cars, Greeley rose. If them cars was parked in front of the Getz woman's place, he sure as hell didn't want to miss the action. Tucking the price of the beer but no tip under the wet bottle, he double-timed up the sidewalk. What a joke, *him* following squad cars. How many times in his sixty plus years had cop cars followed—and lost—him. He moved fast, dodging tourists. This village with its too cute cottages and shops always made him feel smothered. Too cozy for his taste, but a good place to rip off innocent shopkeepers and not get shot at.

Ahead, them cop cars was pulled up smack in front of the Getz place. Cops in the yard and moving around behind the house. He was slipping into the shadows of a porch half a block down and across the street when a car careened out of a side street racing away. Greeley stared.

Cage?

Sure as hell was. Cage Jones, driving fast, dodging other cars. Big hulking guy like Cage

Jones was hard to miss, that long face and long lip. He hadn't seen Cage since they'd got back from L.A. more'n a month ago, done their business in San Francisco, and parted. But he'd read the San Francisco papers, paid attention to the hearing, all right. Cage due to be sent back, and he walks out of that San Francisco jail easy as you please, big smile and a fake ID. What a laugh. Had to hand it to Cage, though it would have suited Greeley's own plans better if he'd stayed locked up.

But what, exactly, was he doing at the Getz house? What the hell did Cage have in mind, coming there? He ought to be staying as far as he could from Wilma Getz; the woman meant nothing but trouble, specially for Cage.

Well, that car had sure as hell been coming from her place, cop fear written all over Cage's bony face, him bent over the wheel, ducking down, driving as fast as he dared and not get stopped—but the next racing figure left Greeley open-mouthed. And then he grinned a cold, knowing smile.

As the cops burned their searchlights into the fading evening, flashing along the crowded cottages, sure as hell looking for Cage, he saw a streak of gray with white markings run through a beam high up along the roofs, then vanish. That damn tomcat. He'd seen Joe Grey for only an instant, but he knew that cat, all right. Well, the cat had sure as hell followed them cops.

77

In a moment he saw the cat again, sailing from an oak tree onto the Getz woman's garage roof, could see the cat's white markings as he crept along the edge of the roof. The next minute he vanished in the thick shadows of another oak. Greeley, hunkering down in the bushes, stayed out of sight, trying to put it all together, figure out what Cage had in mind, coming here.

Cage was a damn fool to come down here to Molena Point—well, he sure wouldn't go home, cops knowing where he lived. Greeley hoped to hell he wouldn't. Because that was where *he* was headed, for a little visit to Cage's place—though he sure didn't look forward to playing nice to Cage's sister Lilly. Sour old spinster, meaner than a snake.

But even if Cage was fool enough to go to ground there in his own house, with Lilly, he'd wait, make sure the cops had searched the place first.

Meanwhile *he'd* have that big house all to himself, if he hurried. And if he could sweet-talk Lilly just right. That Jones house, that was what he'd come for.

He hadn't seen Lilly Jones in some years, not since long before them little burglaries he and the black tomcat had pulled off together in the village. He'd never got caught—though them two village cats knew who did it, all right. They'd *saw* black Azrael go down through a skylight, saw his black tail disappear inside. Nosy little bastards spying on them.

Well, them cats'd kept their mouths shut and with good reason. If he'd got caught, and his black tomcat, too, that damned Azrael would have mouthed off at the cops. And that would have let the cat out of the bag, Greeley thought, laughing. Cops find out there were talking cats in the world, cops *heard* Azrael cursing them, they'd be forced to believe it. And that would sure as hell blow Joe Grey's secret.

That was when he'd met Sue, met her at her South American Shop, and first thing you knew, they were all over each other and headed on back to the tropics to get married—though the honeymoon hadn't lasted long before Sue split. Thanks in part to Azrael. That black tom sure had hated her, sure as hell drove her out. Well, but Greeley, he'd been glad to see the last of her, himself, she was such a teetotal. Hell, he wasn't made for marriage anyway.

Black tomcat was gone now, too. Greeley didn't know where. Evil little bastard, always into voodoo. Sometimes he'd even scared Greeley. He didn't miss Azrael, but he sure missed his skill at break-and-enter. Cat could get into Fort Knox if he had the time to work at it, as good with the windows as Greeley himself was with a safe. They'd made a good team, and Greeley did miss having a partner the cops would never make.

His marriage to Sue might be finished, too, but at least they'd parted friends. When she'd moved back to Molena Point, she was still willing to do a little business on the side, if it profited her. And his own line of work, at the moment, had fit right in, her exports to the States, that shop and its replicas of devils and idols; those little geegaws she'd helped him bring back had set him up real nice. Well, Sue'd get her share when this was all over— what he told her was her share.

Sure as hell, he was past the age when he relished the diving like he once had, and his lungs was going real bad on him. And Panama starting to hire locals and younger men, the bastards. Damn doctors said lung trouble was to be expected, the amount of whiskey he drank. He'd never heard that! What the hell did they know? Screw 'em all, the medical profession didn't know no more than some jungle witch doctor, maybe a hell of a lot less.

Watching cops move in and out of the Getz house, and cop cars take off, he thought again about Lilly Jones. Strange, pale woman. He guessed she stayed on in the family house because she had nothing better. She didn't work, not that he'd heard. Maybe the parents'd left some money when they died, or maybe Cage saw that she got by, so he'd have a place to come the times he was out—and a place to hide his stash. Had to be pretty well hidden for the feds not to find it. He wondered, uncomfortably, if Lilly knew.

But hell, Cage wouldn't have told *her*. And *she'd* never figure it out. Woman was too dull. Hidebound. Spent half her time in church—until that sister of hers was born. Then, Cage'd said once, Lilly'd stopped going to church. That one, the sister, even as a child, was just as pale and silent as Lilly. Even as a child, near as dried up. No more spirit than a sick chicken.

Wilma's shoulder hurt badly, felt like it was swelling, getting tight against her shirt. Cage had twisted her arm so painfully behind her, she wondered if he'd dislocated it. She'd fought him with little effect, and cursed herself for not staying in better shape. But Cage was built like an ape. Well, if she couldn't fight him, she'd have to outwit him somehow.

How many dead women, in the last hour of their lives, had clung to that same futile hope? Imagining they would outsmart their abductor?

She'd blown it when she'd let him slip up on her. How the hell did he get out of jail? What kind of scam had he pulled this time? It had been around four in the afternoon when she was grabbed from behind and shoved in the backseat of her car, where he'd jerked her down and tied her hands behind her, taped her ankles together. She'd wanted badly to ask him how he'd escaped; every time she tried to turn and face him, he'd shoved her down again. The prodding in her back had felt like a gun but could have been anything: flashlight, cigarette lighter, the blunt end of a screwdriver. She prayed he hadn't found her own gun, hadn't jimmied the glove compartment. She didn't dare try to look up over the backseat in that direction.

But now he had her keys, surely he would look. She could only hope he wouldn't want to be caught with her gun. She had managed to flip her credit card in the gutter, distracting Cage again so he wouldn't see it. Slashing at him she'd cut her hand a little on the card's ragged corner. At least, with it folded, someone finding it might be less likely to use it. Maybe someone honest would find it, if it was found at all. Cage had then slapped three lengths of duct tape over her mouth. She'd waited sickly for the blindfold, but he hadn't put one on her. Did he mean to kill her before it would matter what she saw?

How had she ever supervised this man?

But he'd needed her then, needed her goodwill, needed her influence with the court. He didn't need her now, and he could let all the hate out.

She presumed that no pedestrian, no shopper had been near enough to see him throw her in the car. He'd kept his back to the sidewalk while he tied her, his body hiding her. The tape was going to hurt like hell when it was ripped off—if she was alive when it was removed. If it *is* ever removed, she thought, fear escalating into panic.

There were two of them. The other man had

slipped into the driver's seat, shoving the seat back as far as it would go; it pressed hard against her legs. He was tall, thin shouldered, looked younger: smooth neck under longish brown hair. Tan T-shirt tight across his bony shoulders, dirty brown cotton cap pulled low.

Cage had had a partner on some jobs. She must have seen mug shots or read a description, but that was ten years ago; still, there was something about this guy that rang a bell. He started the car, gunned the engine, and pulled out with a squeal of the tires. Drove three blocks to a less public side street, parked, and got out. When Cage got out, too, she managed to twist around and sit up. They stood by the front of the car, talking. There was no one on the narrow little residential street behind the mall, no one visible but Cage and his partner. Yes, this man was younger, maybe twenty-five. Six foot two or three. Lean, long face, high cheekbones. Tanned arms, tanned neck and face. She could see no prison tattoos. He swung into a blue Plymouth that sat parked just ahead of them, a car maybe ten years old and grimy with dirt. She was craning to see the license plate when Cage slipped into the backseat again and pulled a long, dark rag over her eyes, tying it tightly behind her head, and shoved her down on the seat again.

"Stay down. Or you're going to hurt, bad." He slammed the door. She heard him open the driver's door, felt the car rock, heard the door slam and the locks click. He started the engine and pulled out; she could hear the other car take off behind them, the driver gunning the engine. Didn't he know any other way to drive? Cage made a sharp left, and when she struggled up again, hoping to hear better and to retain a sense of where they were headed, he reached over the back, hit her hard, and shoved her down.

"Stay down, bitch, or I'll fix you so you can't get up."

She could only swallow her rage. She thought about her .38 locked in the glove compartment, and she could almost hear Clyde say, "You had to know he'd escaped. Why the hell weren't you carrying! You have a permit for a concealed weapon, and a perfectly good shoulder holster." She could just hear him, and Max, too. In her mind, she pointed out to them that she hadn't known Cage was free, that it was Sunday, broad daylight, in an ordinary shopping mall. She could just hear her niece, too—"You are a retired federal officer, you had every right . . ." Worst of all, she imagined Dulcie worrying when she didn't come home.

As he increased speed, and his attention was on the traffic, she squirmed around until she could reach the door handle behind her, but it wouldn't unlock; he'd engaged the childproof locks. And she didn't relish rolling out of a moving car. There was no hope of running out of gas; she'd gassed up when she hit Gilroy, before breakfast. At least she wouldn't go to her grave hungry, she thought wryly.

Listening, and memorizing the turns, she was sure they were headed for the freeway. And in just a minute the car picked up speed, climbing, as if going up an entry ramp, and then they were whipping through heavy traffic, passing roaring trucks. Heading south, she was certain. Toward Molena Point? If this was Cage's vindication for her testimony in court yesterday, why hadn't he killed her in Gilroy where he could dump her back in the hills somewhere? But what else could this be about?

Could Cage want something from her, or plan to use her as a hostage for some reason? She couldn't imagine what. In the past, when Cage was on parole, she'd usually been able to reason with him, on his own level, to his own degree of tolerance; on several occasions, she had even been able, with careful efforts, to sidetrack or delay his crimes.

Now, with the tape over her mouth, she couldn't even talk to him. And then she thought, what about Mandell? Did Cage plan to find Mandell Bennett, too?

But Bennett was a far warier adversary; he was younger and he kept himself sharp for his work. Mandell was bigger and stronger than she, and he would be armed. Again she was ashamed of letting down her natural wariness and becoming complacent.

But there was one thing in her favor. To her knowledge, Cage Jones had never been a killer. Thief, burglar, robber, manipulator. If he'd ever killed, there was no hint of it in his record.

Well, but she hadn't dealt with Cage in ten years. Ten years in Terminal Island among the vicious prison gangs—a ten-year hitch for which she and Bennett were largely responsible—could make a big difference in the attitudes of a felon. She felt a shaft of late-afternoon sun strike her face and knew for sure they were moving west; she welcomed for that brief moment the warmth and light through the blindfold.

When she'd left the last store, heading for her car, the low sun had shone sharply in her eyes. Now, as they traveled west, it would be shining in Cage's eyes. Too low for the visor to block the glare? Was he wearing dark glasses? If not, and the sun was half blinding him, could she do something to make him swerve and crash? But the odds of doing that weren't good. Tied up in her own car, she'd be unable to escape such a wreck.

Certainly no one was looking for her, not yet. No one in Molena Point would expect her at any given time—except Dulcie, she thought, feeling sad, and yet knowing hope, too. When she didn't come home, when she hadn't pulled into the garage by dark, her friends, if they called, would simply think she was delayed, as any woman shopping might be, or that she was in heavy traffic. But

Dulcie would be pacing, the little cat would be growing frantic. Knowing Dulcie, it wouldn't be long until she started raising some hell. She'd call Clyde, then Charlie. One way or another, she'd alert Max Harper. Max would go by the house and, when she didn't appear long after dark and they couldn't rouse her on her cell phone, he'd have every cop in northern California looking for her.

She wasn't carrying her purse, only a fanny pack; her purse was locked in the trunk, and her phone locked in the glove compartment with her gun. Maybe Cage hadn't used her key, yet, to gain access, to find her weapon and her phone, and play back her messages. And what was the difference? So someone was worried about her? That would be of little interest to Cage. Let them worry.

Did anyone else know Cage had escaped? Had it been in the papers, or on the news? In fact, had the jailers themselves done a head count and realized he was gone? Or had he pulled off something so slick that he hadn't yet come up missing? Slipups could escalate; jails were overcrowded and short-handed; men traded identities, bought their way out with help from friends. Knowing Cage, that's what he would have tried. But whatever had come down, or would, right now, Wilma put most of her hope in one lonely and worried little tabby; thoughts of Dulcie stirring up some action helped considerably to soothe her.

Cage's window was down, and the hot air grew

cooler, the light through the blindfold dimming as evening drew down. When the car took a right off the freeway, she eased up to listen; she could hear less traffic now. Soon they made another turn, and their speed decreased as they climbed up a bumpy road. Sniffing the air, she caught the scent of dry grass, then later of pine and eucalyptus trees, so they had to be heading up into the coastal hills. There was a lot of empty land up there along the higher ridges, above the small horse farms and ranches. Was Cage making for some sparsely populated region where a body could be dumped and maybe never found?

Oh, Dulcie. If they don't find me, you mustn't grieve. I love you. Please, go live with Joe and Clyde, or with Kit and the Greenlaws. Take care of yourself. Please, do what's best for you. The pine scent was sharper now, carried on a welcome cool breeze that hushed, high above her, through tall trees. There was no longer any light through the blindfold; she rode in darkness, bumping along to . . . where?

10

At dusk, up on the open hills where the hot grass blew brown and rattling, ten feral cats paced nervously along a broken stone wall, watching the hills below for the hunting beasts that roamed the hills and for invading and curious humans; the clowder of cats was always alert and wary as they roamed among the estate's fallen rooms and ragged walls and overgrown weedy rosebushes. Below them down the falling hills, all the world lay open, wild and empty, and close around them among fallen stone and hidden cellars where the shadows lay thick, all was silent and still. There was nothing to disturb them, this hot summer evening, but the ten cats paced, lashing their tails, wary and nervous: The human woman had come again into the ruins: the wraithlike young woman who came too often, hurrying stealthily down from the scattered small houses in the hills high above, a pale creature, half child, half woman, as skinny as a starving bird. Always, she crept into the rotting, overgrown old travel trailer that had ages ago been hidden among the fallen walls. She would lurk in there like a mouse in a rusting can, as if seeking privacy and quiet, as if wanting to hide there.

The trailer seemed a part of the vines that covered it, as if they had grown right into its metal skin. It must have been hauled up the little dirt road countless years ago, and pushed by men in among the half-fallen walls and left to rot. Even when their feral band had first come to live in this place, they had not, beneath its heavy mantle of ivy, discovered the trailer for nearly a week. It was not visible, even to a cat, from more than a few feet away. Willow had found it, her inquisitive nose following the stink of mildew.

Once they had discovered and investigated it, and had determined that no beast had taken up residence there, they had slipped away nervously, and had afterward avoided the rusting box, giving it a wide berth. But the thin, pale girl-woman, walking so sad, always wary and sad, liked to hide there.

The trailer could not be seen from the narrow dirt road below; that road hadn't been used since the cats had come to live there. Nor could the top of it be glimpsed from the wooded hills above; Cotton had gone up there to look. No human ever came down through these woods from the far houses except the human girl slipping down into their own realm of shadows like a lost spirit from some ancient Celtic ballad. This band of cats knew the old myths, for they were part of their own history. These little, wild cats knew that they were out of place in this world. They were survivors in a world where such beasts were said not to exist, where humans no longer believed in such creatures. They were trapped in a world they didn't understand and that would never understand them. With their human intelligence and human perceptions, they had learned to survive, to take what they needed from mankind and remain apart. But now, looking down to the sea, stained with the reds of sunset, and to the glinting rooftops of the far village, their thoughts were filled with the unwanted concerns that had reached out to touch them. Willow paced the wall, the faded calico hissing with agitation, and warily the others watched her, knowing well her strange perceptions, and sharply attentive to her fear. For Willow and Coyote and Cotton had friends in the village. This last winter when the weather was cold and wet, three village cats and their humans had saved them from a cage and set them free— three cats like themselves, who could speak with humans. Three who had chosen to live among humans.

Now, something was not right among those three; sharply Willow sensed Dulcie's unease. "What?" she whispered. "What is this distress for tabby Dulcie, what has happened that makes her pace and shiver?" She looked at Cotton and Coyote, but they couldn't sense what she felt—though on the wall beside her, the two toms paid attention. As had the other ferals, all seven, who had vanished uneasily among the stones and caverns.

Clyde Damen was more than uneasy. Switching lanes fast in his old open roadster, dodging village traffic, he swerved in front of a bread truck, so the driver slammed on his brakes, blasted his horn, and yelled obscenities; but then the man stared down at Clyde's classic yellow Chevy and grinned with admiration and motioned Clyde ahead. Clyde gave him a thumbs-up, went in front of him and wheeled across Ocean, heading for Wilma's cottage. He didn't know how he'd explain his swift arrival to the law. He'd think of something to tell Harper. He'd say he'd called Wilma to see if she was home and wanted to catch dinner, that when she hadn't answered he'd decided to run by, and there were Harper's squad cars all over. Looking frantically for a place to park among the patrol units, he ended up two blocks away, squeezing the roadster in between a couple of old pickups, swinging out of the car, and hurrying back to Wilma's.

Impossible to stay out of sight, there were uniforms everywhere—except not trampling her flowers, even the rookies knew better than to trash Wilma's garden. Hitting the front walk of the low stone house, he headed for Officer Brennan, whose large girth guarded the front door. Behind Clyde, two patrol cars took off burning rubber, and a third sped away up the narrow street in the opposite direction.

He started to speak to Brennan, but then he saw Dulcie and Kit at the far end of the house, huddled in shadow beside the back steps, looking small and miserable. Glancing at Brennan, who had turned to speak to someone inside, he hurried across the yard and picked up Dulcie. He reached for Kit, but she gave him a wild look and bolted away, up the nearest oak. Holding Dulcie close, he slipped around the far side of the house looking for privacy where they could talk.

"I called you," she whispered, climbing to his shoulder. "You didn't answer . . . I left messages . . ." Her face was close to his, her green eyes wide with distress.

"Dispatcher called me," he said, cuddling her.

"She's gone," Dulcie whispered. "She hasn't come home, but someone . . ." Her tail lashed against him, her ears laid back in worried anger. "Her packages are here, her overnight bag. Her car's here. There were two men inside—Cage Jones and someone else," she said, hissing. "They tore the house apart, they were in the bedroom, we saw them. Searching for something. What could they want? Kit and I watched them going through her things; when they ran out, I heard a car on the next street but couldn't see it, don't know what kind or which way it went. I called the station . . . Ten minutes later I heard it again, fast but quieter . . . as if they'd doubled back . . .

"Those men . . . They're the only ones who know where she is, who know what happened to her. Your cell phone . . . I have to call Mabel back, tell her what they look like! I didn't tell her." Frantically she pawed at his jacket pockets. "Where—"

"Tell me what they look like, Dulcie. I'll call. If a cop comes around the corner—"

"How can you? You had no chance to see them,

they were gone when you got here. Shove the phone under a bush. Make it snappy."

Glancing around for uniforms, Clyde punched in 911 for her, knelt, and laid his cell phone deep under a camellia bush among a carpet of dead brown blooms. As she talked, he paced, watching the front yard and the back, but only when he had pocketed the phone again and picked up Dulcie once more did he relax. "You sure she hasn't been home?" he whispered. "Maybe went out again? If this is a false alarm, Dulcie, if—"

"Came home and what? Tore up her own house? Tipped over the furniture? Trashed her desk?" She stared bleakly into his face. "No one in the world but those two men know where she is. And now they're gone."

"She was going to stop in Gilroy," Clyde said. "She called me early last evening, wanted to know if she could pick up anything for me."

Dulcie sighed. "She called Lucinda after supper. She sounded fine, then." The little cat leaned against his cheek, swallowing.

"Dulcie, did she check out of her hotel?"

Dulcie's eyes widened.

"Come on . . ." Holding the dark tabby close, he made for the front of the house, up the steps past Brennan, and burst into the living room where Harper was helping Detective Garza lift prints. Both men turned to stare at him, scowling.

"This is a crime scene," Harper said. "You know

better than to come in here. And how did you know? Ten minutes since the call came in." The tall, thin chief was dressed in his usual frontier shirt and jeans, Dallas Garza in faded jeans, a dark turtleneck, and an ancient tweed sport coat.

"Did she check out?" Clyde asked. "Check out of the Hyatt this morning? The one at the wharf."

Max just looked at him.

"Did she check out?"

"Seven, sharp." Max studied Clyde, frowning, stared at the cat in Clyde's arms, shook his head, and turned away, his leathery face unnaturally drawn. "She's been home," Max said. "Or, it looks that way. Overnight bag's here. Packages. Car in the garage. Either before or after she got home, the place was tossed." He turned to look hard at Clyde again. Harper and Clyde were as close as brothers, but right now, Max's head was filled with questions. "Caller wouldn't identify herself, said the door was unlocked. Said she came in, saw two men in the bedroom, they saw her and ran out."

"*Who* called? Couldn't you—"

Harper shook his head. "No caller ID. Said she was a neighbor." Max frowned, compounding the wrinkles on his long, thin face. "I've never known Wilma to leave a door unlocked. Or the kitchen in a mess like that. Even the way she unpacked . . . Go back and take a look, see what you think."

"I don't know how she unpacks, Max. Call Charlie, Charlie would know." Wilma's niece had

95

lived with her aunt for several months; she'd know things about Wilma's personal habits that even he or Max might not.

"I can't reach Charlie. She was going to ride with Ryan this evening. Can't get Ryan, either. They'll have their phones off." Since Charlie had finished the manuscript and drawings for her first book, she'd been riding every evening, making up for lost time, sometimes waiting for Max to get home so they could have a gallop over the hills together, but more often going alone or with Ryan, enjoying the horses before she got back to work on new commissions for animal portraits and on her own drawings and prints.

"I heard," Clyde said uneasily, "that Cage Jones escaped. Doesn't his sister live in the village?"

Max nodded. "That house Cage and Lilly's parents left them. Couple of hours ago, the minute we knew Jones had walked, Dallas and Davis picked up a warrant, searched the house. His sister Lilly says she hasn't seen Cage, didn't know he'd escaped." Max shrugged. "Said she doesn't listen to the news much—now, we'll double back, have another look. Though it's not likely Cage would hide her in his own house—if he *was* fool enough to kidnap a retired federal officer."

Max turned to Wilma's desk, stood looking out the front window. "Sure like to talk with the woman who tipped us." He looked at Clyde, scowling. "Could be our phantom snitch, but I can't figure how that adds up," he said irritably. "How the hell can she or her partner always be in the right place at the right time!"

Clyde felt Dulcie's claws kneading nervously on his arm. Harper's frustration at the unidentified but accurate tips he'd been receiving for several years was both stressful and comical. Clyde shook his head. "Doesn't make sense, does it?" he said innocently. "I don't know, Max. If they weren't always right, if they hadn't been a help in so many cases . . ."

"I'm not sorry to have those two," Max said. "Even if their seeming clairvoyance does drive me up the wall!"

"Is that what you think? Some kind of . . . ?"

"I don't know what the hell I think," Max snapped. He continued to watch Clyde, then shook his head. "Made up my mind not to think about it. Take the information and run with it, not ask questions." The chief reached to his pocket for a cigarette, something he hadn't done for a long time. "Sometimes, it's damned hard not to run those two snitches to ground, or try to. I wish to hell . . .

"But what's the good, wishing," Max said. "I just hope Wilma knows that Jones conned his way out of jail. What kind of shop are they running, releasing a guy on false ID!"

"Not the first time that's happened," Clyde said. "And Jones won't know that Wilma was going to shop in Gilroy. Anyway, the minute he got out, wouldn't he run? Head for another state?"

"Guess you haven't heard the rest."

In Clyde's arms, Dulcie had gone as rigid as a stone, pressing her head into the crook of his arm.

"Bennett was shot two hours ago," Max said. "As he left the office."

Clyde squeezed Dulcie so hard she had to swallow back a mewl. "How bad?" He loosened his grip on Dulcie and contritely stroked her.

"He's in intensive care. They got him in the shoulder and chest. San Francisco General. There's a statewide bulletin out, I just talked with the sheriff up there, he's got deputies all over Gilroy, all over the outlet mall. Mabel e-mailed them a picture of Wilma, that one in Wilma's bedroom of her and Charlie at our wedding."

"And her car's here?"

"In the garage." Max shook his head. "So far, nothing. Couple of tiny spots of blood on the side of the backseat, down next to the door. No more than a scratch would produce. Sample's gone to the lab. Haven't dusted the car for prints yet . . ." Max's phone buzzed. He clicked on, listened and scowled.

Clicking off, he looked at Clyde. "Dispatcher has a description of the two men, the call just came in. From the same woman. Description matches Cage Jones, and I think I know the other guy." He sat down at Wilma's desk, looking tired. "The same snitch," he said again. "Mabel had her hands full dispatching on a drunk call." He looked up at Clyde. "Why didn't that woman give Mabel those descriptions the first time she called?"

"Maybe she was in plain sight when they ran out, maybe she was too busy hiding from them." He felt Dulcie's ragged little attempt at a purr as she eased closer against him. "What's the game plan? If Jones has Wilma, what can you do and not put her in danger?"

But Max was on the phone again, moving men into position, then motioning to Dallas; Clyde looked around at the trashed living room. He felt sick inside. And scared. Max was saying, ". . . use the gas and electric company uniforms, get one of their emergency trucks. And a water company truck, three men. I want to watch the house for as long as it takes. We're not rushing in."

Clyde listened, thinking how unstable Jones was. If Wilma was in there . . . He stroked Dulcie, trying to calm her. Trying to calm himself. He didn't like the way she felt under his hand, her tabby body hard and rigid, the way a sick cat feels to the touch. He stroked her gently, worrying over Wilma and worrying over the little tabby. Why the hell had this happened! Why the hell hadn't Cage just skipped, gotten out of California!

Max looked around the room. "Davis is on her way up to Gilroy. Everything about this break-in looks like a distraction. Could be, she was never in the house at all. Possible they brought her car and her bag back to confuse and delay us."

"I'm heading for Gilroy," Clyde said, and he felt Dulcie's paws tighten on his arm.

"The hell you are," Max said. "You'd be in the way, make the sheriff mad. Let them do their work."

"I'll stay out of the way. I won't hassle Davis, either. I just want to be there." He expected Max to give him a stronger argument. When he didn't, Clyde headed for the door, wondering how to keep Dulcie from demanding that she go, because clearly, as she brightened up and cocked her ears, that was what she was thinking.

"You taking that cat?" Max called after him, raising an eyebrow.

"Thought I'd drop the cat off with Lucinda," he said over his shoulder. "With all the commotion, the house torn up, she seems really stressed. She'll be safer there."

In fact, Clyde meant to do just that. Clutching Dulcie, he beat it to his car as Max turned away to answer an officer's question. Crossing the garden, beneath the oaks, he glanced up into the branches where Kit stared down, her yellow eyes huge. With the living room windows wide open, she'd heard every word. But she wasn't coming down to him. She backed away when he reached up. Changing his mind about taking Dulcie to the Greenlaws', he shoved her up into the branches beside Kit.

"You're staying here," he said softly. "Try to stay out of trouble," he said, knowing it was a useless suggestion.

"Wait," Dulcie whispered. "Wait, Clyde."

"Hush. We can't talk here."

"They can't hear us, with your back to the house. They can't see *us,* in here among the leaves." Dulcie looked into Clyde's face, her green eyes questioning. "Please, Clyde . . . I don't *know* what to do." He had never seen the little tabby unsure of herself; Dulcie was just as decisive and hard-headed as Joe Grey.

She looked at him deeply, her green eyes huge and afraid. "I want to go with you. And I . . . I want to look in Jones's house. If he took Wilma there *after* Harper searched, a second search will be dangerous for her. If Kit and I can get in first, before Harper's men . . . If she's there, we can find a phone in there, we can call, tell them what room and if she's tied up, tell them if she's hurt, and who's in the house . . ." She looked at him intently. Clyde shook his head.

"It's that," she said, "or I go with you to Gilroy to help look for her."

11

Clyde looked up into the shadowed leaves of the oak tree at Dulcie's stubborn green gaze. These three cats sure complicated life.

"*Wilma's* in danger!" the tabby snapped. "You think I'm going to sit here polishing my claws? Jones has already tried to kill Bennett!" She hissed angrily at him, then spun away through the branches. "Come on, Kit." And before Clyde could argue, the two cats were gone, leaping from that oak into the next and up a pine tree, and away across the rooftops. Clyde stood staring after them, then headed for his car. Damned cats never listened. He tried to remind himself that Cage Jones would have no reason to hurt a neighborhood cat if he saw them sneaking around his house. They were cats, cats were no threat to an escaped con. Praying for their safety, and thinking that before he headed for the freeway he'd better gas up, he was nearly bowled over when something hit him from behind. Swinging around to punch his assailant, he felt claws digging into his shoulder, as if Joe had leaped down on him from the roof. "Keep your claws in! I suppose you heard everything."

"Of course I heard everything. I came straight over from the station. We don't have much time before the shops close. Where's your car?"

"You're not going to Gilroy."

"Says who? Get a move on. It's already past seven."

"I can't take you in the stores, they'll call security."

"They have a discount pet store, you can pick up one of those fancy pet carriers that look like luggage. I can sniff out her trail through the mesh door—if there's any scent to follow." Clinging to Clyde's shoulder, Joe peered around into his face. "I'm the only one who can track her scent. Unless they bring in dogs. If we don't get moving, we might never know if she *got* to Gilroy!"

"I take a cat carrier in those stores, security'll be all over me. A big bag like that, perfect for shoplifting! Bad as that backpack in San Francisco. That store cop nearly—"

"We spent three hundred dollars in that store."

"Three hundred of *my* dollars."

"And we royally entertained the store guard—supplied him with a nice little story to tell his wife and neighbors."

Clyde sighed, and pulled the tomcat off his shoulder, tearing his shirt in the process. Setting Joe up in an oak branch, he sprinted for his car—only to feel Joe brush past his leg, see a gray streak sail over the door of the yellow roadster and hunch down on the leather seat.

Swinging in on the driver's side, Clyde started the Chevy and turned to look at Joe. "I can't take you to Gilroy in an open car, on the freeway, it's too dangerous."

"Just as dangerous for you. So put the top up."

"A soft top is going to protect you at freeway speeds? And it's getting dark. That discount mall is nothing but parking lots. Reckless drivers in a hurry to get home. Too many cars, Joe. And you wouldn't *stay* in a carrier. I can never trust you. You could get—"

"Crushed under someone's wheels," Joe snapped. "Picked up by strangers. So stop by the shop, pick up a hard top. You have a hundred cars you can choose from."

"There isn't time."

Joe flexed his paws just above Clyde's expensive new upholstery, the soft yellow leather as creamy as butter. "Not a scratch on it. Yet," he said softly. "Really beautiful. Wasn't this the most expensive leather they had?"

Clyde wanted to wring Joe's furry gray neck. He waited for Joe to retract his claws, then eased the vintage roadster into gear and headed for Ocean Avenue, for his automotive shop.

The tomcat watched him narrowly. "One trick," Joe said, "one act of subterfuge, and you'll have dead mice in your bed every night for the rest of your natural life. Ripe, smelly mice specially aged for your benefit."

Clyde turned into the broad drive of Beckwhite's Automotive and stepped out of the car. "You will behave in Gilroy. You will do as I say, every minute. Or I swear, Joe, I will leave you in a cage at the county animal shelter."

Joe looked back at him with chilling feline disdain.

Turning away, Clyde activated the overhead door of his big repair and maintenance shop that occupied the north half of Beckwhite Automotive. The handsome Mediterranean building provided, besides Clyde's several spacious repair and storage garages and work bays, a vast, elegant showroom along the south side: tile-floored exhibit space for the latest models of BMW, Mercedes, Lexus, and a dozen far richer imports, as well as high-priced antique models. Clyde leased his space in exchange for handling all repairs and regular maintenance on Beckwhite's customers' vehicles. Joe watched, peering through the roadster's windshield and the big doors as Clyde disappeared into a back garage.

In a few minutes, a new white Lexus SUV eased out from the back. Clyde pulled it onto the front drive, put the roadster in the shop, scooped Joe up from the front seat, and dropped him in the SUV. Threatening the tomcat with mayhem if he clawed, or even shed upon, its soft black leather, he shut the big shop door behind them, and headed for Gilroy.

After two blocks, as he turned onto Highway 1, headed for 101, Clyde fished his cell phone from his pocket and dropped it on the leather seat. "Try Charlie. Max couldn't reach her."

"She always carries her cell. Where would she be, that she wouldn't answer?"

"Riding, Max thought."

Frowning, Joe punched in Charlie's number. When she didn't answer, he tried the number for the Harper's small, hillside ranch. In both instances there were four rings, then the voice mail clicked in. Pressing disconnect, he stared at Clyde.

"Try Ryan."

Joe went through the same routine: same pattern of four rings, then a message recording.

"Riding," Clyde said again; but a worried frown darkencd his brown eyes.

The old man slipped away after watching the police action around the Getz house, having seen and heard enough to know that Wilma Getz had disappeared. This made him smile. Sure as hell, Cage had her. Served the old bitch right.

He guessed he'd better get on over to Lilly's while he still had the chance, before Harper sent someone to search the house again, because that cop would be sure to do it. He'd have to make it damn fast, knowing Harper. He hoped to hell Cage wasn't there.

Not likely, though, with cops crawling all over. Specially as that car Cage'd been driving when he left here, that old blue Plymouth thick with dirt, that'd be easy enough to spot if there'd been a witness. Someone must've seen it, to call the law. Well, Cage wouldn't go home, Cage was smarter'n that. Maybe he'd stashed Wilma there, and now would take off down the coast. Or head north. Either way, Cage knew how to lose a cop on them back roads. Thinking about that, Greeley headed up the hills on foot, toward Cage's place, moving fast, thinking how best to approach Lilly Jones, how best to handle her.

The Jones house stood above the village on the ridge of a canyon that cut down from the Molena Point hills, an old brown house, tall and narrow, an ugly frame structure with straight sides, surrounded by brittle-leafed eucalyptus trees that, in the faint wind, shook and rattled against the siding. Ten small windows in the front, five above, five below.

Greeley walked for several blocks, circling the house, looking for Cage's car. Didn't find it. Back at the house, he studied the drive that sloped down to the garage beneath the two floors; the drive was covered with dust and leaves. Didn't look like Cage or anyone else had pulled in there for a long time. He was about to approach the five brick steps that led to the front door when a water company truck turned onto the street, parking a block down. A pair of uniformed utility workers got out and knelt by the curb.

Removing a heavy metal lid, they peered in,

making notes, fiddling with the meter or the pipes or whatever; they took their time, then moved on to the next meter box. Pretty late in the day for water company personnel, unless there was an emergency. Was this a stakeout, waiting for Cage? He couldn't hear what they were saying, but a chill of unease filled Greeley.

But what difference, if they *were* cops? They weren't watching him, they had nothing on him. It was a free country. He had started toward the steps again when a gas company truck pulled up from the other direction, parking in front of a low white house. Three men dressed in gray jumpsuits got out. Moved in between the houses, one after another, as if checking the meters or connections. Men who, in Greeley's opinion, got to work too fast for city employees.

Well, he'd just arrived in town recently, he'd gone to school with Cage. He could come to the house if he liked, maybe come to see Lilly, see how Cage was doing. What business was that of Harper's?

Mounting the steps, he rang the bell, stood listening for sounds from within, for the shuffle of feet approaching, for Lilly's slow, deliberate movement. Cage's sister'd never liked him much, even when they was kids in grammar school, him and Mavity and Cage—and that Wilma Getz. Lilly was some older, in high school then. Tall, bone thin, dry as dust even when she was young.

The door creaked open, and Lilly Jones stood there tall and plain and wearing the kind of shapeless cotton dress his own mother had called a housedress; Lilly was more dried up and skinnier than ever.

"Evening, Lilly. It's me, Greeley Urzey. Heard Cage was out of prison and I come over to visit."

Lilly looked at him like she might look at a frog skewered on a stick. "Cage isn't here. I don't know where he is. What did you want?"

"Like I said, to visit. Been a while since I seen Cage." Greeley gave her what he considered a winning smile. "You going to ask me in? It's been a long time, Lilly. It's hot out, I'd sure enjoy a drink of water. It sure is mighty hot, even this time of evening. Water, or that good lemonade you make. You always made the best lemonade, back when we was kids."

Lilly looked resigned or too tired to argue. She backed away from the door, motioned him in, pointed to the couch. The woman wasn't big on graciousness. But then Greeley guessed maybe he wasn't so smooth, either, in the manners department. Mavity said that often enough. But what the hell difference, anyway?

"I can make you some frozen lemonade," Lilly said shortly. "That's the best I can do. There are some magazines there on the table. But he isn't here, Greeley. And he won't be."

This, Greeley thought, was going to take a while.

She'd kill time in the kitchen fiddling with the lemonade, and then the long process of drinking the sour stuff and trying to draw her out. He glanced around the tired-looking, faded room figuring out just what questions to ask her, how best to pull this off. Old woman was prickly as a cactus. Looked like she hadn't changed a stick of furniture in the room since he and Cage was kids slipping up the stairs to Cage's room and locking the door behind them.

When Lilly finally returned with the lemonade and handed him a glass and sat down, he took his time sipping and smacking, telling her how good it was. She looked at him coldly.

"What did you come for, Greeley?"

"Cage didn't call you? Well, he figured he might not be able to, said he'd try. He needs some clothes and things, plans to . . . be gone awhile. He's out, you know."

"I thought you hadn't seen him."

"Well, he told me to be careful what I said. Until I saw you was alone, saw that the cops wasn't here."

"Hiding from the law again," Lilly said dryly, not seeming at all curious about why or how Cage was out on the streets.

"Well, yes, ma'am. He didn't have no clothes, and—"

"He can buy clothes."

"He told me to come on down to the house, told

110

me to check his closet, pretty much told me which ones to get. And his razor and toothbrush, like that . . ."

"Surely he has money to buy what he wants."

"I guess he doesn't want to be seen just now," Greeley said diffidently.

"I should think not. He almost killed a man today."

That shook Greeley, that she knew.

"That federal officer could die," Lilly said. "Cage belongs in prison."

Greeley wondered, if *he* was in this much trouble, would *his* sister, Mavity, be as hateful as Lilly Jones? He gave Lilly a gentle smile. "Cage said there was some kind of suitcase or duffle bag. Said to pack up his stuff, whatever I thought he'd need. If it's all right with you, of course . . ." He was growing uneasy. This old woman was going to run him off—or try to.

It would be a sight easier if he had the house to himself. If he could search in his own way, take his time. But he hadn't figured out, yet, how to accomplish that.

Lilly looked at him silently for a long time. He waited for her to tell him to get out, but then she settled back, watching him. "Tell me where he is. Tell me exactly what happened. Tell me why he shot that federal officer. If you tell me all of it, we'll see about the clothes."

12

Dulcie and Kit, too, were headed for the Jones house, racing up into the hills, skirting the canyon, where a fitful wind blew at their backs, pushing them along and ruffling their fur. Shouldering through tinder-dry weeds, they bounded into bright flower beds, then tangled grass, then across the back garden of the four senior ladies, on and on, up the ridge through all manner of backyards; at the crest of the hill, they circled around to the street, to the front entrance of the Jones house, just as Greeley had done.

The tall, brown, boxlike dwelling stood on the highest blunt ridge, nearly smothered by eucalyptus trees, a two-story structure with no architectural grace, though the trees hid most of its faults, the silvery-leafed giants crowding so close that their wind-tossed branches rattled against the siding, slapping the cracked wood.

The lumpy front yard was dry and bald, with a thin scattering of scruffy grass. There was no sign that anyone watered, or cared about growing things. Dulcie paused to pull a thorn from her paw, gripping it in her teeth and jerking hard, then spitting it out. A few parked cars stood along the street or in the narrow, cracked driveways. One imagined garages too full of trashy personal treasures to accommodate even a bicycle. No person could be seen in the yards or at the windows. In a few houses, though, lights were on. Above the darkening rooftops, the evening sky was still silvered with the fading day. Venetian blinds covered the windows of the Jones house. All were closed, so the cats could not see in; a faint light burned in what seemed to be the living room.

A block away, a water company truck was parked, as if out late on an emergency call, two uniformed men bent over the curbside meters. One was Officer Blake, a tall, balding, string bean of a man. The cats didn't know the other officer. Down at the other end of the block, three PG&E employees were working, as if perhaps attending to the same emergency: two were older officers the cats had never seen. The cats knew that Max Harper had men on call for surveillance, when he might be shorthanded. Despite the late-afternoon heat, the windows of the Jones house were all closed.

"Must be like an oven in there," Dulcie said. "Could Lilly have air-conditioning? Oh, not in this old house." Most folks on the coast didn't bother with artificial cooling; usually a sharp evening breeze took care of any unusual heat. Kit counted the windows and studied the size of the house, staring high above them. "Why would she live alone, in such a big old place?"

"It belongs half to her and half to Cage," Dulcie

said. "When he was on parole, Wilma suggested he get something smaller, put the money in savings, but he didn't want to do that. I guess the house is paid for, so Lilly lives rent free. Their parents bought it years and years ago, when they were first married . . . I'll bet they never dreamed it might be a place for their son to hide from the law."

Circling the house, sniffing the front porch and along the narrow, leaf-covered driveway that slanted down to the basement garage, they caught not the faintest scent of Wilma.

"If she isn't here," Dulcie whispered, "where has he taken her?"

Kit studied the house, her yellow eyes burning with thoughts of getting inside. They checked the basement vents, but all were solidly screwed in place. They slipped up the eucalyptus trees, one after the other, to inspect the attic vents, but these, too, were securely fastened.

The back blinds and the upstairs blinds were all open, as if Lilly was concerned only with privacy from the street. Peering in from the trees through upstairs windows, they made out four sad-looking bedrooms and one old-fashioned bathroom. When they looked into the main floor from the back of the house, they found an equally outdated kitchen and bathroom, all grim, neglected rooms; it appeared that no one had painted those box tan walls or replaced any rug or piece of marred furniture since the place was built.

Was that because Lilly didn't have the money, or because she didn't care? Not likely Cage would care. There was a younger sister, but she had married and moved out shortly after the parents' deaths. The cats pressed their noses to a living room window, trying to see through the cracks of the closed Venetian blinds; they could see nothing, but voices reached them . . . A TV? No, these were live voices, one scratchy and familiar. Dulcie looked at Kit. "*Greeley? Greeley Urzey?* It can't be. Why would he be here? What would Mavity's brother be doing here?" Tense with questions, she pressed her ear to the dusty pane.

"It's Greeley, all right," she said, listening. "Mavity told Wilma he was in town. Moved right in with her, freeloading as usual. But why would he be here? He doesn't know . . . Oh," she said. "He'd know Lilly!" The idea of a connection between Greeley and Lilly Jones, or Cage Jones, didn't seem to wash until she remembered that Wilma had gone to school with Cage as well as with Mavity and Greeley. She thought Cage and Greeley had been friends, then. All children together, so very long ago.

"Here," Kit whispered, edging along the sill. "You can see in here, where the slat's bent."

Crowding against Kit, Dulcie peered between two slats.

Faded brown couch, faded chairs long overdue for recovering. One frilly lamp lit with a low-watt, dull bulb. Mothy-looking afghans folded over the upholstered chair and couch backs, as if to hide excessive wear. And on the walls, dusty-looking needlework pictures of flowers and square-faced dogs crammed between a collection of huge, ugly masks. What an unsettling combination, the prim, prissy needlework and the rude, primitive faces, crudely made and garishly colored: the faces of devils with their mouths open and tongues sticking out, the heads of snarling jungle beasts with fangs bared and dark holes for eyes, each aboriginal face adorned with jutting feathers.

Even in the history and art books Dulcie liked to browse through in the midnight library, she had never seen uglier masks. The effect of so many huge, violent faces leering down into that stumpy, fussy, old-fashioned room was totally off-putting—as if evil spirits had thrust through the walls, an out-of-control primitive world breaking into that dull, proper house.

Greeley Urzey sat on the couch, a fusty, rumpled old man as out of place in the prim room as were the wild masks. He and Lilly spoke so softly that, even with their excellent hearing, the cats could make little of the conversation.

"Why is he here?" Dulcie said. "He and Cage went to school together, but . . . Could this have to do with Wilma? Greeley hates Wilma . . . Is Greeley part of this? Is Wilma locked in there, and Greeley guarding her?" She looked helplessly at

Kit. "We have to get in . . . Maybe the basement?"

Kit shivered, not wanting to be shut in that house with Greeley Urzey. That old man knew about speaking cats, and he knew they were close to the law. For that alone he hated them.

"Come on," Dulcie said, dropping from the windowsill, down to the bushes, to circle the house again. But as they rounded the corner, Kit paused in a flower bed. Resigned to Dulcie's determination, she looked up past a scrawny jasmine vine to a high, small window.

"Bathroom window?" Kit said. "Would she bother to lock that? No human could get through that."

"And I doubt a cat can get up that vine," Dulcie said, "without tearing it from the wall—spindly thing doesn't look strong enough to hold a mouse." But, testing it, she started up anyway, heading gingerly for the little window.

Tied in a hard, straight-backed chair, Wilma couldn't move without the tight ropes cutting into her arms and ankles. The worst was the tight bandana binding her eyes. She fought panic at being unable to see where she was, to see what—or who—was near her.

At least he'd removed the tape from across her mouth, had ripped it off, surely taking half her skin with it, saying, "You can yell now, bitch. Yell all you want, there's not a soul to hear you or to care."

There'd been a time when Cage wouldn't have dared call her bitch. The room was so hot, the blindfold and her jacket so constricting she felt locked in a straightjacket. She was not a woman given to hysterics, but she felt very near the edge. Only her deep anger at Cage kept her fear at bay. She could not deal with him if she fell apart. *If* he ever returned, to be dealt with. If he did not simply leave her to starve or die of thirst. She was painfully thirsty. She tried not to think about water. She felt close to pure terror, and she must not let that happen. She had dealt with criminals most of her adult life. She was not going to give way now.

Cage had driven her car up into the hills somewhere, up a long, winding gravel road. Blinded, able only to listen, she had tried to sense where they were, tried, as well, to catch some familiar scent on the breeze, the way an animal would do.

He had parked on a gravel drive or yard. When he cut the engine, she'd heard the other car pull up behind them. Forcing her out of the car, Cage had untied her ankles long enough for her to walk across gravel and then rough, rocky earth, his hand bruising her arm as he roughly guided her. She'd smelled eucalyptus and pine trees, and had heard above her the faint swish of wings, then a few birds chirping. He'd pushed her up three wooden steps and through a door that slammed behind them. She heard him lock it, didn't hear the other man enter. He forced her across a rough wooden floor, pushing her to avoid her falling over furniture. The place smelled of dust and sour, rotting wood. When he shoved her into the straight-backed chair, she'd tried to talk to him, had felt so hindered because she couldn't see him.

"What is it, Cage? What do you want from me? How did you get out? Whatever you did, it had to be pretty clever."

He'd refused to be suckered by that. And had refused to remove the blindfold.

"For heaven's sake, tell me what this is about. Maybe I can—"

"Where is it!" he'd barked.

"Where is what?"

"You know what! That day you searched my place, you and Bennett and the frigging DEA!"

"That was ten years ago!"

"Don't matter. You have it, or had it, and I want it back—or want what you got for it."

"I have no idea what you're talking about. I don't *know* what you want."

"You know damn well. You two took it, and I want it now. All of it."

"I honestly don't know. You'll have to tell me, or we'll be here forever."

"That day after the friggin' feds left, you and Bennett were there by yourselves. There a long time, Lilly told me. You went through the house again and I want what you took. That's stealing,

stealing by federal officers. How do you think that would look. The newspapers would love to get hold of that."

"So tell them."

"First, I'm giving you a chance. Trying to treat you nice in spite of what you did. Lilly was there, she's my witness. It's mine, bitch. I want it back, now."

"What did Lilly say we took? I can't imagine your sister lying."

Lilly Jones was the opposite of Cage in every way. She had always seemed an honest, straight-laced woman who believed in obeying the law. Opposite even in looks—Cage big boned, over-sized, and bullish. Lilly frail, and as thin as a sick bird. Lilly Jones spoke little; when she did speak, her attitude was wooden and impassive, stolid to the point of insensibility. The younger sister, Violet, was even more withdrawn. But at least Violet had had the good sense to marry and get out. Or, it had seemed to be good sense at the time. Wilma heard later that she'd married an abuser. Violet had not been in evidence during the time Wilma supervised Cage, so she had never met the girl.

She realized suddenly that Cage had her purse, she could hear him going through it, and he began to comment on the pictures in her billfold. Until that moment she had convinced herself that she could talk Cage out of whatever this was about;

she had assumed that only *she* was in danger. Now, suddenly, she was far more afraid.

"Pretty redhead." Cage's voice told her he was smirking. "Maybe if you don't want to give me what's mine, don't want to save yourself, you'll like to save them that's close to you."

She hadn't answered, had gone cold inside, and felt herself tremble. She heard him toss her purse aside, and then a small rustling as if he was flipping slowly through the packet of photographs she'd tucked in the bag.

"From these pictures," Cage said, "looks like this redhead lives up in the hills. Lives pretty fancy, too, them horses and all. Nice big house like that, that tall peaked roof and glass and all, should be easy to spot from the road, even if you don't have her address in here. Isn't that Hellhag Hill rising up behind?

"Why, here's another picture, and she's getting married. That's you, there, the flower girl or whatever. Must be a real close friend. Or a relative? Why, I believe that there's your niece, the one they call Charlie."

"Whatever you want from me, Cage, you touch her, you'll never get away, the law will track you wherever you hide—and then they'll burn you."

Cage hit her hard, across the mouth. That was the first time he'd ever hit her. During the years that she'd had him on parole, then later on probation on a different charge, he would never have dared do that. He gave a cold laugh. "Bennett got his. You don't want the same, bitch, you'll tell me where you hid 'em." He'd gone silent for a moment, then, "If you sold 'em, you'll hand over the money pronto if you want to go home again. And if you want that redheaded niece safe. Is that how you bought that house of yours, that fancy stone house? With my money? You did, you'll pay for that, too."

"What did you do to Bennett?"

"How you think it'll look to the feds, turns out you bought that house with stolen goods? Illegal to take that stuff out of the country. Illegal as hell just to have it. You and Bennett think of that?"

She'd longed to jerk off the blindfold and get a look at him. If he'd hurt Bennett . . . And if he hurt Charlie . . . Unable to see his face, she cringed from helplessness. But how could anything have happened to Mandell? Mandell was quick, and he always went armed . . . No, Cage had to be bluffing. How could he have had *time* to get at Mandell?

She and Mandell had had dinner together in the city just last night, a wonderful Chinese meal at Tommie Toy's. They'd talked for a long while over tea and dessert. Surely, at that time, Cage was safely in jail—in jail until sometime this morning, apparently. But not a federal prison, just a city jail, overcrowded, understaffed, far easier to figure a way out . . . If he had found Mandell after he escaped . . .

"That big house of your niece's, looks to be about half a mile this side of Hellhag Hill, right along the crest there. Easy to spot, easy access in and out, too." He'd grabbed and shaken her. "You want to tell me what you did with 'em?"

When she remained silent, he hit her again, harder. He said nothing more. He turned, and left the house. She heard both cars drive away, crunching little rocks under their tires. She thought the other man was Eddie Sears, Cage's old partner. She'd seen Eddie only once in person, ten years ago. And she had seen a mug shot or two. Thin, long face. Younger than Cage, thirty-something. Brown hair. When the cars left, she'd fought to get free. But now, what seemed like hours later, she was still fighting.

13

The frail vine sagged under Dulcie's weight, but as it tore she scrambled up fast; the trellis was fragile, too, swaying and cracking. The smell of the jasmine blossoms was too sweet. She was clawing up at the little, double-hung window when beneath her hind paws a slat broke. She fell, clawing at the sill, ripping down the rusted screen. As she was snatching through to the window's mullions, she managed to dig her claws into a little crosspiece and hang there, desperately swinging.

"Hurry!" Kit hissed unsympathetically.

Reaching and stretching, she clawed at the top of the frame until she got a grip. The window slid under her weight, dropping like an elevator. She swung up fast, bellying through the torn screen, pulling and tearing her fur, then regained her balance crouching atop the double-hung window, staring down into the dark little bathroom. She heard Kit storm up the trellis behind her, moving so fast that when two more rungs gave way, Kit's momentum carried her to the sill—with a desperate leap she was through the window, right in Dulcie's face. They dropped to the sink together, then to the floor as softly as they could. They'd worry later about how to get out. Boldly, Kit took the lead, slipping through into the hall—seeming not to remember how she had, not long ago, been trapped while snooping in a felon's house and unable to escape.

The Jones house smelled of old wood, old dust, old clothes worn too long, an unpleasant mélange of stale scents trapped in closed spaces. Following the voices, they looked from the hall into the living room, then slipped in, bellying beneath an unoccupied armchair into dust that threatened uncontrolled sneezes. Peering out, Dulcie looked up at the masks and shivered. How could anyone live among the hideous faces that leered down from the dark walls? The primitive masks had, she felt sure, come from South or Central America; she had seen many like them in the library, in books on primitive art. Interesting that Greeley had lived most of his life in Central America.

Dulcie knew only one other human who had spent much time in those countries and who cared enough about such artifacts to collect them, and that was Greeley's ex-wife. Sue loved Latin American art, though the items with which she filled her shop were smaller than these masks and more appealing, bright, fanciful carvings and weavings of a cheerful nature, whimsical pieces far removed from these bone-shivering presences that reeked of all the devil myths Dulcie had ever heard—though the concept of the devil had come late to Latin America. These images, she thought, would be based on other spirits, on some equally evil underworld putrefaction. Whatever the case, the collection unnerved her, seemed to speak to something deep and ancient within her feline memory, to stir some timeless presence far too menacing. Why would Lilly Jones want to live among such monstrosities?

Above them in the too hot living room, Lilly and Greeley made dull and hesitant small talk, the topic of conversation at the moment being the weather. The dry old woman behaved as if she and Greeley were quite alone in the house, not as if a hostage were locked in one of the rooms; she did not seem nervous, did not pause to listen for sounds from some other room.

But if Wilma was here, did Greeley know that?

Could he be here to take delivery of Wilma, to take her away somewhere? But, then, why wouldn't he simply tell Lilly to take him to Wilma? And, *would* Lilly Jones hide Wilma at the risk of her own arrest? From what Dulcie knew of Lilly, she did not seem the kind to take risks, even for her own brother.

Except, Lilly would be more afraid of Cage than of the law. Cage could be mean and coersive, and Lilly was reclusive and weak, not nearly bold enough to defy her brother. Dulcie sighed. Nothing would make sense until they knew why Cage wanted Wilma. Dulcie's housemate wasn't some heiress with unlimited funds for a ransom. What could she have, or know, that would make her so valuable to Cage Jones?

But maybe Greeley was here looking for some-*thing,* and not for Wilma at all.

But what? And why now, just when Wilma had vanished?

Greeley had abandoned the weather as a topic, and was digging for information, feeling Lilly out with questions about as subtle as a Great Dane in a crystal store; but at last he got down to specifics, wanted to pack Cage's clothes and take them to Cage, and bring some papers, too, that Cage had put away. Could Lilly get those for him? He'd be glad to get them himself, save her the trouble. He said Cage had mentioned a small box he wanted, and that Cage had told him where to find it. The old man seemed as nervous as a cornered rabbit in his eagerness to break away from Lilly, to get at the rest of the house on his own. He kept at it until Lilly said, "What are you looking for, Greeley? What do you think Cage has hidden here that you want so badly?"

Greeley widened his eyes in surprise. "Just what he told me to get, Lilly. Oh, you can't think Cage has hidden something illegal? Oh, my. If them cops search the house, looking for him, and they find something incriminating . . ."

"I told you, they have already searched."

"But they'll be back," Greeley said darkly. "Now that Wilma Getz has disappeared, they'll be back here looking for her. You can bet on that. And if they find something illegal in your house . . ." Greeley shook his head. "That would make you an accessory, Lilly. There's a terrible long prison term for that.

"Of course, if it's something he's brought across the border, carried up from Panama, that makes it a federal offense, with an even longer prison term—for Cage, *and* for you, if you knew about it."

"That doesn't make sense," Lilly snapped. "An innocent woman, alone. No one would put an old woman in prison. What a foolish thing to say."

"Norma Green went to federal prison when she was eighty-seven, for passing forged checks. Eileen

127

Clifton was sixty-eight. Sentenced to twenty years by the feds for taking her kidnapped granddaughter across a state line. Her *granddaughter!* Anything that goes across a state line . . ."

Kit's ears were back, her yellow eyes narrowed with disbelief; Dulcie swallowed back a hiss of disgust.

"Them federal judges are sticklers for the law, Lilly. Don't make no difference, your age. If you know that he's hidden something here, you're aiding and abetting. Them judges will see you do federal time, sure as hell is filled with brimstone. Well, I'd just hate to see them even book you, even take you off to the local jail . . ." And Greeley kept laying it on, about how bad the prisons were, about the sexual bullies and prison gang wars. It was hard to know what Lilly was thinking, with that sour poker face. When Dulcie could stand it no longer, she cut her eyes at Kit and they slipped out from behind the chair into the shadows of the hall.

Trotting swiftly through the shadows from one room to the next, they didn't look for whatever Greeley was after, they wanted only to find Wilma; poking into closets, they prowled a room used for sewing, two unused bedrooms, a dark room dedicated to storing boxes and other junk, and a large linen closet, skillfully and silently sliding open closet doors, poking their noses behind the brittle shower curtain of a second bath—all to the background of Greeley's wheedling and Lilly's sour, one-line refusals. And even as they inspected each depressing room for Wilma, it was hard not to keep an eye out for whatever Greeley had come here to find.

Slipping up the stairs from the hall to inspect the second floor, they made quick work of the four other bedrooms, the last of which was redolent with Lilly's lilac scent, Lilly's clothes and shoes in the closet. Nowhere was there the faintest scent of Wilma, no hint that she had been in this house.

They found Cage's room, though, and he had been there recently—same sour male smell as in Wilma's house. Cage had, within the last few weeks, slept in the front bedroom; a few of his clothes hung in the nearly empty closet.

Interesting that Lilly had said no word, when Greeley claimed that Cage had sent him for his clothes. But still, nothing really made sense; Dulcie hated when things didn't add up.

They tossed Cage's room more thoroughly than the others, though Wilma certainly hadn't been in there; they found nothing valuable that Greeley might want. Heading back down the stairs to the first floor, the drone of Greeley's voice met them, accompanied by a faint clicking. And when they peered around from the hall, they saw that Lilly was knitting—having grown totally bored with Greeley's wheedling—her needles flying through some project fashioned in pink yarn, she was so engrossed she seemed hardly to notice Greeley.

Some women knit when they're nervous, when they need a calming diversion. Some knit when they're angry. As the cats watched the needles flying and the rows of pink stitches building, Lilly seemed to grow calmer. Greeley, apparently running out of hot air, sat watching her, stone faced, then at last he rose.

"I'm sorry to have troubled you," he said stiffly. "I hope, Lilly, you are doing what's best for your own welfare."

The cats smiled as Lilly hustled him out the door; behind her back, they fled for the kitchen; and there they waited crouched on the worn linoleum until they heard her return to her knitting, sighing with relief to be rid of him, her needles once more clicking away madly. They prowled the kitchen, pausing to sniff thoroughly at a door that smelled strongly of musty basement and of gas and oil from the garage.

Could Wilma be down there, so securely confined that Lilly felt no need to go downstairs and check on her? Could she be drugged, or so hurt that she could not escape? In her terror, Dulcie leaped and snatched at the doorknob, clawing and swinging, making too much noise. She couldn't see if the separate dead bolt was locked. But, fighting the door, she heard the knitting stop, heard the hush of Lilly's footsteps on the carpet. Frantically, both cats fought and kicked—until Lilly entered the kitchen, then they slid behind the refrigerator, a tight squeeze, the motor hot against their fur.

They listened as Lilly opened a cupboard, apparently getting herself a little snack; they could smell vanilla cookies, could hear her munching. When, rattling the package, she headed for the living room again, they followed on her heels. Dulcie's mind was on the basement, on the windows at the back of the house where the cliff dropped away and the daylight-basement looked out at the ravine. And, slipping past the living room as Lilly again bent over her knitting, they made for the bathroom. Onto the counter, and then they were up and out the window, leaving tabby and tortoiseshell fur caught in the torn screen. Ignoring the trellis, they broke their fall among the bushes and fled for the back of the house. Only there did they pause to lick their paws, bruised from the doorknob, and their bare tender skin where the screen had pulled out hanks of fur.

"Will it ever grow back?" mewled Kit who, six months ago, couldn't have cared less how she looked. Now she sounded as foolish as the vainest house cat.

"It will," Dulcie said dryly, studying the basement windows and, for a quick escape, the grassy canyon that dropped away below them.

The canyon was far narrower here than where it fell away behind the seniors' house. Pine and eucalyptus trees grew up its sides, climbing to within a few feet of the basement, casting their shadows across the dirty basement windows. There were no screens.

Each cat leaped to a low sill and began to work at a slider, trying to jimmy its old brass lock. It took maybe ten minutes and made way too much noise, too many choruses of dry scraping, before Kit's lock gave way; under her insistent claws and then her pressing shoulder, the bottom half rose up with a loud, wrenching screech that turned the cats rigid. They expected any minute to hear the door in the kitchen fly open and Lilly come rushing down the stairs.

When they decided she hadn't heard them, they leaped into the basement, into a mildew-smelling, clutter-filled storage room behind the garage. They could see, up front, past a row of deep, built-in cupboards, an old Packard that was just the kind of car Clyde would covet, a vintage model badly wanting Clyde Damen's loving restoration. Dulcie stood very still, scenting for Wilma, but not daring to call to her. Kit pressed close, her round yellow eyes big with unease in the shadowy, musty space; then at last they began to search, going first to the oversized cupboards.

14

With her hands tied, Wilma couldn't reach to rip away the blindfold. She couldn't move, tied to the chair; tilting it back and forth, she was able to rock along crablike, jerking across the rough wooden floor, the chair legs banging. Feeling out with her toes, for barriers, she soon found a wall. Getting the chair turned, she rocked along beside it until she came to what felt like a heavy wooden dresser. Yes, she could feel the corner with her arm, and then the drawer handles.

Bending her head against the top drawer, she wriggled and worked until she caught the blindfold on the handle. She pulled and fought until she had jerked it and it slipped down around her throat— her release from darkness left her heart pounding. The thin light of evening filtered in through dusty windows. She looked warily around her.

The house was a crude cabin. Rough wooden walls, small, dirty windows. One wall of dark stone, behind a rusty woodstove, two faded armchairs before it. To her right opened the three small windows. Hobbling her chair toward them, she pressed her face to the grimy glass.

The cabin stood in a grove of pine and eucalyptus trees. She could see only woods, and a bare dirt yard. One small outbuilding away at the edge of the graveled clearing, a rusty old car parked beside it. To her left, where the woods thinned, she could glimpse open hills washed golden by the last rays of the sun as it settled into a low line of fog— surely that fog lay over the sea, over the Pacific. She was very likely high in the Molena hills. She caught glimpses, closer to the cabin, of a narrow dirt road leading away and down to vanish among the falling golden slopes, a road surely making its way to the sea. She searched along the far fog line for the roofs of Molena Point, but could find no hint of them.

In the far corner of the room was a kitchen alcove and a wooden table. A window above the sink faced the woods away from the sea. On the long wall between her and the kitchen was a heavy door that looked like it would lead outside; she thought she had come in that way. Awkwardly tipping and turning the chair, she headed for the kitchen. If these were her last hours on earth, she damned well wasn't going to die of thirst.

When she had gained the sink counter, she stood up as best she could, bent nearly double in the chair, and, leaning over the stained yellow Formica into the rusting steel sink, she pressed the tap handle with her chin.

Water gushed out. She drank awkwardly for a very long time, soaking herself, drenching her shirt, cool against her hot, sweaty skin. She rested, letting the water run, then drank again, rested and drank until at last she felt satisfied; then clumsily she pressed the faucet off and balanced back, steady on the floor again. She looked around her at the dark kitchen corner, the cracked brown linoleum and ancient dark cabinets, the worn Formica; no surface looked clean. A newspaper lay on the counter. The headline and photograph caught her attention; she remembered the article from earlier in the week:

Woman Killed in Her Home, Police Seek Burglar

The picture was of a smiling Linda Tucker in a low-cut dark dress, a professional photographer's portrait taken perhaps for a birthday or other special occasion. The paper was well worn, the stain of a cup or glass at the lower corner. This was the only paper she could see; there were no other newspapers or magazines in the room, not even on the table beside the two worn chairs. Had this one paper been saved for a reason? Or had it only been kept to wrap the garbage?

The kitchen alcove was so small, and the heavy table so close to the cabinets, that, tied in her chair, she had no room to maneuver; every time she rose to move, the chair legs sticking out behind her rammed into the cabinets or the table. The drawers were in the tightest corner. She was able, just, to reach behind her and open the top one. Feeling gingerly through its contents, she found only forks and spoons, no knives. Shutting the drawer, she had hunched down to the next, was wriggling forward, pulling the drawer out, when a sound beyond the kitchen window startled her so that she nearly toppled the chair. The sound came again, a hushed scraping. She twisted around trying to see.

Was someone out there? Someone who would help her, or someone she must hide from? Nothing moved beyond the glass; in the darkening evening she saw nothing but the dense pines. It couldn't have been a branch blowing; the soft wind had died.

The sound did not return; she sat staring into the woods, both disappointed and relieved. But then, knowing there might not be much time, she turned her attention again frantically to the kitchen drawers—paper napkins and long narrow boxes of foil or waxed paper with little metal saws along the edge that might cut rope. She considered those briefly—little saws that could leave her arms painfully scraped and bloody, inviting infection if she remained there long.

Putting that option aside as a last resort, she was fumbling lower into the next drawer when she heard the hushing sounds again. As she twisted toward the window, something dark flicked away, so fast in the gloom that she couldn't tell what it was. The shadow of a person? A small animal? A squirrel? No fox or weasel would be that high off the ground, and it had moved so fast.

A cat, peering in at her? And now, even as she watched for that presence to return, another noise alarmed her, a sound from the ceiling, a loud thudding. Was there a second floor, then? She'd seen no stairs. But someone was there, someone was in the house, above her.

The rows of identical shops bordering Gilroy's parking lot seemed to Joe Grey, in the mall's vapor lights, yawningly dull and commercial; yet at this moment the discount mall drew the tomcat more powerfully than rats scrabbling in a barrel. As Clyde parked in front of Wilma's favorite restaurant, to see if in there he could get a line on her and also could find Davis, Joe crouched, ready to leap out and head across the parking lot to the shops that, too soon, would be closing.

Clyde slapped his hand on the lock. "You stay in this car, Joe. You will not get out of this vehicle. Not for any reason. Not unless and until I say you can get out." He stared hard at Joe. "You got that?"

Joe looked at him defiantly. "You can't be serious. This is what we came for! So I can—"

"Not without me. Not until I tell you. *Comprende?*"

If Dulcie had been there, she might have felt just as rebellious as Joe, but she would have looked meekly reprimanded, knowing that you can catch more birds with subterfuge. Joe stared pointedly at the clock, which even now rolled its lighted digits to the next minute. "Twenty minutes! That's all we have!"

"You get out of this car, in this traffic and confusion, and get hurt or in trouble, and you're going to blow the search. Did you think of that? I told you I plan to stay over, get a motel room. The stores we don't cover tonight, we'll hit in the morning."

This might sound reasonable to a human. It made no sense to the one doing the tracking. "The scent is fresh *now*. By tomorrow morning the cleaning people with their vacuums and chemicals will have trashed every trace. Vacuuming compound, cleaning substances, to say nothing of the personal scents of dozens of assorted humans."

"Five minutes, I'll be back. Then we'll hit the stores." Clyde leaned over, his face close to Joe's. "I have to open some windows or you'll die in this heat. I expect you, on your tomcat honor, to stay inside this car." He looked up again, scanning the parking area. "That could be Davis's unit, over behind that truck. I'll just see what she's found, then we'll get to work." Another hard glare and he was gone, leaving the windows halfway down, locking the doors simply as a small deterrent to passersby.

Not that anyone with common sense, seeing the glaring eyes of the enraged tomcat, would stick his hand through. Joe watched Clyde enter the restaurant and wave, and glimpsed Davis, sitting in the back. The squarely built Latina was in uniform as usual, though the day was hot as hell and such formality was seldom expected of Harper's detectives. She didn't look happy to see Clyde.

Juana Davis was a good detective, she'd do a thorough search for Wilma—as good as a human could accomplish with no talent for scent detection. Sitting with Davis in the booth were two sheriff's deputies. As Clyde sat down beside Juana, Joe considered the car's open windows. He looked across the parking lot to Liz Claiborne's, which was Wilma's favorite store and had, most likely, been her first stop this morning—if she ever got this far, he thought, rearing up with his paws on the glass, wondering if the security alarm would go off.

It didn't. He propelled himself over and out, and there was not a sound. In a nanosecond he was across the lot, between parked cars, slipping into Liz Claiborne's, padding in on the heels of a hurrying shopper. Ducking behind a rack of dresses, immediately his nose filled with the smells of new cashmere sweaters and women's perfume, unwelcome indeed as he sought the one scent of importance.

15

Dulcie and Kit left the Jones house running shoulder to shoulder, smug with information but deeply disappointed that none of it was about Wilma; they had found no scent of her, no hint that she'd ever been in Cage's house. The only place they hadn't been able to search was the attic; though after they left the basement, they'd tried. There was no way to get up into that under-roof space without going back in the house and trying to drag a chair under the trapdoor, which would have brought Lilly quicker than fleas to a stray hound. Leaving the attic without searching it worried Dulcie. A prisoner could die under that roof, it would be hot as blazes in there.

They had, before they approached the roof, thoroughly searched the jumbled basement, swinging open musty cupboards, peering behind tangles of old furniture and stacks of cardboard cartons. How many years of discards were dumped in that crowded space? Old clothes, a dressmaker's dummy, a treadle sewing machine, a gigantic waterfall dresser, an abandoned refrigerator (with failing hearts, they looked inside; nothing but mold). Boxes of rusty tools: crowbar and wrenches, screwdrivers and hammers tossed in with cans of rusting nails.

In the garage, they had searched the old car, too. Looked like it had seldom been driven. Tires half flat, dust on every surface. They'd leaped in through its open windows, which, they supposed, Lilly left down to prevent the mildew that had taken hold anyway, along with a hidden nest of mice that smelled as rich as steak, and the thick gossamer homes of several generations of spiders. There was no human scent. Jumping out again, they had returned to the other end of the basement; they were crouched to escape through the basement window when Kit turned aside to paw at the loose linoleum in a closet they had earlier investigated, the one where the door wouldn't close. Pawing and scrabbling, suddenly she lowered her ears and lashed her tail with excitement. Dulcie pushed close, to see.

Raking the linoleum up against the wall with surprising strength, Kit skinnied underneath. "Look here! And someone's been here!" They could both smell it: The linoleum and concrete smelled of Cage Jones.

Sunk into the concrete floor beneath its grimy linoleum covering was a metal safe. A very old safe, rusting but sturdy and heavy. Cage had come down here recently, had surely pulled the linoleum back and handled the safe, and had probably opened it. The finger smears through its coat of dust smelled of Cage, and the dust around the dial was streaked, as if he had spun it; there were also smears along the edge of the lid, as if he had lifted it. What had he kept there? Was this what Greeley was looking for?

They had tried for a long time to open the safe, without luck; as superior as was a cat's hearing, Dulcie and Kit were not artful at sorting out the tumbler sounds and then spinning the dial accordingly. That was Greeley Urzey's forte, it was Greeley who was skilled at safecracking. For that old man, this would be the work of but a minute. They could catch no scent of what the safe might contain, or have contained, could smell nothing but the metal itself, and dust, and Cage's stink. No odor of old musty money, nothing like the way bills smelled that had been hidden for a very long time—they knew that nose-twitching smell; some of Lucinda Greenlaw's little fortune had once smelled like that from being hidden for many years.

Nor was there any hint of other musty paper in the safe, such as secreted bonds or stock certificates; aside from Cage's scent, only the sharp metal smell. Turning away, they had let the linoleum spring back and were pressing it into place, wondering if they should try to paw dust over it, when a noise sent them out of the closet and streaking for the window. Even as they leaped to the sill, behind them the door to the stairs flew open.

They heard Lilly gasp as they exploded out onto

a pine tree. Scrambling up its far side, claws digging into the bark, they climbed as fast as a pair of terrified squirrels. Behind them they heard Lilly's footsteps cross the gritty floor.

They had peered around to see her approaching the open window, and had drawn back. For a long moment, she stood looking out. There was no sound. And then, as if perhaps fearful that a burglar had been there and might return, Lilly slammed the window shut. They heard her attempt to lock it.

"That," Kit whispered, "doesn't make any sense. If she thinks there was a person inside, how does she know he isn't still there? How does she know he won't step out of a cupboard and mug her?"

Lilly tried for some time to lock the window, then fetched the rusty hammer and jammed it in above the lower pane of the double-hung window so it wouldn't open.

"What if she saw us?" Kit breathed.

"So? We're cats! What if she did? Come on!"

Scrambling to the roof they had peered over, checking the vents again, but none was loose. Padding across the scorching shingles listening for sounds from the attic space below their paws, they called Wilma, called her name over and over, at first quietly and then louder than was safe. Only silence greeted them. If Wilma were gagged as well as bound, she could give no answer—unless she could knock, kick out with a bound foot, make some noise. They tried for a very long time but could detect no sound at all beneath the hot shingles. They gave up at last, licked their scorched paws, and abandoned the roof, praying Wilma wasn't down there. Leaping into the pine they backed down its rough trunk and dropped to the ground, into thick dry pine needles. Dulcie, shaking needles from her fur, glanced toward the far end of the house—and there was Greeley, standing in the next yard watching them, looking straight at them, an evil smile on his wizened face, a leer as cruel as the devil masks upstairs. The cats fled straight down the steep wall of the canyon. Leaping down through tangled grass and weeds, tumbling and sliding to the canyon floor, they ran, their hearts pounding. Not until they were two blocks away and well concealed within the canyon's bushes did they stop and look back to the cliff-side houses.

He was still there, in the Jones's backyard, looking straight down at them, staring directly toward the bush where they crouched, his piercing, knowing look filled with rage.

"What's wrong with him?" Dulcie asked. "What does he think?"

"He thinks," Kit said, gulping air, "he thinks we found whatever he's looking for? Found it in that basement?" The two cats looked at each other, and shivered and crouched lower. They remained there, as still as rabbits gone to ground, waiting for Greeley Urzey to turn away.

They were still waiting when along the street high above them a police unit flashed quietly between the houses and stopped in front of the Jones house. Greeley saw it, and slipped back into the shadows.

As Dallas Garza and Officer Crowley stepped out of the squad car, the two cats slipped up the cliff again, keeping out of sight, up a eucalyptus tree to the roof, where they crouched, peering over as Dallas rang the bell. They heard its harsh ring, heard faint sounds from the basement, then an inner door close, heard footsteps on the wooden basement stairs as Lilly came up to answer.

Lilly Jones hadn't seemed pleased to find the detective at the door. "You just searched my house, you were here not two hours ago. You went all through it. Why would you search again? Let me see your warrant."

Patiently Dallas handed her the warrant; though the cats could see only the top of his head, Dallas's dark, close-cut hair, they knew that his square face would be bland, his dark eyes unreadable. As Lilly studied the warrant, Garza's gaze wandered past her and through the open door. "We're looking for Wilma Getz," he said bluntly.

"Wilma Getz?" Lilly paused as if sorting that out. "The librarian? Why would she be here? I hardly know her."

She glanced past him at two PG&E employees who were heading around the side of the house.

"What do they want? It's too late for city employees to be . . . Are they with you?" Her dry, lined face was a study in distrust. "What is this about, Detective?"

But then, quite suddenly, her anger faded into a look close to relief. Perhaps she'd thought of Greeley's unwanted visit and felt comforted to have the officers present. Dallas looked at her patiently. "May we search again, Lilly? You will accompany us?"

Peering down, the cats watched Lilly step slowly aside, allowing Garza and tall, thin Officer Crowley to enter. As she stepped in behind them and closed the door, three more utility workers joined the first two, moving to surround the house.

Watching Lilly, wondering how difficult she was going to be, Dallas followed her, and Crowley, into the dim, depressing house. Lilly, saying nothing, led them into the living room.

"I don't understand, Detective Garza. What is this about Wilma Getz? Why would she be here? Why would it be necessary for you to search, again? Would you explain, please?"

Frowning, Dallas wished he could read her better. He kept his expression steady, infinitely patient. "Lilly, Wilma has disappeared. Cage broke into her house. He was seen, there was a witness. It's possible he may have kidnapped her."

"Why in the world . . . ?" She looked at him for

some moments. At last she turned, scowling. "Come on, then, if you must." And she led them down the hall and on into the rest of the house.

And as Dallas searched the dim rooms, above, on the roof, Dulcie and Kit waited and listened. *Please, go in the attic,* Dulcie thought. She could not get that hot, airless space out of her mind. *Oh, please, Dallas, the attic. Go in there, the one place we can't reach.*

They heard the two officers moving around in the rooms below, heard doors open and close, an occasional question from Dallas and Lilly's terse reply. After what seemed ages there came a sliding sound, as if the ceiling hole to the attic had been opened; seconds later they heard an officer moving around close beneath their paws, heard hollow footsteps across the bare attic floor. Dulcie imagined Dallas ducking beneath the low attic roof, hunched uncomfortably. Listening to the detective's progress across the wooden floor, her little cat heart pounded hard. But then at last they heard Dallas descend again and speak to Crowley, then replace the attic door, sliding it back into position. They had found no one. They listened as the officers moved about the rest of the house and then headed down the wooden stairs to the basement; and the cats padded silently across the roof to the pine tree and scrambled down, to watch through the basement windows.

16

"Even if Dallas finds the safe," Dulcie said, peering from the pine tree, into the basement, "he won't open it if the warrant is just to look for Wilma and Cage."

The kit's yellow eyes narrowed. "He needs to know Greeley's looking for something in there, just like Cage searched Wilma's house. If we had a phone . . . There's a phone in the kitchen, we can slip back in the house and call his cell . . ."

"No way," Dulcie hissed. "Phone Dallas while he's in the house with us? We push our luck, and . . . I don't like to think about that."

Kit sighed and settled reluctantly among the branches, watching Dallas search through the boxes and abandoned furniture, his hand never far from his weapon. When he opened the empty closet where the safe was hidden, the cats hissed with surprise: The closet had been empty, just the loose linoleum with the safe beneath it sunk into the floor. Now it was filled with boxes, a bucket of tools, the old rusted fan that had lain atop a trunk, and a tangle of old boots. Dallas stepped back, looking. He knew that clutter hadn't been there when he'd searched the house earlier. The detective turned, his back to the wall, taking another long look into the shadows and dark spaces. He stepped to the door that led to the stairs, closed it, and shoved a heavy carton against it. Then he searched the garage.

When he found no one, he moved to the windows. Finding the unlocked window, he examined the sill, then slid it open, looking out into the dark woods. Above him, the cats crouched, unmoving. Leaning out the open window, he used his flashlight, in the darkening evening, to study the earth beneath the sill. Dulcie and Kit were glad they had trod only on pine needles. At last Dallas eased himself out the window and shone his light back and forth across the yard, looking for footprints.

"Did Greeley cover up the safe like that?" Dulcie whispered. "Or did Lilly? Is there something in it *she* doesn't want found? Did she put that stuff on top after she heard noises and came down, thinking someone was in there?"

"Someone was there. We were."

"Someone human," Dulcie said. "Maybe she thought it was Greeley. But what would she hide in there? Her jewelry?" Dulcie smiled. "She doesn't look like the type to ever wear fancy jewelry . . . And would Greeley go to all this trouble for a few pieces of an old woman's jewelry? I don't think so."

"And," Kit said, "what does all this have to do with Cage?"

Dallas was moving the boxes and trash from the closet; when he'd emptied it, he knelt, lifted the loose linoleum, and pulled it back out of the way. Yes, he'd known the safe was there, the cats could see that. And now that someone had taken the trouble to cover it, his attention was keen.

He tried lifting the lid, then turned the dial until it clicked, and tried again. Maybe his warrant covered this, maybe not. The detective was as curious as a cat, himself. When spinning the dial once didn't work, he remained crouched, lightly fingering it.

"Does he know how to crack a safe?" Dulcie whispered, and the tabby smiled. "Looks like he's tempted."

"Would that be legal?"

"To finger the tumblers, and crack a safe?" Dulcie twitched her whiskers. "Not likely," she said, enjoying Dallas's temptation.

They watched him resist, and at last he rose and began to replace the clutter that had been piled on top, putting everything back just the way it had been, his tanned, square Latino face drawn into a frown. Then he headed for the stairs, moved the barrier, and disappeared. As his footsteps ascended, the cats scrambled up again to the roof and softly across it, then crouched above the front door listening to Dallas and his officer taking their leave, Dallas thanking Lilly for her courtesy and help with a dry sarcasm that was rare for the laid-back officer; the cats watched them head for their squad car as Lilly closed the front door hard with a chill finality, a clear message that she was tired of people tramping through her house. As the officers' car made a U-turn and headed back down the hills toward the village, Dulcie and Kit streaked away across the rooftops, heading home, their minds a tumble of new facts and more than a few questions.

Racing from shingles into pine or oak trees and down across more roofs, up and down over a jumble of peaks, Dulcie hoped Max Harper was still at the cottage, and that by now there was news of Wilma—good news. Dulcie let herself think of no other kind. The evening was warm, as soft as velvet, the late sky holding more light, now, than the dark village streets below. But when the courthouse clock struck nine, her heart sank. On a normal evening Wilma would be home, they'd have finished supper and would be tucked up together on the velvet couch, or, on cold nights, in bed by the woodstove, contentedly reading.

Dulcie's creamy stone cottage shone out of the darkness, and there were lights at the windows. The tabby ran so fast she hardly hit the shingles, and twice she tripped over her own paws. But, then, warily they stopped on the roof of the next-door house, looking.

There were only two police units, now, at the curb. And two officers stringing yellow tape around the edge of the garden. *As if this is a murder scene,* Dulcie thought sickly. As she approached the house, she began to shiver.

But of course Harper would want to mark the premises off limits, to preserve any possible evidence they might have missed. Taking heart, she leaped from the neighbors' roof into the oak tree by Wilma's living room window.

Just beyond the open window, Max Harper sat at Wilma's desk, busy with paperwork. Dulcie drew nearer along the branch, and could see that he was filling out a report. Both cats tried to read it upside down. Behind them a car pulled to the curb and Dallas stepped out, alone; perhaps he had swung by the station to drop off his officer. He hurried in through the open front door. The whole house seemed to be open, though the heat that had collected within would take half the night to dissipate; the walls would stay hot long after the late breeze had cooled the rooms. Dallas drew up a chair beside the desk, glancing inquiringly at Max.

Max shook his head. "Nothing. You?"

"No sign of Wilma, and Lilly doesn't seem to know anything. One or two details were strange; I'll fill you in later. Anything on the Tucker and Keating murders?"

"Reports just came in," Max said. "Linda Tucker case, the only sets of prints besides the Tuckers' belonged to the cleaning lady and to a plumber who was in the house three days before.

"The Keating case, Elaine's husband had a poker

game last week. All we got were the Keatings' prints, and those of five poker players. We'll need a day or two to get that bunch in for questioning."

Harper didn't seem terribly interested in those possible suspects, and the chief's indifference shocked Dulcie. "What's he thinking? Is he off on some other track?"

But Kit's yellow eyes had widened with dismay. "Does he think . . ." She looked at Dulcie and shivered. "Does he think the husbands did it? Oh, that would be too bad."

Dulcie watched Kit with interest. The young tortoiseshell cat, after helping gather information on so many cases, and hearing about other murders from Joe and Dulcie, should be inured to such matters—but she was not hardened to the thought of a husband killing his wife, and Dulcie understood. The fact that these men might have murdered the partners they had vowed to love and cherish, seemed to hurt something deep and tender in the young tortoiseshell. Kit had never, as a kitten, known a loving and nurturing family; did not remember her mother or her littermates. A close and loving family seemed to Kit rare and wonderful; she looked on family as having a sacred bond of love and decency, and the thought of murder within that family bond hurt her deeply. Dulcie looked at Kit, hunched miserably on the branch, and she licked Kit's ear, trying to soothe her; but suddenly both cats startled to attention as

Max, pushing back his chair, stood up from the desk.

He shoved his papers in a folder and looked at Dallas. "I'll stop by the Greenlaws, see if they've heard from Wilma, if they have anything that could help." The lean lines of his face fell into a deeper dismay. "They have to be told she's missing; I don't want them hearing it on the news if some reporter picks it up. Will you call Ryan again? I'll keep trying Charlie. Those two . . . They get off with the horses, they never turn on their phones, the rest of the world doesn't exist."

"I'll keep trying," Dallas said. "Or I'll take a run up there."

Max nodded. "Maybe by the time we get hold of them, we'll have better news."

Dulcie and Kit watched Harper head up the walk to his squad car; as he pulled away they were already racing across the roofs, heading for Kit's house. Kit wanted to be there with Lucinda and Pedric, to be close to comfort them when Max told them that Wilma was missing. She wanted to be there for them just as, when she was little and lost and frightened, Lucinda and Pedric had comforted her, had held her close, petting her; had snuggled her in their soft bed and given her nice things to eat. Now her humans would need comforting, would need what Pedric called "a wee bit of moral support."

Though Kit couldn't bring them good things to eat—unless Lucinda and Pedric had developed a taste for fresh mouse.

17

That soft tapping wasn't caused by the wind; Wilma listened to the sounds above her hoping it was a squirrel in the attic, or a raccoon, or maybe a crow on the roof, pecking at the shingles. But she knew better. Those were human footsteps, walking softly across the second floor of what she had thought was a one-story shack. Her fear of whoever was there and might come down while she was tied up and helpless sent panic through her that was hard to control, filled her with a shock of terror that dwarfed the fear she'd felt when she'd glimpsed, out the window, that dark, small shape careen away. Though surely that had been only a squirrel or a cat, nothing big enough to threaten her. She wished it had been Dulcie, or Joe, or Kit.

But no one knew where she was. In the moving car, she had left no scent trail, nothing for a cat to follow. Even those three clever feline friends had no way to find her.

Cage had told her he'd searched her house, and that filled her with terror for Dulcie; thinking he might have hurt Dulcie.

But Dulcie wouldn't have gone near him, wouldn't have let him approach her, if she had come home and found him there. And he'd have driven away, leaving no trail for a cat to follow.

Driven away in her car, or in the other one? For a moment, she banked all hope on the quick reactions of one small cat, praying Dulcie had seen the car, that she had reported her car stolen or seen the license number of the other car and called the station.

But that was too bizarre, a far too timely solution to a messy situation. Too much wishful thinking. Still, if Dulcie had made the car, there were police patrols all over the village, and the station was just blocks away. One of Harper's units might have been able to find and follow Cage.

Awash in panic because, very likely, no one knew where she was, and no one was going to know, she ceased her awkward search for a knife and uselessly fought her bonds again, jerking and struggling as she listened to the footsteps overhead, soft shoes or slippers padding around on a hard floor. She looked for a place to hide, certain that every time she moved the chair, whoever was there would hear the awkward thumping.

The windows were growing dark; when night fell, the woods and yard and inside the cabin would be black as sin; there would be no moonlight to seep in among the masses of tall, dense pines. If whoever was there came downstairs in the pitch-black dark, when she couldn't see them . . .

Bending awkwardly to fight open the lowest drawer behind her, conscious of every small scrape and thump as she tilted and rummaged trying not to lose her balance, she searched with increased panic for a weapon to free herself.

Indeed, in the low attic room above Wilma someone heard her struggles and visualized what she might be doing down there, someone who moved softly about the dim room, someone filled with questions, with fear, and perhaps with a cold, hidden rage.

And from outside the house, others, too, watched Wilma, observing her through the window as she fought for her freedom: Three small, wild beings looked down from the stickery branches of a pine tree and in through the dusty window, watching the captive woman struggle.

The pale calico looked at her companions. "I *know* her. That's Wilma, that's Dulcie's Wilma." Amazed and puzzled, Willow slipped around the pine's dry trunk to its far side where the tall, gray-haired woman wouldn't glimpse her, wouldn't see in the gathering night, her pale calico coat gleaming. Both she and white Cotton would stand out now, easy to observe. Only Coyote with his dark brown–striped coat would blend into the night's shadows.

But Coyote was saying, "You never saw Dulcie's Wilma," and the big, dark cat lashed his tail with disgust, his long, tufted ears flicking with annoyance.

"I know her from how Kit described her," Willow said. "You heard her, Cotton heard her." She looked at white Cotton, but that tom remained silent.

"No one can know a human from a description," Coyote said. "There could be hundreds like that."

"There are not hundreds like her! I do know her," Willow hissed. "You think humans are all alike? She's tall and slim, she has long silver hair. Look at her, her hair tied back with a silver clip. Jeans and a red sweatshirt. All exactly the way Kit said." She glared at the dark long-haired tom whose black face stripes and tall ears made him resemble a small coyote. "I'm not stupid!" Willow snapped. "I know Dulcie's Wilma."

Coyote looked back at her uncertainly. Maybe she did know, who was he to say? He knew little enough about human creatures.

But it was Cotton who crept closer along the branch and looked in at Wilma for the longest time, saying nothing. And then, with a flick of his tail and a twitch of his ears he leaped away into the undergrowth; when Willow called softly after him, he said over his shoulder, "Hunting. I'm going to hunt."

"But—"

"What do I care for humans and their senseless problems?" And with that, Cotton was gone. Willow looked after him, hurt and disappointed.

But again, Willow peered around through the

branches at Wilma, her bleached calico coat ghostly against the dark trunk. "Those men not only tied her to a chair, they blindfolded her. Well, but she's gotten that off! Good for her! But what do they want with her?" She looked hard at Coyote. "How rude Cotton was! We have to help her, we have to free her."

"I don't—"

"Just like Kit freed us!" Willow hissed. "It's payback time, Coyote. Couldn't Cotton see that? We have to free her before they hurt her!"

Coyote stared at her, his ears back stubbornly. And Willow, swallowing, knew she had spoken too directly. It hadn't taken much to send Cotton off. If she got Coyote's back up, he'd leave, too, and she'd have no help at all.

Coyote was a good cat. So was Cotton. They just didn't find any value in humans. Neither tom trusted humans, and with good reason.

Most of their band felt no connection to humans. They had all grown up feral, wild and wary, keeping to themselves. Well, maybe she was glad Cotton had gone. The white cat was so bossy, always wanted to do everything his way. At least Coyote was gentler; and Coyote had a deep social feeling for their own kind, a love of their own wild rituals. Maybe she could play on that. Maybe she could manipulate Coyote into helping—if only she knew *what* to do, knew *how* to help.

But there wasn't much time. Those men might

soon be back. *If they're coming back,* she thought. She was all nerves, watching Wilma struggle. With that chair tied to her, the tall lady could hardly turn. Willow could see the knives that Wilma hadn't found, she wanted to tell her where, to leap in and touch her hand with a soft paw and guide her.

But she could not; she could not bring herself to try the things Dulcie and Kit took for granted; she dare not try to open that window, or go voluntarily into a human's house. Instead, she turned a limpid gaze on Coyote. "We were in that cage two weeks, captive, just like she's captive now. I thought we'd never get out. *Her* friends helped get us free.

"I was so scared, locked in there," she said, trembling. "We all three were. Now she's trapped like we were, and *she* doesn't even have anything to eat, like we did. Or any water until she managed to turn on the faucet." She looked hard at the dark, striped tom. "She's brave, Coyote. She's a fighter—as strong and brave as a cat herself."

Coyote watched her narrowly. "So? What can *we* do?"

"It was her friends who saved *us,*" Willow repeated. "It was her friend, Joe's Grey's human, who cut off the lock for us. We can't leave Dulcie's Wilma. How could we? But, how can we help her?"

Finding the blade of a long butcher knife, Wilma cut her finger. Swearing under her breath, she felt for the handle, then, bending and twisting, nearly dislocating her spine, she pulled it to her and hauled it out.

With the big knife securely in hand, she was twisting it around with the blade toward her bound wrists when she heard the overhead floor creaking, louder, then footsteps approached, echoing hollowly, as if coming down hidden wooden steps.

It sounded like the stairs might be behind the stone wall where the woodstove crouched. Frantically she cut at her bonds—and of course cut herself again, she could feel the slick blood. Angry at her clumsiness, and shaky with her effort to sever the rope, she was looking directly at the stone wall when a figure emerged from behind it.

A small figure, stepping hesitantly. A woman, young and pale and as insubstantial appearing as a ghost. A frail and displaced-looking creature, stick thin, dressed in an oversized man's shirt and a long, faded skirt from which her white ankles protruded like two bones. White feet shod in worn leather sandals. She stood looking at Wilma, then slowly approached; and even in the gathering shadows, Wilma could see her fear, her eyes wide in the fading light. She said no word; she watched Wilma warily, then focused on the knife Wilma clutched behind her; she reached gently out to Wilma, as if meaning to cut her bonds—and jerked the knife away. Snatched it roughly from her hands and backed away fiercely clutching it, her eyes hard now.

"Please," Wilma said. "What are you doing? Please, cut me free."

"I can't. They'd kill me."

"They won't kill you if I'm free, and we get out of here, if we run before they get back."

The girl shook her head; something about her looked familiar, something about her frail thin body. Wilma studied her, trying to make out her age. Could this thin, pale woman be Cage's younger sister? She looked as Wilma remembered her, but Violet would be around twenty-five. This girl looked maybe sixteen. "Violet? *Are* you Violet Jones?"

A faint nod, as she backed away.

Wilma looked at the cheap gold band on her finger. "Violet Sears, now? Eddie Sears's wife?"

Another nod, tinged with a downward, closed glance of shame.

"If you leave me tied, Violet, and they kill me, you'll be an accomplice to murder. You'll go to prison right along with Eddie and Cage. Federal prison. For a very long time."

"If I untie you, Eddie will kill me."

"What does Cage want with me? If I knew that—"

"You stole from him. What he had in the safe. He told you that, I heard him tell you that."

"*What* did he have? He won't tell me anything. I

have no idea what he thinks I took, no idea what he wants."

Violet said nothing, only looked at her.

"If you free me, maybe I can help him. Find out who did steal from him. I can't do anything tied up."

No answer.

"I know how to help Cage. If I'm free I *can* help him."

But the girl didn't buy it. She shook her head and turned away, heading for the hidden stairs. Wilma didn't want to believe she would leave her there, helpless. But she guessed she'd better believe it.

She hadn't seen Violet since she was a child. She might have glimpsed her on the street and not realized who she was. She'd heard that Violet was born just months before their mother died, that Mrs. Jones had died from complications developed at Violet's birth. Other village gossips liked to say that Violet wasn't Mrs. Jones's daughter at all, but was Lilly's. That the shock of Lilly giving birth out of wedlock had killed Mrs. Jones.

Wilma hadn't lived in the village when Violet was born, but Molena Point, like all small towns, enjoyed a complicated network of—as some put it—domestic intelligence. A web of personal histories and sensitive facts embroidered liberally with imaginative conjecture.

Lilly Jones had always been reclusive, and more so after the baby came. She was never seen in a restaurant or at the library or at village celebrations; nor was the child seen except walking alone to school and home again, alone, always alone. Lilly was about thirty when the baby came. She was around fifty-five now, though she looked far older. Watching Violet head for the stairs, Wilma felt too stubborn to plead, and she knew that was stupid, stupid not to try.

"If you leave me, Violet, Cage will kill me just the way he shot Mandell Bennett."

Violet turned, her eyes widening with shock. "Cage didn't shoot anyone."

"Turn on the news, you'll hear it. And if he kills me, too, that will be your fault. You'll be an accomplice. It's a federal offense, to be involved in the murder of a federal officer. You'd do hard time, Violet. Time in a federal prison. Those women would make mincemeat of you."

Violet looked back at her, her narrow face sour and ungiving. Saying nothing, she rolled up the sleeves of her oversized shirt.

Her thin arms were red and purple with bruises. She pulled up the long tails of the shirt to reveal a mass of red and purple marks across her stomach and back, and one broad and ugly red bruise. "If Cage don't kill me, this is what Eddie will do."

Wilma had never gotten used to the signs of abuse. No matter how often during her working career she had witnessed this and worse, such violence sickened her. "What Eddie does to you . . . That's all the more reason for us to get out of here. I promise I'll find you a place to hide, a good place. And I'll see that you're protected."

"Not the cops!" But Violet approached again, slowly, and stood watching her.

"Not the cops," Wilma said. "If we *can* get away, if time hasn't run out, there are others you can trust. Private organizations. Abused women who have escaped, themselves, and who understand, who will hide you and protect you."

To promise this battered person protection, promise her a secure shelter away from Eddie Sears, was very likely useless. If Violet ran true to form, if she was like most battered women, she would just go back to him. Wilma knew too many who did; she knew too well the terrors, and the hungers, of an abused woman. To try to help a battered woman, to try to bolster her courage and self-respect, often had no effect at all; many wouldn't listen, they were just as addicted to abuse as were their abusers.

But she had to try. If she meant to live, she had to try. Because it looked like Violet Sears was the only chance she might have.

She looked at the week-old newspaper on the counter, wondering if it was Violet who had kept it—maybe out of some twisted fascination? Or because she felt a kinship with the murdered woman?

Or was it Eddie who had dog-eared the page, reading it over and over? She looked at the picture of Linda Tucker, then looked at Violet.

"I knew her," Violet whispered. "I knew who she was, I'd see her in the grocery when we lived in the village, when Eddie let me go out to the store. I saw the look in her eyes, and I knew . . . She always wore long sleeves, and her shirt collar buttoned up. I knew . . . ," Violet repeated in a whisper. She looked at Wilma, desolate. "Now there's been another one. Tonight. Another murder, a woman at home alone, in her bed. The paper calls it a break-in murder." Her eyes narrowed. "Those weren't break-ins.

"This woman who died tonight, she was the same as Linda Tucker. I'd see her, too, in the grocery or drugstore . . . The same look, same cover-up clothes. We knew each other. We'd look at each other, and we knew."

She pressed her clenched fist to her mouth. "There was no burglar to murder those women. Eddie . . . He just keeps reading about Linda Tucker, reading it over and over."

She looked for a long time at Wilma. "He's been reading that paper all week, like . . . like he would read a dirty book. Real intent, drinking beer and looking at her picture and reading about what her husband did to her."

"You have to get away from him, Violet. We can get out of here now, together, and I'll help

you. Now, quickly, before they come back—
before they kill us both."

The village streets and unlit doorways were inky
between soft spills of light from shop windows.
Only above the rooftops where Dulcie and Kit
raced did the last gleam of evening reflect a silver
glow across the shingles; the two cats flew over
peaks and dodged between chimneys and crossed
above the narrow streets on the twisted branches of
old and venerable oaks—but they were not as fast
as the squad car.

When they landed on Kit's own roof, Max
Harper's big white police car was already parked
at the curb, heat rising up to them with the faint
stink of exhaust; the chief still sat at the wheel,
talking on his cell phone. Quickly the cats scrambled down an oak tree that overhung the street,
then crouched on a low branch, listening.

Harper's voice was coldly angry. ". . . and call
me back, Charlie! Now, at once."

Shocked, Dulcie and Kit stared at each other.
Max never talked to Charlie like that. The Harpers
had been married not quite a year, they were still
newlyweds, he loved his redheaded bride more
than life itself. Loved every freckle, loved her
unruly carroty hair, loved her sense of humor and
her quick temper. The tall, lean police chief loved
Charlie Harper in a way that made both cats feel
warm and safe. Now, did Max feel guilty that

Charlie's aunt Wilma had disappeared, on his watch? Was that what made him cross? That didn't make any sense; it wasn't his fault.

But a lot about life didn't make sense, a lot about humans didn't make sense. They watched him step out of his unit and head up the brick steps to the wide porch; as they trotted across an oak branch to Kit's little cat door in the dining room window, and pushed through into the house, they heard the door chimes and watched Lucinda hurry to answer.

Opening the door, the tall old lady laughed with pleasure. "Max! This is a nice surprise. Come in." Then she saw his expression and drew in her breath. "What? What's happened?"

18

Beyond the Greenlaws' open windows, an owl hooted; and a pleasant breeze wandered through the big living room of the hillside house, cooling the hot night as the tall, lean, eightysomething newlyweds welcomed Max Harper; they stood waiting quietly for whatever bad news Max had brought them. Across the room, on the upholstered bench before the big front windows, Dulcie and Kit listened, trying to look as if they'd been there a long time, quietly napping. This was going to be terrible, Kit thought. It was scary enough that Wilma had disappeared; she didn't want Lucinda to become sick with worry over her good friend.

Kit worried about Pedric, too; but Pedric Greenlaw was tougher. Equally thin and frail looking, but wiry and hardy, Pedric Greenlaw's dry humor had seen him through all kinds of crises in his younger days, and through some questionable scrapes with the law, too. His checkered past had left him with a quick turn of mind, fast to act and shocked by very little.

Now, though Lucinda turned pale as Harper laid out the details of Wilma's disappearance, Pedric asked clear, precise questions: *Had* Wilma left San Francisco? Had she checked out of her hotel? At what time? Which stores did she favor? Did she usually pay with her credit card, which could be traced? Had the sheriff been notified? Max hid the little twitch at the side of his mouth and patiently answered Pedric's questions; Pedric should know he had done these things, but that was how Pedric Greenlaw approached a problem.

The cats smiled, themselves, as the captain explained that everything in Wilma's house had been fingerprinted and photographed, all possible evidence duly bagged, and that the house would be sealed. Ordinarily, much more time must pass in a missing person report before the police undertook this thorough an investigation, but there had been a witness—and in Wilma's case, ordinary procedures went out the window.

"Detective Davis is on her way to Gilroy," Max

said. "And so is Clyde. I couldn't stop him; I just hope he stays out of Davis's way."

Lucinda glanced across at Dulcie and Kit, clearly wanting to know if Joe Grey was with Clyde. Kit twitched her ears in a little private yes that seemed to brighten Lucinda's mood. The Greenlaws had great faith in Joe Grey. No cop could track scent, as Joe would do.

"What?" Max said, watching her. "Why the smile?"

"I . . . That will give Clyde something to do," Lucinda said, "to keep him from worrying so much."

Max nodded. "Charlie would want to head up there, too. If I could reach her. I guess she and Ryan are riding."

"We saw on the news," Pedric said, "that Cage Jones escaped this morning. Pretty shoddy way to run a jail. And then the paper said Wilma's partner was shot. We've been worried about Wilma. Lucinda called the house and her cell—"

"Wilma's quick," Max said, "and careful." But his face had gone closed with the extent of his concern.

Lucinda said, "Do the seniors know any of this?" The four senior ladies, who had bought a home together, were close friends of both the Greenlaws and Wilma.

Max nodded. "Mavity came into the station to ask advice about evicting her brother. Greeley's become a real headache, and she wants him out of there. She told Mabel that she'd been trying to call Wilma, she said if they heard from her, they'd call the station. Apparently Mavity and her housemates hadn't seen the paper or had the news on, they didn't know about Jones's escape, and Mabel didn't tell her."

Lucinda nodded, then shook her head. "Poor Mavity. Greeley camping in their nice house, letting those women feed him—poor all of them." She spoke with sympathy, but with a laugh, too. "I think I'd spice up Greeley's supper with a touch of rat poison."

"Every time Greeley shows up," Pedric said, "he brings trouble. I hope Mavity booted him out for once and all."

"Mavity got down to the station," Max said, "nearly lost her nerve, but finally filed a complaint."

Lucinda shook her head. "This news about Wilma will be hard for those ladies, they're all close to her."

"Maybe Wilma's disappearance," Pedric said, "as terrifying as it is, will load Mavity up with enough worry that she'll stop tolerating that old crook. Mavity will stand for just so much frustration before she pitches a fit."

Max rose, and so did Lucinda. He put his arm around her. "All agencies are alerted and looking for Wilma. An APB out for Jones. Sheriff's men all over Gilroy. Wilma isn't . . ." He paused when his cell phone rang. He answered, then put the caller on hold, looking up at them. "Wilma was a federal officer, Lucinda. She knows how to handle herself."

Lucinda and Pedric walked Harper out, watched him move quickly down the steps, pausing on the stone walk to speak with the waiting caller—and the cats slipped out behind them. They were crouched to race for Harper's patrol car, intent on hiding in the back and hitching a ride wherever he was headed, when Lucinda snatched them up by the napes of their necks—an indignity usually reserved only for kittens.

"It's hot!" she whispered crossly, turning her back to Harper, and ignoring the cats' anger. "Think about it! You get locked in that car, you'll suffocate."

"We never—" Kit began.

"Yes you did!" Lucinda looked hard at the tortoiseshell. "You've done it before, both of you! Slipped into cars, and at great danger!" She held them close against her. Neither Dulcie nor Kit would insult Lucinda by trying to get away—at least, not if they could argue their way out of a scolding.

"We just meant to listen to his call . . . ," Kit lied, whispering into Lucinda's ear. She looked beseechingly at her thin, wrinkled friend. "We just wanted to listen . . ."

Dulcie had the good sense to keep her mouth shut.

Frowning, Lucinda put them down again, giving them another stern look; she stood and watched as they slipped into the bushes behind Max.

". . . hardly dark," he was saying, "and the other two happened around midnight. What's the coroner say? Does Bern see similarities? Dallas is at Wilma's place. Get him over there."

The cats looked at each other. What was this? Another murder, a third one?

"*No* witnesses, no one heard anything? Who did you send?" Then, "Tell her to print everything! Every damn surface! Light switches, dirty dishes, soap dish, whatever! Everything in the kitchen where you found her—salt shaker, table legs, trash can, every damn surface she can find! Stuff in the trash, jars and cartons in the refrigerator, stay there and print if it takes her a week. I don't like this—this isn't going to continue, not on our watch! Keep someone with the husband; I'm on my way."

Crouched in the bushes, the cats burned with questions. Who was the victim? Where? As Harper punched in a number, Kit took a sneaking step toward his squad car, but Dulcie nudged her, looking up guiltily at Lucinda. "You promised her, Kit," Dulcie whispered, her green eyes fixed hard on Kit. "You came flying home to comfort Lucinda and Pedric, not to worry them—you go off on some wild hair now, you'll have them pacing all night!"

"What about the times you left Wilma worrying!" Kit said, turning away; she was slinking back toward the front door when Harper's phone rang again. She paused; both cats watched him as he listened and then swung into his car. They heard, through the open windows, his voice falter, suddenly broken and rough.

"What time was this, Ryan? You checked the whole house? The barn? She hadn't gone riding without you? Did you . . . ?"

A truck roared by, blocking all sound, prompting Max to roll up his windows. The cats watched a long, indecipherable discussion. When no more trucks passed, he put the windows down again. "Are you carrying?" he said.

Another longer silence. Then, "Lock yourself in your truck, Ryan. Do it now. And stay there; I'm on my way." But before he spun a U-turn, they heard him call the dispatcher. He told Mabel to put out a "be on the lookout," for Charlie. "Call Garza, tell him the Peggy Milner murder's all his, I'm headed for the ranch."

The cats listened, deeply afraid. Behind them in the open doorway Lucinda and Pedric stood with their arms around each other, Lucinda clutching the doorjamb, both of them shocked into silence, thinking of Charlie, of Max's redheaded bride, watching helplessly as the chief took off fast, burning rubber.

19

Max left the Greenlaws' moving fast through the village, emergency lights flashing, seeing only Charlie's face, her green eyes searching his, feeling the cloud of her red hair against his cheek, her presence filling his whole world; for a long and painful moment the earth had dropped away, leaving only Charlie and, around her, an empty and chilling void.

He had Ryan on the speaker. "The kitchen door was unlocked," she was saying; her cell phone cut in and out a couple of times, then came in clearer. "I know she locks that door when she goes out to the barn." Ryan's voice shook, her Irish/Latina temper blazing. "Who the hell . . . Her car's here, Max. She's fed the horses and brought them in from pasture, put the dogs in a stall to feed them, and shut the door.

"Sandwich fixings laid out for our dinner, sliced roast beef and potato salad in the refrigerator. Coffeepot's been plugged in for hours. Boiled dry. And, Max, she left her work out. She would never do that. Scattered everywhere, computer on, drawings and manuscript all over."

No, he thought, Charlie wouldn't leave her work strewn about. The first thing she did when she finished for the evening, before she went to take care of the animals, was to put everything away: backup computer disks, manuscript in the file, drawings safe in the long drawers of the map cabinet. All in its place, ready for the next day's work.

"Maybe," Ryan said, "when she got my first message that I'd be late, maybe she decided to get back to work. But she . . . She isn't here," she said uncertainly. "Dallas called me earlier, told me that Cage Jones has escaped . . . And then I heard it on the news . . . Could this be part of it? Dallas described what . . . What they did to Wilma's house."

"You were in the kitchen, Ryan? Did you go into any other part of the house?"

"I've been through every room, closets, the works."

"What time was this?"

"Just now."

"You checked the whole house. Did you . . . ?"

"Nothing seems disturbed. Kitchen isn't messed up, just looks like Charlie was interrupted, that maybe she stepped outdoors for a minute, which could explain the door being unlocked. If she played her messages, she knew I was delayed. Cement truck was two hours late, there was a wreck on Highway 1 and we . . ."

"You never did talk with her, then? Just the messages?"

"That's right. Cement truck arrived, we had to

pour and finish out a three-car garage, then pour foundations . . . ," Ryan said helplessly. "It was dark when I got here, no lights on in the house. Only the automatic security lights outside. Both dogs were barking, in the barn.

"The instant I parked and opened the cab door, Rock leaped out over me—he never does that any more. Roared out of the truck snarling and barking and headed straight for the barn. Circled and circled, and then flew around back. He was on to a scent, Max. Wanted to take off through the woods. I grabbed his collar, pulled him back until I could see what was going on.

"There were tire marks behind the barn, fresh ones. Rock was going wild. They were close together, not a truck. Some kind of small car . . . a track that came down the bridle trail! Came down to the barn, turned around, and went back up again. And there were fresh footprints, three sets. I thought . . . One set was smaller, like Charlie's paddock boots."

Max thanked his stars it was Ryan who'd gotten there first, not someone who knew nothing about investigation; she had learned well from her uncle Dallas, and would disturb as little as possible. He imagined Charlie going into the barn, someone stepping from the shadows, grabbing and dragging her, Charlie fighting . . .

Turning onto Ocean he flicked on his siren, moving fast. Despite Ryan's worry over Charlie,

177

Max could hear the pride in her voice at the behavior of her untrained dog; he marveled, too, that Rock would be so responsive. But Rock was bred to that—the Weimaraner was a sight-and-scent tracker and retriever used on all kinds of game. A well-bred specimen like Rock was a powerhouse of intelligence and determination.

He spun a turn onto Highway 1, cut across two lanes, and took off for the hills. Ryan said, "The ground in the alleyway between the stalls was all scuffed up; I kept Rock close to the stalls. It was all I could do to hold him, pulling and snarling. And the horses were nervous, snorting, shying when I approached their stalls. The two dogs were wild, leaping at their stall door. I didn't dare let them out, I was afraid they'd take off, and what good would that do?"

The Harpers' two half-breed Great Danes were long on enthusiasm but, except for basic obedience training, were still too unruly to be of any specific use. If someone had tried to take Charlie by force, Max thought they would have attacked if they'd been out of their stall. And Ryan was right, they would sure give chase if someone had Charlie. Feeling ice-cold, he fought the sinking fear that threatened to overwhelm him.

"Those tracks, Max . . . Where could they go, up the bridle trail like that? There are just woods up there, and patches of open hills. Just that narrow trail . . . Shall I saddle up and . . . ?"

"No! I'm almost there, just turning off the highway."

In Gilroy, Joe ducked under a dress rack when he saw Clyde coming into Liz Claiborne's, and he fled for the dressing rooms, where Clyde might not come pushing in. Winding in and out of each little cubicle, sniffing at the carpet, he sorted through a hundred scents of powder, perfume, hair spray, and less appealing odors; he nosed at garments discarded on the benches and floor. Talk about messy shoppers. He had just caught Wilma's scent and found her booth, when a young clerk came back to the dressing rooms. She, too, wound in and out picking up rumpled clothes.

When, in Wilma's abandoned booth, she picked up a navy blue windbreaker that some earlier customer had left, Joe stared up at her from beneath it. He looked as innocent as he knew how to look, while gripping in his teeth a lipstick-stained tissue that bore Wilma's scent. Above him, against the wall, hung three pairs of jeans, two sweaters, and a blazer that Wilma had tried on; he had reared up on the little bench to make sure.

When the clerk picked up the jacket and saw the tomcat, she let out a yip—but then she laughed and knelt to stroke him. "Aren't you a handsome fellow. Where did you come from? What did you do, just wander in? Did someone bring you in, some shopper?" She glanced behind her down the row of dressing rooms, then toward the door, as if expecting someone to come looking for their lost cat. Then she petted Joe and baby-talked him until she had finessed a rumbling purr from the tomcat.

She was an exceptionally pretty brunette. Long, silky hair and big brown eyes, and she smelled like fresh green grass. When she tried gently to remove the tissue from his clenched teeth, he snarled at her until she withdrew her hand. But he had not intimidated this lady.

"What do you want that for, you silly cat? Maybe you like the smell of lipstick? Cats," she said, laughing. She was obviously a cat person, and for that Joe was grateful. "You are a pretty fellow. Where *did* you come from? What are you doing in here besides stealing tissues?" Laughing again, and despite his earlier growls, she boldly picked him up.

Making nice again, he purred against her shoulder and gave her the look that Dulcie called "lovey eye." He made up to her so shamefully that he soon had her practically purring herself. When she came out of the dressing rooms carrying and stroking him, Clyde was standing at the cash register talking with a clerk. Seeing Joe, he did a double take, then quickly collected himself.

"There he is," he said, as if deeply relieved. "I've looked everywhere." He grinned at the girl, and reached out to take Joe from her arms. "Cat got out of his carrier.

"What a bad cat you are," Clyde cooed, staring deep into Joe's angry yellow eyes. He did not try to remove the tissue from Joe's teeth. "I looked and looked for you. Come on, kitty, baby—such a bad cat. Come on, Joe, baby. Come to Papa now."

This performance earned, the moment they were alone in the car, an incensed scolding. *"Kitty, baby? Come to Papa?"* The tomcat was so furious that, when Clyde tossed him into the front seat, he deliberately scratched Clyde's hand. "If I weren't so good-natured, I'd have bloodied your face! If you ever again call me kitty baby, I swear I'll kill you, Clyde. Slowly and painfully, as I would disembowel a gutter rat!"

But then, because he was totally wired after what he had found, proof that Wilma had been there, Joe broke into a grin. "Actually, that was some rare performance you gave in there. Juvenile. Insulting. But crudely amusing."

Clyde stared at the tissue that Joe had laid carefully on the seat. "What did you find? You think Wilma handled that?"

"I know she did. Wiped her lipstick and powder on it, maybe before she slipped a sweater over her head. She tried on jeans, two sweaters, and a green linen jacket, all of which she left hanging neatly in the dressing room, her scent all over them. Good-looking jacket, but not her color."

Clyde dangled the tissue carefully by one corner, took a clean tissue from the box beneath the dash, wrapped the evidence in it, and placed it in the glove compartment. "This is evidence to us, Joe. But how do I present it to the law? What would I tell Davis?"

"*I* don't know. All I know is, Wilma was there, and recently. Could you say the smear of lipstick looked like Wilma's, so you picked it up just in case?"

Clyde raised an eyebrow.

"Let me think about it," Joe said. "Maybe I can come up with something." He twitched a whisker. "Tell Davis you've been training me to follow scent, like a tracking dog? That I found it and you're really proud of me, that it's the same color lipstick as Wilma's, and you bet if they ran the DNA . . ."

Silently Clyde looked at him.

"Guess that wouldn't fly, either," Joe said.

"I guess not."

"I personally think the concept has possibilities. A cat's sense of smell isn't as good as a bloodhound's, but it's far superior to a human's. I could—"

"Leave it, Joe."

Joe shrugged, and looked at the clock on the dash. "Ten of nine. I have time for one more shop." And he leaped out before Clyde could grab him, was out the window heading for a store that, he'd noticed, featured print denim jackets, just the kind of thing Wilma liked.

Clyde shouted at him, then followed him, running—but before Joe hit the shop door, he stopped. He did a sudden, cartoon cat skid, spinning back to the curb, to the gutter where the tiny, bright corner of a credit card had caught his attention with a hint of Wilma's scent and the faint, metallic smell of blood.

Pawing aside a crumpled paper bag, he uncovered the bent plastic card. Yes, it smelled of Wilma, all right. It had been folded the way Clyde folded his outdated credit cards when new ones arrived in the mail. He would fold the old card once, break it in half, then fold and break it again before he threw it away.

This card wasn't broken, just bent. The name Wilma Getz was embossed clearly below the red band that bore the name of a chain bookstore for which Wilma received bonus credits. It was the red stripe across the top that had caught Joe's attention.

The asphalt beneath where it had lain featured what was clearly a blood spot, dry but fresh. In this heat it wouldn't take long to dry. He tried to calculate. Maybe an hour? He had no way to ascertain exactly how long since that blood had been spilled, but surely no more than three hours. He was no forensic pathologist, he was just a simple hunter who'd had a fair amount of experience with spilled blood. Taking the card in his teeth, he backed out of the gutter looking up at Clyde.

Gently Clyde reached for it, lifting it gingerly by one edge. He looked at its brightly colored logo and at Wilma's embossed name. "What's that on the corner? Is that blood?"

"Blood."

"You sure?"

Joe just looked at him.

"Human blood?" Clyde asked. He had total faith in Joe's ability to distinguish human blood from, say, mouse blood or the blood of some canine unfortunate enough to have run afoul of the tomcat.

"Human blood," Joe said.

"That could be the blood in Wilma's car, then. Can you tell if it's Wilma's blood?"

"That I can't tell."

Clyde looked around them, but no one was near to witness their exchange. "This," Clyde said, "is what we came to find! This, we can show Davis. How the hell did you see this, how did you find this under that trash?"

"Saw the red stripe, then caught her scent. My superior sense of smell, and my superior wide-angle vision, combined with a far more sensitive retina that enables me to—"

"Okay! I've read the books. You smelled it, then you saw it." Reaching down, Clyde gripped Joe firmly, both out of friendship and to keep him from leaping away again as they headed for the car. Joe refrained from pointing out that if he hadn't left the

184

car, against orders, he would never have found this piece of evidence.

Before Clyde started the engine, he laid the credit card in a clean tissue, folded the corners over, and placed it, too, in the glove compartment. Then he called Davis's cell, switching on the speaker out of deference to Joe.

She picked up on the first ring, grunted when she heard Clyde's voice. "I'm sitting in Chili's with a couple of CHP guys. Sheriff's deputy just left. I'll meet you by the register."

Driving the short distance across the parking lot, Clyde pulled into a slot in front of the restaurant, then looked down at Joe. "That was a long shot on Wilma's part."

"Maybe that was all she had time to do. She'd know there'd be a report out for her when she didn't show up, that her name would be on every police computer . . ."

"The street sweeper could have picked it up, anyone could have." Clyde removed the wrapped credit card from the glove compartment, leaving the lipstick-stained tissue. "Here comes Davis up to the front. Get in the carrier; you're not staying here." He gave Joe a stern look. "If I can smuggle you into Chili's, you damn well better behave yourself. No yowling. No thrashing around making a scene."

"When have I ever yowled and thrashed around making a scene, as you put it? I want to hear what Davis found. Order me a burger. Rare, with no—"

"I know how you like your burgers. Shut up and get in the carrier."

20

Joe slunk into the cat carrier growling at Clyde, watched Clyde fasten the latches, and felt the carrier rudely snatched up and swung out of the car; the next moment they were entering Chili's, into a heady miasma of broiled hamburger, French fries, and various rich pastas that hit the tomcat with a jolt. He hadn't realized he was so hungry. Clyde greeted Davis and they settled into a booth, Clyde dropping Joe's carrier on the leather seat, which smelled of uncounted occupants and of spilled mustard.

"Have you eaten?" Clyde asked her.

"No," Davis said. "Nothing but coffee, I'm awash in it."

Joe, if he sat tall in the carrier, could see the sturdily built detective across the table, her short black hair smooth and clean, her dark uniform regulation severe. Where most detectives wore civilian clothes, easy and comfortable, Juana Davis preferred a uniform. Joe's theory was, she felt that it made her look slimmer. "I'm starved," she said, picking up her menu.

When the hostess came, glancing apprehensively into the carrier, Clyde said, "Just got off the plane. Trained cat, very valuable. He does movie work." The yellow luggage ticket hanging from the handle was an excellent touch, and seemed to impress the thin, swarthy waitress.

"What movies has he made?" she asked with a considerable accent.

"Oh, he's done over a dozen films as a bit player, but only two so far where he starred, where he had top billing." Clyde mentioned two nonexistent movie titles, hoping she hadn't lived in the U.S. long enough to know the difference.

Davis, sitting across from Clyde, remained straight-faced. When the waitress had taken their order and disappeared, Davis said, "I'm not going to ask why you brought your cat. Or why you took him into Liz Claiborne's." She looked at Clyde for a long time. He said nothing. "Are you going to explain to me what happened in there? I heard a pretty strange story from the deputy who just came from talking with the manager."

Clyde looked at her blankly.

"About the tissue," Davis said patiently. "And about that tomcat running loose in the store."

Clyde gave her a disingenuous look that to anyone but a cop would reek of honesty. "He got out of his carrier. Guess I didn't fasten it securely. Cat picked up a used tissue somewhere while I was describing Wilma, asking if she'd been there. I thought I had the carrier door fastened."

Davis did not respond. Joe wished she'd show some expression. As warm and thoughtful as Juana Davis was on occasion, that cop's look could be unnerving.

"Juana," Clyde said, "Wilma's like my family, you know that. I'm really worried about her, I had to just go in and ask, had to do something. I . . . with Wilma gone, I didn't have anyone to leave the cat with.

"But then," he said with excitement, "when I left the store, luck was with me. Incredible . . ." He reached in his pocket, drew out the wrapped credit card, laid it on the table, and opened the tissue. "Looks like, for once, my stupid civilian nosiness paid off."

Davis looked at the credit card, at Wilma's name, at the dark stain that appeared to be dried blood. She looked up at Clyde. Still a cop's look, silent and expressionless, a look designed to unnerve the toughest convict.

"It was in the gutter. Among some trash, right where I parked my car."

Juana's rigid demeanor and her unreadable black Latina eyes made her look more severe than she was.

"I figure," Clyde said, "either someone robbed her and dropped this—except why was it bent? Or that Wilma was mugged and kidnapped, and had time to drop it herself. To bend it and drop it. A car-jacking, maybe? You think that's blood on there? Could she have slashed someone with it, then dropped it hoping it would be found?"

Joe was glad he was concealed inside the carrier so Davis couldn't study his face as severely as she was studying Clyde's.

"My guess is," Clyde said, "she was shoved in a car outside Liz Claiborne's, had the card in her hand, slashed at her abductor, and dropped it as he slammed the car door and took off."

"Why would she fold it?"

"To make a better weapon? That sharp corner?" Clyde took a sip of his coffee. "I don't know, Juana. I only know it's Wilma's, it has her name on it, and it's an act of fate that I found it, that I ever saw it."

Davis studied the credit card. She picked it up by the edges and, taking an evidence bag from her pocket, dropped the card in, marked it with date, time, and location, and sealed it. She looked at Clyde again, then looked across the table at Joe's carrier. Joe yawned stupidly, scratched a nonexistent flea, and curled up as if for a nap. Davis and Clyde were silent until their order came. A burger for Clyde, the same for Joe, sans the fixings. A chicken sandwich for Juana, which probably fit into her perpetual diet.

Clyde opened the carrier, shoved the burger inside, and fastened the mesh door again; he tore into his own burger as if he hadn't eaten in days.

Joe inspected his order to be sure there were no pickles or offensive spreads, pulled off the bun, and scarfed down the hot, rare meat.

Clyde said, "What have you found out? Can you tell me? Sheriff have any leads?"

Joe stopped eating to watch Juana. Suddenly her dark eyes revealed a depth of anger that neither Joe nor Clyde often saw in the steady officer, a controlled rage that frightened them both; she didn't like what she'd found. Wilma was not just a missing case, she was Juana's friend, too.

"Sheriff's deputies had already done the rounds when I got here," Juana said. "Three clerks, in two stores, recognized Wilma from the picture we faxed. One clerk saw her leave, saw her go up the sidewalk with her packages but didn't see where she went. Didn't know if she got in a car. Sheriff has copies of her Visa charge slips. He checked the motels in the area, in case she decided to stay over. Showed them her picture. Nothing.

"No one's found her car, no sign of Jones or Sears. We don't know that Sears is with him, but he's usually in Jones's shadow. Sheriff is checking convenience stores, gas stations. CHP is all over the freeway watching for her car, and for Jones or Sears. APB out for the state. If she's not found soon, that'll be all the western states."

"What does Sears look like?"

"Slighter built than Jones, thin face. Younger,

thirty-two. Longish brown hair, muddy brown eyes. Jones is a hulk, six four and built like a truck. Gorilla face, long lip." The detective was tense and edgy. Joe waited uneasily, as did Clyde. There was something more, something she wasn't telling Clyde. Rearing up against the carrier's soft top to observe her, Joe shivered. Davis was mad as hell, and about something more. Joe was surprised when Clyde unfastened the carrier, reached in, and began to stroke his back, as if to comfort them both.

"I just got off the phone with the dispatcher," Juana said.

Clyde's hand stiffened. Joe went very still.

"It's Charlie," Juana said. "Charlie's disappeared. Charlie Harper's missing, too."

Clyde gripped Joe's shoulder so hard the tomcat hissed. But then he rubbed his face against Clyde's fingers, which felt suddenly icy.

"Charlie and Ryan had planned to ride," Davis said. "Ryan was delayed on the job. By the time she got there, Charlie had fed the horses and put them up, and started to make sandwiches. Looked like she went outside again on some errand, or at some disturbance. The door left unlocked, and she hadn't finished in the kitchen. From that point, no one knows. Ryan got there, she was gone. No note, no phone message. Her car there, engine cold.

"Max is there. Karen is making casts, taking the prints. Ryan found the tracks of a small car or maybe an old-style Jeep behind the stable, leading away up the bridle trail, back into the woods." Juana looked at Clyde gently, her cop's reserve falling away. She was close to Charlie and the chief, the small department was like family.

"Whatever the hell this is," Juana said, "I hope the bastards burn—that we can make them burn."

Even as evening fell, the cabin and the little cubbyhole kitchen remained intolerably hot, the walls pressing closer, so that Wilma felt there wasn't enough air. Sweating, confined by the tight ropes, panic gripped her, making her feel almost out of control. She wanted to scream and to beat at the walls, to tear at the rope, tear it off, and she couldn't even get a grip on it.

She seldom lost it like this. She was trained *not* to panic, but her training had gone to hell; she wanted to scream, and keep screaming until someone somewhere heard her.

Violet had taken the butcher knife, jerking it from Wilma's clenched hand with surprising strength, and was carrying it away with her, toward the stairs. Wilma watched her retreating back; how thin her shoulders were, every bone visible beneath the flimsy shirt.

"You don't think I can hide you," Wilma said, trying not to beg. "You're wrong. You don't believe the federal authorities can keep you safe. I know they can. Witness protection has hidden thousands of folks with far more dangerous men after them than Sears, and those women are doing fine."

Violet paused, but didn't turn to look at her.

"You're destroying what may be your only chance for freedom, Violet. I can get you into a safe house far away, out of the state. New identity, new name, all the papers. New driver's license, new social security number. You can start over, free of Eddie's abuse, do as you please with your life."

As she tried to gain Violet's attention, she prayed that in Gilroy her credit card would be found. But that was a real long shot, you couldn't lay your life on a card lying in the gutter, a card that would probably be swept up by the street sweeper and dumped in some landfill.

"We can hide you in a little house or apartment in the most unlikely small town, somewhere no one would think to look. We'd alert the sheriff there to watch out for you, he'd be the person you could go to anytime if you were afraid. You could be living where no one would beat you, threaten you, hurt you, Violet."

"He'd find me," Violet said in a flat voice. "There's nowhere he wouldn't find me."

"He won't find you if he's in prison. If you help me get him there, he can't follow you. I have enough on Cage and Eddie to put them both behind bars for a long time."

Violet turned, a question in her eyes.

"Believe me. A long stretch in the federal pen."

"What happens when Eddie gets out? He wouldn't be locked up forever. He'd know I helped you, he'd come after me."

"Not if he can't find you." She was losing patience with Violet, but she couldn't afford to snap at the girl. Violet, with no sense of self-worth, could easily become useless to her. "What's the alternative?" Wilma said gently. "You're going to sit here like a lump waiting for him to come back and beat on you for the rest of your life? Or kill you? If he's in jail where he can't get at you—"

"I don't believe you can lock him up. He never—"

"He has aided and abetted Cage's escape, the escape of a federal prisoner. He has kidnapped a retired federal officer. Both are offenses with long mandatory sentences. Mandatory, Violet. The judge *has* to send him away."

Violet looked hard at her.

"If the law can make Eddie for theft, too, if Cage and Eddie have made some big haul—if that's what Cage is looking for, that added to the other offenses could put Eddie in prison for the rest of his life."

"And Cage, too?" Violet asked warily.

"Of course, Cage, too. That's the law. Both locked up where they can't hurt you."

Violet was very still; Wilma watched her, trying not to let her hopes rise. No matter how much psychology Wilma had studied, it was still hard for her to relate to the masochistic dependence that made an abused woman love and cling to her tormentor. Wilma was too independent to understand the self-torturing, or guilt-ridden pleasure, an abuse victim took in harsh mental lashings and harder physical blows, even in wounds that could be fatal. Such an attitude disgusted her, went against her deepest beliefs. Disgusted her because these women had abandoned their self-respect, were committing self-abuse by their complicity.

She wanted to shout and swear at Violet, almost wanted to strike the woman. No wonder such women were ill treated. Violet's cowering submission made a person *want* to hit her.

Violet looked at her for a long time.

"I can help you," Wilma repeated; she was tired of this, tired of everything. "I will do all I can to help you, will use every kind of assistance that the federal system has to offer." She prayed she wasn't promising more than she could deliver. "But you have to want to be rid of him—and first, you have to help me."

Violet's blank expression didn't change. She didn't speak; she turned back toward the wall and disappeared behind it. Wilma listened in defeat to her soft footsteps mounting to the upper floor.

But then, swallowing back discouragement, she reached awkwardly behind her again to fight open the next drawer, to scrabble blindly for another tool sharp enough to cut her bonds.

21

When Cage Jones grabbed Charlie Harper, the only witness was the white cat—the only witness who could speak of what he had seen in the alleyway and behind the Harper stables. The other animals could not.

It had taken more courage than Cotton thought he possessed to go to that ranch seeking out the tall redheaded woman and ask her for help for the captive human. He had never in his life approached humans except to steal their food in the back alleys where his clowder had sometimes traveled.

But he had once seen Kit speak with the redheaded woman, and that lady had seemed gentle and respectful of his kind, so he'd thought maybe it would be all right. He had heard her promise that if ever his small, wild band should need help, she would come. Cotton remembered.

But now the redheaded lady needed help, perhaps to save her life.

Approaching the ranch, three times he had nearly turned back. But at last, shivering and ducking away from nothing, he had come down through the woods, avoiding the bridle trail, not wanting even to leave paw prints.

When he slipped into the stable, the horses had stared over their stalls at him with only mild interest, but the two big dogs in their closed stall had huffed and sniffed under the door, then had barked and kept barking, and in a moment he heard the door of the house open. When he looked out of the stable, redheaded Charlie Harper was coming across the yard to see what they were barking at. He'd tried to steel himself to speak to her, but he was so frightened he had ducked into the stall that held saddles, shivering, not daring even to peer out—and the next moment he was filled with guilt because his presence had brought her there.

He'd heard a vehicle approach from behind the barn where there was no road, only a horse trail. Little rocks crunching under its wheels. The dogs were barking too loudly for Charlie Harper to hear it stop quietly beyond the closed back door. But Cotton had slipped out of the saddle room's open window and around to the back, along the side of the barn, concealing himself among the bushes as best he could considering that he was blindingly white and seldom able to hide very well.

Peering around the corner of the barn, he'd watched two men step out of an old rusty vehicle. It was the same strange, rusty car that had been near the house up in the woods beyond the ruins, where the silver-haired woman was tied up.

And these were the same two men he'd seen there, the one bulky as a bull, the other, thin with long brown hair. The two men stank the same, too.

Sour sweat, and the whiskey humans drank; Cotton drew back in the bushes as they slipped around the building to the front, where the big doors stood open. Cotton followed.

The minute they saw Charlie in the stable they raced in and grabbed her, scuffling and swearing and fighting, and Charlie Harper was shouting and the dogs were barking and leaping against the stall door and the horses plunging in their stalls; the big man laughed at Charlie's rage—then Cotton found his nerve and leaped into the thinner man's face, clawing and biting. But the big man was gone with her, dragging her out the back door to the old car. And the thin man grabbed Cotton off his face and threw him; he landed twisting and screaming in a pile of straw.

Leaping up, he raced out the back again, to see them shove her into the back of the old car they called the Jeep, and tie her hands and feet together. They muttered and argued between themselves, then the thin man snapped, "That rotting trailer won't hold her, you could jam your fist through those walls. Damn woman'll kick them apart, kicks like a mule."

"Not if we tie her up good, she won't. Get a move on, I don't wanna be stumbling around in the dark up there in that mess."

"Ain't near dark yet. And we can't get the Jeep in there, not anywhere near enough. Have to drag her—"

"So we drag her," the big man said. "What's your problem?"

"She's that cop's wife, is what! The damn chief. You think of that, Cage! It's a federal—"

"It ain't no federal offense to mess with the *wife* of a cop, for Chrissake. That ain't the same as—"

"How the hell do you know? You don't know what you're talking about!"

But Cotton heard no more. He couldn't stop them; they could easily kill him, and then maybe no one would know what had happened to red-headed Charlie Harper, or to the gray-haired human. And Cotton knew only one thing to do. Despite his terror of the human world, he spun away out of the stable, across the yard and away through the pasture, running full out, hitting only the high spots across the open fields, heading for the village. Not only fear drove him now, but rage. Running and panting and his heart pounding too hard, the feral tom was a dazzling white streak exploding down across the brown hills, as incandescent as a small meteor. Something in Cotton, recalling his own captive misery last winter, couldn't bear that those two women who were not like other humans were now captive and helpless. He could only pray that he could find Kit, who would know how to bring help, could only pray that he could find his way to her through the village among the confusion of houses and shops and so many moving cars and hurrying people—

among all the millions of smells that would hide the scent he remembered, of the kit's home.

He tried to remember which way, from the night Kit had led their escape away from the vicious cage, to her tree house and then out of the village to safety on the open hills. Kit's tree house could be anywhere among the hundreds of village houses. No clear direction came to him; he had been too terrified to pay proper attention. The evening was still light, the sun low and orange ahead of him as it dropped toward the orange-tinted sea. On and on down the hills the white tom raced, rigid with fear that he would never find the tattercoat kit, that his terrified search among humans would come to nothing, and that those two special ladies would be lost.

It was dark when Max sped home, driving too fast, his siren and emergency light blasting a furor of alarm in the still evening. Half a mile before his turnoff he extinguished both, quelling the loud, bright announcement of his approach. Skidding a turn onto his own dirt lane that led in from the highway to the house, he slowed. The time was nine thirty.

Ryan had called him ten minutes earlier, ten minutes that had seemed like a lifetime. He had no clear idea how long Charlie had been missing. Swerving his car onto the grass shoulder between the lane and pasture so as not to obliterate other tire marks, he parked near Ryan's truck and Charlie's SUV, and for a moment he imagined that Charlie was there, that she would step out of the kitchen or the barn waving to him.

He saw only Ryan, standing alone in the lighted door to the stable. He heard three more units swing into the lane behind him, the crunch of tires on gravel.

Getting out, he walked on the rough grass, motioning for his men to park on the shoulder; he stood looking around the yard, scanning it for fresh tire marks and footprints, still imagining that Charlie would appear, stepping sassily out of the barn. He was empty inside, all his cop's professional detachment vanished; empty, and shaky, and lost.

An hour before the Greenlaws knew that Wilma was missing, Mavity Flowers learned the news when, her mind set on evicting her brother, she headed for Molena Point PD.

Greeley had been dead drunk at dinner, slopping food on himself and laughing raucously, and he'd stunk to high heaven of booze and unwashed clothes, was so disgusting that Cora Lee had sent twelve-year-old Lori upstairs with her supper. The child had eagerly picked up her plate and vanished; she'd seen enough drinking in her own family; Greeley's behavior brought back too much pain.

Days ago Mavity's housemates, Susan and

Gabrielle and Cora Lee, had ceased being polite to Greeley. Gray-haired no-nonsense Susan Britain was ready to sic her two big dogs on Greeley. It wouldn't take much; neither the Lab nor the dalmatian liked the old man. Blond Gabrielle had stayed as far away from Greeley as she could manage, and had talked about moving out. Cora Lee had simply looked at Mavity, her lovely, café-au-lait beauty and dark eyes very sad, and Mavity could do nothing less than get Greeley out of there. Disregarding the sinking feeling in her middle at the thought of abandoning her own brother, she had called the department to ask how to get rid of him.

Mabel Farthy had answered; Mabel was the only dispatcher Mavity knew very well, and with whom she was comfortable. Angry as she was, it still took a lot of courage to boot her own brother out on the street, but she didn't know what else to do.

Greeley had told her that, as her brother, he had every right to move in. The downstairs apartment was vacant, wasn't it? So what was the problem? When he'd first arrived, showing up one evening without calling, without letting her know he was even in the States after she'd heard nothing from him for six months, she'd told him to go to a motel. That had shocked her housemates—but that was two weeks ago.

Arriving unannounced, just at supper, he had

marched boldly into the house sniffing at the good smells of roast beef and gravy and all the other fixings; then they were all at the table, Greeley tucking his napkin into his collar and belching. Susan and Cora Lee and Gabrielle made a fuss over him at first, as they would any guest; Susan said he must be tired, and gray-haired Susan Britain had served him generously of the good roast. Cora Lee had poured wine for him, over Mavity's disapproving scowl. That was the first night; later, for a while, the ladies were too well mannered to be rude, but at last they lost their patience.

Mavity had put a folding cot in one of the two small basement apartments they were renovating as rentals, apartments that they meant, later on down the years, to accommodate live-in help. She'd made him promise to stay just the one night and then go on about his business. She didn't know what business that was and she didn't want to know. Now he'd been there two weeks, dug in like a mule refusing to leave its stall. She'd left the other apartment locked up tight, the one they'd already cleaned up and painted and furnished real nice, and had told him it was rented.

Now, after Mabel Farthy suggested she come on down to the station and sign a complaint, Mavity and Mabel stood on either side of the dispatcher's counter sipping the coffee Mabel had just brewed. Mabel was in her late fifties, pudgy, but with a bright blond wash on her short hair, and an honest way of dealing with folks.

"Captain Harper and both the detectives are out on cases," she said. She sounded unnaturally distressed, and it took a lot to upset Mabel. "The chief is . . ." She paused, watching Mavity. "You don't know?"

"Know what?" Mavity said nervously.

"You're not to repeat this—I'm sure it'll turn out all right," Mabel said gently.

Alarm filled Mavity.

"You haven't heard about Wilma."

"That wasn't Wilma, the break-in and—"

"No! Oh, no. She's . . . Nothing like that." Mabel had taken her hand. "She's only . . . Mavity, Wilma is missing."

"Missing! She can't be missing, she went up to the city. Didn't . . . ?"

"She checked out of her hotel this morning. Her things are at her house, suitcase, packages. Her car. But . . . Captain Harper isn't sure Wilma ever got home."

"I don't understand. If her things are there . . . Where would she go?" Mavity felt cold all over. "I don't understand what you're saying." Wilma had just gone up to the city for a court hearing, that was old stuff to Wilma. "She was going to stop in Gilroy. You'd better tell—"

"He knows that. Davis has gone up there. This afternoon, someone was in Wilma's house, searched it, left it a mess. Captain has an APB out for her, all the law-enforcement agencies across the state. I think the captain and Detective Garza are still at the house. You didn't talk with her today, haven't heard from her? Any messages, anything that could help?"

"I haven't seen or talked with her since . . . since last Thursday," Mavity said, thinking back. She was so distraught that, when at last she'd left Mabel, she'd found it hard to drive home, had to concentrate hard on what she was doing. And at home, after she'd told Susan and Cora Lee and Gabrielle, and despite the fact that she'd filed the complaint against Greeley, she'd gone down to ask if he might have seen Wilma. Not that he'd care if Wilma was in trouble, not after she'd booted him out of her own house last year, Greeley dead drunk and dragging that horrible black tomcat in there to torment Mavity, herself. Greeley barging in and embarrassing her when she'd just come out of the hospital and Wilma was taking care of her. And then Wilma telling him to leave, Mavity thought, smiling. No, Greeley had no love for Wilma Getz. But still, he might have taken a phone message and not bothered to pass it on, or might have glimpsed her on the street. She knew she'd have to ask him.

She'd heard him on the back deck of the downstairs apartment, had found him sitting in the chaise swilling beer, the radio on, singing along with it, out of tune and loud enough so everyone in the neighborhood could hear him. Coming onto the deck, she saw him toss his empty beer can down into the canyon—with how many others?

Strange thing was, when she'd told him Wilma was missing, the news upset him more than she'd imagined. The old man stopped guzzling and came alert, and right away started asking questions about what she'd been doing in San Francisco. But Mavity got the feeling he already knew the answers. And when she told him about Cage Jones escaping from jail, Greeley had got real nervous. But again, as if he already knew and wanted to see what she knew.

Well, the escape had been in the afternoon paper. Mabel had shown her the clipping before she left the station. She wondered why Greeley *had* asked her those questions. And what was he so fidgety about? Nothing made sense, Greeley didn't make sense—but then, with the amount of booze he drank, what did she expect?

Greeley and Cage Jones had grown up together, went to school together in the village. She didn't know if they'd stayed in touch; she didn't know much about Greeley's business, all those years down in Central America. She *had* wondered where he got the money to buy himself that fancy PT Cruiser, just three days ago. She'd asked him, "How you going to make the payments, Greeley? You plan to get a job?"

"Paid cash for the car," Greeley said, laughing an

openmouthed laugh at her. "Got a deal on it. I always did like a green car."

"Where, Greeley? Where did you get the money?"

"Savings. Not that it's any of your business." Greeley had never in his life had any savings; he spent it so fast the money might be programmed to dissolve.

After he bought the car and she'd asked about the money, he started drinking even more and got louder and worse tempered, and that was when she'd gone down and talked with Mabel and had been so relieved when Mabel said she'd send out a patrol officer, get Greeley out before the neighbors started calling in complaints about him. Mabel had said it wouldn't hurt Greeley to spend the night in a cell, that the captain kept a nice clean jail, and she'd sent Mavity back down the hall to that nice young Officer McFarland who'd helped her with the restraining order. Mavity had left the department feeling guilty that she'd really done it, but feeling a whole lot relieved, too.

22

The village streets were filled with heavy evening traffic, the blaze of moving headlights blinding and confusing the white tomcat. He had been on these streets only once before, and then it was midnight, the town was silent and empty as he and Willow and Coyote had followed Kit from that cage to freedom. Kit had told them how she crossed when there was heavy traffic, by trotting close behind humans. But now Cotton couldn't bring himself to do that. The sidewalks were alive with people, their hurrying feet threatened to trample him even as he hid in the shadows of steps and alleyways.

Scrambling up a vine to the rooftops, he felt safer, alone at last. How did Joe Grey and Kit and Dulcie stand the human mobs? Breathing with relief the fresher air of the warm, open roofs, Cotton felt his pounding heart slow; he stopped panting and looked around him across the angled peaks, trying to get his bearings.

Far ahead rose a familiar collection of metal chimneys and the railing of a penthouse veranda that seemed familiar, as if Kit had led them that way. He recognized the tall tower, too, with the clock in it, he had seen that from the window of Kit's tree house. Looking away to the northeast, slowly the night of their escape came back to him.

Crowded into that smelly cage, he and Willow and Coyote had nearly lost hope. Then Joe Grey and Dulcie had been captured, too, and jammed in there with them, five cats crammed in, and their rage building dangerously. But at last Kit and Joe Grey's human had found and freed them:

Clyde Damen cut off the lock, and they had exploded out of there and out the window, running with terror—and then with wild, incredible joy, running and running, following the tortoise-shell kit. She'd led them to a flower-decked alley, to a plate of delicious food that had been set out just for cats. He and Willow and Coyote had thought it was some kind of trap, but Kit swore it was not, and she had eaten and eaten, and when at last they tried, too, she drew back so they would have the rest. Cotton licked his whiskers, remembering the taste of the fine salmon and cheeses. They had filled themselves right up, and then Kit led them to her tree house, where they had curled up safe and warm. That had been their first deep, deep sleep since they were trapped, not jerking awake with fear at every sound.

Now, taking his bearings from the clock tower, Cotton reared up to search the rooftops and the islands of trees; and it was then he glimpsed a little peaked roof, too small for a regular house. It rose high among the oaks beside a big house. He raced ahead eagerly between chimneys and balconies and across girding branches: raced to find the kit, to find help for the two women who knew about cats like them, who were not afraid to talk to cats. What cat would ever have thought that he, Cotton, would launch himself on such a terrifying journey in order to save two humans?

• • •

Max Harper was thankful he'd hired Karen Packard. She'd taken over the stables and yard as efficiently as a far more seasoned investigator. Her careful, intelligent presence helped very much to ease his wrenching pain over Charlie's abduction, as the slim, dark-haired young rookie took prints in the stable and house, and now in the alleyway of the stable poured casts of the intruders' footprints. Karen was thirty-six, a tall, fine-boned woman with long dark hair and caring green eyes. She'd done some clothes modeling to work her way through the law-enforcement program at San Jose State. She'd told him, when he hired her, she'd rather dig ditches than do one more modeling job; she didn't like the atmosphere, didn't like the people, didn't like their values and the meaningless glitz. You couldn't put it more clearly than that, Max thought with a crooked little smile. Now, Karen pursued every aspect of her job—investigation, paper work, surveillance—with an eager, single-minded commitment that would not be understood in that world of what she considered to be high rollers.

Running a brush over Bucky's back, Max smoothed on the blanket and set his saddle in place, reached under for the cinch, automatically fending off Bucky's companionable nip at his backside. It might seem a cowboy thing to do, to set out after Charlie on horseback, but there was a

210

lot of wild, tangled country up there, and no way you could get a truck or a car up that trail; it had been iffy even for whatever smaller vehicle those men had used. He had observed, even in the near dark as he walked up along the shoulder of the trail, tire marks careening up over the shoulder, and broken branches that would have scraped hard along the vehicle. Hitting Charlie's bound body? His mind was filled with Charlie, sitting across the table from him, laughing over some silly joke; grinning down at him from the back of her mare; standing out in the pasture calling the dogs, the wind blowing her long red hair; her hair tumbled on the pillow as she lay warm against him.

As he tightened the cinch, Ryan put Rock in the pasture so the eager dog couldn't follow them. Max fetched the shotgun from his unit, nestled it into the saddle scabbard, and checked the clip in his automatic; then he and Ryan mounted, Ryan on Charlie's mare, and headed up the dark trail. They would avoid using much light, which might be seen for some distance through the woods, and their cell phones were on vibrate.

He didn't like employing a civilian in this way, but none of the uniforms at hand was any good with a horse and he wanted someone with him in case they had to split up. Ryan, having grown up in a police family, knew more about the work than most rookies, and she was competent with a firearm; her uncle Dallas had overseen the training of Ryan and her two sisters as soon as he considered them old enough to be responsible. Dallas was their dead mother's brother. It was their father's brother, their uncle Scotty, who had taught Ryan carpentry. Ryan had never played with dolls, the little girl much preferring to tag along after Scotty on his construction jobs.

Moving quickly up the trail through the dark woods, they had to use their torches occasionally, shielding them heavily, flicking them on only to pick up a tire track, making sure the vehicle hadn't turned off somewhere. Though that wasn't likely; with no side roads, the rough terrain would slow it considerably. They were less than five minutes out when they heard a huff behind them—and Rock came racing, the big dog a pale, panting streak looming like a ghost out of the night, charging into their shielded beams.

"Oh, God," Ryan breathed. "He climbed the fence." The heavily woven wire of the pasture fence was constructed to confine the Harpers' two big mutts, as well as the horses; it was six feet high, and the Harper dogs had never thought to climb it. A Weimaraner was another matter, Max thought, half angry, half amused.

The big silver dog was royally pleased with himself, and raring to go; he had his nose to the trail and paused only to look up at Ryan, as if for direction, then sniffed at the breeze, drinking in a scent that drew him. He was all tension, ready to forge ahead, not wanting to obey when Ryan told him to hold. Max watched the two of them, frowning.

Ryan didn't know whether to scold Rock and waste time taking him back or wait and see what he'd do. She wondered if Rock's original escape from his sadistic owner had been accomplished by climbing over the woman's chain-link security barrier. The expression on the silver dog's face reflected such joy at his accomplishment that she couldn't scold him. She looked through the darkness to Max. "Do I take him back?" But she didn't want to do that.

Max knew this was foolish, the dog wasn't trained. But, "Let him try," he said softly. "Keep him quiet."

She had only to nudge the mare ahead and Rock's nose was to the trail, then scenting up high, drinking in the still air—and like a shot he took off.

They booted the horses ahead, fast. What the hell were they doing? Max thought. This wasn't a tracking dog, Rock had had no such demanding training. But Max shook his head. *Give him a chance, let's see what he has. He's bred for it, and he's sure as hell on to something.* Max's gut was churning, his mind filled with Charlie's face; he daren't blow it, bringing the damned dog. But they moved on quickly, following the ghostly dog; and the cop who never prayed was praying now, and was willing, tonight, to take any help they could get, no matter how off the wall.

They kept the horses to a fast trot, it was too dark to safely gallop, the trail too rough; he wasn't going to cripple a horse, which would only slow them. He hoped to hell the trees were thick enough to hide their shielded lights. They followed Rock as fast as they dared, losing him sometimes, then catching a faint movement far ahead, the crack of a twig as he ate up the ground. Was he tracking the vehicle only because Ryan was following it, obviously distressed? Or could he be on a deer? But a deer wouldn't stay to the trail this long. Max couldn't believe Rock was following Charlie, but that was what it looked like: the big dog taking her scent from the air, moving fast and intently, never swerving from the narrow path.

They knew that Rock was exceptionally well-bred, from a long line of dogs developed to follow by scent as well as sight, to track and retrieve on land and on water. This was an all-around breed, intelligent and powerful, that Max had grown to admire. But, tracking without training? Watching him, Max could only speculate on what was happening in that intent canine mind. Rock was fond of Charlie, and he was keenly sensitive to Ryan's feelings; clearly he knew that something was wrong. Before they set out, he had been attuned to their tension, watching them, nervous and alert, as they'd saddled up. Now, staying to the bridle path, repeatedly scenting the air above the tire tracks, Rock moved so fast he was leaving them behind.

Ryan daren't shout at him; she whispered to call him back but he paid no attention. Max was afraid he'd run straight into their quarry and give them away—but suddenly, at the top of a ridge, he slowed. Stood frozen.

They strained to see among the dense, dark trees, to hear the smallest sound. Approaching Rock, they could see him sniffing the ground in a circle, as if he'd lost the trail. They pulled the horses up at a distance so as not to disturb whatever he had—but the horses hardly had time to rest before Rock started again, stepping slowly now, his head raised to taste the wind. At the same instant, Max's cell phone vibrated, sending unease through him and then a surge of hope that Charlie had been found, that he'd hear her voice. Snatching the phone from his pocket, he answered softly—and went rigid.

A female voice—but not Charlie.

"Charlie's kidnappers are headed for the ruins," she said, and the voice was so familiar that he shivered. "For the Pamillon estate. They plan to hide her there, leave her tied up in an old overgrown trailer, all covered with vines."

"If you know where she is, *then help her!*" he whispered. "Where are you? Can't you untie her, help her get away! Where—"

"I'm not there. I . . . heard them say that's where they'd take her. I'm not anywhere near there."

"Then how did you hear them? Who are they?"

"Cage Jones. And a younger man, slimmer than Cage. Long hair and faded brown eyes."

"Will you tell me who you are? Tell me how you . . . ?"

The caller hung up.

He knew who the woman was, as much as he could ever know. This snitch, who had given him so many tips, had never identified herself and very likely never would. Feeling numb, he punched in the code for Garza, got him on the first ring.

"Ryan and I are on the trail above my place," he said softly, "headed up into the hills, following the tire tracks. The snitch just called—the woman. She said it's Cage Jones and, from her description, I'd guess Eddie Sears. Said they mean to hide Charlie at the old ruins, that she overheard them. Some overgrown trailer up there. That ring a bell?"

A negative from Dallas.

"She said it's covered with vines. Send four units up the old road, no lights, radios off. Have them wait at the edge of the ruins, stay in their cars. No radios, no noise."

"They're on their way."

When Max hung up, he called Karen. She had nothing new, she was still taking prints while waiting for her casts to dry—tire casts and three good sets of footprints, one set that she thought would be Charlie's. "Did Rock follow you? He got out of the pasture. I'm sorry, Max. He wouldn't come to me. I didn't know dogs could climb—I swear I saw him do it."

"This one can," Max said wryly. "He's here. Damn dog's tracking her." He told her about the snitch's call and that four units were headed for the ruins. "When you finish, Karen, get on back to the station, get those prints into the works."

Hanging up, he pushed Bucky to a slow, sure-footed lope, catching up with Ryan. She'd dismounted and was holding Rock back, to wait for Max. When she turned the dog loose he took off again, tasting the air now with even sharper excitement, his four-inch tail wagging madly, wagging the way it did when he dug out a ground squirrel. Then suddenly he stopped again, dead still, nose to the ground and snuffling hard.

Ryan slid off the mare, threw her reins to Max, and pulled Rock away so he wouldn't destroy the new configuration of tracks. "Shoe prints," she said softly. She praised Rock and hugged him, and she and Max studied the torn-up ground, their coats wrapped over their lights.

The Jeep had stopped there, and the prints of two men were all around its tracks, in a confused tangle. Had Charlie made a successful try, and gotten away? Max searched for her footprints, his hands sweating, his belly in a knot.

The young officer who came to evict Greeley Urzey from the seniors' basement apartment took considerable verbal abuse in both English and Spanish. Jimmie McFarland was one of the youngest men on the force, baby faced, with soft brown hair and innocent brown eyes. Jimmie knew enough Spanish to greatly admire the grizzled old man's vocabulary.

Greeley Urzey was not well educated, but McFarland knew he'd lived and worked most of his adult life in Panama. He'd apparently learned quickly what he needed to get along, including a nice repertoire of retorts. As Officer McFarland invited Greeley to quietly leave the premises of the seniors' house or spend the night in jail, Greeley told him half in English and half in Spanish that he wasn't sleeping in their jail and just what they could do with that facility.

McFarland had looked at Greeley steadily, trying not to smile. "You want a lift down the hill? It's a motel or the jail, take your pick." McFarland wasn't about to leave Greeley hanging around the seniors' place and have to come back for him. No cop likes a domestic dispute, even an apparently nonviolent one—though he didn't much want the old man in his squad car, either; he smelled like a drunk billy goat.

"I have a car!" Greeley had snapped, snatching up his wrinkled leather duffle and heading around the house to the street, to a new, green PT Cruiser that surprised McFarland. McFarland waited for him to start the car and head down the hill, then followed him, wondering if he should run the plates, see if the car was stolen. He pulled over, making a note of the plates, and watching as Greeley swung into the parking area of the first vacant motel he came to, parked the PT Cruiser, and carried his battered old satchel through the motel's patio and into the lobby.

After ten minutes, when Greeley did not come out, McFarland called the motel desk to make sure he'd checked in.

He had. Breathing easier, McFarland left, thinking about the beginning Spanish lessons he was taking, wondering if the advanced course would provide a more colorful approach, if it might include some of the old man's impressive vocabulary.

McFarland had had a good day. He had, with the two detectives and Karen working the urgent missing cases, been given free reign with the village murders. He had acquired, by means he might not want to relate to the chief, enough evidence to bring in both Tucker and Keating for questioning—for visits that, he hoped, would result in arrests. As for the third murder, he was convinced that it, too, would turn out to be a domestic, though as yet they had nothing solid.

As Greeley signed the register and palmed the key to his room, up in the hills his sister, Mavity, was airing out the apartment that he had occupied.

Setting down her arsenal of vacuum cleaner and dust mop, scrub mops and chemicals and buckets, she flung open windows as violently as if the wind coming up the canyon could blow away Greeley himself. Her attack of cleaning included new contact paper in all the drawers, which gave her an excuse to go through them to see if he'd forgotten anything of interest. She had already searched Greeley's duffle, two days earlier.

That was part of what had upset her so, and made her pursue the restraining order. She had been searching his bag for his stash of whiskey, meaning to throw it out. She felt no guilt in poking around. It wasn't her fault her brother was a drunk, but she did feel responsible for the fact that he was disturbing her friends. She hadn't found his bottle, but she'd found something far more interesting.

In the bottom of the bag was a small white paper box, maybe two by three inches, embossed with the logo of a Panamanian jewelry store; the box was old and stained, as if perhaps it had been used for many purposes. Inside, packed carefully between layers of yellowed tissue paper, was a little gold devil. An ugly little figure with an evil leer—devil, or some other idol, one of them pagan idols from Central America. It looked like real solid gold, and it felt warm and rich like gold; it was so heavy it startled her.

But it couldn't be real gold, the real thing would be worth thousands, maybe more. It had to be a museum copy. She remembered Greeley telling about little gold figures, ancient artifacts, he'd said. She couldn't remember the name he called them. Did he say they were pre-Columbian? From the time before Columbus discovered South America? Didn't seem possible anything could last that long, anything so small. Sacred trinkets, Greeley'd said, fashioned by vanished tribes. He'd been only a little drunk at the time, just enough to be in one of them showy moods when he liked to tell what he knew, and embroider on it. He said them little gold figures were in great demand, now, that even one would be worth a fortune.

With Greeley, she never knew what to believe.

She didn't know much about history or archeology, and she didn't remember those long-ago dates. Huacas, she thought suddenly. That was what he'd called them. The real gold huacas, Greeley said, were illegal to own, in Panama, except by the national museum. He said the museum made copies, though, and sold them to the tourists. Surely this was one of the copies. But why was it so heavy?

Greeley wasn't above stealing, if he could get away with it, or thought he could—but Greeley couldn't steal this kind of state-guarded treasure. If what he said was true, such a theft was far more sophisticated than anything that old man was capable of. Greeley's thefts ran to cracking the safe of a small mom-and-pop store and making off with a few hundred dollars. Not some high-powered international operation; that wasn't Greeley's style, he wouldn't know how to go about such a thing. All his talk that night, that had been whiskey talk, colorful storytelling, more than half from Greeley's sodden imagination.

All their lives, her brother had stolen, ever since they were kids. She was forever surprised he didn't spend more time in jail; it was just short sentences and then out again. Well, she had to admit, in spite of his thieving ways, he'd held down a good job for forty years—but only because he loved the diving. She never ceased to wonder that he could be so responsible at his work and so worthless in the rest of his life.

That day she'd found the huaca she'd stood there in the basement apartment looking down at that evil gold devil, wondering. It *was* an evil little thing; its stare had given her the creeps, made her think of voodoo curses, the pagan magic that Greeley liked to tell about.

Wilma said those countries weren't all pagan, that they were Christian, too. Catholic. But Mavity had seen pictures of those South American churches, their voodoo idols all mixed in with the saints and the virgin. That, in her book, wasn't any kind of Christian.

Quickly she had wrapped the gold devil up again, closed it away in its box, and put the box back in the duffle. Hurrying, she'd latched the worn leather bag and left the room, her hands icy, the image of that devil face too clear in her mind.

Now, she cleaned the room vehemently until she'd eradicated the sour smells. She carried the sheets and towels into the little laundry at the end of the hall, put them in the washer with plenty of Clorox. When she gathered up her cleaning equipment and locked the door to the apartment, she left the windows open, to air the place. She felt no guilt at possibly sending Greeley to jail. If he didn't obey the restraining order, a cell was what he deserved.

23

Charlie's whole body was sore from the battering Cage gave her, and from bumping along in the Jeep; her face felt bruised and raw where he'd struck her, hit her three times for trying to roll out of the vehicle. And then when it blew a tire and skidded on the narrow trail, jamming hard between two trees, she'd prayed it was stuck. She'd thought at first the sharp report was a gunshot, it had sent her ducking down, filled with hope—but it was only the tire exploding when the wheel hit a deadfall. The men's rage would, under other circumstances, have been amusing. They were near hysteria by the time they got the wheel off, then found that the spare had no air, that it, too, had a hole in it. The situation was entertaining, but turned heart-stopping when they grew so enraged that she didn't know what they might do to her.

But they hadn't taken it out on her. They had sworn and argued, then at last had set about patching the spare, irritably bickering. Now, bumping along again, she was terribly hot and thirsty, her sweaty T-shirt plastered to her, the too-tight ropes burning into her. The worst discomfort was the gnats; millions of gnats had found her, and were feasting. Their bites made her wild with itching, and she couldn't scratch. Her last thread of composure was almost gone. And she was ashamed, so ashamed that her disappearance would have Max frantic, would cause all kinds of trouble. Ashamed that she hadn't been watchful, that she'd let her guard down, had come out of the house completely unprepared for a prowler. She knew better. After several previous threats to Max, she knew better than to become complacent. She had stepped out thinking the dogs were barking at nothing or at some small wild animal; and now Max would have to deal with the trouble her fool-ishness had caused. Worst of all, she knew he'd come after her, that she'd put him in unnecessary danger.

No matter how she twisted and worked at the knots, she'd not been able to loosen one. With her feet tied, and her hands tied behind her, even if she'd been able to roll off the Jeep, she couldn't have run, couldn't get away, could only hop stupidly, like a trussed-up chicken.

When the men had finally gotten the spare tire patched and on the wheel, and had taken turns pumping up the tire with an ancient hand pump, they'd shouldered and fought the Jeep out of the trees and moved on again up into the pine forest. The woods were black as midnight, the headlights dim. She lay helplessly bumping along again on the dirty metal floor trying to understand what this was about.

She knew Cage's name, the other man had called him that, receiving a vicious blow across the mouth, a strike that had made him spit blood. Cage Jones—the man Wilma had gone up to the city to testify against. In some way, this whole thing was about Wilma; that knowledge riveted her with fear. Was this retribution against Wilma, for her damning testimony? What else could it be?

Early in the evening, when she brought the dogs and horses in from pasture and fed them, she'd been imagining Wilma on her way home down 101 in the heavy afternoon traffic, her car loaded with boxes and bags of new clothes and early Christmas presents. She'd thought that when she and Ryan got back from their ride, if there was no "getting home" message from Wilma, she'd give her aunt time to unpack and have a cool shower, a drink, and some supper, then she'd call her and they could talk about Wilma's weekend.

Tending to the horses, then going in the house to fix sandwiches for herself and Ryan, she'd amused herself imagining what Wilma had bought. New jeans, of course. New sweatshirts. But she hoped something frivolous, too. When the dogs began to bark, she'd stepped out on the porch, stood in the falling evening listening. Deciding maybe there were raccoons in the barn again, or the fox who often came to sneak dog food and that enraged the mutts, she had just slipped into the barn to see—

It happened so fast. She was grabbed from behind, the dogs going crazy, the horses plunging in their stalls. She was swung around hard, losing her balance, to face a huge man.

He had clamped his meaty hand over her mouth so she couldn't yell, had dragged her out behind the barn and tied her up and gagged her, and then thrown her in the Jeep. There was a second man, thinner. Neither spoke until they'd driven for some time and were well away from the stables, up the narrow trail. She'd leaned up to look over the back, trying to see behind them, hoping uselessly that someone had seen them and followed. But every time she tried to look back, Cage reached around from the driver's seat and knocked her down.

And who would have seen? She'd been alone at the ranch. There was no one to know she was missing, or to know what had happened. She'd bounced along miserably on the hard metal floor, through the darkening woods, with Cage watching her so closely, against any attempt at escape, that she just about lost hope. Until the tire blew and her hope rose again.

But that hadn't lasted long and they were off again, she still steaming at her helplessness, at her inability to help herself.

But now . . . Did she hear something behind them? The faintest noise? Stealthily she slid up again along the side of the Jeep to sneak a look. The sky straight above them was still silver, but the dense woods through which they rumbled were so dark that surely Cage, looking back from the driver's seat, could no longer see her clearly. Far back down the trail, she thought she glimpsed a flash of light. She saw it for just an instant, saw it again, flicking, then it vanished. Had she heard, above the Jeep's rattling and grinding, another sound? A distant door close, an engine start?

She tried to judge how far they had come. They'd been climbing constantly, the Jeep's engine straining, climbing very steeply in some places. When she could see through a gap in the trees, beneath the lighter evening sky, the black hills fell away, but then they were gone again, hidden by the pine forest.

There wasn't much up this trail but forest, and patches of open hills. Some scattered old houses far up, a fallen fence line. And, nearly straight ahead, this trail would pass close to the Pamillon ruins.

Was Cage headed there? Did he mean to dump her there? *Kill me and leave me under the fallen walls or in some caved-in cellar, where no one will find me? Leave me there to get back at Wilma?* Certainly Cage hadn't kidnapped her for a ransom. He wouldn't get much, she thought ruefully, she wasn't some heiress worth millions.

Oh, but Max would pay. He'd pay with the ranch, the horses, the cars, and every smallest thing he owned, go into debt for the rest of his life, if that was the only way to save her—except that Max was too clever for that, Max would never be so foolish, he was far sharper than these two cheap crooks, he would never let them twist him around.

Wouldn't he? To save my life?

And she knew he would.

Was this revenge against Wilma? Did Cage think he could make Wilma suffer far more if he killed her niece? Or, she thought, could Cage want something from Wilma, something besides revenge? *Am I a hostage? Is this some kind of trade? But trade for what? Certainly he can't buy his freedom from the law with a hostage. The U.S. courts don't make that kind of bargain.*

This was all too unlikely, too bizarre. It had been such a peaceful afternoon, she'd so been looking forward to a quiet ride, to spending some time with Ryan. And then . . . everything had gone to hell.

The sky was going dark now. Cage, still grousing over the flat tire, which was all Eddie's fault because it was Eddie's Jeep, hadn't glimpsed her peering over the back. She caught her breath when she saw another light, a flash as brief as a firefly, one pinprick, then gone. But then another, farther down the hills, where she thought their ranch lay. Then the trail behind them was hidden by a thick stand of pine. The Jeep came up over a rise and dropped down again, and Cage swung around in the seat, turning his light on her; he caught her looking, and before she could duck, he smacked her in the face so hard he sent her sprawling. She lay unmoving, hurting, detesting Cage Jones. And thinking about the lights.

Someone was at the ranch or was approaching it. Or did those lights belong to someone following the Jeep? Ryan must have arrived by this time and found her gone. Found the door unlocked, the tire tracks, the animals upset. If she had, there'd be cops all over, and Max would be following their tracks.

They topped the rise and turned, bumping over rocks. She glimpsed broken stone walls, they *were* in the ruins, the old Pamillon estate. *Did* Cage mean to kill her here? She *had* to get away, get back down the trail to Max—If Max couldn't get a vehicle up that trail, he'd follow her on horseback. *Not alone on horseback, Max, please. They're both armed. Please* . . . There was a shotgun between the front seats, she'd seen it when they threw her in the Jeep, and Cage had a handgun.

Stop it, she thought. *Max is no fool. If he comes on horseback, they'll never see him, never know he's there.* Twisting her hands in ways she hadn't thought they'd bend, she again tried desperately to free herself; she felt blood flowing, making her hands slick as she tried uselessly to undo the knots. Cage pulled the Jeep deeper in among the fallen walls, stopped, and killed the engine.

The Jones house had been dark when Greeley arrived back there, though it was only an hour since he'd left, since he'd seen them cats tossing the place. What the hell were they doing? What were the little sneaks looking for? They couldn't know what this was all about. Approaching the Jones's front windows, he could see no light now. Had Lilly gone to bed? Not until he stepped around the side of the house did he see that one lamp was burning low, just about where Lilly had been sitting earlier. Was she *still* in that same chair, mindlessly knitting away? Moving around to the front porch again, he rang the bell, hoping she might be in a better mood this time around. Hoping to hell them cats was gone, dirty, nosy varmints.

Well, he was damn glad to be shut of that cop, rousting him out of Mavity's place like that. As if a cop had that kind of rights. Like some Gestapo bully. Stateside cops were as bad as them Panamanian La Guardia, didn't give a damn for people's rights. Unless you lined their pockets. In

Panama, if you didn't buy your freedom, the Guardia'd just as soon shoot you. Cheaper than feeding you, in jail. Well, hell, it made no difference. You get thrown in a Panama jail, only way out is in a pine box—if they bother to put you in a box, if they don't just throw you to the sharks.

He'd stayed in that motel patio, after that cop followed him from Mavity's, until he was sure the rookie was gone. Watched him drive away, talking on the radio like he was heading on another call. Watched him as far as he could see the cop car, then he'd retrieved his own car and headed up the few blocks to Lilly's place. Oh, he'd checked in to the motel, all right. Waited till that cop called them, then said he'd changed his mind.

He didn't know how he was going to convince Lilly to let him stay, but he'd figure it out. Once he got settled in one of them upstairs bedrooms, he could search the house at his leisure, do it while she slept. Do it before Cage got back. Sure as hell this would be his last chance before Cage barged in here to get the stash.

If Cage got it first, he'd turn right around and head back to the city, to the same fence. And once that fence started moving Greeley's own share to collectors, the feds would hear about it and them bastards'd have the dogs out.

He rang the bell again, fidgeting. What the hell was Lilly doing? At last he heard her padding to the door and he had to think how best to con her.

She wasn't an easy woman. So far, she sure hadn't been what you'd call cordial.

He'd thought of phoning her first, asking real nice if he could stay there a day or two, that his sister had a problem with the apartment he was in. Maybe tell her the water pipes broke? But Lilly'd of hung up on him, sure as pigs had curly tails. He'd thought of pretending to be Cage, telling her to give Greeley a room, but their voices were too different, no way he could pull that off. He heard the knob turn, and she opened the door with the burglar chain on, peered out through the little crack at him. One good lunge with his shoulder and he could break that puny chain, send the door flying. Instead he gave her a big smile. "It's me, Lilly. I come back. I . . . I have a kind of a problem. You think I could come in? Come in and maybe tell you about it and maybe get warm for a minute?"

"It's still ninety degrees, Greeley."

"Well, it's a lot hotter in Panama," Greeley said pitifully. "My blood's thin. And I sure do need some help. For old times' sake?"

"What old times?"

"It's Mavity," Greeley said. "Something happened to her apartment where I was staying. She'd rented it and those folks showed up early to move in, and I had to leave. She didn't have no more room; I just need me a place to stay for the night. Until I can get a motel, until the tourists go home.

Motels are all full, I got me no place to sleep." He hoped to hell she didn't check. "I'd be gone again first thing in the morning . . ."

She stood scowling down at him for a long time. They were the same height, but with him standing a step down on the porch, she was some taller. She looked real sour at being disturbed, sour and stubborn. He could have been starving or sick, she would have looked just as mean. When she shut the door, he thought that was the end of it, that he'd lost the first round.

But she'd only closed it to slip the chain. She opened it again, still scowling. She stared at him for another long minute, then stepped back, opening it wider. He gave her a pitiful, grateful look and moved inside, doing his best not to grin. He thought of going back to the car to get his duffle but was afraid she'd change her mind and lock the door. There wasn't nothing in it he really needed.

She didn't ask him into the living room, didn't ask him to sit down. She led him along the hall to a little bedroom on the first floor. "You'll have to use the guest bath," she said, pointing back toward the bath near the front door. "I'll set out a towel. You'll find sheets in the top drawer of that dresser. When you leave in the morning . . ." She gave him a hard look. "What makes you think you can get a motel tomorrow if they're all full tonight?"

"I made me a reservation," he lied. "It's Sunday

233

night, some of them tourists don't leave till Monday morning. I got me a room for then, all fit and proper, soon as they're made up, so I won't burden you."

Looking unconvinced, Lilly turned and left him.

He found sheets in a drawer, and spread them on the bed, listening hopefully for the sound of Lilly going upstairs to her room. He waited for a long time, but when he went to use the bathroom, the reading light was still on in the living room and he could hear the clicking of her knitting needles, could see her seated shadow reflected against the wall between two devil masks, her shadow hands twitching and jumping as she cast on stitches or whatever the hell knitters did.

He had to brush his teeth with his finger and lavender hand soap. Didn't know why he bothered. The towel she'd left him was thin and had a hole in one corner. Why the hell didn't she go on to bed? Returning irritably to the fusty little bedroom, he fidgeted and stewed, sat on the bed with the pillows behind him and thought about Cage's stash.

He and Cage had brought most of it up from Central America packed in boxes of old books that were heavy. And the boxes stacked in with furniture, in one of them big, metal overseas containers. They'd had a regular mover in; that was when Sue left Greeley and he'd give up the apartment.

When they got back to the States and the stuff was delivered to where Cage was staying in the city, they'd made sure it was all there, then tossed the books in half a dozen Dumpsters. Sold the furniture. Cage said maybe some of them books was valuable, but how valuable could a bunch of old musty books be?

They'd waited a long time, years, for gold to hit eight hundred again, because that should nudge their prices up, too, but it never got that high. Inflation was up, though, and that was good. Then finally they'd lost patience and started making plans. Cage was inside at the time, he wrote that when he got out, they'd do it. If Greelcy'd fly up, get his half wherever he had it, Cage'd take him to the best fence. Greeley never was much good at that part of it. He'd been good at making the heist, real good, and Cage owed him that, big-time.

Gold was what all them Latin American countries had been about, back in history, gold that brought them Spanish ships, had nothing to do with saving souls. Inca idols of solid gold near as big as a house, a whole garden made of life-size gold figures and animals, hard for a fellow to believe. Made what he and Cage brought back look like peanuts—but it was still worth plenty if they'd got full price. Fence, and his dealers, everyone took their damn cut.

Still, though, he'd have enough to set him up real nice, all he'd ever want. No more diving; he was tired of working for Panama. Buy him a nice little finca up in northern Panama, couple young Indian girls to do the cooking and warm his bed, a pretty nice retirement.

Sitting on the bed, he waited for over an hour, fidgeting, until he heard Lilly go up the stairs. When he looked out, the living room was dark. Standing in the hall he saw a faint light upstairs, from a room to his left. Returning to his room, he listened for some time more as she moved around above him getting ready for bed, listened to the water running in the upstairs bath. Didn't like to think of that old turkey naked in the bath. Listened until the water gurgled out of the tub, and finally there was silence, sweet, unbroken silence. When he peered again up the stairway, all was dark above. He hoped she was a sound sleeper. Hoped to hell she didn't come sneaking down and catch him. Because if Cage knew he'd searched the house, Cage'd kill him.

But by the time Cage found his stash gone, he, Greeley, would be where Cage wouldn't ever find him. He sure wouldn't find him through the Frisco fence. Greeley wouldn't use him again, he had another contact, had lucked on to that one and had managed it all right; kept that guy under wraps, staked out and waiting. A short layover in Miami, sell the stuff and get his cash, and he was out of the States, where Cage'd never come looking.

24

Wilma watched Violet vanish behind the wall and listened to the soft hush of her footsteps on the bare, hidden stairs, footsteps with, it seemed to her, a stubborn finality. What a hard, cold young woman Violet was, despite her frail looks and uncertain ways. Wilma felt she had made no real connection with Violet, though certainly she'd tried.

Couldn't Violet, with her deep fear of Eddie, relate to Wilma's own fear and to the danger she faced? Wilma had seen no sympathy in her, no recognition of their mutual peril and vulnerability. Certain that she'd lost what might be her one chance for freedom, Wilma felt herself falling into a hopelessness that was not typical of her, that was not the way she looked at life. Cage could return at any moment, and the fear that he would kill her churned in Wilma's stomach so hard that it brought bile to her throat. This was a kind of terror she had never known, nothing like the quick surge of fear that prodded one to action. That defensive fear sharpened a person, honed one's perceptions and one's responses. Instant, reactive fear was what she should have felt when Cage slipped up behind her undetected and shoved her in the car; her normal fear instinct should have triggered fast

237

action, triggered a counterattack of violence, of the moves and blows in which she had been trained. Instead, she'd caved, had been too slow. And the helpless fear that washed over her now did no good at all.

Leaning backward into the drawer again, she resumed her frantic search for a knife. At one point, she had considered the stove that stood just beside her. It was gas, and she'd thought of lighting a burner, of trying to burn the ropes off. But that was a last resort, a move of terrible desperation. Third-degree burns hurt like hell, and could further incapacitate her.

There had to be another knife, no one could cook with only one. In order to search a drawer, she had to grasp its handle in her tied hands, and twist and hump the chair forward enough to pull the drawer to her; and the space was so small she couldn't turn fully. Digging behind her, she sorted through unseen kitchen implements, a grater, a peeler, pushing them aside. Ladle and measuring spoons jumbled together. As she searched, she listened for sounds from above, and for the sound of the car returning. But suddenly—was that a blade beneath her fingers?

Yes! A paring knife. Small wooden handle, and not very sharp. Excitedly, she drew it out.

Holding it by the handle, the tip of the blade pointed toward her, she rested her bound wrists on the edge of the open drawer and, with that support, attempted awkwardly to slip the blade between her wrist and her bonds. It took her many tries. The knife kept slipping, she couldn't get a grip that would allow her to twist it in the right direction. Twice she dropped it, but both times was lucky that it fell into the drawer—she daren't drop it on the floor or she'd never be able to retrieve it. Working stubbornly, and cutting herself several times, she was able at last to slip the blade between wrist and rope in a way that gave her traction. The relief of that small accomplishment was amazing. She was sawing away at the rope, intent on gaining more pressure, when Violet spoke, making her jump.

She hadn't heard the young woman come down, no smallest sound on the stairs this time. She twisted around to glance across the room at her.

Violet stood beside the woodstove watching her with a cold resolve that had not been evident earlier. Its meaning was indecipherable; clearly the girl had made up her mind. But to do what?

Had Violet decided to release her, had she found the courage to run? Or did she mean to escape alone, leaving Wilma, thinking that the returning men would be too preoccupied with their captive to come after her?

Wilma didn't dare speak, the girl looked as unstable as quicksand. Looked as if, at one word, she could come apart. Then, who knew what she might do? Watching Violet, she sawed hard at the

239

frayed strands and jerked, trying to break free—but swiftly Violet moved across the room, reached over Wilma, and snatched the knife away. Jerked it from her grip, bending Wilma's wrist and thumb back with more strength than she'd thought the girl possessed. The pain was sickening. Had Violet learned that excruciating trick from Cage, or from Eddie? As Violet stood gripping the knife, Wilma remained still, her head bent, fingering the frayed rope. Waiting.

When Violet leaned over her again to examine the rope, Wilma grasped it and jerked—she felt it break. Her hands were free. She lunged, tackling Violet, the chair still tied to her. They went down in a heap, Wilma on top tangled in the chair. Lying across Violet, holding her down, she wrestled the knife from the girl. And with her knees hard in Violet's belly, she managed to cut free her ankles, then to free herself from the chair.

Twisting around, forcing the chair down on top of Violet, she untangled herself as Violet flailed and fought. With the cut rope she jerked Violet's hands behind her and tied her wrists, then pushed the chair away. Sitting on top of Violet, she pinned Violet's kicking legs and used the other piece of rope to tie them.

Leaving Violet secured for the moment, she rummaged through the kitchen drawers until she found a jumble of tools. Pliers, screwdrivers, a wrench, a roll of black electrical tape, even a flashlight that worked. Pulling open the last drawer, she withdrew a hank of old, worn clothesline cord.

Taping Violet's wrists, she tied the cord around them and around the girl's waist, then freed her ankles.

"Get up."

Violet didn't move.

Wilma shoved her. "You're getting out of here whether you want to or not. What you do later is your business. Is there a car? Where are the keys?"

"They took the Jeep. Both cars are there. I don't have keys, Eddie never leaves keys. He won't let me have a car when he's gone."

"You're lying. Where are the keys?" Wilma crossed the room and looked out; there was just enough light left to make out two cars parked close to the house. Neither was new, but new enough that they might be hard to hot-wire. She could make out a third vehicle farther away, by a shed. "That old station wagon—does that run?" It was one of the big old fifties models, with tall tail fins that made her think of a shark.

"It runs."

"Are you sure? Does it have gas?"

"He keeps it full, he uses it to . . . He keeps it full. But if we take a car, they'll find it and they'll kill us both."

"You think I have a choice? I stay here, I'm dead anyway." Wilma stuffed the tools in her pockets.

Holding the flashlight like a weapon, she jerked Violet up. "Get moving."

Violet was dead white as Wilma forced her across the room and out, down the wooden steps; hurrying across the dirt yard, she shone the light on the old station wagon. It was thick with dirt over the rust. She wondered what Eddie used it for. Forcing Violet backward against the rear of the car, her hands taped behind her, she tied her to the bumper with the long clothesline, and then wound that through the bumper, and tied her feet together.

Jerking the rusting driver's door open, Wilma lay down on her back under the steering wheel and got to work. Thank God Clyde and Max, when they were wild young men, during their rodeoing days, had taught her to hot-wire a car.

It took her maybe five minutes, making sure it was in neutral and the brake on. She felt a crazy thrill when, crossing the two bare wires, she made the engine turn over. Carefully she goosed the gas pedal until she had it running smoothly, then she slid out.

Untying Violet, but leaving her hands and feet bound, prodding her with the flashlight, she made her hop around the car and into the passenger seat.

"Stay there on your own side, Violet, and don't mess with me. This flashlight, if I hit you in the right place, can be just as lethal as a gun. Where did they go in the Jeep?" She had thought, when the men left, that their vehicle hadn't headed down the hill in the direction of the coast, that they'd turned away behind the house, moving south.

"Another road," Violet said shortly.

"Where? What road? Where did they go?" She prodded her so hard that Violet sucked in her breath. "You might as well tell me. Whether you want it or not, I'm giving you your freedom."

"A narrow path through the woods," Violet said sulkily. "Only the Jeep can get through there." She looked away at a ninety-degree angle to the wider road that Wilma could make out in the darkness, to a narrow line snaking away into the woods. That would be the bridle trail where Charlie rode sometimes. The big station wagon wouldn't get ten feet along that track before it was stuck. Backing around, she took off down the wider road, moving without lights beneath the paler sky, down through the black land that fell away before her. This had to be the old dirt road she knew, that should lead to the Pamillon estate.

"Where does this go, Violet?"

"To the village. To the ruins, first. You know where that is?"

"What ruins? How far?" Wilma felt her heartbeat quicken.

"Parmean or something."

"Pamillon?"

"I guess. All fallen down."

Wilma's spirits soared. She wasn't lost, she was close to home, she was free and had wheels. She just wished she had a more formidable weapon. Cage and Eddie would be after them soon enough, the minute they got back and found them gone. "Where did they go in the Jeep? When will they be back, Violet?"

"I don't know where. It's just woods and then ranches. I don't know what they're doing and I don't know when they'll come back. Maybe they won't, maybe they'll hit the highway somewhere and keep going." Violet glanced at her. "Maybe they've run."

Wilma hoped so. "Can we get through the ruins to a main road, is this road clear?"

"They come and go this way. There are side roads, but I don't think they use them."

"Do you know the ruins? Know how to get around in there?"

Violet didn't answer.

Wilma didn't know what had made her ask that, what had made her think that Violet would wander there. But, from her sullen silence, maybe she did know her way among the fallen walls. Wilma glanced at her but returned her attention quickly to the dark and narrow twisting road. Dare she try lights, at least the parking lights? She knew there were drop-offs here, with nothing to mark them.

But the tiniest moving light would be a beacon, a dead giveaway. As she came around a sharp curve she hit a rock, jolting them so hard she was knocked sideways in the seat. Before she could see anything, they hit another. She thought they had gone off the road, but then the way smoothed again.

"Washed-out places," Violet said shakily; she kept watching behind them, peering into the dark, looking for Cage and Eddie. The next bump was so violent they went skidding, the car sliding and tilting. As Wilma steered into the skid, Violet slid into her, using the momentum to ram Wilma into the wheel, making her lose control. Fighting the wheel, she felt the ground drop; the car fell with a terrible jolt, they were over the side, plummeting. The car came to a halt, hitting on its side, ramming her head against the window.

Violet lay on top of her, both of them jammed against the dash and the driver's door, which was now underneath them. She couldn't turn off the key—there was no key—and the engine was roaring. Afraid of fire, she shoved Violet aside hard, and jerked the wires loose every which way, breathing a shaking sigh when the engine quit.

She thought they must be on a ledge. She was afraid to move, the car was still rocking. The only sound was a faint ticking as the vehicle settled. Violet had fallen back on top of her, and lay there, limp. Wilma thought she was knocked out cold. She came to life suddenly, scrambling up and lunging for the passenger window above them, stepping on Wilma's shoulder to boost herself through. Wilma didn't grab her, she let her go, she didn't want a battle that would send them over. The car rocked alarmingly as Violet leaped away. She heard Violet run, her footsteps soon lost in the night.

Gingerly Wilma lifted herself out from under the steering wheel and groped for the flashlight, sure she wouldn't find it. She almost jumped when she felt its rubber-covered handle. Gripping it, envisioning the car balanced precariously on the edge of a cliff, she stood up slowly on the driver's door, then stepped up into the crack between the two seat backs. As her head and shoulders cleared the passenger-side open window, the car teetered.

She didn't see Violet in the darkness, didn't hear her; now there was no sound. She could see, above her and above the edge of the drop, the jagged ghosts of broken walls.

Before climbing out she felt in the glove compartment carefully, not expecting to find anything useful, praying for a gun but knowing that Eddie and Cage weren't that careless.

She found nothing but papers, probably old repair bills. Switching on the flashlight for an instant, shielding it in her cupped hand, she took a quick look at the cliff.

The earth looked solid enough beneath a black mass of boulders, she could see no dark empty spaces yawning directly below her. Switching off the light, she eased herself out the window onto the door. As she crept onto the fender, the car shifted. She slid to the ground landing among the boulders, thought it would fall again, but then it settled. Closing her eyes until they adjusted again to the dark, she climbed up the rocks that loomed black above her, her every muscle already aching and sore.

She stood at last on the road feeling incredibly free—free of ropes, free of the precarious car, free, for the moment, of Violet; hindered now only by the jabbing pain in her leg and hip, and by the aching sting of her cuts and bruises. Beneath the paler sky the land lay inky black; if she was indeed above the village, and if that faraway silver line was the sea, then those tiny clustered lights might be Molena Point. The thought of *home* had never seemed so safe and dear.

But she wasn't there yet. Alone and hurting, she set off limping down the dark road thinking longingly of a hot shower, a stiff drink, and a rare steak—and entertaining herself with what she'd like to do to Cage Jones. But then her thoughts turned to Dulcie. She prayed that the little cat, in her panic when Wilma didn't come home, hadn't gone off alone looking for her.

But, no, first Dulcie would have called Max or Clyde. That would have the whole department looking for her, would have the law in Gilroy searching, going through the shops, talking with the clerks. Maybe they would find her credit card and know she'd been there, know something was wrong. She looked hopefully down the hills, longing to see the dark silhouettes of police units climbing without lights up the dark road—and yet, why would they come here? No one knew she was here, there was nothing to bring them looking for her in this desolate place.

Around her there was no sound, just the empty night and the looming hulks of broken walls—and, hiding somewhere among the tangles of stone, Violet Sears. Was Violet waiting, still meaning to harm her? Perhaps wielding some sturdy piece of metal she'd picked up among the rubble? But why would she bother, now that she had escaped? Wouldn't she run head down the dark hills to freedom?

Or, if Cage and Eddie appeared suddenly, she would hide among the invisible tangles of stone and rubble and sudden drops. Maybe Violet *knew* the lay of these ruins, maybe she *knew* where to hide. Living so close, might she have come here during the day, when Eddie was gone? But then, eased of her stress, each time she would return, lacking the courage for escape?

Limping, hurting so badly she wondered if something was broken, and not sure how far she could walk, Wilma made her way slowly among the fallen walls, debating whether to start for the village or wait until the pain dissipated.

25

Slipping through the dark village streets, then through heavily shadowed, overgrown gardens, Cotton had at last found the oak that held Kit's tree house. Thankful to have left traffic and people behind him, reassured by the night's silence in the quiet neighborhood, he'd scrambled up the oak—and found himself face-to-face with Kit herself, and Dulcie, standing in the door to the tree house. Observing the street below, they had watched him for some time.

Already the two cats knew the redheaded lady was missing. And when Cotton described her capture, panting out his urgent news, within minutes Kit was across a branch to a window of the big house and inside, shouting and nearly mewing into the telephone to Police Captain Harper.

He'd told them how he and Willow and Coyote had seen the older, gray-haired woman through that kitchen window, how he'd gone for help and seen the two men grab the redheaded one and tie her up, and drive away with her up the dirt trail through the woods, and how the big man talked about the ruins—

"But Wilma . . . !" Dulcie had exploded, lashing her tail, her green eyes wild. "Where exactly *is* that house? Why did . . . ?"

He had told them all he knew. And now when Kit finished the call, and went right in to talk with her humans, Cotton was ready to race away. But he was too curious—and the next thing he knew, the thin old woman, Lucinda, was bringing him food, and he *was* very hungry. He ate with one eye on the woman and the man, and listened to Kit argue boldly with them.

"You can't be sure where they're taking Charlie," Lucinda said. "It's late and dark, and you—"

"Cotton is sure," Kit said. "He heard them, they said 'to the ruins.' We—"

"The police can get there faster, Kit. Those empty hills at night are wild with coyotes and bob-cats. You *do* remember the cougar?"

"The cougar is not there now, we haven't smelled him on the hills for a long time. We can *be* there in the time it takes to argue!"

"There could be shooting. You could end up in the middle of gunfire, and what good would that do Charlie or Wilma? Max will have half the force up there, armed officers who—"

"We have sense enough to stay out of the way!" Kit hissed at Lucinda. "You know you can't keep us in, we—"

"If you *must* go, if you absolutely *must,* then Pedric and I will take you."

"But you can't. There will be too many police cars, they'll be all over that little dirt road. They'll have it blocked and . . . How will you explain being there? How would you explain that you already know about Charlie and Wilma? It won't be on the news yet. Maybe it isn't even on the police radios, maybe they're using their cell phones so no one else will pick it up. You can't—"

"We'll take you as far as we can. I'll just get my keys." Lucinda stared hard into the kit's blazing yellow eyes. "Wait for us! Promise me! Think of the time you can save."

"Cotton won't ride in a car!" Kit shouted. "Cotton won't get in a car! He's feral! He won't—"

But he had gotten in. And that had amazed Cotton himself. And now here he was riding in the backseat beside Dulcie trying to put down his panic at being shut inside the noisy, moving vehicle while Dulcie and Kit thought nothing of such a journey. The old woman drove. Her husband, Pedric, sat beside her with the kit on his lap.

Cotton was glad that Dulcie sat close to him to give him courage, purring to ease his nerves, and licking his ear. But then as they moved up among the dark hills, she reared up with her paws on the window, staring out into the night. And now he was beginning to get the feel of the moving car; it wasn't as loud or as bumpy, or as windy and cold as when he and Willow and Coyote were hauled down from the hills in that metal cage tied on the back of a motorcycle. That had been more than a cat could bear, trapped and caged and carried down the mountain in that violent, bumpy ride and the icy wind battering them trying to tear out their fur. They'd all thought that was the end of them.

It was Dulcie and Joe Grey who had come looking for them and gotten trapped, too; and it was Kit who had rescued them all. So he guessed he could try to be as brave as she was. Well, this car *was* nice and warm. And the motor wasn't so loud; its voice was almost a purr.

But then soon the ride grew bumpier once they turned off the smooth road onto the dirt one that led, winding, up the hills. Dulcie was still rearing up; in the front seat Kit stood up in Pedric's lap, to look out, too. And she said all in one breath, "Cop cars, Lucinda, without lights. Slow down and put out your lights or we'll give ourselves away and give the cops away. Turn them off now!"

"They're off, Kit!" Lucinda snapped, pulling to the side of the road, onto the rocky edge. At once, Kit put her paw on the door handle.

"Kit . . . ," Lucinda began, holding down the master lock.

"Please, Lucinda. You've brought us this far; we're as safe now as we ever can be. You can't—"

"I know," Lucinda said sadly. "We've had this argument before. I can't run your life; I'm overprotective, and you can't live that way."

"Let them go," Pedric said.

Lucinda flipped the lock. Kit leaped out the door, and Cotton beside her. Only Dulcie paused, looking at the bright tears on Lucinda's cheeks. Then she, too, was gone.

But away among the rocks Kit reared up to look back. "We'll be fine," she whispered. "Go home, Lucinda. Go before the uniforms see you and come asking questions." And, spinning around, she followed Dulcie and Cotton away fast, streaking up the hill toward the jagged, fallen walls that loomed above them against the dark night sky.

On the second floor of the ruined mansion where the front wall had crumbled away, the big, old-fashioned nursery stood open to the night like the stage in an abandoned theater. Beside a broken rocking horse, Willow and Coyote crouched, looking down the black hills, watching yet another car move up the road without lights. Already, half a dozen cars were parked along the shoulder, dark and still. Police cars. The two cats watched this car stop, saw the door open and a white cat streak out beside two darker companions.

"Cotton!" Willow hissed. "That can't be Cotton. Riding in a car? But . . . that's Kit and Dulcie." They watched the three cats race up toward them and vanish among the tumbled stones. "Cotton went to find Kit and Dulcie?" Willow whispered, ashamed that she had doubted him. "When we saw Wilma through that window, I thought he ran away to hunt, that he didn't want to be bothered. But he—

"He went to find them," she said. "Even though he hates humans and fears human places. He hates that village where we were captive—but he went there, all alone." Admiration for the white tom filled Willow. Beside her, Coyote was silent; and when Willow looked at him, he was scowling. Willow's eyes widened. Was he jealous? She had never known Coyote to be jealous.

But there was so much else to think about, so much happening, first that car going over the side and the thin young woman scrambling out and climbing up to the road and running, and then the silver-haired woman following her more slowly, and limping. The young one called Violet seemed very afraid. Her every movement sent messages of fear, like the movements of a cornered mouse. And then the cop cars had come, and parked, never turning on lights.

"There," she said, glimpsing Violet. Spinning around, she raced through the cluttered nursery to the back where the wall still stood intact. Leaping to the sill of a broken window, she looked deeper into the interior of the ruined estate. "Violet's headed for that old trailer, the place she goes when that man has beaten her."

"She thinks she's safe there," Coyote said. "She doesn't know he watches her go in there."

"Here comes Wilma," Willow said softly, "following her. We have to tell them those men know about that place, that they will find them there."

"We can't talk to humans!" Coyote stared at her, shocked.

"We'll tell Dulcie and Kit, they'll tell them . . ." But even as she spoke they heard a car coming from the woods along the horse trail, heard the rattle of that rusted, open car, and there was no time to find Dulcie; Willow leaped away down the broken stairs and out the back, heading for the old trailer. Behind her, Coyote didn't move, he stood staring after her. Glancing back, Willow gave him a scornful look, and slid away into the ivy.

Wilma moved warily and painfully downhill, approaching the derelict mansion, looking for Violet's pale, swift shape, imagining her flashing away like a ghost among the ruins to some secret hiding place. The Pamillon estate had remained without repair for more than a generation, awaiting disposition of a title so tangled among two dozen heirs that even a vast array of attorneys seemed unable to sort out the many wills and trusts in a way that would establish legal succession. Pausing to get her bearings, shielding the flashlight and switching it on just long enough to be sure she wasn't headed for a sinkhole, she flicked it off again, startled when she glimpsed Violet's thin white shirt vanish among the jagged walls. Quickly she followed.

In the shadows of a collapsed garden shed and tangled ivy trellis, the girl stood unmoving, as

255

ethereal as a ghost; Wilma approached her, expecting her to run.

She didn't run, she stood shaking, white as paper in Wilma's shielded light. Wilma studied her thin face and then took her icy hand. "Come on, Violet. We have to hide. Show me where."

Violet stared into the shielded light. "There's a place, but there are spiders and—"

"If we can hide there," Wilma said, listening to the faint rumble of a distant, ragged engine approaching from the south, "then get on with it! They're coming."

Violet listened to the Jeep crunching over gravel and rocks and brushing through the trees, breaking branches. She stiffened when it did not turn up the hill toward the house but continued on through the rubble, heading directly toward them.

"Move it," Wilma snapped. "Now!"

Violet spun, and ran.

26

Willow and Coyote watched the two women slip quickly in among the vines that hid the old trailer. The shelter stood in such a tangle that only a cat might find it, prowling the rubble as they had, a hunting cat slipping through the heavy growth. They didn't know how Violet had discovered it—but that man knew about it, too. More

256

than once he had followed her there; months earlier he had watched her slip in there to hide, had waited for her to leave, and then he had pushed into the mildew-stinking trailer to see where she'd been.

The next time she went there the cats had expected him to go in and drag her out, but he didn't. He watched her, then turned away smirking in a silent, ugly laugh. As if, once he knew her secret, he meant to wait until just the right time to sneak up on her and—what? Thinking about that made them shiver; they feared that sour, sneaky man.

Now they watched the two women disappear quickly beneath the ivy and the metal roof, escaping from the Jeep. Did they think they were safe? A voice behind Willow made her spin around.

"Did she get away?" Cotton said softly. "Did the silver-haired lady get away?"

Willow leaped at him, happily licking his ears. "Did *you* bring help? Did *you* bring the cops? There are cops all over, sitting in their dark cars. But how . . . ?" Then behind him she saw Dulcie and Kit, and she leaped at them, too. "Quick, you have to tell them. Tell Wilma to run, that the Jeep is coming and those men know where they are. Oh please—" But Dulcie and Kit and Cotton were three streaks racing into the old, hidden trailer.

• • •

The trailer was dark inside and smelled of rot and mildew; the door Wilma had come through flopped on one hinge, hanging out into the mat of vines. Safely inside, she shielded the flashlight with her cupped hands and switched it on.

"Where'd you get that?" Violet said.

"In the glove compartment." She shone the light around the tiny trailer, across surfaces heavy with dirt and rust and rat droppings, over damp wood spongy with rot and smelling sour; everything was thick with mold. Who knew how many varieties of lethal spores Violet breathed in here. If she came here often, no wonder she looked pale and sick— though more likely it was the stress of living in fear of her husband that left the girl so frail.

Going in ahead of Wilma, Violet had curled up at one end of a single bed that was built between a minuscule kitchen counter and a closet that held a smelly toilet. The bed was covered with a filthy spread and smelled sour. Wilma sat down on a narrow bench, one of a pair flanking a small table that had been folded out from the wall and was supported by a flimsy leg. The trailer, cooler than the outdoors, rang with the sounds of crickets, dozens of crickets hidden in the dark around them celebrating the hot, humid night. Wilma sat with her elbows on the table, her chin on her hands, trying to quiet her fear, ignoring the pain in her leg and hip, encouraging her pounding heart to settle to an easier rhythm. A demanding mewl brought her up startled, swinging around to the open door.

Dulcie stood looking in at her. The dark little striped being was hardly visible in the night, but for her lighter nose and ears and the gleam of her green eyes. Crouching, she sprang at Wilma, landing on her shoulder, clinging to her, licking and nuzzling her face. Laughing, Wilma cuddled and hugged Dulcie, kissing her ears. "You're all right! You don't know how I missed you, how I worried, how bad I felt for you . . ."

Dulcie couldn't talk in front of Violet. She couldn't have talked anyway, she was too choked up, all she could do was mewl. But then, getting hold of herself, she whispered faintly against Wilma's ear, her words so soft that Wilma could hardly make out what she was saying.

"They're back. They know about this place! Get away. Cage knows where she hides. Run! Run now!"

Wilma rose fast, holding Dulcie tight. "I hear them, Violet! The Jeep, they're coming, headed straight here, I hear them talking . . . Run!" And she was out the door, clutching Dulcie, and away, letting Violet decide her own fate. In the dark behind her, the crickets had stopped. The noise of the Jeep was like thunder. Wilma ran, dodging fallen rubble, her every painful step jolting her. She could hear someone running behind her.

Violet caught up with her, they fled together as headlights veered at them, then vanished. Had they been seen? The engine roared as if goosed, roared again and died.

Silence. Wilma watched Violet warily as they crouched behind a fallen wall maybe thirty feet from the trailer, half that from the Jeep. Dulcie clung tightly to Wilma, her heart pounding against Wilma's chest. They heard the men step out, their shoes crunching on broken stone. Wilma prayed Violet wouldn't move—wouldn't intentionally give them away. The girl started to rise. Wilma shoved her down and twisted her arm behind her. "Be still. Not a sound."

Violet moaned at the pain of her twisted arm. "Let off a little! I won't do anything! There's someone in the back of the Jeep, they're forcing someone out . . ."

Dulcie breathed one word in Wilma's ear, turning her cold. "Charlie. They have Charlie."

There was commotion around the Jeep, the prisoner was fighting them. Cage yelled, "Bitch! Damned bitch. Hold her, for Chrissake!" Then a dull thud and a woman's muffled moan. But then Charlie snapped, "Go to hell!" That brought Wilma up, rigid.

Both men were facing them, they could see the pale smear of Cage's face and shirt, his heavy shoulders against a stone wall as they dragged Charlie away from the Jeep. "Untie her feet,"

Eddie grumbled. "I'm not carrying her, she's too damn heavy."

"Shut up and take her shoulders, I'm not untying her. Hurry the hell up!"

Wilma hugged Dulcie close and then jerked Violet up. "Come on. Now." Pulling Violet, she slipped away fast among the broken walls. They moved as silently as they could through the scattered rubble. Wilma didn't dare run and risk stumbling noisily over the rocks. But suddenly she was aware of small shadows running with them. Kit? Yes. And she could see Cotton, white in the blackness. No time to think what other cats there were. Intent on getting away, she forced Violet ahead, brutally prodding her, hoping the sounds of their running were drowned by Cage and Eddie's arguing as they dragged Charlie into the trailer.

Hauled roughly out of the Jeep and across ragged stone into what appeared to be a cave, Charlie saw, high among the fallen walls, a hint of swift movement, something small and quick. And despite the men's arguing, she caught the faint whisper of voices, distorted by Cage's swearing and Eddie's whining replies—but now, all was still. Could that band of feral cats still be here, in the ruins? For a moment, hope filled her.

But those shy little cats; even if they were here, how could they help? They were so wild, and so fearful of humans. They wanted nothing to do with humans except to steal food, to scavenge from the alleys and escape. They would be escaping now, running from invading humans, would have been alerted by the first sounds of the Jeep, terrified by the men's angry voices.

She had spoken to them once, spoken as a friend to three of them. But still, she thought they were too shy and far too fearful ever to help her.

Dragging her across a hard floor, Cage dumped her on what seemed to be a dirty, rumpled cot. He flicked on a small, weak flashlight. They were in some kind of little shack, or maybe a trailer.

Yes, it was a trailer, a small old camping trailer, every surface rimed with mold and dust. She tried to picture where she was in the ruins, could only be sure it was somewhere behind the main house she had seen looming against the sky when Cage dragged her out of the Jeep. She had walked these ruins, she and Max, and they had ridden up here to picnic, as had she and Ryan, leaving their horses tied while they explored the broken rooms and cellars—but they had never discovered this trailer.

The first time she'd ever seen the ruins, she and Max and Dillon Thurwell had hidden here from another killer, hidden in one of the cellars just under or just behind the main house, a cellar with broken concrete stairs leading down to it. If she could free herself, could she find it again and hide there? She didn't like the fact that it would be a dead end, only one way out, but it would be better than nothing. Strange that she was a prisoner here a second time. That first had been enough.

When Cage tried to tie her bound legs to the bed, she twisted and kicked him hard, her feet striking him in the chest. He grunted, sucked air, and hit her, knocking her against the wall so violently that her vision swam—hit her again and she went dizzy; fighting to stay awake, she could feel herself reeling and falling as if into a black pit.

From her hiding place, Wilma watched the two men drag Charlie into the trailer, swearing and arguing; she burned to get her hands on Cage. Kneeling, she felt among the rubble of fallen stones until she found a long, well-balanced rock. And she headed for the trailer.

"Wait," Violet hissed, grabbing her arm. "They're leaving. Look, they're coming out. They . . . they've left her there." She looked at Wilma. "Who is that woman?"

Wilma didn't answer. She watched the men moving away, glimpses of their dark figures shifting against the broken stone walls; she expected that any minute they would turn back, to further hurt Charlie. But they hurried on, to the Jeep. She heard the engine start, listened to it pull away without lights, heard it head uphill, its engine whining—she felt Dulcie jump down, the little tabby gone before Wilma could grab her. "Dulcie . . ." She could see nothing in the blackness. Dulcie had vanished.

"The house . . . ," Violet said. "They're going back to the house, and they'll see we're gone. They'll be back and they'll find us." She rose to sprint away, but Wilma grabbed her. Violet hit her hand with a painful chop and jerked free, and ran; Wilma could hear her stumbling through the dark, toward the mansion. She stared after the girl, half hating her for not wanting to help Charlie, half glad to be rid of her. She rose and, carrying the rock, headed for the trailer and Charlie.

She daren't switch on the flashlight. As she hurried, stumbling through the rubble, listening to the Jeep's roar grow fainter, she felt Dulcie brush her ankle, warm and furry.

"Good riddance," Dulcie said softly.

Wilma picked her up, glad to hold her close again. "Where did you go?" But Dulcie said nothing. Pushing in through the curtain of ivy and stepping up into the dark trailer, Wilma, meaning to rush to Charlie, switched on the flashlight.

She stopped in midstride.

Four cats were crouched on the cot, over Charlie where she lay tied up. All four were busily chewing at the ropes—like some strange, impossible fairy tale. Chewing at Charlie's bonds just as, not long ago, Kit had chewed at similar bindings to release a younger hostage, freeing twelve-year-old Lori Reed when she had been kidnapped. Wilma watched, not knowing whether to laugh with delight or weep at the cats' bold kindness. It had not been easy for these wild little cats to come in here, to put themselves so close to humans—but now, the minute the light flicked on, the three feral cats froze, staring up at her with eerie reflective eyes. And they were gone, dropping soundlessly from the bed and melting into the shadows.

She supposed they vanished out the door, though she saw and heard nothing. Only Kit remained on the cot, diligently chewing at Charlie's ropes and glancing sideways up at Wilma, her golden eyes caught in the light, her tortoiseshell fur dark against Charlie's red hair. Then Dulcie leaped from Wilma's shoulder to help.

Quickly, Wilma removed the dirty bandanna from around Charlie's mouth, and began to work on the half-chewed ropes, jerking them apart where the ferals had chewed almost through them. It was the look on Charlie's face that made Wilma laugh, a look of terrible wonder and disbelief.

Charlie struggled up as Kit chewed through the rope that bound her hands. Wilma jerked the last rope off, and Charlie swung off the bed—and they ran, Charlie and Wilma, Dulcie and Kit, up across the ruins. "Where can we hide?" Wilma said. "Where are . . . ?"

The roar of the returning Jeep barreling down the road silenced her. They stopped and turned, heard it pull up close to the trailer, Cage swearing.

"We still have the niece," Eddie said, "and the

aunt'll come back for her. She'll do whatever we say when she knows we have her precious niece."

"This way," Kit hissed, and the little cat ran, slipping past the Jeep in blackness, Charlie and Wilma stumbling behind her.

"We can't see you," Charlie whispered. But Kit mewled softly, then mewled again. Cage was still swearing as Kit led them away between dark and fallen walls, up four steps and into the kitchen of the ruined house, then through the kitchen and the living room, tripping over rotting furniture. "The captain," Dulcie said, "has men down there, six units parked along the road. We can just . . ."

But the Jeep had pulled around the house, they heard it skid to a stop before the broken front door; they had time only to duck behind the tumbled furniture, into the deepest shadows.

"Damn women," Cage growled, slamming the door of the Jeep. "How the hell . . . You take the first floor, I'll look upstairs. How the hell did Violet get the keys to the wagon! You gave 'em to her, Eddie! I told you—"

"I never!"

"Don't lie to me! Violet cut her loose and took the damn car keys. Why the hell did you . . . ?"

"She wouldn't dare, and she didn't know where them keys were. Even if she did, she ain't got the balls to take them."

"You shoulda beat her before we left there the first time, made sure she couldn't run. Come on . . ."

"They wouldn't hide in here, right in the house. There's basements and things."

"Them black, caving-in cellars? Not Violet. Scared of spiders, scared of the dark. And where the hell's the station wagon? You think they went on down the hills?"

"Told you, car was damn near out of gas. Running on fumes. Told you I was out of canned gas. No, they hid the wagon somewhere; could be anywhere in this mess." The other car door slammed, and their footsteps crunched across stones, the twin beams of their torches flashing up the steps and across the porch, then blazing straight in through the front door and across the tangles of fallen furniture.

Cage stood in the doorway looking in, seeming, in the flashlight's reflection, as big as a giant. "You go find the station wagon. I'll take care of this bunch. Still don't know why you left the keys in it. If you can't find it, look for tracks, try to make yourself useful."

"Told you I didn't leave the keys in it!" Eddie stood on the porch behind Cage, shining his light back into the ruins as if hoping the station wagon would miraculously appear and he wouldn't have to go searching for it in the dark.

"You didn't leave them in it, then you gave 'em to Violet! Or you told her where they were. I swear, sometimes—"

"There," Eddie shouted, jumping off the porch, swinging his light and running.

Cage turned and looked. "What the hell!" then took off after Eddie. When they were gone, Wilma rose and went to the window, stood watching them.

"They found it," she said as Charlie joined her. They could see the men's two lights shining down the embankment, could hear their voices clearly in the still night. Eddie began to laugh. "Guess that did 'em."

"What the hell?" Cage's torchlight shining down silhouetted his tall bulk. "What you mean, that did 'em? Ain't nobody in the damn wagon. Damn women got out." As he turned, staring back toward the house, Wilma grabbed Charlie's hand, ready to go out the back.

But Charlie pulled away and moved to the front door, staring into the night.

"Come on!" Wilma said, grabbing her. "Before they come back." Outside, at the wreck, the men were quiet for a moment, as if looking over the damage to the old car. When Wilma tried to pull Charlie with her, Charlie jerked away roughly.

"What?" Wilma snapped.

"Look," Charlie said softly, slipping out onto the porch. "Watch, maybe half a mile back along the tree line—where the trees part. Watch the little dip, with the sky a shade lighter behind it. Watch right there, something's coming, I saw movement farther back . . ." She gripped Wilma's hand. "Horses. Horses on the trail . . . Max . . ."

Wilma could not hear horses. This was Charlie's

wishful thinking. She had dropped Charlie's hand and was starting to turn away when . . .

"There," Charlie hissed. "There, see!"

Wilma glimpsed something moving past the little dip, then it was gone. Two riders, making for the ruins.

Terror filled Charlie's voice. "Cage has a handgun, and there's a shotgun in the Jeep. If he hears them . . ." She pulled Wilma through the front door and down the steps. "Go! Go down to Max's men, tell them to come fast, on foot, and quietly . . ."

"But you can't . . ."

"Go!" Charlie snapped. "Take the cats!" She snatched up Kit and shoved her at Wilma. "Go with her, both of you!" And she moved away through the blackness, toward the Jeep. Wilma wanted to drag her back, but knew she could make things worse by charging after her and alerting Cage. She could only go for help, as fast as she could go, down through the rubble and the dark road.

27

"Damn bitch!" Cage hissed, staring down the cliff. "How the hell did she get loose! That bitch Violet. Why the hell did you give her the keys! She cut that bitch loose and now she's wrecked the wagon! Look at it! And both of 'em gone!"

"I didn't give her no keys, I told you! Maybe they hot-wired the car."

"That's sure as hell lame! Violet couldn't hot-wire nothing, she hardly knows which end of a hammer to use! What'd you do, have extra keys made? I thought I could trust you!" He looked so hard at Eddie Sears that Eddie took a step back.

"I swear, I never had no keys made. I never *drove* the car, it's your car . . . I thought you planned a few more heists and then would dump it . . . I swear, Cage . . ."

"If you never drive it, how'd it run out of gas? Where'd you drive it to? What else have you been lying about?"

Eddie's voice shook. "I swear, Cage, I never. You drove it two weeks ago. If I'd used it, you know I'd of put gas in!"

"And why the hell didn't you work Violet over beforehand? Look at the mess you've made."

"I should of," Eddie said, backing away. "Should of beat her up good." But then he rallied. "That old woman'll show herself. She'll come out when she knows you have her niece, when we drag the red-head out where the old bitch can see 'er."

As the men left the edge of the cliff, heading for the trailer, in the blackness beside a fallen wall Charlie slipped toward the Jeep. She could hear, above her, the soft hush of hooves on the trail and the occasional click of a shod hoof against stone as the riders approached and, once, the faint jingle of a bit. In another minute, Cage would enter the trailer and see that she was gone and come roaring back. Enraged, would he return to the Jeep to grab his shotgun? Max would be nearer, then. They'd hear the horses and shine their lights on Max like jacking a deer. She daren't shout to warn him, daren't telegraph his presence.

Racing toward the dark silhouette of the Jeep, she couldn't tell where Max would enter the ruins. Would the horses spook among the unfamiliar night shadows, shy and make a fuss, rearing and backing, and give Max away? As well broke as their mounts were, this was no easy place for a horse in the pitch dark and looming shadows, when he couldn't see where he was stepping, and with dark figures moving mysteriously in the night.

Peering into the Jeep, then slipping inside onto the seat, she snatched up Cage's wadded jacket. Yes, beneath it, between the two narrow front seats was the sawed-off shotgun. It took her precious moments to find the bracket that held it in place, then to discover how it worked. She was sweating and shaky when at last the gun came free.

Carefully fingering it, she could find no lever. She decided the shells must be ejected by the movable portion of the stock, like Max's shotgun.

Everything was harder in the dark, more so with as little as she knew about shotguns, and her increasing urgency as the horses drew closer; she heard one of the horses snort.

Laying the gun across her lap and wrapping the coat around it, she snapped the stock to eject a shell. She felt the shell fly out inside the coat, against her thigh. With shaking fingers she found it and snatched it up. She explored the parts of the stock and barrel as best she could, then pressed the shell into what she prayed was the feed. She had no idea how many shells the gun contained, but her guess was, if it was loaded, it would be fully loaded. Maybe six to ten rounds? She didn't like to depend on a guess. Feeling for the safety, she found the little button pushed in; pressing it to a protruding position seemed logical for it to fire, if the in position sent a bolt through the firing mechanism. She was praying hard that she was right when she heard the two men burst out of the trailer. They came pounding straight toward the Jeep. They weren't swearing now, they were silent and fast, only the sound of their running and stumbling on the rocks. At the same instant, she heard a low exclamation from the trail. She heard the horses milling, as if they'd been pulled up short. She was scrabbling her hands over the dash trying to find the light switch—and the men were there, racing at the Jeep. She found the switch and pulled it.

Twin beams like lasers cut the blackness,

catching Cage with a shock of light; he loomed out of the dark, diving for the Jeep, blinded by light, then dropped down behind the fender, taking cover as he reached beneath his jacket. Eddie had ducked down on the other side; Charlie saw the top of his head, his cap moving as he began to circle, to get behind her.

Standing up in the Jeep, she braced herself against the dash, the stock of the gun jammed hard into her shoulder, her stomach flipping as she tried to hold steady, to keep her hands from shaking.

When Wilma ran down the dark road, looking for the nearest patrol car, the two cats didn't follow her, but had leaped away, in the opposite direction. She prayed for their safety; she could never have made them come with her, she'd only have wasted precious time. Running, searching for the first dark vehicle, she thought she'd spent half her life saying prayers for those three cats. Ahead, she saw a dark shape that had to be a patrol car; she stopped when a dark-clad figure stepped out, and she caught the glint of a handgun, stood with her hands out away from her sides, waiting. "It's Wilma Getz," she said softly. "Don't shine a light, they'll see you. Max is coming on horseback. And Charlie . . ." She caught a flash of the officer's badge, the line of his dark uniform, the tilt of a familiar jaw. "Is that Jimmie? Jimmie McFarland?"

"Yes, ma'm." Young Jimmie's soft, bright voice sounded truly glad to hear her. She paused when a second officer emerged, stepping around from the far side of the unit, and she saw the broad curve of Brennan's belly.

"Fill us in," Brennan said quietly, staring up into the unbroken dark of the old estate. "How many men? And where? Where's Max? He called us from the trail. Where does it come out?"

"To the left, above the Jeep," Wilma said, taking Brennan's hand and pointing with it to where the Jeep stood.

"Get in the unit and stay there," Brennan said, and he and McFarland moved away. She wanted to go back into the ruins, but knew she would only hinder them. She slipped into the hot squad car and had hardly pulled the door to, making no sound, when far up among the rubble a pair of lights flashed. Headlights. Someone was in the Jeep.

The diffused gleam of the Jeep's lights washing out across the ruins cast into stark silhouette the broken walls and gnarled oaks—and the small shapes of the feral cats, one poised atop a ragged tower, a pale cat padding across the sharp slant of a collapsed roof, and a stark white cat treading the top of a wall high under the stars. All watched the scene below. Curiosity, anger, and fear filled them. Then along the wall, two more cats appeared, dark creatures, rearing up, a pair of yellow eyes and a pair of green catching the light. Kit and Dulcie, fearful and intent, watched as Charlie stood up in the Jeep, her shotgun leveled behind the light—and as Cage Jones lunged to grab her.

Standing in the Jeep, her back to the dark where Max was approaching, the stock of the shotgun jammed against her shoulder, Charlie swallowed. "Stop, Cage. Stop now!"

Cage laughed. "Gun ain't loaded, missy. And it'd be double-aught bird—if the gun was loaded. It ain't."

"Want to find out?"

Cage laughed again and lunged for her. She fired. He staggered and fell back, and grabbed the fender, bent double, rocking the Jeep. She felt Eddie's weight rock it in the other direction and she spun around. He ducked, and disappeared beyond the light, then she heard him running in the blackness. She didn't dare fire where she couldn't see. Eddie was gone, pounding away as Cage clung to the Jeep, his face a mass of blood that turned her stomach. Slowly he slid down the fender, clutching it with bloody hands.

She waited for him to fall, but suddenly he twisted up again, righted himself and came up over the fender straight at her. She fired again, point-blank. He went down. This time, he stayed down.

How strange, the way that shot had echoed. Too

275

loud and with an unnatural thunder, not like the first round.

But now the night was so still, only the echo of the shots ringing, the blackness unbroken except for the acid path of the headlights, beneath which Cage Jones lay crumpled.

Holding the gun at ready, knowing he couldn't be a threat now but alert in case he was, she swung out of the Jeep.

He lay writhing in a way that sickened her. Where was Eddie? Her shots had stopped Cage from slipping up on Max in the dark, but where was Eddie Sears?

She heard no sound of running. And, now, she did not hear the horses. "Eddie's out there," she shouted. "Cage is down. Eddie ran."

But the shots had warned Max. Somewhere in the dark, he was ready.

She didn't think Eddie Sears would go after Max, not alone. Eddie was a coward, and this wasn't Eddie's battle. He'd be crazy to shoot at a cop. But still she stood scanning the night, watching for a dark figure slipping back toward the riders. She was thinking maybe she was stupid to think Max would be caught off guard, when Max said, behind her, "Thanks, Charlie."

His hand brushed hers as he shone a light on Cage; he knelt with his gun on Cage, checking his breathing and searching him for a weapon. Then, standing again, he switched on his radio. "Need a medic for Jones. Eddie Sears ran." He looked at Charlie. "Is he armed?"

"He didn't fire at me, but . . . I don't know."

He relayed that information, and then he held her close, warm, so warm. He smelled of male sweat and horse and gunpowder. She lay her head against him and only now knew how weak she felt, how scared.

"It's all right," he said, stroking her hair and shining his torch into the night, searching—and watching Cage.

And then McFarland and Brennan were there; they took charge of Cage. Other lights moved through the night, throwing looming shadows as officers searched for Eddie Sears. She heard the horses behind her and then Bucky loomed over her, and beside him her own Redwing—and then out of the darkness Rock leaped at her, the silver hound all over her, wagging and whining, jerking the long lead rope that Ryan held.

Ryan sat Redwing, looking down at Charlie, holding Rock's rope, and holding Bucky's reins. In the glancing reflection of the headlights, Ryan had that long-suffering look on her face as Rock made a fool of himself.

"He tracked you," Ryan said.

Charlie looked at her. "You've never trained him."

Ryan shrugged. "He tracked you."

Max said, "Where's Wilma?"

"She's all right, she went . . ." She nodded

toward where the patrol cars were parked. Lights were flashing now, men running, dark shadows dodging among the ruins as if someone had spotted Eddie Sears.

Max was on the radio. "Wilma down there?"

"I'm here," Wilma said.

Max handed Charlie the radio. She nearly dropped it. "You all right? Where are you?"

"In a nice comfortable squad car drinking someone's leftover coffee and starving to death. Are *you* all right? What was the firing?"

"I . . . I shot Cage Jones. He . . . Could we talk about it later? I'm beginning to feel . . ." Charlie swallowed. "I think I need to . . ."

"Later," Wilma said, and the radio went silent. Charlie listened to the sounds of running feet and rocks being dislodged and the faint, harsh mumble of the radios as officers searched for Sears; she prayed that no one else would be hurt. Max looked down at her and, with the back of his hand, wiped the tears from her face. She wondered why she was crying. Max put his arms around her, and it was all right, everything was all right.

28

From atop a crumbling wall, the five cats watched dark-clad cops scour the ruins, shining their lights into caves and crevices, talking to one another in those low, machine voices. They saw, farther up the hill, Max Harper kiss Charlie, and then Charlie mounted the big buckskin—the horses were nervous from the shooting, sidestepping, and fussing. Charlie rode away into the woods with the other woman to calm the frightened mounts, the cats thought. Willow and Cotton and Coyote understood that; they needed comforting, too. The three sat close together, gently grooming one another.

They had done things tonight that were not natural to them, had participated in frightening events foreign to their world, and now they needed one another. But they were warm with satisfaction, too. Cage Jones had gotten what he deserved, and that made them purr. But beside the three ferals, Dulcie and Kit were tense with excitement, watching the action as if eager to leap into the fray, convinced that, with cops all over, Eddie Sears would soon be caught, too.

"Like a mouse in a tin can," Kit said. And Willow and Cotton smiled. In the ferals' wild and threatened lives, retribution was highly valued—

and suddenly Eddie Sears appeared from out of nowhere running straight at them, racing for their wall, dodging, searching for a place to hide, and the cops were nearly on him. The three ferals slunk down, ready to vanish. But Dulcie and Kit crouched, with blazing eyes, their ears back, their tails lashing as Eddie veered along the wall looking for a way through—and the two cats flew at him: twin trajectories hitting him hard, raking him harder. Emboldened, the other three followed. Eddie Sears, covered with enraged and clawing cats, ran screaming, batting futilely at the slashing beasts.

"Don't shoot," Wilma shouted, swinging out of the squad car and running up the road. Maybe no one heard her; there were officers all over, converging on Sears. "Don't shoot," she cried, "he's not alone!"

"What is that?" McFarland hissed, throwing his light on something wild and screaming that rode Sears's shoulder, raking his face. McFarland dove at Sears's legs, hit him low and hard and dropped him. As Sears went down, the beast that covered him seemed to break into separate parts and vanish, exploding away in the dark.

McFarland knelt, cuffing Sears's hands behind him. *What the hell* was *that?* He shone his light into Sears's face. It was clawed and bloodied. McFarland shivered and felt the hairs on the back of his neck stand up, stiff.

He was securing Sears's legs when he glanced up and saw Wilma standing over them. She looked at him, looked at Sears. She said nothing, just turned and headed away, back toward the squad car. McFarland knelt atop Sears, watching her, amused by the shadow of a grin that she couldn't hide. Then Brennan joined him, and they got Sears to his feet. "What was that?" Brennan said. Around them in the night, officers were gathering, their lights coming down out of the ruins. "What the hell was that?"

No one knew, or maybe didn't want to say what they thought they had seen. Until rookie Eleanor Sand arrived. "I think," she said, "it was cats."

"Cats?" the men looked at her, and laughed. "*Cats,* Sandy? What kind of cats? Sandy, girl, you've lost it."

"I think there are feral cats up here," she said. "I've been up here, seen them. Domestic cats gone wild."

"Sandy, no cat would do what we just saw."

"What kind of cats would . . . ?"

"They'd have to be rabid to do that."

Eleanor laughed. "No. Those cats act all right, usually. But they stay away from people. Maybe tonight, with all the confusion, they felt threatened."

It was then that Charlie rode up on the buckskin. "I think Eleanor's right," she said softly. "Maybe tonight, with all the excitement, everyone running,

281

the lights . . ." She looked around at the circle of unbelieving cops. "If those feral females were protecting kittens, as wild as they are, they'd attack anything."

The men stared at her and shook their heads.

"Wild cats with kittens . . . I've read that cats in wild colonies birth their kittens all at one time. And that they will band together to protect them." Charlie shrugged. "Maybe Sears, running like that, got too near their lair." Turning Bucky, she headed back up toward the woods, her joy in retribution equally as fierce as that of the five little cats.

Her only disappointment was that, entering the woods where Ryan sat astride Redwing, she could tell her nothing of what had really happened, she could share none of the wonder with Ryan. Nor could she, she thought sadly, share this with Max.

Dulcie and Kit listened to the ambulance come screaming, they watched as the rescue vehicle slowed and made its way through the estate, watched the medics get to work on Cage Jones.

Ought to let him die, Dulcie thought as she fled for the squad car and Wilma. She glanced behind her once, to the broken wall where Kit sat with the three ferals, all of them smiling. Then heading down the road, Dulcie leaped in through the passenger-side window, into Wilma's arms, snuggling with her and purring so loudly that Wilma smiled.

But after a while, Dulcie said, "You're hurting, aren't you? I can tell, the way you sit. I bet you're all bruises." Dulcie quit purring and laid her ears back. "Hurting, and all alone, while Cage Jones is being patched up and pampered and covered with a warm blanket and given a sedative for pain."

Wilma laughed. "I'm not alone, I have you. I could use something for my headache. A whiskey and a rare steak would fix that."

"Makes my fur bristle to think of all the tax money the state of California is going to spend, making that man comfortable."

"That, Dulcie, is the way it works."

"Money that could be used to clean up our house, which he trashed. Why spend money on that scum?"

"Only in a dictatorship," Wilma said, "would Jones be left to die unattended."

"Maybe so, but that's all he deserves. Well, I'm only a cat. I don't have to think like a human. Maybe cats cut a sharper line between good and evil."

"Maybe," Wilma said, stroking Dulcie's ear. "Maybe cats should rule the world."

The traffic was light considering what this freeway usually handled. By nine forty-five the late work traffic had dispersed. Beyond Clyde's open window the worst heat had abated, and the night was warm and soft; the heavy Lexus SUV provided a ride so smooth and silent that a guy could go to sleep, Clyde thought. Not like the vintage cars he restored, that let you know their engines were running. The way he babied them, his engines always purred—but louder and with more character. Tonight, he could have used a bit of engine growl to keep him alert. He didn't even have Joe's acerbic conversation. In the open-top carrier on the seat beside him, the tomcat slept deeply, his soft snoring rivaling the smooth rhythm of the Lexus. It had been a long day for the tomcat.

From Dulcie's frantic phone call to the station saying that Wilma was gone, from the moment Joe raced to her house, and then their hasty trip to Gilroy; from Joe's sleuthing in the discount shops, to playing dumb for Detective Davis, all that on top of the village murders that the gray cat had fussed over for days, Joe was done in. In the car after supper, looking out from the carrier, his last words had been that he'd catch a few winks, a small restorative nap to recharge the batteries, then be rarin' to go again.

The calm evening drive would be peacefully restorative for Clyde, too, if he hadn't been strung tight with concern for Wilma and for Charlie. Not in the mood for local radio or a CD, his mind was filled with a succession of scenes that ran by him like clips from old movies. Wilma the first time he ever saw her, when he was eight and Wilma in her twenties, the day her family moved in next door to him, Wilma in jeans and an old T-shirt, her long blond hair tied back, working alongside the two men her folks had hired to unload the rented truck. The tall blonde carrying in big cardboard boxes marked "kitchen," "bathroom," "Wilma's room," all the rooms of the house. Clyde's mother had said they were probably paying the moving men by the hour, so everyone helped. Times were hard then for many families, certainly for his own folks.

A memory of Wilma playing baseball with the little kids, in the street, Wilma hitting a home run over the neighbor's garage; they never did find the ball. Wilma making Christmas cookies in the shape of cowboy hats and horses for him; she was always so beautiful, her blond hair so clean and bright. Long years later, when it turned gray, she didn't dye it like other women, she enjoyed that silver mane. Wilma taking him to San Francisco for the weekend when he was twelve, to the zoo, to Fisherman's Wharf for cracked crab and sourdough. And the trip through the San Francisco PD because she knew the chief.

And then when Charlie had first come to stay with Wilma after she'd quit her job in the city, packed up her belongings in cardboard boxes, driven down to start a new life in the village. First time he ever saw Charlie she was lying on her back underneath the van, changing the oil in her old blue van, swearing when oil dripped in her eye.

For a long time he'd thought he was in love with

Charlie. Maybe he had been. It had hurt bad when suddenly Charlie and Max were a pair, no hints, no working up to it that he'd noticed. They'd been training Clyde's unmanageable Great Dane puppies for him, up at Max's ranch, working the two on obedience where there was room for them to run.

It was a situation that neither Charlie nor Max had planned, Clyde was sure of that. It just happened. After Charlie told him, he'd never let either of them know how much it hurt.

But he'd gotten over the hurt, had seen how good they were together, had realized that in some strange way they belonged together, and he'd been glad for that, glad they'd found each other—and now Charlie was missing. Clyde felt his stomach twitch and churn, hurting for Max, felt tears of rage burn.

This wasn't coincidence. Did Cage Jones have both women? He understood how Jones's twisted mind might decide there were issues that warranted kidnapping Wilma, that was sick enough. But why Charlie? A hostage, additional pressure on Wilma? But for what? Both Max and Davis thought the hostage theory was valid, and that Wilma's kidnapping wasn't for retribution alone. Clyde slowed at the Prunedale cutoff, but then gave it the gas, deciding to keep straight on through Salinas, which was a safer route. In this light traffic, the trip should be less than an hour.

Not until he'd slowed going through Salinas did he hit the phone's button for Molena Point PD.

When the tomcat heard the ringing on the speakcr, he jerked awake and pushed up out of the carrier, stretching tall and yawning. Stretching again as he listened to Mabel Farthy's brief answer.

"It's Clyde; I'm just coming through Salinas, headed home."

Mabel's voice was bright with excitement. When she said, "Wilma's safe! Charlie's safe!" Clyde almost wrecked the car.

"They . . . Hold a minute," Mabel said, as she switched to another line. She was gone maybe twenty seconds, then cut back in. "The captain's there with them, Dallas on his way. Jones is in custody, headed for emergency, gunshot in the face. Hold . . ."

Another short delay, then she came back on. "Sears is in custody, too."

"Where?" Clyde snapped. *"Where are they?"*

"Don't go up there, Clyde. Half the force is up there on a narrow road, can hardly turn a car around, you'd only be in the way."

"Up *where?*"

"Hold again . . ." Over a minute this time. As Clyde sped up, west of Salinas, a truck passed him, cutting close. He let off the gas until there was again ample space between them. Mabel came back on. "Gotta go, three lines flashing . . ."

"If you don't tell me where, I'll keep calling, jam your lines."

Mabel sighed. "Pamillon ruins. Come on into the station, Clyde. They should be down here by the time you get back. They . . . Gotta go," she said, and cut off.

He turned the speaker off, grumbling. Beside him Joe sat erect in the carrier, staring at Clyde, then staring out the window, then back at Clyde, his look saying clearly, *Step on it. Get this heap moving.*

"I'm not wrecking us to get there faster. The excitement's over. They're safe. Thank your cat god or whatever, and keep your fur on."

"But they . . . Dulcie and Kit . . . She couldn't tell us what's happened to them. Where they are, Clyde? What if . . . ?"

"I'm not driving any faster. We'll be there in twenty minutes."

The tomcat began to wash his paws. "There was a time, you'd have floor-boarded this buggy."

"There was a time I'd kill a quart of whiskey, get up the next morning and hunker down on the back of the meanest bull in the string. I'm older now and smarter."

Silence.

"Does it occur to you that my more sensible driving keeps your worthless neck safe? Or does that not mean anything?"

Joe Grey sighed, curled up in his carrier, lifted a

disdainful paw, and pulled the top over. He remained thus secluded until Clyde bypassed Molena Point and, at around ten forty, turned up the hills, toward the Pamillon estate. Then Joe came alive, staring high above them at the scattered car lights, pricking up his ears at the wail of an ambulance that came zigzagging down, forcing them onto the shoulder. The minute they stopped, he crouched, to leap out.

29

The house was silent around Greeley, no sound from the dark upstairs rooms. Probably Lilly was asleep, but he waited a while longer to make sure—he'd waited long enough for her to stop knitting and go to bed, he guessed a few minutes more wouldn't matter. He'd conned her into letting him stay overnight, but she hadn't shown no hospitality; hadn't offered one of the upstairs rooms, which were likely bigger.

Well, this downstairs cubbyhole suited him better, farther away from her room. Having spotted the safe earlier as those two cats prowled the basement, he meant to start there. Finesse open the safe, and that was likely where he'd hit pay dirt. If that turned up empty, he'd have to plow through that whole damn basement full of junk, and maybe the rest of the house, too. He wondered if she was one of them early risers, up before daylight. He hoped to hell not. The time now was just after one.

He wondered if Lilly knew where the stash was. Not likely. He'd never known Cage to tell her nothing.

Well, he'd find them trinkets before she was out of bed, he had to. Find them, and be out of there before first light. And the old man's face brightened in an evil smile. Maybe he'd leave her a note, thank her all proper for her hospitality.

He had one more little drink, from the bottle he'd brought in his coat pocket, waited a few minutes more, listening to the silence of the house, then, swinging off the bed, he opened the door without a sound, and slipped out.

It was eleven thirty when Clyde pulled off the narrow dirt road onto the soft shoulder below the Pamillon estate, to make room for a police car coming down. Above them in the blackness, flashlight beams glanced across broken walls and twisted trees in a surreal tangle; they could see cops moving about, and half a dozen people gathered where the lights were concentrated and still. They passed the Greenlaws' car parked off to the side, just after the ambulance went by, and they stopped, Clyde grabbing Joe before he could drop out the window.

Lucinda looked out the driver's window at Clyde. "Wilma's up there somewhere. She's safe.

And the cats—we brought Kit and Dulcie, they would have taken off up the hills by themselves . . . I never could have locked them inside, any more than I could lock a person in. You know how hard-headed they are . . ."

"But so much has gone on," Pedric said. "We don't dare go up there and be in the way. All we can do is sit and worry. It's been mighty hard to hear gunshots, when the cats are up there . . ."

Joe Grey stood up again with his paws on the window. "They'll be among the rocks some-where, hiding," he said softly. He hoped to hell they were.

Lucinda reached across and touched Joe's cheek, then Clyde pulled away, heading on up, studying the turmoil of flashing torches, trying to make sense of what was happening. Joe rode with his paws on the door, ready to leap out.

Clyde gave him a look, and restrained the tomcat by the nape of the neck as he parked behind a row of squad cars. "Let's take a little time here." Killing the engine, his hand tightening on Joe, he sat scanning the blackness as Joe hissed, and pawed to get free. "Just stay still a minute and look," Clyde said. "There, on that nearest wall." Above them, surrounded by twisted oaks and picked out by the flashing lights, five cats prowled along the wall, were lost, and then silhouetted again against the night sky.

"Dulcie and Kit?" Clyde said.

Joe nodded, twitching his ears with relief.

"And the other three? The ferals?" Clyde said with amazement. "What other cats could it be? But they . . . those wild creatures wouldn't stay there, with all that's going on!"

"Let me loose, Clyde, before I hurt you. The excitement's over, someone's coming down with a prisoner. Let me go!" They watched a squad car approach. "Look, there in the back . . ."

The squad car passed them, two officers in front, a thin man in the back, behind the security screen, sitting rigidly, as if shackled.

"Eddie Sears?" Clyde said, smiling. "But where—"

"Let me out now." Joe twisted around, lifting an armored paw.

Clyde freed him and Joe was gone, leaping down, racing through the night to Dulcie.

Clyde looked after him, sighing. He remained in the car until three more police units passed, heading for the village. He watched two riders come out of the woods, breathing with relief when he saw Charlie. But where was Wilma? *Was* she safe? A cold hand touched his heart. Snatching the keys out of the ignition, leaving the windows down for Joe to get in, he hurried up the dark little road trying to look everywhere at once, watching for any eruption of violence. He was passing the last squad car when Wilma's voice spun him around. "Clyde?"

She opened the door and stepped out, and the next minutes were a tangle of hugs and both of them talking at once; but then suddenly Wilma was shivering and had to sit down again. Sliding into the backseat she moved over to make room for him. "I guess it's catching up with me." Her hands in his were cold.

"I'd guess it *would* catch up with you. What did Cage . . . ?"

Wilma looked at him. "It'll take a while to tell. Charlie shot him. She shot Cage. She's shaky, too. Pretty upset."

Clyde held her hands. "I guess this will take a lot of telling. Have you had anything to eat?"

"Coffee, and a sweet roll Brennan gave me. Before that . . . Breakfast in Gilroy around eight this morning."

"You need a rare steak and a drink."

"I'd kill for exactly that. But where's Joe! You went to Gilroy . . . Where's Joe Grey?"

Clyde pointed up to the wall, where six silhouettes lingered, two of them sitting close together, Joe's white markings bright in the flashing lights.

Wilma laughed, and relaxed. "Those other cats are the ferals. That, too, will take a bit of telling. You won't believe what they did. I hardly believe it."

"You need to eat. Tell me over dinner. You don't need to hang around? Let me go up and see Charlie, then we'll get you a steak."

• • •

From atop the broken wall the six cats watched Clyde step out of the squad car and head up to where Charlie stood, safe in Max's arms. Cotton was worn out; the white tom had never pursued the kind of madness he had tonight. Approaching the village, he'd been scared out of his skin, and he still wasn't sure why he'd done it. But now that it was over, he was proud he'd found the courage. Now, he wanted only to sleep.

Willow looked at Cotton stretched out limply along the stone wall, and wanted to snuggle down with him. Until tonight she hadn't known which of the two tomcats she favored; she thought she loved them both. But now she knew. Cotton was brave and staunch, Cotton made her heart race.

Coyote might be more dashing and handsome; certainly he would have no trouble finding his own lady. Maybe among their own ten, or maybe he'd slip back to their old clowder and lure away one of the discontented young queens. Coyote was her friend, they would always be close, but Cotton was her chosen.

Coyote watched her, and knew. He felt sad and a little lonely. Felt shy beside them now—but he was often shy. He looked away to the high boulders where the others of their small group were hidden, then lifted his nose to look south. Some miles away, their old clowder might still be ranging. He thought about the young queens there, and he wondered, and his green eyes lit up with speculation.

Joe Grey and Dulcie and Kit glanced sideways, watching the little scene, and they smiled. Dulcie and Kit felt sad for Coyote, but Joe knew the challenge that gripped the striped, long-eared tom. The hunt was everything, the hunt for game, the hunt for a mate. And, in Joe's life, the keen and wily search for human prey, the hunt that drove him ever more powerfully. He glanced at Dulcie and twitched a whisker. The hunt that absorbed them both, a hunt no other cat in the world but the three of them would understand or care about.

Looking up the hill, they watched Clyde hug Ryan and hold her for a moment as they talked, then Clyde sat down on a fragment of broken wall beside Charlie, who was wolfing down coffee and a sandwich. There was some laughter, a few tears, and a lot of hugging. But then at last Clyde rose and headed back for his car.

Wilma stepped out of the squad car and stood with Clyde beside the Lexus, looking up at the cats. At once, Dulcie tensed to leap down. With a lick at the ferals' ears and a nudge of noses, a special nuzzle for Cotton by way of a thank-you, Dulcie dropped from the wall and streaked for the road where Clyde and Wilma stood waiting. Joe followed close on her heels. Behind them Kit made her own farewells, then raced for Lucinda and Pedric.

Parting from the wild band was hard for Kit—but she'd already made her choice many months ago about how she wanted to live her life. In her deepest heart, she'd already left their wild ways—she did not want to change her own life, she wished only to see them sometimes, here among the ruins. If they remained here. With a wild band, who knew where they would go? She could only wish them well, wish them happiness. Nuzzling each cat, she spun around and raced away following Dulcie and Joe, her little cat heart hurting, but not regretting.

From the top floor of the Pamillon mansion, from the old nursery, Violet Sears had stood for some time watching the scene below. She felt sick when Charlie shot Cage. She knew he deserved it, but he was still her brother. She watched Eddie run, and saw those cats leap on him. That had shocked and deeply frightened her.

She had watched the police clean up Eddie's wounds and force him into a squad car, and she didn't know how she felt about his arrest. Maybe she felt nothing.

Eddie would be in jail now. For a little while, she was free of him. She shivered at the thought that she was on her own; she didn't know what to do about that. How would she live? Where would she live? There had always been someone else to decide about her life. Their parents. Lilly and

Cage. And then Eddie. She thought that woman, Wilma, wouldn't really help her. She stood watching the dark scene before her, shivering and afraid.

Watching Clyde step out of the squad car and head up in her direction, Charlie had suddenly and inexplicably found herself crying. Pressing her face into Max's shoulder, when he turned back to her after briefing Brennan and a handful of other officers, she felt weak and shaky—but she was safe now, safe in Max's arms. He held her away from him and wiped her tears. She looked up at him, ashamed of her weakness, embarrassed at crying in front of his men. He handed her a paper bag.

"Hunger'll take all the starch out. Here's Brennan's lunch. Roast beef and coffee and you'll be yourself again."

"I can't take his lunch, he . . ." Knowing how Brennan loved his meals made her tear up all over again.

Max laughed. "He kept one sandwich of the three, and a slice of cherry pie. He gave his coffee roll to Wilma."

Charlie glanced across at Brennan and blew him a kiss. The portly officer looked embarrassed, grinned at her, and turned away. She had sat down on the remnants of a tumbled stone wall and was wolfing down the second of the sandwiches and slurping hot coffee, nearly scalding her mouth, when Clyde sat down beside her.

"Glad you got out of that."

She nodded, her mouth full.

Clyde laughed. "Wilma's pretty hungry, too. I'm taking her for a steak. Want to come?"

She swallowed. "Going to ride back with Max, take the horses back. I think Ryan's going with Dallas, her truck is at our place."

He nodded. "How did the snitch know where you were?" he said softly. "She called Max, but how did she know?"

"The white cat, Clyde. That feral cat. He . . . Against all odds, that wild little animal went down into the village. Went to Kit for help. Dulcie was there at the Greenlaws' with Kit, and it was Dulcie who called."

Clyde shook his head. "Seems impossible."

"But then," she said, "the other two ferals . . . all three of them and Dulcie and Kit chewed my ropes. They had me almost loose when Wilma found me." She swallowed the last of the sandwich, washed it down with more coffee. "And there's a lot that we don't know yet, that Dulcie and Kit will tell us. But you . . . You and Joe . . ."

"Same thing," Clyde said, grinning. "A lot to tell. Too much for now, Wilma's starving." He hugged her and rose, stood a moment with his hand on her shoulder. "She's pretty upset that Jones dragged you into whatever he wanted from her."

"She doesn't know what he wanted?"

"Not a clue." He leaned down to hug her again. "Have a good ride home."

She watched him stop to talk with Ryan and make a date with her for the next night, then head down to fetch Wilma.

"Where'd the sandwiches go?" Max said, coming to join her, looking at the wadded-up paper bag. "I was gone no more than three minutes."

Charlie laughed.

"That hold you until we get home? Take about an hour. You've had a long day, you feel up to the ride?"

"Oh *yes*. Can you do that, can you leave, with . . . ?"

"Dallas is here. Prisoners are secured. Wilma's safe, with Clyde. We'll take her statement in the morning. Right now, I think it's time for me to take your statement."

Flushing, she moved away to the horses. Leaving Max to wrap up a few details, she stood with Ryan, leaning against her mare. "You found me gone, and you called Max."

Ryan nodded and put her arm around her.

Charlie said, "Guess I owe you supper."

"Guess you do," Ryan said. "If you two take the horses back, I'll never see that potato salad and roast beef you had laid out."

"Guess I can make more potato salad," Charlie said, hugging her back, and as Max turned to join them, she tightened Redwing's cinch and mounted up.

30

It was midnight when the old man descended to the basement and, working silently, moved the piled boxes out of the closet, shoving them in among the rest of the detritus that crowded the concrete room. He guessed Lilly had gotten nervous about that safe, so visible and all. The fact that it was covered up told him there was something to be nervous *about.*

Kneeling over the locked metal box he tried to remove it from the closet, but it was sunk deep in the floor. Probably bolted, the bolts removable only from inside, once it was open. When he couldn't budge it, he took from his pocket a small, rechargeable electric drill and a miniature periscope, a tiny light on a long, thin, flexible neck, an eyepiece at the end.

The sound of the drill wasn't loud. But twice he stopped to listen to the house above him, just in case Lilly woke and started down. The big old house remained silent, and within minutes the drill had gone through the thick metal lid, leaving a quarter-inch hole into which he slid the periscope.

Slowly he turned the safe's dial, watching through the periscope as the plates moved, slowly working out the combination until, after maybe twenty minutes, he was able to apply that information and lift the heavy lid.

Staring down into the metal box, Greeley was very still. His expression didn't change. An observer could have read nothing on the face of the grizzled old man. He knelt there in his wrinkled clothes and old worn shoes, shaggy gray hair, three days' growth of stubble, looking down blankly into the empty safe. Only slowly did his rage burn to the surface, like a flame that started deep inside a building, belatedly flickering and blooming until it blazed red and violent through the walls.

Rage. Disbelief. A deep and painful disappointment. He knelt there a long time, looking. At last he closed the safe again, spun the dial, and rose. He put back the boxes on top as they had been, shut the closet door, and turned resolutely to search the rest of the basement, but without much hope.

Knowing Cage, he limited his survey to places that would be relatively fireproof, because Cage had once lost a nice haul in a fire, in an old, tinder-dry apartment. He investigated a patched area of concrete where another safe might be sunk, but could find no way into it. Carefully he examined the concrete walls, the concrete floor beneath the stairs. He looked over the stacked boxes and old bits of furniture, but they were all tinder, not what Cage would choose. At last he turned away, discouraged, and left the basement, moving up the wooden stairs in his stockinged feet just as he had come down.

Back in his room, shutting the door silently behind him, he sat down on the bed, put his feet up on the spread, poured a good jolt of whiskey into the plastic glass he'd taken from the bathroom, and drank it down. You could bet that bitch parole officer had been here, just like Cage must've thought. Her and her partner, her and that hard-nosed Bennett—served him right coming in here and stealing, served him right he got shot.

He thought about them cats. That one cat that lived with the Getz woman. Had them cats spied on Cage, watched as he opened the safe and then told her? And she'd waltzed right in here, her and Bennett, and cleaned it out? With *them* cats, anything was possible.

It did not occur to Greeley that Wilma and Mandell Bennett had made that official search of the Jones house with the DEA agents some years before tabby Dulcie had come to live with her. In fact, before Dulcie was born. Sitting on the bed finishing the whiskey, the old man began to feel trapped, driven into a corner by an unfair and twisted fate. He'd been counting on that gold. Not so much because he needed it; he had already cashed out half his own share, before this trip, more than enough for all the cars and whiskey, and even women, he could handle in what remained of his lifetime; and he didn't care about fancy houses and clothes, he cared only about his own pleasure. No, it wasn't that he needed Cage's half of the haul. He wanted it purely because he'd set his mind on it—because this theft had been the big one. The one spectacular prize before he retired, before he kicked back and enjoyed life. This job was big enough to have the entire Panamanian government panicked into closing its borders, if they'd knowed about it.

That was the beauty of this heist. The Guardia didn't know, not a clue. A theft from thieves didn't get a lot of police action. If those guys he and Cage'd stole from had run to the Guardia, *they* were the ones who'd be in the *carcel*.

And now, that bitch parole officer had cheated him out of every penny.

Sure as hell no one else had known about the stash. Cage wouldn't of told anyone, he was too closemouthed. Greeley wondered if he'd told Eddie Sears, but Cage never had trusted him. Cage's sister Violet, she didn't count for nothing, skinny little thing afraid of her own shadow. Ditto Lilly Jones. Lilly didn't have the imagination or the balls to think of stealing anything. The very idea of cracking a safe would give the old girl a sick headache.

No, it was that Getz woman. Fancy stone house and new car. Not hardly, on her federal retirement. Likely socked the rest of the loot away in some kind of securities or some little-old-lady annuity, safe and untouchable.

But right now he had to search the rest of the house. Cage *could* have hidden the stash somewhere else, and he'd be a friggin' fool to miss it. Slipping out of the room to toss the main floor, he used a little penlight that wasn't much. A nuisance searching in the dark. He went through the refrigerator-freezer, which might be impervious to fire but was the first place a burglar would look. He was turning out the living room, checking the electrical plugs for tampering, when he heard a noise at the front door. The lock clicked, the knob turned, and as the door opened Greeley drew back behind the couch, crouching down as sneaky and undignified as them damned spying cats.

"I still have no idea what Cage was after," Wilma said, settling back into the leather booth, sipping her whiskey and water, gazing into the fire that Moreno's Bar and Grille kept blazing even in warm weather. The cozy restaurant was nearly empty at this hour. A rare steak was on the way, with fries and onion rings. "Was he dumb enough to hide stolen stocks or securities there in the house? There's no theft like that in his record, but that doesn't mean much. Who knows what Cage might have pulled off that was never connected to him."

Clyde frowned. "Stocks or securities that could

be traced? Whatever it was, it had to be pretty valuable to leave it there all those years while he was in prison."

"Or," Wilma said, speculating, "maybe something he thought would increase in value? I wonder if he has that much foresight."

"Or," Clyde said, shaking his head, "he meant to hide it until the law forgot about it?"

Wilma laughed. "Cage won't be around that long. If it's of interest to Treasury agents, they don't forget." She yawned, beginning to relax, feeling the aches and tension subside. The cozy retreat, and Clyde's company and the promised steak, had made her feel almost normal again. That, and the fact that Dulcie and Joe Grey were tucked up on the leather bench beside her, Joe with his head on her lap, treating her to a rare show of affection. She was greatly touched that the tomcat had put aside his macho disdain of cuddling.

Clyde made a pattern of rings on the table with his glass. "What will happen to Violet? I guess she's glad Eddie's in jail. Or she should be."

"I don't know that she's glad. I half-expect she'll go back to him when he gets out, even years down the road." The subject of Violet tired her. "I don't have much patience for a woman who won't help herself, and I don't think she plans to do that."

Clyde shook his head. "Maybe she'll change."

"If she has any sense, she'll get out of Molena Point and go where Eddie won't find her, go while she has the chance. I told her I'd help her." She stroked Dulcie, then looked up at Clyde. "At least Mandell is mending."

On their way down from the ruins, she had called the San Francisco hospital on Clyde's cell phone and had been able to speak with Mandell. He was out of intensive care and wanted to get into physical rehab as soon as possible. He said that when he got his hands on Cage Jones, he planned to be in top form.

"I'll be right beside you," Wilma had told him. "Have you been able to figure out what Jones thinks we took?"

"Nothing my secretary could find in his early files. She went through everything. But those years he was in Central America, who knows what he did down there? Didn't you and Cage go to school with some guy who later moved down to Panama? A diver for the Panama Canal?"

"Greeley Urzey. Greeley was older, but it was a small school. When Cage grew up, he and Greeley ran around together for a while. They were in Panama at the same time."

Mandell had been silent for a few moments, then, "Something I read, some years back. I keep thinking about it, but can't bring it clear. Be glad when I'm off this pain killer and I can get my mind straight."

"About crimes down there, some unsolved crime?"

"Seems like something spectacular. How would I forget that?"

"Let me do some checking. I'll run it by Max."

Talking with Bennett, she'd had the speaker on. Both cats, when they talked about Greeley and Cage, had been glued to the phone. But when she'd said good night to Mandell and hung up, she had studied their two sleek little faces, Dulcie's green eyes and Joe's yellow eyes as innocent as the gazes of kittens, the two cats looking back at her blandly and saying nothing.

Mandell had described how Cage had shot him, how he'd gone into the office as he often did on weekend mornings to catch up on paperwork, worked from seven until midmorning, then had gone out for a good breakfast. When he stepped out of the courthouse elevator in the parking garage, checking around him as he always did, he felt the impact a second before he heard the shot. He took a second shot in the shoulder and heard a car speed away, glimpsed Cage's face as the car swung up the ramp. He had tried to run after it, then to use his cell phone, then he must have blacked out, which embarrassed him; he could remember nothing more.

"Woke up in the ambulance," Mandell had said, "thinking strange thoughts . . . about my Cherokee ancestors who I never knew. I could see them marching as prisoners across the continent into that dry hot land they hated. Woke up hot and parched, thinking I was marching . . . Strange," he said, "what the human mind will do."

Wilma thought of Mandell again after dinner, when Clyde dropped her and Dulcie off at home, thought that it would take Mandell time to recover, that he would be pretty laid up for a while, and no one to do things for him in his little bachelor apartment.

Clyde insisted on going through the house with her. The trashed rooms were heartbreaking, daunting. She tried to put that out of her thoughts; she'd clean up tomorrow. The first thing she did was go to her car, unlock the glove compartment, and retrieve her .38, which was locked there, just as she'd left it.

"It would be nice," Clyde said, "if you'd sleep with that where you can reach it. And," he said, "if you would consider putting a lock on the bedroom door, to narrow the odds of someone walking in on you. Dulcie can't play watch cat all night." He stroked Dulcie gently. "She stands guard all night, she'll never get her beauty sleep."

Wilma laughed and gave him a hug. "I'll keep it close, and I'll call a locksmith in the morning." And within half an hour of Clyde's leaving, she and Dulcie were tucked up in bed, a chair propped under the doorknob, which at least would make some noise if someone came in. She didn't see how it would be needed, now that Cage was in the hospital, and Eddie in custody, but she'd promised

Clyde. She did straighten up the bedroom. Then, stretched out in bed between smooth sheets, she relished the clean feeling from her shower, the feel of Dulcie snuggled warm beside her, extravagantly purring, and the thick stone walls of her own house secure around her.

31

There was no need now for stealth on the dark bridle trail; the two riders headed home using their torches to throw wide beams of cheering light among the trees that crowded their passage, bright paths that delineated tire marks ahead, broken by the hoofprints of their horses and the paw prints of the big Weimaraner. On her sorrel mare, Charlie welcomed the quiet, empty night around them as she tried to get centered again, after seeing Cage Jones's bloodied face when she shot him, the explosion of bone and blood, seeing Cage twist and fall. Her mind and spirit were sick with that moment, with the shock of shooting a man.

But the alternative could have been her own death, and Max, too.

"Takes a while," Max said, watching her, riding close and putting his arm around her.

"Does anyone really get over it?"

"You live with it. Better than not stopping him."

"I know. But it's hard to get used to. Do you

remember, when I read C. S. Lewis aloud, where a damned soul wouldn't change itself, so it went out like a snuffed candle? Just vanished? And someone, maybe an angel, said, 'What would the alternative have been?'"

"I remember that."

"I keep seeing Jones's face, all bloody. And a moment before, when he raised his gun at me, so vicious and filled with hate." She looked at Max. "The devil's face, it seemed to me," she said, looking at him shyly.

"That's not crazy," he said softly. "Evil is evil, Charlie."

She leaned into Max, their legs bumping against each other, the horses fussing because they were forced too close together. There had been moments this evening when she'd wondered if they would ever be together again, if she would ever see Max again. Tonight, when she'd thought that Cage had killed Wilma, when she'd thought that they would both be dead by morning, hope had nearly deserted her.

She sat up straight, looking away through the trees where the lights of the ranch shone, welcoming them home, and she squeezed Max's hand. And as they headed down the last hill through the woods, loud barking greeted them and the three dogs came running—their own two unruly half Great Danes, and Rock, dancing around the horses. Beside the house, Ryan's red truck stood parked beside a squad car. The air was filled with the aroma of something spicy cooking.

The door opened, spilling light from the kitchen, and Ryan stepped out, the smell of simmering chili filling the night. Dallas came out behind her and crossed the yard to help with the horses. That, too, was a rare treat, that Dallas would rub the horses down, give them a flake of hay and extra grain, see that they, too, were comfortable. Handing her reins to Dallas, she slid gratefully from the saddle, made her way tiredly across the yard beside Max, and went into their bright house. They were home, safe and together.

In the upstairs master suite of Clyde Damen's house, all the windows were open, the predawn breeze blowing through smelling of the sea, cooling the bedroom and study. Beneath the high rafters, in the king-size bed, Clyde slept sprawled across the sheets, clad only in Jockey shorts, snoring. The gray tomcat slept close against Clyde's shoulder, on his back, his four paws in the air, much as he had slept when he was a kitten. He snored, twitching in his sleep. He woke at dawn still half worn out from dreaming, irritable and hungry. He nudged Clyde, his cold, insistent nose jerking Clyde from sleep. Clyde rolled over, glaring. Then, turning, he stared incredulously at the bedside clock.

"It's five o'clock. Five A.M.! Do you realize—"

"It's Monday. You going to work?"

"Six," Clyde said, rolling over. "You know what time the alarm rings. Go back to sleep. If you can't sleep, go up on the roof. Wake up the neighbors. Leave me alone."

"I'm hungry. Weak with hunger."

"You are not weak with hunger. You ate half my steak last night and nearly an entire order of fries. I'm surprised you didn't throw it all up in the middle of the bed. If you—"

"Weak," Joe repeated. "The excitement . . ." He looked hard at Clyde. "Stress. That kind of thing is really stressful for a cat, all that shooting. Stress can kill a cat. I feel—"

"You are not going to die of stress. Or of starvation. You might die of strangulation if you don't shut up. Your problem is, you're turning into a first-class pig. If you think you're hungry, go get some kibble. Paw open the cupboard, you've done it enough times. And use a little consideration, don't spill kibble all over the floor."

Joe didn't want kibble. He wanted something hot and freshly cooked. He wanted comfort food, something to warm his little cat heart and soothe his frayed nerves. He wanted restorative fat and cholesterol, a real tomcat breakfast, the kind only Clyde could make. Letting himself go limp on the pillow, paws drooping, he looked up at Clyde pitifully.

For an instant Clyde's dark eyes widened in a

312

flash of concern, but then he caught himself. Glaring, he turned over and pulled the pillow over his head. Joe sighed. Some woman could give Clyde an equally pitiful look and he'd fall all over himself, but when a poor little cat tried it, nothing. Joe lay, sighing his last, until he almost believed that he was fainting away—and finally his perseverance did the trick; Clyde sat up scowling at the clock, glared at Joe, muttered something unnecessarily rude, and swung out of bed. "Who can sleep after that performance? What do you want for breakfast!"

Joe considered several menu options while Clyde retreated to the master bath and turned on the shower. "Damn cat! Damn rotten spoiled tomcat!"

Grinning, Joe padded down the stairs, slipped out through his cat door, and stood looking up and down the street. When he saw no neighbors about, and no one looking out a window, he took the morning paper in his teeth and hauled it through his cat door. Dragged it through to the kitchen and with some difficulty wrestled it up onto the kitchen table. The paper was getting heavier every day. If they didn't solicit all that unnecessary advertising to bulk it up . . . Unfolding it as he waited for Clyde, he scanned the front page.

There was nothing about Wilma's or Charlie's kidnapping, or about the arrest of Cage Jones. Max and Dallas had been adept, indeed, at keeping things quiet. There were still a lot of loose ends in this case, and it didn't need to go public yet.

The front page covered the third break-in murder, though, recapping how Peggy Milner had been killed in her kitchen. How a neighbor had seen her in there, but when she went to Peggy's door, and knocked and called out to her and Peggy didn't answer, the neighbor had called 911. Peggy had been fixing a late supper for one, as her husband was working late. She had been stabbed. The neighbor said the sight sickened her. There were, so far, no other witnesses. The article followed up with recaps of the Linda Tucker and Elaine Keating killings, pointing out similarities between the three incidents. The byline on the article said "Jim Barker."

Barker was a tall, neatly groomed, sensible guy with three little girls and a keen sympathy for the problems the police faced when information was aired too soon. He covered the police blotter with common sense and real interest, not with a chip on his shoulder like some egocentric newsmen. Joe remembered some very snide articles by other reporters questioning the conduct of Max's officers, and, more than once, claiming it would be foolish to spend city money on drug dogs and working police dogs, for whom Joe had the highest respect.

He wondered sometimes if Molena Point would ever get a police dog. That would be a fine addition to the force—except that a canine officer could sure destroy Joe's rapport with the law, could mess up his investigations and totally destroy his clandestine surveillance. A trained evidence dog would pick up the faintest cat scent at a crime scene, and might single him or Dulcie or Kit out as having been there, might come down really hard on them. And a dog would know the minute a cat entered the PD, would know where they were, under which desk, behind which chair. No, dogs would be a problem in Harper's department. Anywhere else, they'd be an asset.

Clyde came down the stairs and turned on the coffeepot. "And what is your royal highness's pleasure this morning?" Rudely, he picked Joe up from atop the front page. "Do you have to hog the entire paper?" Setting Joe on his own side of the table, Clyde laid out a place mat and silverware for himself. "Omelet? What do you want in it? Ham? Bacon? Mushrooms? Cheese?"

"That would be fine."

"That *what* would be fine?"

"What you just said. You can hold the mushrooms if you want, if you're really—"

Clyde sighed and jerked open the refrigerator.

"That door gasket isn't going to last another six months if you—"

"Can it, Joe. I haven't had a lot of sleep."

Joe yawned in Clyde's face to demonstrate that he had missed just as much sleep.

"You slept all the way home," Clyde said, cracking eggs into a bowl.

"I merely had my eyes closed. I was thinking." The tomcat returned to the front page, perusing the article that pointed out the similarities among the three murders. It left out only those sensitive facts that Harper would not have wanted published, such as the identification of fingerprints and the list of suspects—of which, Joe knew, there were few. Jim Barker said that at this point the police were looking at no single burglary suspect who might be involved in all three cases. The paper went on to say, in a sidebar, that the Molena Point police kept a current list of the names and addresses of all calls for domestic disturbance or abuse.

An accompanying human-interest article at the bottom of the page dealt with the plight of abused women. It quoted a psychologist's assessment of the fears of such women, and their reluctance to make a fresh start. It suggested steps they might take to separate themselves from their abusers if they chose to do so, including agency, shelter, and private foundation names and phone numbers. Jim Barker had done an admirable job for Max in helping to alert other women before it was too late. He had, at the same time, as was surely Harper's intent, alerted other possible wife killers that the department was aware of their brutal tendencies.

As Clyde dished up their omelets, Joe pushed the

paper around, facing Clyde's plate. Far be it from him to hog the morning news. Twitching an ear at Clyde by way of thanks for an elegant omelet, he glanced down at Rube's empty place on the floor, as he had done every morning since they'd had to put the old Lab down. And, as he did every morning, before he started to eat he said a little cat prayer for Rube that he supposed was just as valid for dogs.

Then he set to on the omelet, as ravenous as if he couldn't remember his last meal. He ate slurping and enjoying, then at last gave his whiskers and paws a hasty wash, another flick of the ears for Clyde, and he was off—up the stairs, onto Clyde's desk, up onto the rafter and out through his rooftop cat door. He paused in his tower for a hasty drink where the water was cool from sitting out all night; then he was out his tower window and across the roofs heading for Molena Point PD.

32

Following the smell of sugar doughnuts, Joe padded silently into Molena Point PD on the heels of Mabel Farthy, who was carrying a bakery box. Behind the dispatch counter, a thin, redheaded young officer Joe didn't know looked over at the tomcat and raised an eyebrow.

"It's all right," Mabel told him. "The cat has

clearance." The officer laughed and rose to leave, going off shift, turning the electronic domain back to Mabel. He reached out tentatively to pet Joe, stood stroking him as he filled Mabel in on late night's events.

Last night's excitement had all happened on Mabel's eight-to-twelve shift. The after-midnight calls had been tamer: a few drunks, a loud teenage party, and two domestic disturbances that made Joe prick up his ears, though both had been settled peaceably. When the officer left, Mabel sorted through the faxes, yawning. Her dyed blond hair wasn't quite as neat as usual, and her uniform was a little mussed. She hadn't had much sleep, having been on duty last night and then doubling back this morning. She yawned again, came out from behind the counter, and went down the hall with the doughnut box. Joe could hear her filling the big coffee urn. From the counter, he watched her move on to Max's office, heard her fill his smaller coffeepot from the bottle of water on the credenza, and the special brand of coffee he liked. Outside the glass front door, cars were pulling into the parking area that the PD shared with the courthouse offices. Soon, among other arriving officers, Harper and Dallas came in, heading down the hall, and turned into Max's office.

Dropping soundlessly off the counter, Joe slipped along behind them and inside, under the credenza. Maybe they knew he was there, maybe they didn't. Harper poured two mugs of freshly brewed coffee, handed one to Garza, and sat down at his desk. He turned on the computer, then opened the three hard-copy files that lay on his blotter. Garza sat down on the leather couch and removed a clipboard and file from his briefcase. Beneath the credenza, on the Oriental rug, Joe curled up, so full of omelet he didn't even hunger for a doughnut.

The third murder, having occurred last evening, just before Max learned that Charlie was missing, hadn't received much of the chief's attention. Among the papers Dallas took from his briefcase was a copy of the coroner's report on Peggy Milner.

"It was the next-door neighbors," Dallas said, "the Barbers, who made the call." He rose to refill their coffee mugs. "Bern says the knife we found didn't kill her, though very likely it was used on her. Apparently, no prints, it was wiped clean. I sent it to the lab to see what they can do. There are flecks of dried blood between the blade and the handle. Bern says a wider, heavier weapon killed her, struck her in the throat."

Max made a sound of disgust. Beneath the credenza, Joe shivered. The older he got and the more he learned about humans, the better he liked his own feline cousins.

"Milner is an insurance representative," Dallas said. "Got home late, said he'd had three evening appointments. I took the information off his client files and time sheet, and we've talked with two of the three. Third guy, a builder, is up the coast this morning picking up some plumbing, should be on his way home by now. The first two check out okay. The builder was Milner's first appointment last night, just about the time his wife was killed.

"Bern thinks the killer wore leather gloves; he found flecks of something like leather in the wound, maybe from an edge of rough-cut leather. Waiting for the lab on that." Dallas sipped his coffee. "Again, like the other two cases, no sign of a break-in. The front door was unlocked. Milner said she often forgot to lock it." Dallas shook his head. "No sensible woman, in a house alone, leaves the door unlocked."

"Unless she's expecting company."

Dallas nodded. "There's no indication, so far, that she had an outside interest."

"Nothing from the Milners' other neighbors?"

"Only the Barbers. They can see the Milner kitchen window from their kitchen. Mrs. Barber saw Peggy in there preparing her dinner. Ten minutes later Mrs. Barber was watching TV, and when she saw there was a movie on that Peggy liked, she phoned her.

"There was no answer. She tried again in a few minutes, tried three times. The light was still on in the kitchen, but now the blind had been pulled. She said it was unlike Peggy, not to answer. Told her husband she was going over to see what was wrong. He said not to do that, told her to call 911. She told him that was silly, and she went on over. Walked in the unlocked front door, found Peggy on the kitchen floor, bleeding. Ran home, and her husband made the call."

Dallas looked down beneath the credenza where Joe Grey lay curled up pretending to sleep. "You might as well come out of there, tomcat, make yourself at home." He looked up at Max. "Cat's staying out of the way this morning. Funny, he almost seems to know when things are real busy."

Joe smiled to himself, rolled over beneath the credenza, and appeared to go back to sleep.

"Thanks for last night," Max said, "for putting the horses up and fixing supper with Ryan. You two could have stayed and eaten with us."

Dallas laughed. "We ate half the chili while we were putting it together. You two needed time alone."

"Charlie wasn't too worn out to spoil her appetite. She ate almost that whole pot, and half a dozen tortillas."

Dallas smiled. "I have to admit, my half-Irish niece makes pretty good Mexican soul food."

"Charlie drank one beer with supper, fell into bed. I'd hardly put out the light and she was gone, snoring in my arms." He looked a minute at Dallas. "That dog, last night. I never saw an untrained dog track like that. He went wild when he saw Charlie down there; Ryan had put my lariat on him, and he was jerking and fighting to get to Charlie."

"Ryan and I talked about that. I think Rock's worth training."

"Could be. He had a bad start in life, but he has plenty of potential. What about the neighbors on the other side of the Milners'? Anything there?"

"No one home. That's a second residence. Karen and James Blean. Gone most of the time. Peggy Milner takes—took—care of their yard and watered it for them, and she had a key to their garage."

Max looked at Dallas with interest.

"I got the key from Milner last night, took a look. Not much in there, a few garden tools, a small workbench, a new roll of hose. No cupboards, nowhere to hide a weapon."

Max nodded.

"No attic access. Some paint cans stacked under the workbench, and one of the cans had been opened recently. I asked Milner about it. He said his wife had borrowed a bit of white paint to touch up a scratch on their kitchen wall; he showed me where.

"There was no paintbrush. Milner said she'd probably taken a little on a tissue, then flushed it, that she didn't like to clean paintbrushes. Looks like it could have been dabbed on with a tissue."

A bit of paint surely amounted to nothing, had nothing to do with the murder, but the officers' interest brought Joe alert. Maybe he'd have a look, himself, at that garage.

"I left the door unlocked, put one of our locks on it, in case we want in again."

The tomcat, rising, yawning as if he'd had enough of their boring voices, sauntered away into the hall; he slipped out of the PD on the heels of a sleazy attorney with a beard and a battered brief-case, some crook's mouthpiece; he headed for the Milner house, making no attempt to gather his two accomplices. Dulcie would be snug at home with Wilma; and Kit needed Lucinda and Pedric just now. As bold and brash as the tortoiseshell was, she was tender inside and easily upset by the rough treatment of those she loved.

It was three in the morning when Greeley, crouched down behind Lilly's sofa, listened to the front door open, and close, and a woman's soft step head for the kitchen. Too light a step for Lilly, and anyway, she ought to be asleep upstairs. He stayed where he was when the light went on in the kitchen.

He had tossed most of the main floor, had been deciding whether to slip on upstairs when he'd heard the key in the door. He hated to give up the search now. The thought of walking away from that kind of money galled him, even if he did have that much already salted away. It had been tire-some, the effort it took to open three puny checking accounts, getting fake social security numbers and drivers' licenses, just so he qualified for three safe-deposit boxes. But he didn't trust nowhere else short of a bank box, nowhere the IRS wouldn't come nosing, before he got the cash out of the country.

Two million in Mexico'd buy all he ever wanted, a little place down the coast where it was warm and the living was easy—and buy a knife in your back in a damn minute, too, if anyone knew what you had. And, the way customs was now, it would be hard to get that kind of money down across the border. Feds in your way, no matter what you did.

He could smell coffee from the kitchen, and toast. Who the hell could this be? She had a key, he'd heard it in the lock. Rising from behind the couch, he slipped down the hall, stopping in the shadows. She hadn't heard him. She was sitting at the table, a cup in her hand. Young and skinny and pale as a ghost.

"Violet?"

She stared up at him, frightened.

"You're Violet?" He went on in, sat down across from her. He'd known her when she was a teenager, just as fleshless and bony then. Hadn't seen her since she'd married Eddie Sears, still in her teens—likely to escape living with Lilly and Cage. Probably it wasn't no better with Eddie.

Had she been here last night, when he'd searched the basement? Might she have watched him?

Woman looked like she could slip around silent as a ghost and you'd never know she was there. He looked at her for a long time. She pointed to the coffeepot.

"There's plenty," she said softly. "I thought Lilly might be up."

"I didn't know you were living here."

"I'm not. Well, maybe I am now. From this morning. Is Lilly still asleep?" She didn't seem interested in who he was. Maybe she knew, though, maybe she remembered him from years back. But she sure didn't seem interested in what he was doing there, now.

"I expect she's still asleep," he said. "She let me have a room last night; the motels was all full." He rose and poured a cup of coffee. Perching on the edge of his chair, he blew on it and drank it quickly. He wanted to ask what she was doing there; she made him real uneasy. But then, later, when he found out Eddie was in jail, and Cage in the hospital, he guessed she'd had nowhere else to go.

Nervously finishing his coffee, he rose again. "Have to be getting on. Tell Lilly thank you." He went to get his jacket, and within minutes was relieved to be out the front door and away.

Checking into the Seaview Bed and Breakfast, he couldn't get the rate down even on a Monday morning. Whole damn village was the same, take all a man's money and ask for more. Now, with

Cage in the hospital, he didn't want to leave Molena Point. He didn't give a damn if Cage cashed it in, but no one except Cage could tell him where the stash had been, and who else might have taken it, if Wilma hadn't. Only thing he could do was wait till Cage got out of the hospital and away from that police guard—if he didn't die—and then follow him when he went looking.

One thing sure, Cage'd come out of that hospital mean as snakes with his face all shot up, the kind of mean that he'd kill you if you sneezed wrong. And, Greeley thought, smiling, that Charlie Harper who'd shot him, she'd be smart to get out of town before Cage found her.

33

The house next door to where Peggy Milner was murdered was a charmingly remodeled cottage that had only recently been a shack with an uncertain future. In this village where folks would pay a million for a teardown, the expense of such a renovation was not unusual. The disturbance of the remodeling had sent droves of mice out into the neighborhood, and Joe and Dulcie and Kit had had their share.

The resulting small, cream-toned retreat was now far more appealing than the two-story gray box that loomed beside it, where Peggy Milner had drawn her last breath. The garden had been redesigned to feature low-maintenance lavender and Mexican sage. A narrow side yard was enclosed by a woven-wire fence four feet high topped with a two-by-four crosspiece, meant to confine the Bleans' small terrier when they were in residence. The yard within stunk sharply of dog. Joe, coming up the block, had already endured the sour stink of the neighbors' garbage cans clustered on the street along with plastic recycling boxes of newspapers and cans and bottles, a miasma of rotten food, wet baby diapers, cleaning liquids, and wet paint.

He had circled the Milner house, making sure there wasn't a uniform or two standing guard, had strolled casually beneath the yellow crime tape, looking up at the windows. When he saw no movement within, he moved on to the Blean house. He circled it, too, though he wasn't interested in getting inside. It was the garage Joe wanted, where Peggy Milner and her husband had had key access.

Leaping to the top of the low fence pondering possible methods of entry, Joe gave a whiskery grin. Right there in the dog yard was just what the tomcat wanted: a small doggy door installed next to the narrow, pedestrian door. Smiling, he had dropped down into the dog yard when he realized that the little door would likely be blocked from inside by one of those sliding panels that people installed when they planned to be away, to prevent the entry of raccoons or skunks—or inquisitive tomcats.

He nosed at the plastic flap, expecting it to stop against a hard surface. Wondering if he could claw that sliding panel to the top of its metal tracks and push in under it, he nearly fell through when the flap gave freely. Quick as a flash, he slipped inside.

The Bleans' garage was nearly empty. It was light and pristine, the white walls finished as nicely as the inside of a house. He caught the scent of fresh paint, from the can that Peggy Milner had recently opened. The space was lit by a long row of high windows looking out on the dog yard. Beneath these stood a small white workbench. No tools hung on the wall behind it. No gardening tools adorned the other walls, and there were none of those tall storage cabinets that people installed to hide clutter. He found, when he leaped atop the workbench, a neat row of small garden implements laid out beside a rolled-up hose that was still in its package. He dropped down again to consider the shelf underneath.

The paint smell came from there, from one of a row of gallon cans, each featuring its own hand-written label indicating living room, kitchen, master bath, and so on. Talk about neatniks. Clyde could take a lesson here. He could see where one can had been opened, a tiny line of paint still glistening at its edge, from where Peggy had touched up her own wall. Dropping off the low shelf, he circled the garage, not sure what he expected to find. The fact that Peggy Milner's husband had had access to this private and uninhabited space, out of sight of the neighbors, interested Joe just as it had interested Harper and Garza.

Dallas had found nothing, but Dallas didn't have a cat's keen sense of smell. And as Joe circled, the scent of paint followed him, as if it was not all coming from the can beneath the workbench.

The smell grew stronger near the door that would open into the house. And stronger, still, when he padded toward the corner, following a foot-high, four-inch-wide, oversize baseboard that ran the length of that one wall. He remembered, from slipping in here after mice while the builders were working, that this space had been open, then, with telephone, electrical, and cable lines running through it—an electronic life-support system from the meter and cable boxes into the dwelling.

In the corner, the smell of water-based paint came strongest, and he found a freshly painted area, dry, but still fresh. The smell was faint enough that, he supposed, a human could easily miss it.

Studying the surface at an angle, he could see where the protruding baseboard had been cut and then resealed; and beneath the smell of paint, he caught a faint scent of caulking or patching.

Dragging a paw softly over the barely dry surface, he felt a subtle, raised line beneath the fresh paint. When he looked closely, he saw not only the patch line but brush marks.

He found no paintbrush in the garage, used or otherwise.

Maybe the cable man had been here. Or the phone guy, making some change that necessitated cutting into the baseboard. Maybe they had used their own brush, and had taken it with them?

Or maybe not.

The Milners had had the garage key. If a serviceman were to be admitted, Peggy would likely have come over to let him in, and she would have told her husband. Under the circumstances, wouldn't he have made sure to tell the cops?

Well, Peggy Milner wasn't talking. He stood a moment, considering, his heart pounding hard. *If it was just painted, where's the paintbrush? Why would someone . . . ? Where . . . ?*

Muttering to himself, he headed out through the doggy door, leaped to the top of the fence and over, and fled up the street to the nearest neighbor's garbage cans, where, among multiple offensive stinks, he'd caught a whiff of paint.

He found no paint can in the recycling box. Leaping atop the closed garbage can, pawing at the handles that fastened the lid in place, he flipped them up as easily as any raccoon could have. But it was impossible to get a purchase on the lid itself and push it off while standing on it. He gave up at last, dropped down, and with a flying tackle threw his weight against the side of the can, praying no one was watching. Over it went, the lid flying, the contents spilling into the street.

Did he hear someone running and shouting? Nosing in panic among the stinking mess, he pawed aside items he didn't care to identify—he'd taste these smells for hours—spoiled food, bleach, and . . .

Paint! There! Pawing aside wadded paper, he snatched up a little, damp paintbrush stuck to the lid of a tomato can.

Taking the brush carefully in his mouth, he looked for a tube of patching compound or caulking. Behind him, the running had ceased. He was still looking when softer footsteps approached behind him, making him spin around.

A small boy stood staring at him, a kid of about seven. Short black hair, a red-and-blue baseball jacket. He looked up at the house behind them. "If Mrs. Hallman sees what you did, cat, you'll be cat skin." He stared at the paintbrush. "What've you got?" Lunging, the kid tried to snatch it . . . But Joe Grey was gone, scorching into the bushes and behind the houses, into a thorny thicket of blackberries. That should stop the little brat.

He waited maybe twenty minutes while the kid tramped around outside the thicket pawing at the vines. Joe smiled when the kid got hung up and scratched himself good, and then at last wandered away.

Slipping out again and along through the back-yards, Joe headed once more for the Blean cottage. But this time, before he went over the fence, he slipped beneath a holly bush, lay the paintbrush against the holly's trunk where it wouldn't get any dirtier, then stood there debating.

He'd been seen doing something very uncatlike. Even a seven-year-old had to wonder why a cat would steal a dirty paintbrush. Who would that boy decide to tell about the weird gray cat? If this kid turned up while Garza was talking with some neighbor, and if the kid opened his busy little mouth . . . Joe shivered.

But it couldn't be helped. Anyway, who would take the word of a seven-year-old boy? Why would anyone believe that a cat would want a dirty paint-brush? He looked out to the street and, when he didn't see the kid, Joe irritably dismissed him.

He had to find a phone, he didn't want to leave the brush there very long. Maybe he could get into the Blean cottage through the inner garage door and use that phone.

But why would there *be* a phone in there? Why would anyone bother to pay a monthly phone bill when they weren't there very much, when they could just use their cell phones? Even for rich folks coming down once a year on vacation or the occa-sional weekend, to pay for a landline seemed foolish. He looked next door to the Milner house, wondering if he could get in there, instead.

Rearing up, slipping the paintbrush higher among the prickly branches of the holly bush, he had crouched to make a dash for the Milner house, thinking first to check the windows and then the roof vents, when a patrol car pulled into the Milner drive.

Talk about serendipity. Talk about happy accident and smiling fate! Dallas Garza stepped from the car and headed directly for the Blean cottage, moving carefully through the deceased's flower garden, clutching a key in his hand.

At about the time Joe watched Dallas cross the garden, apparently to have another look at the Blean garage, up in the hills in the Cage Jones house Lilly Jones sat at her little writing desk methodically paying the monthly bills and making her phone calls; she was relieved that that Greeley person had left, but not at all happy that her sister, Violet, had moved in on her. And without even a phone call. Well, but the poor thing had nowhere else, the helpless creature never had had any gumption. Lilly supposed she could put up with Violet for the short term. In the long run, what difference?

Nor was she unduly upset that Cage was in the hospital in intensive care; she was not wringing her hands for her brother. If Cage's wounds to the throat and face and chest were critical enough to seriously restrict his respiratory functions, that was his fault and his problem. Fate would do with Cage what fate would do.

She had spent the hour since her breakfast dusting and vacuuming. If that woke Violet, that was too bad. She hadn't asked Violet to move back home, into her old room. She might feel sorry for Violet, but the girl's presence compounded Lilly's own problems.

Still, in some respects, Violet's proximity might make life easier for her. Thinking about Violet, back again and living there, and then about Cage in the hospital, perhaps dying, Lilly Jones smiled with a dawning contentment, and returned to paying her bills.

Watching Dallas approach the garage, Joe snatched the paintbrush from where he'd shoved it up into the bush and, trying not to drool on it, fled beneath the lavender and Mexican sage to the gate of the dog yard that Dallas would have to open to reach the garage side door.

Dropping the brush where Garza couldn't miss it, he fled again, unseen through the bushes and, behind Garza's back, up a pepper tree.

He watched Garza pause before the gate, looking down at the paintbrush. Frowning, Dallas took a tissue from his pocket and carefully picked it up. Then he scanned the yard all around, looking up and down the street. At last he crossed the dog yard, unlocked the garage door, and disappeared inside. Joe's nerves were doing flip-flops.

He knew he should get out of there, but he was unwilling to miss the crucial moment. Skinning over the fence, he crouched beside the doggy door and, lifting a paw, cautiously pushed the flap in a quarter inch and peered through.

Dallas had placed the paintbrush in an evidence bag, which he still held. He stood looking carefully around, then knelt to examine the lower shelf of the workbench and the gallon cans of paint, much as Joe had done. He ran a finger around the lip of the can that had been opened, then held the paintbrush to the can.

Apparently, from the look on the detective's face, the paint matched. Dropping it back in the evidence bag, he circled the garage studying the walls and rafters—and sniffing the air as intently as had Joe himself, and that made the tomcat smile.

It didn't take the detective long to find the source of the scent, to locate the patched and repainted portion of the oversize baseboard. Running a finger lightly over the floor, he examined a tiny spill of white dust on the concrete that Joe himself had missed. When Dallas rose quickly to leave, Joe backed out into the dog yard, squeezing beneath a dog-scented bush as Dallas raced past him—after this caper, he was going to stink of dog pee.

He heard the car door open and slam and thought

Dallas would take off, but almost at once the detective was back, carrying a camera. The minute he was inside the garage again, Joe peered in, watching as he photographed the repaired wall and the white dust on the floor. He watched as Dallas, wearing thin gloves and using a penknife, carefully lifted the minute particles of dust and dropped them in a small plastic sandwich bag, which he sealed in an evidence bag. Then with his knife, Dallas pried away a six-by-six-inch section of drywall board. It came out easily, the new caulking sticking to the edges. Shining the light into the end of the small utility tunnel, presumably picking out cable and electrical and phone wires, Dallas smiled.

Again he photographed, this time directly into the hole. Half a dozen shots, then he reached in, nearly to the elbow. He drew out two leather gloves, handling them by the corners of the cuffs, and dropped each into an evidence bag. He retrieved a small, folding hatchet of the kind that a hiker might take camping.

With the hatchet secured in an evidence bag, he examined the hole again and, finding nothing more, he rose. He bagged the paint can and, with a last look around, he headed for the door. This time Joe was quicker. As Dallas locked the door behind him, Joe Grey was on the roof above him. But when Joe glanced up the street, he saw the nosy kid poking around in the spilled garbage.

Below him, Dallas was heading for his car when he paused in the Milner drive, looking back up the street, watching as the boy happily rummaged.

Frowning, the detective headed there. Joe remained frozen as Dallas found a stick and began to rummage, too. The kid stared at him. "What you think you're doing?" When Dallas opened his coat and thrust his badge at him, the kid took off for home. Methodically, Dallas sorted through garbage. After maybe ten minutes, he reached deeper in with the stick and eased out a small, crumpled tube.

Studying the tube and then bagging it, Dallas looked again at the garbage, then looked up and down the street as if wondering how this particular can had gotten tipped over, when all the rest stood undisturbed. Watching him, Joe could only pray that that little kid was royally scared of cops, too intimidated to venture forth with some story about stray tomcats.

You say a word about cats, kid, I'll skin you. You think those blackberry stickers hurt! You haven't a clue, what a tomcat's claws can do.

Well, Dallas had hard evidence now. The gloves and hatchet, the paint can and tube and portion of drywall would go to the lab. Considering that Peggy's husband had had access to the garage, Dallas would surely bring him in on suspicion, maybe would have enough to hold him. In the meantime, there was other unfinished business—

the arraignment hearings in the other two murders; Greeley's unexplained search, and learning what *was* missing from Cage Jones's house—what Cage had stolen, and lost. If Joe was right, that theft had been, indeed, an audacious piece of work on Cage's part. And, with a wry smile and a flick of his ears, Joe Grey left the scene of the Milner murder, his hunting instincts keening for action.

34

Wilma and Charlie worked all morning in the gathering heat, straightening up Wilma's trashed cottage; at noon, Charlie's cleaning-and-repair van pulled up, and Mavity and two other members of Charlie's team emerged carrying their cleaning equipment, ready to give the house a good polishing.

"I'm sure glad you went into this business," Wilma said, hugging her niece. "I would never have sprung for having someone come in to clean, I'd be doing it all. But it's so hot—should we take Mavity to lunch with us? She's already done half a day's work on their first appointment."

Charlie considered, and shook her head. "Let her work, she wants to make the house nice again for you. We'll bring back dessert for all of us, that will be a treat." She stepped into the kitchen as little, gray-haired Mavity Flowers, in her ubiquitous and oft-washed white uniform, came in though the back door, loaded down with brooms, mops, and buckets; her two tall, younger crew members entered close behind her carrying bins of cleaners and polishes; both were strong young women dressed in jeans and T-shirts. Mavity hugged Wilma, then looked at her, frowning. "You okay?"

"I'm fine," Wilma said. "We're both just fine, now. They can't put down the Getz women. We're just going to run out for a bit of lunch, Mavity. If you'll put on a pot of coffee, we'll bring back some desserts. Crème brulée?" she said. "Key lime pie?"

Mavity grinned. "You know I love them both." She put down her equipment, hugged Wilma again, then turned to get to work.

Stepping into Charlie's SUV, Wilma carrying her dry cleaning to drop off, they headed toward the shore. "It's Monday," Wilma said, "the Bakery will have flan."

Charlie glanced at her, laughing.

"I can't get filled up. I know it's all in my mind. I only missed lunch—and dinner by a few hours. You'd think . . ."

"Stress," Charlie said. "I feel the same. I ate three bowls of chili last night, pancakes and bacon and eggs this morning. Panic hunger, or some fancier name. I only know I want one of the Bakery's famous crab sandwiches."

"I could eat two, *and* dessert."

Moving up the steps of the old gray dwelling that

now housed the Bakery, Charlie asked for a table on the wide, covered porch where they could cool off in the sea breeze and watch the surf a block away. Ordering iced tea, they settled back, looking at each other like two wanderers who had been lost, and had only just found each other again. It took a little while to ease back into the normal world. There was a strong family resemblance, two tall, slim women, one gray haired, one redheaded; the same lean features and steady eyes.

This morning while they'd cleaned, they had avoided talking about their ordeal. Now Wilma said, "You're doing all right? About the shooting?"

"As good as can be expected. Max says everyone goes through this."

"Everyone does. It gets better, with time. Just remember that he could have killed you, killed both of us and Max and maybe Ryan, if you hadn't shot him."

Charlie shivered. "We still don't know what he wanted. What he thinks you took, what he had hidden."

The waitress came with their tea. They ordered crab sandwiches, salads, and three kinds of dessert to go. When they were alone again, Wilma said, "Dulcie says Greeley searched the Jones house."

"Is she saying *Greeley's* involved in this? Those cats! Did he find anything? What did they—"

"Dulcie and Kit found a safe," Wilma said. "Which, of course, they couldn't open."

"When was this?" Charlie said softly. "Greeley can crack a safe."

"I'm not sure when. After we were kidnapped. I don't have it all sorted out yet."

"Weren't Cage and Greeley in Central America together?"

"They were both down there, Greeley working in Panama. I can't be sure when Cage was there— only the times he was not was when he was under supervision or in prison. He was always secretive, said he couldn't remember the dates. Said he was all over Central and South America, couldn't remember exactly when and where. Even if he'd given me dates and places, it would have been hard to corroborate. Certainly, most of the time, Lilly didn't know where he was."

"The interesting thing is, why did Greeley show up here, just now?"

Wilma nodded. Their order arrived, and they were silent for a while. Charlie said, when her first pangs of hunger were appeased, "When Mavity called this morning to ask what time they should be at your place, she sounded really distressed. She said she'd kicked Greeley out, called the station and gotten a restraining order. She said he'd been so drunk, so loud that she didn't have a choice. I let her talk it out, or try to.

"She really rambled," Charlie said, "not at all like Mavity, said she was so embarrassed, the way he behaved in front of her friends. She confessed she'd gone through Greeley's suitcase, she was embarrassed about that. She said he had some kind of little gold idol, an ugly little man. She called it a devil, said it gave her the shivers. Sounded like those museum copies that Greeley's ex-wife brings back from her trips. But Mavity said this was far heavier. She said she's looked at those, and they don't weigh half what this did . . ."

Wilma had stopped eating. "Those little pendants that Sue brings back for the South American shop." She was silent for a long time, looking at Charlie, and thinking. "Charlie, on the way home, let's swing by the library. It won't take a minute, I'll just run in."

Charlie nodded. Wrapping half her sandwich in her paper napkin, and asking for the bill, she quickly paid it, gulped her tea, and rose, picking up the cardboard box filled with the Bakery's famous desserts.

They were back home at Wilma's twenty minutes later, Wilma loaded down with half a dozen heavy coffee-table books on pre-Columbian art, Charlie carrying the bakery box. Pushing in through the front door, they smelled fresh coffee. It was not until the five of them had finished coffee and the desserts that Wilma sat down with Mavity in the living room surrounded by library books. Getting Mavity settled with the heavy books, Wilma thought, amused, that she'd set aside the next few days to be alone and quiet, to enjoy a little recuperative R and R, and instead, here she was, digging into clues, unable to leave the puzzle alone—every bit as curious as the three cats.

In the library, as she'd hurried toward the stacks, one of her coworkers had stopped her and started laying on the sympathy about her "ordeal," asking nosy questions about the kidnapping. You could keep nothing secret in a small town. Little dumpy Nora Wahl had told her with great authority that what she needed to do "right now," was to "get right out with your friends again, Wilma. *Do* things, *go* places, don't stay shut up in the house brooding. Go out among people right away, get your mind off all that trouble, keep busy and you'll soon forget it."

Wilma had told Nora curtly that that wasn't the way to heal anything, to try to forget it and hide from it. That *that* wasn't the way her mind worked, thank you. That what she needed was a little privacy. And she had headed into the stacks, leaving the library assistant startled into unaccustomed silence.

Now, sitting on the couch next to Mavity, with Charlie on the other side, she watched the little grizzle-haired woman leaf through color photographs of gold pendants and gold ceremonial artifacts that had been dug from ancient graves.

"Ugly," Mavity said. "But . . . I don't know . . ." She looked up at Wilma. "They hold you, don't they? Do *you* think they're ugly?"

Charlie said, "I think they're fascinating, strong. But maybe that's an acquired taste. The faces are ugly, but the work itself . . ."

"Yes," Mavity said. "I think I see." She studied Charlie. "You're the artist, you know about these things. These were made by ancient Indians?"

"Yes, with really simple tools. The whole of that continent was so rich with gold, great veins of gold that they could just dig out. When the Spanish conquered those people and killed them, they took their beautiful gold sculptures and melted them down, destroyed thousands upon thousands of these pieces, casting them into Spanish coins."

"But how did Greeley . . . ?"

"His is most likely a copy," Wilma said. "The museums make copies, to sell."

"It was so heavy," Mavity repeated. "So very heavy, for such a little thing."

"If it is gold," Wilma said, "it was illegal to bring it out of the country. In Panama, it's illegal even to own real gold huacas, unless you register them. You can't sell them. Only the Panamanian government, and the museum of Panama, can legally own them."

"Then if it is gold, where could he . . . ? Oh, he didn't steal it, from a museum! Greeley isn't that clever."

Charlie said, "Would there be more? Would he have more of them?"

Mavity's eyes widened. "Greeley . . . Greeley isn't some international thief like you read about, able to get into a museum." She looked hard at Charlie, and at Wilma. "That's just not possible."

"We're guessing a lot here," Wilma said. "But . . . maybe not a museum. 'The most recent grave discovered,' " she read, " 'was found less than a hundred years ago.' " She looked up at Mavity. "People stole gold artifacts from it, before the Panamanian government found out and stopped the thefts." She scanned the columns again, then, "No one knows where those pieces ended up. Possibly, it says, in private collections."

"But," Mavity said, "if Greeley stole something so valuable, even from a private collection . . ." She shook her head. "My brother's just a petty thief. I don't think he'd know how to go about that kind of sophisticated theft."

"Maybe Greeley and Cage together?" Wilma said. "Cage might be capable of that, if he planned carefully."

Mavity sat back, marking her place in the book that lay open on her lap. But then, leaning forward again, caught almost beyond her will by those riches, she read aloud the description of a golden garden in ancient Peru, a garden paved in gold, with life-size gold corn growing on gold stalks, life-size gold sheep and their lambs, huge gold jars filled with emeralds, full-size gold women; she read of gold fountains with running water where gold birds bathed, and there were even gold spiders, other gold insects, and gold lizards.

"Like a fairy tale," she said. "Such wealth seems impossible. To even imagine . . . Oh my, how valuable even that little devil must be, if it's real. And how many centuries old?"

"Maybe five centuries," Wilma said, "or less. Some were made later."

"I don't think," Charlie said, "the Indian cultures had devils. They had underworld men, but I think the idea of the devil came with the Spaniards, with the Christian religion."

Wilma nodded. "And the native religions incorporated the Christian devil into their own beliefs—but those underworld figures looked like devils. Dulcie said Cage has masks with devil faces hanging on the living room wall. I think those are more common. After Christianity was introduced, the Mexicans and many other cultures made devil masks of . . . Oh, painted papier-mâché or wood. Masks for festivals and holidays."

Charlie said, "Would that be why Cage kidnapped you, because he did have such a treasure, and someone stole it while he was in prison?"

Mavity said, "And Greeley has at least one."

Wilma put her arm around Mavity. "If Greeley stole from Cage, why would he search the Jones house? We don't know that Greeley stole even that one little figure."

"So heavy," Mavity repeated, her little wrinkled face pulled into lines of concern. "So very heavy when I picked it up. And the way the metal felt . . . Warm and heavy, not like some bit of cheap jewelry . . ."

It was not until Mavity had left, she and the two younger women driving off in the blue van with Charlie's logo on the side, that Charlie said, "How much of this do Dulcie and Joe know? And where is Dulcie? I haven't seen her all morning. Clyde said that when you didn't come home last night, Dulcie was a basket case. So where is she now? I'd think she'd be staying close."

"She was snuggled up with me all night, as close as she could get. We woke up early, I had coffee in bed, and then we had a nice breakfast." Wilma frowned. "Maybe the cats are at the station."

"Maybe," Charlie said. "Max and Dallas were going to bring in Lilly and Violet Jones for questioning. If the cats knew, they wouldn't miss that." She hugged her aunt, then rose. "I'm going back home for a quiet nap with the dogs. Maybe, if Max can get away, a nice evening ride. Will you rest, too?"

"Of course I will," Wilma said, and she got up to see Charlie out the door—but the minute Charlie's car pulled away from the curb, Wilma was at the computer and online, searching for references to reported thefts of pre-Columbian gold. She spent nearly two hours reading and printing out pages; then, wondering if this information was indeed relevant to the case, or if she had wasted her time, she reached for the phone to call Max.

35

Lilly and Violet Jones, sitting stiffly side by side in Max Harper's office, looked so rigid they might have just been formally charged and their rights read instead of simply invited down to the station for a few questions. Perched on the edge of Max's leather couch, the two dry, pale women looked Harper over as if his invitation to stop by and have a chat had been a summons from hell itself.

The courteous young rookie who had knocked at their door and then chauffeured them to the station had been meticulously polite; Harper had offered the sisters coffee and a plate of George Jolly's homemade cookies, both of which Lilly and Violet refused. Max had made it clear that neither sister was suspected of wrongdoing, but that didn't stop their scowls at Harper and at Detective Garza, who sat in the leather armchair. The only observers the two women didn't frown at were the two they didn't see.

They sure don't like being hauled into the station, Joe thought, watching from beneath the credenza.

Well, Lilly doesn't like much of anything. Mad at the world. And it isn't only anger—there's fear in that woman's eyes, the tomcat thought with interest. *Harper sees it. So does Dallas. Does Lilly fear for Cage, lying so close to death? Or is it something more?*

"Cage *is* better," Lilly was saying stiffly in response to Harper's question about her brother's condition. "It's a wonder, the way that woman shot him—to shoot him in the face like a—"

"If my wife hadn't shot him," Max said coldly, "he would very likely have killed her, and might have killed me, too. *That woman* saved her own life and possibly her aunt's life, and mine."

"And since when," Dallas asked Lilly, "have you grown so concerned about the welfare of your brother? When we talked a few days ago, you said that if he went to jail that was what he deserved."

"Jail and that terrible shooting are two different fates," Lilly said pitifully. "The one what the law dictates. The other so unnecessarily gruesome."

"Is there," Max said, "a more humane way to stop a killer who has a gun pointed at you and his finger tight on the trigger?"

Dallas looked at Violet. "Do you feel the same, Mrs. Sears?"

Violet looked down at her lap and said nothing, and the cats glanced at each other. Was she silenced by the proximity of her older sister, or by her inability to give an honest answer? If Joe read

Violet Jones correctly, she would find happiness only if both Cage and Eddie were to disappear from the face of the earth.

"As soon as Cage is well enough to be released," Max said, "he'll be in jail, here, with follow-up medical visits. We asked you to come in today hoping you could help us understand why Cage and Eddie kidnapped Mrs. Harper and Ms. Getz, and why Cage shot Mandell Bennett." Max's voice was softer again, quietly friendly.

"Cage is fortunate," Max said, "that Mandell Bennett is recovering. He could be facing first-degree murder charges." He studied Lilly. "He seems to think Ms. Getz stole something from your home. Do you have any idea what that might be?"

Lilly pressed her lips together. "I don't know what Cage ever left in that house worth stealing. I have seen nothing worth the trouble. Those masks he brought from South America, I can't imagine who would want those. Anyway, they're right in plain sight for any thief to take. I wish someone would take them." She fixed cold eyes on Max. "If there was something in the house I don't know about, it's surely gone now, or Cage wouldn't be so upset. Someone took it," she said accusingly.

Max remained patient, sternly reining himself in. Dulcie put out her paw, wanting to touch him, then hastily drew it back before it might be seen under the credenza. She had longed to comfort Max when he thought Charlie might have been murdered, he'd been so alone and hurting.

The women remained quiet as Max described the indictment and bail processes Cage would face. A flicker of sudden eagerness in Lilly's eyes, when Max said bail might be denied, made Joe and Dulcie look knowingly at each other. Joe thought, watching the two women, that they were both afraid of Cage's release.

Joe could understand Violet's fear. If Cage and Eddie were both out, no matter how unlikely that was, she might think she couldn't escape from Eddie, that Cage would force her to stay with him. But why would Lilly fear Cage's freedom?

When the dispatcher buzzed Max, and he picked up, he suddenly became very quiet, listening. Immediately, Dallas made small talk to distract the women, speaking softly, complaining about the excessive heat. He received only terse answers.

At his desk, Max was intently taking notes. Joe, peering up, could see the excitement deep in the chief's eyes. The tomcat was ready to leap into the bookcase behind Harper to cadge a look at his notes, when Dulcie nipped him on the shoulder, her green-eyed glare saying clearly, *Don't, Joe. Don't* think *about it!*

She'd told him that he did that too often, leaped into the chief's bookcase to read over his shoulder, she'd told him more than once that Harper would begin to wonder, and that he should be more restrained. Now, both cats stiffened as Max said, "Thanks, Wilma. I sure will."

Max hung up, trying to suppress a smile, and sat looking steadily at Lilly and Violet, studying them until Lilly began to fidget. "I think, for the moment, ladies, our conversation is concluded." He waited, then, "Unless you have something to add."

Neither woman spoke.

"I can only tell you there is a formidable prison sentence for withholding information or evidence. In this case, one would be facing both state and federal sentences." Max watched them for a moment more, then he rose, pushing back his chair.

The sisters looked blankly at him, and stood up. Lilly Jones had gone parchment white. Violet looked even more frightened and uncertain than usual. "There is no need for a driver," Lilly said stiffly. "We prefer to walk home."

As the Jones sisters departed, Max shoved his notes across the desk to Dallas. "You want to get on the computer, see what you can find? This is a real long shot, but . . . Wilma thinks Greeley and Cage might have brought in contraband from Central America—it's all in my notes." And Max moved quickly away to the dispatcher's desk, where he talked with Mabel for a moment, then headed out the front door.

From beneath the credenza, Joe looked up at

Dallas, wanting to get a look at the notes. Dulcie whispered, so softly no human could hear, "I'm going home. Come on. We can find out quicker from Wilma!" And Dulcie slipped away, down the hall, the tip of her tabby tail flicking, and out the wide glass door, behind Violet.

Joe didn't follow. Sauntering out from under the credenza, he rubbed against Dallas's ankles.

Dallas stroked the tomcat absently as he read Harper's notes. Joe was crouched to leap to the back of his chair when the detective folded the notes, and slid them in his pocket. "Well, tomcat! Maybe we have some teeth in this case, after all." Giving Joe an absentminded pet, he hurried down the hall to his own office and flicked on the computer. Joe paused, uncertain whether to follow Dallas and get a look at the notes and see what he brought up on the computer. Or whether to beat it over to Wilma's, where Dulcie would be getting the full story.

But then he thought about Violet and Lilly. Whatever Wilma had told Harper, he'd soon hear it from Dulcie—but whatever those two women talked about while walking home could be lost forever. And quickly he headed for the front door, racing out when a rookie came swinging in. Belting out onto the hot sidewalk, he raced to catch up with the Jones sisters, then padded along behind them, keeping out of sight among the long morning shadows, dodging behind planters and steps, feeling like Columbo without the trench coat.

The women were slow, they had no interest in striding out swiftly, as Wilma or Charlie would do; there was no joy in their steps. It would be hard to live with such a dour pair. Their voices were without inflection, too, featureless, and so low he had to push close on their heels to hear some of their mutters; Lilly was still coldly angry.

"What nerve, *Unless you have something to add!* What did he mean, *withholding evidence?*"

Violet turned to look at her older sister. "Do you know what Cage had, Lilly? What was stolen? *Do you know what they were talking about?* There had to be something, Cage was so angry . . ."

Lilly stared at her and didn't answer; they were silent now as they moved on through the village and started up the long hill.

"And what was that Greeley person doing in our house?" Violet asked at last. "When I came in and saw him . . . Lilly, why did you let him stay there?"

"He was trying to trade on his friendship with Cage to get a free room. Cheap. And pushy. He kept banging at the door. I got tired of it, and let him in. Then I got tired of his whining, gave in to shut him up, just for the one night." Climbing the hill, the women had slowed even more, but at last Joe could see the dark old house rising up ahead, smothered by its pine and eucalyptus trees.

"He could have murdered you," Violet said.

"That little runt? I locked my bedroom door."

"You could have called the police."

Lilly looked at her and laughed, a dry, mirthless sound. "Cage would like that. He'd be wild if there were any more cops in the house. Twice was bad enough. Anyway, he's gone. Guess he's at the Seaview Bed and Breakfast. He made a call there, this morning. I wish he'd pack up and leave town, him with his ugly gold devil—"

"A gold devil? Cage has . . . What was it like?"

"Some kind of trinket from South America, had it in his pocket. Ugly as those masks. What *about* Cage?"

"I . . . He has a devil thing like that, a dangle on a key chain. Could there be two? Eddie says the one Cage has is real gold and worth a lot."

Scowling, Lilly looked at Violet for a long moment, then turned and moved quickly up the steps, fishing her house key from her pocket. They disappeared inside, slamming the door nearly in Joe Grey's face.

Not that he wanted to enter that house and be shut in with those two. Turning away, he galloped down through the neighborhood's overgrown yards, and scrambled up a cypress tree to the hot rooftops, heading for Dulcie and Wilma's house— thinking about Greeley in South America, and about Greeley's little gold devil and that Cage had one like it. Wondering if those trinkets were solid gold, and what they might be worth, and if there were more, and who had them? He had reached Wilma's block and was about to come down the pine tree beside the stone cottage when Dulcie came flying out her cat door. She stared up at him, her green eyes bright, and clawed her way up the pine between its tangled branches.

"I was coming to find you. Wilma—"

"Come on," he hissed, "tell me on the way . . ."

"But—"

"Greeley's in a motel," he said. "A bed and breakfast. He has—" Seeing her impatient stare, he stopped. "What *did* Wilma tell Harper? Come on, tell me on the way!" And before she could answer, he took off across the roofs in the direction of the Seaview Bed and Breakfast, Dulcie close on his tail, bursting with her own news.

36

"Be still one minute, can't you!" Racing across the roofs, Dulcie careened against Joe and took his ear in her teeth, pulling him to a halt. "Just listen! Mavity told Wilma about some kind of gold devil Greeley carries, and Wilma got some library books and showed Mavity pictures. They found one the same as Greeley's, just a tiny figure, among all kinds of idols, some huge. All solid gold, and worth a fortune. Wilma went online and found that a lot of them were stolen, never recovered . . . some about the time Greeley and Cage were there—and every piece worth enough to keep us in caviar for a lifetime."

The shingles were too hot to stand still. They moved on again, trotting. "Could they have pulled off a theft like that?" Dulcie said. "Is that what Cage claims went missing, and Greeley was looking for? They stole something worth a fortune, and then someone stole it from them?" She paused in the shadow of a chimney. "Or did Greeley . . . ? Where is Greeley? Which bed and breakfast?"

"Seaview, on Casanova." And Joe took off again running flat out, Dulcie close behind him. "There," he hissed, flying along the edge of a steeply shingled slope, "that green roof with white dormers." And with a wild leap, he dropped down into a shingled valley between the two rising dormers of a rambling old frame building.

Crouching on the scorching shingles between the steep roofs, they looked down into the inn's tiny patio. A cooler breeze rose up from freshly sprinkled bricks, where a gardener was watering. They were discussing how best to find Greeley's room when the old man himself appeared out on the sidewalk, wiping his mouth with the back of his hand, as if he'd just come from breakfast. He had a large, greasy stain on his pants leg. As he headed for a room directly below them, they drew back against a chimney.

They heard his key turn in the lock, heard his door open. When they didn't hear it close, they peered over.

The door stood wide open, as if to catch the cooler air that lingered in the small patio. From within the room, they heard Greeley open a window, then apparently drop a handful of change on the dresser, maybe emptying his pockets, meaning to change pants—though a grease stain had never before seemed to bother that old man. They heard an inner door close, then water running in the bathroom basin.

"Now!" Dulcie said, flying backward down a trellis, knocking off clematis blooms; ducking into a mock orange bush beside Greeley's door, they looked into the dim room—and moved inside, searching for the best hiding place. They might have only a minute. And Greeley knew them. To that old man, they were not simple neighborhood cats, he knew very well what they were capable of, and that their sympathies lay not with cheap crooks like Greeley, but with the law.

The room was small, dim, dusty smelling, and overfurnished. Huge, dark mahogany dressers, big unmade bed. Wildly flowered, faded draperies left from another era, striped upholstered chair crowding one corner. On an upholstered bench stood Greeley's wrinkled leather duffel. They hopped up beside it, and Dulcie disappeared halfway inside, searching, as Joe leapcd to the dresser behind her, among the tangle of small items from Greeley's pockets.

Greeley's billfold smelled of old leather and old man and was well stuffed with cash. Beside it, a fall of loose change, a little penknife, a wadded-up handkerchief that Joe didn't want to touch. A ring of five keys, including three safe-deposit keys, flat and smooth, without ridges. And a little flashlight and the tiny periscope that Greeley favored for cracking a safe. But no gold devil.

They heard the toilet flush. Dulcie leaped out of the duffle, the small gold devil dangling from her teeth, and took off fast, out the door, Joe beside her. They had barely made it to the shadows beneath a potted tree when Greeley came out of the bathroom. When he opened the closet door, they were gone, up the clematis trellis to the safety of the roof.

They heard items rattling on the dresser below, loose change clinking, as if Greeley was dropping those small possessions back in his pocket. They wondered if he had changed to clean pants? On the roof above the old man, Dulcie dropped the little gold figure on the dark shingles. It caught the morning sun in a flashing gleam: square, scowling face and large nose beneath an elaborate head-dress, its body naked, its maleness boldly explicit. Its entire aspect, as Mavity had said, gave one the shivers.

Joe lifted it by the dark leather string from which

it was suspended, widening his eyes when he felt its weight. "Heavy as a wharf rat," he said, laying the huaca down again.

Dulcie's green eyes glowed; the same triumphant look as when she came tramping across a field dragging a large and succulent rabbit. "It's so heavy, Joe. If it's real, and solid gold . . . then as sure as I have paws, this is what Cage was after, a stash of artifacts like this."

"But . . . I don't know." Joe shook his head. "That's big-time, Dulcie. To steal from a museum, in a country that will shoot you if you sneeze wrong. Greeley isn't that sophisticated. Is Cage? Just how were those burglaries handled?"

"On the Web, one article Wilma pulled up said the unrecovered huacas from the museum had probably been sold to illegal collectors." Her green eyes narrowed. "Think about it. If a person had an illegal collection of stolen goods, and then someone stole from him, would he report the theft?"

Joe smiled.

"And now," she said, "with this information, what will Harper do?"

The tomcat shrugged. "Report it to customs or whatever federal agency deals with this stuff." He laid his ears back uncertainly, but then he smiled. "Will the feds contact Interpol? Talk about heavy."

But Dulcie looked uncertain.

"What?" he said, frowning.

"The feds can have Cage," she said. "Let him burn. But his sister . . . If he did have a stash of gold, and it was in the house while Lilly was living there, won't they arrest her, too?"

"So?"

"So, if she didn't know, and they send her to prison, that would be too bad. She's just a lonely old woman."

Joe just looked at her. Here was his beautiful tabby lady, with her delicate peach-tinted ears and her huge emerald eyes, the most perfect cat in the world, feeling sorry for some second-rate, bad-tempered, and probably lying human.

"Dulcie, if Lilly Jones knew there were millions in stolen gold hidden in her own house—if that's what this turns out to be—and she didn't call the police, if she knew why Cage kidnapped Wilma and she didn't tell Harper, if Lilly Jones just sat on her hands, then why would you feel sorry for her?"

"But what," Dulcie said in a small voice, "if she didn't know?"

Watching his lovely lady agonizing over that stupid woman, Joe Grey picked up the leather cord in his teeth and trotted across the roofs, the gold devil dangling and thumping against his gray-and-white chest.

Where a cluster of chimneys and air vents rose close together, in a little cleft between two steep peaks, several layers of shingles met at odd angles. There, Joe pawed back the shingles, dropped the little gold devil on its leather cord safely beneath them, and watched the asphalt squares flop back over it.

Patting at the shingles, making sure nothing could be seen, he turned back to Dulcie. "How about Jolly's alley? I'm starved." And the cats raced away toward Jolly's, heading for a mid-morning snack—leaving that one small fragment of a vast and ancient culture where not even a seagull or roof rat was likely to find it.

For nearly a week, the cats thought about the little gold man hidden among the shingles. Several times a day Joe or Dulcie trotted across the roofs to that aerial hiding place, making sure the treasure was safe; and all week their minds were full of questions yet to be answered. But not until the following Friday, when their human friends gathered at Clyde's for dinner, did they learn more.

The occasion was Mandell Bennett's release from San Francisco General and his arrival in the village to stay with Wilma for a short recuperation. Wilma wouldn't hear of his staying alone in his apartment with only a handful of coworkers coming in to tend to his needs, though they would have been more than adequate. "What if Jones breaks out again and comes after you? Better to have someone else in the house until you're better. This time, I promise, Mandell, I'm ready—and the department is only blocks away, they can be here in seconds."

She had made up the guest room for Mandell, had all his favorite foods on hand, had arranged for a visiting nurse to come in to help him with bathing and changing bandages; and in anticipation of Mandell's arrival, she and Clyde had planned a party.

37

Only now, in the early evening, had the accumulated July heat managed to penetrate to Clyde Damen's patio; in this sheltered oasis, the high, plastered walls hoarded well the cooler night air. It seemed to Joe that the heat spell would never end; he felt as if the whole world was being smothered by a giant, sweaty hand. Pacing the top of the six-foot wall above the unlit barbecue, he watched Clyde hosing down the brick paving and the plaster benches. Only the outdoor cushions, piled on the porch, had escaped the soaking onslaught of the spray. As Clyde adjusted the hose to a gentler pressure and began watering the flowers in their raised planters, the tomcat sniffed with appreciation the cool, damp breath rising up to him.

"Game for a little shower?" Clyde said, flicking the spray in Joe's direction.

"You want a set of claws in your backside? Only some idiot dog would want to play in the hose." But immediately he was sorry he'd said that. Old Rube had loved the water, had loved to bite and leap at the hose. Together, Joe and Clyde glanced across the garden to Rube's grave, and exchanged a hurting look. The big retriever had been put down just two months ago, and both man and cat still felt incomplete; they missed painfully the black Lab who had for so many years been a member of the family; every memory of Rube was distressing. But it was hard not to think of him, hard not to stir their memories.

Rube's greatest passion had been to swim in the ocean, shouldering through the surf as strong and agile as a seal. Now, Joe's remark had left Clyde so distressed that he turned off the hose, came over to the wall, and stood silently stroking Joe.

"I'm sorry," Joe said.

"I know." Clyde rubbed behind his ears. Joe could smell Clyde's aftershave over the nose-tickling aroma of cold charcoal from the big barbecue; it was too hot this evening to build a fire for burgers or steaks or ribs, though a crowd would soon descend.

A cold supper waited in the kitchen, cold cracked crab, cold boiled shrimp, and an assortment of George Jolly's succulent salads. Charlie and Wilma, as two of the guests of honor, had not been allowed to contribute a delicious casserole or salad as they usually did. Ryan, who would rather build houses than cook, was bringing the beer.

Clyde dried off the chairs and benches with a towel, and tossed the cushions back onto them. He had stepped into the house to bring out the big iced tubs of shrimp and crab when the doorbell rang and the unlocked front door opened; Joe could see in through the kitchen window and straight through to the living room where folks were crowding in, Dallas and Ryan and her sister Hanni, Max and Charlie, and behind them other cars were pulling up.

Everyone but Hanni was dressed in old worn jeans and cool cotton shirts; Ryan's beautiful and flamboyant sister wore a low-cut black T-shirt and a long, flowered skirt, expensive sandals, and dangling silver earrings. No one ever said the two sisters were alike. Except in their lively attitude, Joe thought, admiring both women. The tomcat was amused that he had begun to notice people's clothes in addition to people's attitudes; that was Dulcie's influence. It was true, though, that what people wore told a lot about them. Cats didn't have that problem. Only the condition of one's fur mattered, and that was more for the feel of it; scruffy fur was irritating and distracting.

Ryan wore ancient jeans, sandals, and a nice red T-shirt that set off her short, dark hair, her green Irish eyes and warm complexion. Wilma came in behind her, wearing red, too, Dulcie perched on her shoulder, the other guest of honor following.

Mandell Bennett was using a walker. He looked happy indeed to be out of the hospital, out of intensive care. His short dark hair was freshly trimmed, his print sport shirt still lined with creases from the store. He was laughing, his dark Cherokee eyes filled with pleasure. As people crowded through to the big kitchen, a tall thin man with carrot red hair came in behind Bennett. Mike Flannery was Ryan and Hanni's father, and Chief U.S. Probation Officer in San Francisco. He was Bennett's boss, and Wilma had worked for him before she retired. He had picked Bennett up at the hospital to drive him down from the city, a good excuse to get away for a few days and to see his family.

Lucinda and Pedric came in behind Flannery, the kit snuggled in Pedric's arms. The thin old man was dressed in jeans, an open shirt, and a lightweight cotton sport coat. Lucinda wore a long cotton jumper over a light blouse. As people moved on through the kitchen in a tangle and out the back door, a dozen officers crowded in the front door, laughing. There was not a uniform among them, not even Detective Davis who, like blond Eleanor Sand, was wearing a long denim skirt and a T-shirt.

Ryan stopped to put a six-pack of beer in the crowded refrigerator in the space Clyde had left beside the bowls of deli salads. She handed her heavy cooler to Clyde, to carry down the back steps. Pedric came out behind her. As he passed the patio table where the crab and shrimp were bedded in ice, the tattercoat peered down, licking her whiskers.

Joe smiled at the look of satisfaction on Ryan's face as she looked around Clyde's patio, now as crowded and noisy and full of life as Ryan had intended when she designed it. She always seemed so pleased to see something she had designed and built put to its full use. Clyde, standing with his arm around her, pulled her close. The cats thought they made a warm, handsome couple.

But Joe had thought that about other women. He'd thought that about Charlie, had thought for sure Charlie and Clyde would marry—and she'd ended up falling in love with Max.

And as Dulcie had pointed out, when Clyde did get married, Joe himself would be evicted from the master suite; he was, after all, not an ordinary cat, and newlyweds did need some privacy.

No more king-size bed, no more waking Clyde in the middle of the night just for the pleasure of hearing him complain. No more direct route from bed to the rafters and out the cat door to his rooftop tower.

But, Joe thought, watching his friends celebrating, he'd think about that when the problem arose. He watched Eleanor Sand and Charlie, sitting off in a corner of the patio, on the bench beneath the maple tree. Eleanor's arm was around

Charlie, and Charlie looked weepy, very still and quiet—that shooting had upset her more than she'd let on to her friends.

Of course Max knew how deeply Charlie felt, as did Dallas and Davis. But Officer Sand had recently been through the same thing and, being young and not on the job too long, she, too, had had a bad reaction. Joe wanted to slip closer and listen, but when he caught Dulcie's eye, he hastily turned away and leaped to the top of the wall beside her and the tortoiseshell kit. Across the patio, the three non-speaking household cats were up on the porch, close to the doggy door that would admit them quickly to their lair in the laundry if the party got too noisy. Two of the cats were growing elderly, and the young white cat had always been skittery and shy.

Everyone toasted Mandell, and then toasted Wilma and Charlie and made jokes at their expense. Mandell looked at Wilma. "Have to admit, this is a weird set of circumstances. Devil masks, ancient treasure . . . and I'm sure I haven't heard the half of it." He looked across at Max. "What was the outcome of Eddie Sears's arraignment, wasn't that yesterday? I was really out of the loop, in that hospital. What about Jones? Will he live to be arraigned?"

"Sears is up for two counts of kidnapping," Max said. "Jones, hard to tell. He's still in intensive care, and the prognosis is shaky."

The three cats glanced at one another. They were not all of one mind on their preferences as to Jones's fate. Joe was for a slow and painful death, before Jones cost the courts a bundle of money, trying and convicting, and then incarcerating him. Dulcie wanted Jones to face charges and endure a long, tedious, painful battle in court. Kit looked from Joe to Dulcie and wasn't sure what she wanted. Just, she thought, whatever would cause Jones the most misery. A cat is not big on forgiveness. These two men had no compassion for human lives, and in their humble feline opinions the world would be safer without them.

"We have several interesting communications from Interpol," Max said, "on thefts of pre-Columbian artifacts. When Wilma found some of that information on the Internet, we started making contacts.

"There were three burglaries from the Panamanian National Institute of Culture. At least one, early in 2003, was an inside job. A big haul of gold huacas and clay pots that could date back farther than two thousand years. The pieces were taken from the institute's Reina Torres de Arauz Museum of Anthropology, from locked display cases. Nothing broken, not a lock damaged."

Joe tried to think how long ago two thousand years really was, how many generations of ordinary cats that would be, but the magnitude of that many lifetimes made his head feel woozy. He knew that Dulcie could think in those terms more easily, at least when it had to do with their own mythical history. And the kit . . . She had grown up on ancient tales. Kit looked at ancient history as just yesterday. Joe watched the tortoiseshell as she peered down from a low branch of the maple behind Max, studying the pictures that had been faxed to him by Interpol. And Joe dropped to the bench beside Clyde where he, too, could see.

One picture seemed identical to the gold pendant he had hidden on the roof. There was a handwritten note in the margin, placing its value at over four thousand dollars. That little bit of gold . . . If Cage had stolen as much as would fill the floor safe in his basement, the value would be considerable. No wonder he'd been in a swivet when the pieces vanished.

He watched Kit, staring down from the branch at the pictures. Was she thinking that those gold huacas were very like ancient Celtic relics? Like the primitive gold jewelry and shields from Ireland and Wales that were so entwined with the myths about their own strange race of cats? But that stuff made Joe shiver; their own strange, mythical past made him unbearably nervous.

"The 2003 theft," Max said, "had to be an inside job. No employee was supposed to have both the key and the combination, to any single display case. Obviously someone, or several people, did have them. One guard who had recently been employed, had a long record. He was out on bail when they hired him, waiting on appeal for an earlier job."

"And they *hired* him?" Charlie said.

"This is Central America," Max said. "Interesting that the theft occurred a month before they were to install a new security system.

"The museum had been hit a year earlier, and there was a theft in 1982. And that's where we think this haul may have come from." Max reached for another O'Doul's. "Cage was in Panama in the eighties, as well as more recently." He looked across at Wilma. "And Greeley Urzey was there in the eighties."

Wilma said, "I don't think Greeley, alone, has the skill to pull off that kind of job. But he and Cage might."

Max nodded. "There were several illegal collections of pre-Columbian artifacts in Panama, held by wealthy individuals. Ownership is legal only for the museums. Interpol thinks those collectors bought huacas stolen from the museums, and that then, over the years, some of those collections were burglarized. That kind of theft, Cage and Greeley might have pulled off. And those thefts, of course, would never be reported."

"How would they get them out of the country?" Lucinda asked.

"A lot of ways," Max said. "Customs can't check

everything. They might have been sealed in moving containers, in those big overseas crates. Packed up by a mover in Panama or the Canal Zone and put on shipboard for transport to the U.S. Before 9/11, it would have been far easier to slip contraband through. But," Max continued, "there's a kicker to this. Late last night, we had a call from Seattle PD.

"Five stolen huacas have turned up there, sold by a San Francisco fence about a month ago." He settled back, sipping his beer. "They were sold three days after Greeley's flight got in from Panama—the day after Cage Jones was released from Terminal Island. We're guessing Greeley flew into SFO, maybe under an assumed name. Cage meets him there, or maybe Greeley rents a car and picks Cage up at T.I. And Cage takes him to the San Francisco fence."

The eyes of all three cats glowed. They glanced sideways at one another and found it hard to keep from grinning.

"But," Mandell said, "if Cage sold his take in the city, what was he looking for at the Molena Point house? What disappeared from there, that he thought Wilma and I took?" He frowned, his dark eyes narrowing. "If Cage and Greeley made a large haul together and got it out of Panama, and then split it, that could have been Greeley's half that they sold in the city."

Max nodded. "That's what we think."

"And then," Mandell said, "Greeley came after Cage's half, which he hadn't yet sold."

"But why sell Greeley's share so near the time that Cage got out of prison?" Wilma said. But then she smiled. "Greeley waited for Cage to get out, to make the contact for him. Greeley isn't very sophisticated when it comes to that kind of thing, it's Cage who knows the high-powered fences."

Pedric said, "If they sold Greeley's share, and Cage's half was still in the house, *did* Greeley find and take it?"

Max shook his head. "We don't think so. Greeley was in there after the kidnappings, snooping around. If he'd already found and taken it, why would he go back?"

"And what about the three murders?" Lucinda said. "They weren't connected to this, at all? You arrested one man, the husband?" she said with distaste.

"Two," Max said. "Tucker and Keating. We had enough evidence on both to make good cases. And in the Milner death, we have the murder weapon. We were able to lift one print that he missed when he wiped it."

"Then—" Lucinda began.

"Milner's skipped," Max said. "Parked his car at San Jose airport, made a plane reservation, but we don't think he boarded. He'll be picked up—we hope he will. He's not too sophisticated."

Max said no more, nor did Dallas. Neither

officer mentioned the plastered-over and painted baseboard in the Milner case, the paintbrush, the caulking tube found in the neighbor's garbage. Until the trial, it was best to keep such information to themselves, even among those close to the department. The fewer who knew, the fewer slips could be made. The cats glanced at one another, Dulcie twitched a whisker, and again Joe Grey smiled.

"And there never was a burglar," Lucinda said.

"None." Max grinned. "You're safe in your bed, Lucinda." He looked around at Clyde. "I'm starved. One more toast to the three guests of honor, then let's eat."

But before Max raised his glass, Charlie said, "I think there's another guest of honor who helped stop Cage Jones."

The cats went rigid, staring at Charlie.

"Seems to me," Charlie said, "that a toast to Rock is in order. The poor guy ran his tail off tracking me." Joe and Dulcie and Kit went limp. Charlie's eyes met theirs, laughing, then moved on, her look noticed only by those who knew the whole story. And as Charlie knelt to hug Rock and give him a treat of shrimp, the cats knew he deserved every morsel. Joe smugly washed his whiskers, and Dulcie rolled over on her back, purring. And soon everyone gathered around the table, filling their plates with the good shrimp and crab, Jolly's seafood so fresh it might be still swimming, the salads crisp and well seasoned, the French bread freshly baked, the desserts rich, just as the cats liked them. Rock and the cats, the household cats, too, all had their own plates; Kit ate so much, ending with a lovely bowl of crème brulée, that Lucinda and Pedric were sure she'd be sick before they got her home.

But Kit wasn't sick, she reveled in the evening, loved having all her friends around her, cat and human; after her lonely, bullied kittenhood, she loved being part of this warm human world. When late that evening the friends parted, heading for their cars, and Ryan lingered for a last drink with Clyde, Kit sat on the seat, between the old couple, talking nonstop; she wanted all the answers that had not yet come to light, she wanted it all at once.

She wanted not only to know all the final resolutions to the several cases in question, which no one on earth could yet tell her, but also she worried over her wild friends who had so courageously helped Charlie and Wilma. She worried about Willow and Cotton and Coyote living wild, and she envied them, too. She knew they would choose no other way. Wound tight, Kit talked nonstop until the old couple had tucked her into bed between them and turned out the light, and then she fell asleep all at once, purring.

Kit's frustration notwithstanding, the answers did come, the first, early the following morning. Kit woke to the ringing of the phone. She rolled over on the big bed as Lucinda picked up. Lucinda listened, then turned on the speaker so Pedric and Kit could listen.

"Cage Jones died at four this morning," Wilma said. "The hospital called Max, and Charlie called me. She was crying."

"Oh dear," Lucinda said, swinging out of bed and feeling for her slippers. Beside her, Kit shivered. Charlie had killed a man and, no matter how casual a cat might feel about taking another creature's life, Charlie was a tender human.

"What can we do?" Lucinda said.

"She'll be all right," Wilma said. "She's strong, it just takes time. She knows very well that she saved lives that night. Max said that as soon as he can get away they're going to saddle up and take that week's ride down the coast that they've been planning, take some time alone together."

That same day, Violet Jones moved back into her childhood home with Lilly, and found a part-time job waiting tables. And it was later that week that Greeley Urzey left the village, just disappeared, didn't tell Mavity he was going. "Just like him," Mavity said. "He shows up, makes trouble, and vanishes." Greeley checked out of his motel at five A.M., the day after Cage's fence, in San Francisco, ID'd Cage and Greeley as having sold him illegal gold huacas. The fence had studied pictures from Interpol that identified the pieces he'd bought as having been stolen in several Panamanian burglaries. When federal officers went to arrest Greeley, he was gone. He had sold his car two days before to a private party. If he got on a plane, he'd used a fake ID. The feds were still looking for his trail on the day of Cage Jones's funeral, which was delayed while forensics determined whether Max's .38 or shotgun pellets had killed Cage, though the question was academic. It was a week before the funeral when Lilly Jones disappeared.

Violet called Wilma to say that Lilly was gone. She wasn't crying. She didn't know why Lilly had left; she said they'd been getting along just fine. Her voice was stiff, but Wilma thought that, secretly, she was pleased. She told Wilma that Lilly's bank account had been closed and that she had left a large check, telling Violet to open her own account in order to pay future household bills. Lilly's note said there was no mortgage, and that, with Cage's death, Violet owned half the house. That she would have to pay the taxes, and insurance, and upkeep. Lilly did not leave a forwarding address. She took only a few clothes and the one good suitcase. She explained that Violet couldn't sell the house, of course, without Lilly, but that if Lilly decided to release her half, she would send a legal paper to that effect. She did not take the old Packard, but transferred the registration to Violet. She did not make airline reservations under her own name.

There were no charges against Lilly Jones. But Max gave the information to Interpol. Violet, when she checked with the bank to be sure Lilly's account was indeed closed, learned that Lilly had also relinquished her large safe-deposit box. At this time, two abused village women left their homes, seeking shelter and protection, and Violet, while waiting tables at the Patio Café, toyed with the idea of taking in such women as roomers, for mutual support. She thought about this during Cage's graveside service, which she witnessed apparently without emotion, turning away when it was finished, dry-eyed and composed.

Hidden among the tombstones behind Violet and the few others present, the three cats waited. The morning was hot, overcast, and muggy. The service was short. Lilly's minister did not seem inclined to go on at much length about the life or virtues of Cage Jones. The selections he read from the Bible were blandly generic. Violet spoke no words of cleansing or of memory on Cage's behalf. Cage Jones's funeral was a glum affair. In the arrangements Lilly had made for it before she vanished, she seemed concerned only about doing the minimum civil duty and being done with her brother. The cats, curled up in the shadow of a nearby granite monument, looked sadly at one another. To possess human life, and to have so squandered it that one departed accompanied only by hatred or indifference —that was, in their eager feline minds, indeed a terrible waste. They felt no grief for Cage Jones; they felt only disgust. What each of them wondered about, and grieved over, was the emptiness and waste.

They watched Wilma and Charlie turn away and leave the cemetery with Max and Dallas, watched Violet leave alone. When the handful of people was gone, they waited patiently until the backhoe had arrived and the grave was unceremoniously covered with earth, and then sod laid over it.

Then, alone, Joe Grey approached the grave.

And now, smiling with a sad but perverse sense of humor, the tomcat dug a hole in the center of Cage Jones's grave, dug it in the soft dirt, as any cat would dig, but carefully between the squares of sod. He dug it deep. He dropped the leather thong, which he had carried all the way to the cemetery secure between his teeth, dangling the heavy gold devil—dropped it deep into the hole and buried it, covered it well, as any cat would do.

And he turned away, smiling, leaving Cage Jones alone with his only remaining treasure.

Center Point Publishing
600 Brooks Road ● PO Box 1
Thorndike ME 04986-0001 USA

(207) 568-3717

**US & Canada:
1 800 929-9108**
www.centerpointlargeprint.com